49 ⌇

ORMOND

ORMOND;

OR, THE SECRET WITNESS

Charles Brockden Brown

edited by Mary Chapman

broadview literary texts

Canadian Cataloguing in Publication Data

Brown, Charles Brockden, 1771-1810
   Ormond
(Broadview literary texts)
Includes bibliographical references.
ISBN 1-55111-091-1 (softcover)   1-55111-309-0 (hardcover)
I. Chapman, Mary Megan, 1962- . II. Title. III. Series.
PS1134.07 1999   813'.2   C99-930715-0

Broadview Press Ltd., is an independent, international publishing house, incorporated in 1985.

North America:
P.O. Box 1243, Peterborough, Ontario, Canada K9J 7H5
3576 California Road, Orchard Park, NY 14127
TEL: (705) 743-8990; FAX: (705) 743-8353;
E-MAIL: 75322.44@compuserve.com

United Kingdom:
Turpin Distribution Services Ltd.,
Blackhorse Rd., Letchworth, Hertfordshire SG6 1HN
TEL: (1462) 672555; FAX (1462) 480947; E-MAIL: turpin@rsc.org

Australia:
St. Clair Press, P.O. Box 287, Rozelle, NSW 2039
TEL: (02) 818-1942; FAX: (02) 418-1923

www.broadviewpress.com

Broadview Press gratefully acknowledges the financial support of the Book Publishing Industry Development Program, Ministry of Canadian Heritage, Government of Canada.

Broadview Press is grateful to Professor Eugene Benson for advice on editorial matters for the Broadview Literary Texts series.

Text design and composition by George Kirkpatrick

PRINTED IN CANADA

Contents

Acknowledgements

I have contracted many debts of gratitude during the completion of this book. The University of Alberta supported the project with release time, the intellectual stimulation of the classroom, and the service of several helpful librarians in Inter-Library Loans. The Social Sciences and Humanities Research Council of Canada generously awarded me a Faculty Research Grant to work on this and related projects.

Thanks go also to the many graduate students who worked as my research assistants — Judy Dunlop, Robert W. Gray, Heidi Janz, Victoria Lamont, Karen Overbye, and Jean Richardson — and to Astrid Blodgett for her expert secretarial work.

Judith Sargent Murray's "On the Equality of the Sexes" is reproduced from the *Massachusetts Magazine* (March and April 1790) 132-35 and 223-26.

Selections from John Robison's *Proofs of a Conspiracy Against All the Religions and Governments of Europe, Carried on in the Secret Meetings of Free Masons, Illuminati, and Reading Societies* are reproduced from the Third edition, published in Philadelphia by T. Dobson in 1798 (80-184).

The selection from Jedidiah Morse's "A Sermon Exhibiting the Present Dangers, and Consequent Duties of the Citizens of the United States of America. Delivered at Charlestown, April 25, 1799" is reproduced from the edition printed at Worcester, Massachusetts, Daniel Greenleaf (July 10, 1799) 88.

Charles Brockden Brown as a young man, in pastel and charcoal, over graphite on discoloured blue wove paper by James Sharples. (Reproduced with the permission of the Worcester Art Museum, Worcester, Massachusetts.)

Introduction

> We rejoice to see these reprints of Brown's novels [*Ormond* and
> *Wieland*], as we have long been ashamed that one who ought to
> be the pride of our country, and who is, in the higher qualities
> of mind, so far in advance of our other novelists, should have
> become almost inaccessible to the public.
>
> Margaret Fuller, *Papers on Literature and Art* (1846)[1]

The provocative miniature that graces the cover of this volume is
significant in many ways: depicting a late eighteenth-century European woman cross-dressed in military uniform, the miniature most
immediately recalls the charismatic feminist Martinette de Beauvais
depicted in Charles Brockden Brown's *Ormond*, who dons a soldier's
dress in order to fight alongside her husband in democratic revolutions on two continents. In form it also recalls the token of affection
exchanged between the novel's narrator and its heroine, the value of
which is obscured by the process by which it is torn out of the private sphere of the sentiments and sold into the public world of commodities.

Small enough to be treasured in a pocket close to the heart, but
ornate enough to be displayed and circulated, the miniature fore-
grounds many of the questions at the centre of Brown's complex
novel: in a frame which exaggerates its interiority, the miniature
asserts a certain immunity from the risks and contagions of public
life. Paradoxically, however, it asserts the fixity of the self at the same
time that it announces its inevitable imbrication in the life of another,
most notably the friend or lover in whose possession the miniature
rests. In this way, the miniature complicates the structural opposition
between the private and public spheres that is at the heart of Brown's
meditation on the place of the individual in the national body in the
first two decades of the early Republic.

It also draws attention to the debates about identity, gender, and
sexuality that permeate every page of this disturbing text. While it
may seem puzzling to feature the portrait of a woman on the cover of

---

1 Bernard Rosenthal, ed. *Critical Essays on Charles Brockden Brown* (Boston: G.K. Hall
& Co., 1981) 62.

a novel named after its male protagonist, *Ormond* itself is a cross-dressed text written by a male author in the persona of a female narrator writing, among other topics, about the benefits and risks of private women's attempts to participate in public life, to the mysterious I.E. Rosenberg, whose gender is unknown. This radical approach to gender is one of the qualities that made *Ormond* so powerful when it was first published in America in 1799, and what makes it so fascinating to contemporary readers interested in the intersections between gender and nation.

Brown and the American Literary Canon

Although Charles Brockden Brown is often celebrated as "America's first professional man of letters," "the invent[or] of American Gothic," and a "pioneer voice" in American literature, Brown's relation to the American literary canon has always been problematic.[1] While he has been considered the best American novelist of his generation, when his wild, improbable fictions were first published in late-eighteenth-century America, reviewers were sometimes "patronizing and lukewarm, occasionally hostile, in their response."[2] More than a century later, a critical emphasis on aesthetic unity led New Critics to read Brown's baroque plots, imbedded narratives, over-determined symbolism, and lack of closure as evidence of hastily written blunders of questionable literary value. As a result, at the same time that Brown has been honoured for his prodigious literary output – four Gothic novels, two sentimental-domestic novels, a fictional dialogue, two unpublished novels, one lost novel, assorted short fiction, poetry and essays, all written in a ten-year span in which he also edited three influential early American periodicals – his works have often been dismissed as the hackneyed products of a "Gothic bungler."[3]

---

1 See F.O. Matthiessen, *The American Renaissance* (New York: Oxford UP, 1941 [1968]) 202; "Charles Brockden Brown and the Invention of American Gothic" in Leslie Fiedler, *Love and Death in the American Novel* (New York: Anchor Books, [1966], 1992) 126; David Lee Clark, *Charles Brockden Brown: Pioneer Voice of America* (Durham: Duke UP, 1952).

2 Alan Axelrod, *Charles Brockden Brown: An American Tale* (Austin: University of Texas Press, 1983) xvii.

3 For a rehearsal of critical reservations about Brown's work, see Alexander Cowie, *The Rise of the American Novel* (New York: American Book Company, 1951) 69.

Brown's marginalization has been caused in part by a critical dismissal of the forms in which he worked, the early American novel, and more specifically the Gothic novel, both of which have been much maligned for what have been perceived to be their artistic flaws: their aesthetic fragmentation, generic impurity, two-dimensional characterization, and formulaic plots. Recently, however, new developments in literary study have allowed scholars to reevaluate these long denigrated forms and, as a consequence, Brown's literary stock has never been higher. Most significant to the project of reassessing Brown's work has been the recognition that the aesthetic fragmentation of the early American novel and, in particular, the early American Gothic novel, does not signal their "systematic failure,"[1] but rather serves as evidence that both forms incorporated and revised other literary genres. As Cathy N. Davidson notes, the early American novel "fed upon and devoured more familiar literary forms such as travel, captivity, and military narratives; political and religious tracts; advice books, chapbooks, penny histories, and almanacs. It appropriated drama ... and nonliterary forms such as letters ..., diaries as well as traditionally oral forms of culture such as local gossip, rumor, hearsay, folktales."[2] Maggie Kilgour has noted the same tendency in the Gothic novel which "feeds upon and mixes the wide range of literary sources out of which it emerges and from which it never fully disentangles itself.... The form is thus ... assembled out of bits and pieces of the past."[3] At their worst, then, the early novel and the Gothic novel can be bungled, episodic trash; at their best, they can be highly self-conscious rebellions against the constraints of neoclassical aesthetic ideals of unity in order to explore the ways in which culture has relied on forms to organize itself.

Replying to the New Criticism's emphasis on aesthetic unity, recent scholarship on the early American novel and the Gothic novel has begun to explore how, in challenging aesthetics, the two hybrid forms also challenge the organizing hierarchies of class, gender, sexuality, race, ethnicity, and nation that culture has naturalized. Louis S. Gross and other scholars of the Gothic, for example, have observed

---

1 Elizabeth R. Napier, *The Failure of the Gothic: Problems of Disjunction in an Eighteenth-Century Form* (Oxford: Clarendon Press, 1987) 7.

2 Cathy N. Davidson, *Revolution and the Word: The Rise of the Novel in America* (New York and Oxford: Oxford University Press, 1986) 12-13.

3 Maggie Kilgour, *The Rise of the Gothic Novel* (London: Routledge, 1995) 4.

that the Gothic novel, the product primarily of women writers, homosexual writers, and colonial writers, often explores marginalized relations to dominant structures and questions the binaries that privilege white patriarchal power.[1]

Inspired by Jane Tompkins's *Sensational Designs: The Cultural Work of American Fiction 1810-1865* (1985), which values popular American novels for the "cultural 'work' they were designed to do" and Davidson's *Revolution and the Word* (1986), which argues that early American fiction served as a political and cultural forum to articulate the fears and fantasies of the emerging nation, contemporary critics have started to read early American texts as political works, whether as rich repositories of information about the early Republic's struggles to control and contain racial and sexual difference, or as dramatizations of efforts to define personal and national identity in a time of crisis, and to read recurring tropes of incest, rape, seduction, murder, suicide, pestilence, and other threats to the physical body as a metaphorization of the more political threats to the national body.[2] In *Romances of the Republic: Women, the Family and Violence in the Literature of the Early American Nation* (1996), for example, Shirley Samuels argues that in early American literature, political and familial discourses intersect so that anxieties about political and national identity map onto representations of threats to the female body. Elizabeth Barnes's *States of Sympathy* (1997) extends and complicates Samuels's thesis: rather than reading representations of seduction in early American sentimental and Gothic fiction as allegorically signalling only threats to the national body, Barnes argues that seduction can also signify "the sentimental operations by which patriarchal politics gains access to the national body."[3]

---

1   Louis S. Gross, *Redefining American Gothic: From* Wieland *to* Day of the Dead (Ann Arbor and London: UMI Research Press, 1989) 2; see also Kate Ferguson Ellis, *The Contested Castle: Gothic Novels and the Subversion of Domestic Ideology* (Chicago: University of Illinois Press, 1989).

2   Jane Tompkins, *Sensational Designs: The Cultural Work of American Fiction 1810-1865* (New York and London: Oxford University Press, 1985) xv; Cathy N. Davidson, *Revolution and the Word: The Rise of the Novel in America* (Oxford and New York: Oxford University Press, 1986) passim.

3   Shirley Samuels, *Romances of the Republic: Women, the Family and Violence in the Literature of the Early American Nation* (New York: Oxford University Press, 1996) passim; Elizabeth Barnes, *States of Sympathy: Seduction and Democracy in the American Novel* (New York: Columbia University Press, 1997) 43.

Coinciding with these and other reappraisals of the early American novel and the Gothic mode has been a renewed interest in the significance of Brown's contributions to these genres and a recognition of the importance of his work to our understanding of the early national period. Beginning in the late 1970s and early 1980s with the publication of scholarly editions of all of Brown's works by Kent State University Press and the appearance of a collection of critical essays on Brown, and culminating in 1998, the bicentennial of the publication of Brown's first book *Alcuin*, with the Library of America's publication of a volume of Brown's three most popular Gothic novels and a "Revising Charles Brockden Brown" conference, Brown scholarship has recently experienced a renaissance.[1] In part, this renaissance has been driven by developments in literary theory – most significantly, new approaches attentive to representations of gender, sexuality, race, class, and nation – which have made available a critical vocabulary with which readers can make sense of Brown's haunting fiction.

Feminist scholars have taken up the gender issues in Brown's writing: for example, his dramatized debates about women's education, gender equality, and marriage; his depictions of female cross-dressing; his representations of Republican womanhood; and the perceived foreclosure of his earlier works' feminism in his later sentimental domestic novels. Contemporary queer work on Brown explores elements of Brown's biography, such as his passionate letters to William Wood Wilkins, and his devotion to Elihu Hubbard Smith, or depictions of romantic friendships and homosociality in his works. Julia Stern, for example, has read the female homosociality represented in

---

1 Kent State University's Bicentennial Edition of the *Novels and Related Works of Charles Brockden Brown*, under the general editorship of Sydney J. Krause, with S.W. Reid as textual editor, was published in 1977-87; Bernard Rosenthal edited *Critical Essays On Charles Brockden Brown* in 1981. Library of America published *Charles Brockden Brown: Three Gothic Novels* (New York: Literary Classics of the United States, 1998). The "Revising Charles Brockden Brown" conference, organized by Christopher Looby, was held at the University of Pennsylvania, October 23-24, 1998. Many other projects on Brown are in preparation: *Revising Charles Brockden Brown*, a volume of new essays on Brown, edited by Stephen Shapiro, Philip Barnard, and Mark Kamrath; a critical edition of Brown's letters, edited by John R. Holmes and Edwin Saeger; and a CD-Rom edition of the uncollected writings of Charles Brockden Brown, edited by Fritz Fleischmann, Wolfgang Schäfer, Dietmar Schloss, and Alfred Weber.

Ormond as a viable alternative to the patriarchally authored and frater-
nally fractured polity of the early Republic. In addition to feminist
and queer work on Brown, recent criticism attentive to class in American literature has initiated discussions of Brown's works as explo-
rations of a culture of domestic republican virtue on the cusp of a
new era dominated by market-driven capitalism.[1]

Like all early American prose, Brown's works are intellectually
challenging to contemporary readers because of his intense engagement with late eighteenth-century currents of debate. Inspired by
novels of purpose written in the 1790s by European Jacobin writers
like William Godwin, all of Brown's works are complex considerations of the issues of his day: the location of authority in a democratic
state; the construction of American national character and identity;
post-enlightenment views of gender and sexuality; the balance
between individual freedom and communal responsibilities; and the
shifting values of the era in which America moved from an agrarian
community valuing civic responsibility to a capitalist economy valuing trade. However, because Brown is most interested in dramatizing
the limit cases – where, for example, the rhetoric of self-making pro-
motes a monstrous confidence man; where gender equality produces
a bayonet-wielding "lady who sheds no tears"[2]; and where the
rhetoric of individualism licenses an ideologue to stop at nothing to
achieve his personal desires – his politics have puzzled his comment-
ators.

Feminist critics, for example, either claim Brown as America's

---

1   For recent feminist discussions of Brown's work, see Heather Smyth, "Imperfect
    Dis(clothes)ures: Cross-dressing and Containment in Charles Brockden Brown's
    Ormond" in *Sex and Sexuality in Early America*, ed. Merril D. Smith (New York: New
    York University Press, 1998); and Paul Lewis, "Charles Brockden Brown and the
    Gendered Canon of Early American Fiction" in *Early American Literature* 31: 167-
    88. For queer readings of Brown, see Julia Stern, *The Plight of Feeling: Sympathy and
    Dissent in the Early American Novel* (Chicago: University of Chicago Press, 1997)
    153-238; and Stephen Watt, *The Romance of Real Life: Charles Brockden Brown and the
    Origins of American Culture* (Baltimore and London: Johns Hopkins University Press,
    1994) 33-34. For discussions of Brown's relations to emerging market discourse, see
    Emory Elliot, *Revolutionary Writers: Literature and Authority in the New Republic, 1725-
    1810* (New York: Oxford University Press, 1982); Elizabeth Jane Wall Hinds, *Private
    Property: Charles Brockden Brown's Gendered Economy of Virtue* (Newark: University of
    Delaware Press, 1997); and Stephen Watt, *The Romance of Real Life* (1994).
2   The phrase, adapted from a passage in *Ormond* which describes Martinette's failure
    to cry while burying Roselli (57), is Julia Stern's. See *The Plight of Feeling* 153.

earliest feminist or reject him for being patriarchal and condescending. Some have called Brown's earliest major published work, *Alcuin: A Dialogue on the Rights of Women Part One* (1798), the first extended argument for the rights of women to appear in the United States because it features a bluestocking widow, Mrs. Carter, who attempts to convince a priggish schoolmaster Alcuin to sympathize with proto-feminist demands for more lenient divorce laws, as well as women's rights to own property, pursue professions, and educate themselves. However, the second part of *Alcuin* (not published until after Brown's death), which depicts Alcuin suddenly extending Mrs. Carter's arguments to advocate free love and the dissolution of marriage as an institution, has suggested to other scholars that Brown is actually ridiculing the radical feminist platform of Mary Wollstonecraft and tainting all eighteenth-century feminist positions by association.[1]

Similarly, scholars interested in Brown's relationship to competing visions of liberal democracy current in the infant republic have found his fiction ambiguous. Do his works support Jeffersonian idealism, characterized by a belief in humanity's innate integrity and perfectibility, an agrarian vision of America, a desire for minimal governmental interference, and support for French revolutionary principles? Or do they advocate Federalist restraint, characterized by pessimism about human nature, a belief in the need for governmental regulation to preserve law and order, and a fear of French democracy's extremes and the dissolution of organized religion? Because Brown sent a gift copy of his first novel *Wieland* to Thomas Jefferson, then leader of the Democrat-Republican Party, Jane Tompkins has read its representation of a pastoral idyll destroyed by a menacing outsider as simple

---

1   The question of Brown's commitment to feminism in still hotly debated. For a survey of the debate, see Paul Lewis, "Charles Brockden Brown and the Gendered Canon of Early American Fiction," *Early American Literature* 31: 167-88. Leland Person argues in "My Good Mama," *Studies in American Fiction* 9:1 (1981): 33-46, that *Alcuin* registers "some uneasiness about roles for women. Indeed, despite his thoroughgoing opposition to many arbitrary customs of marriage, the attitudes of Brown's major male characters toward marriage and women are extremely problematical" (33); in "The Matter and Manner of Charles Brockden Brown's *Alcuin*," Davidson contextualizes the publication of *Alcuin* within debates about marriage and free love which followed the publication of Mary Wollstonecraft's biography (Rosenthal 71-86). For a discussion of the equality of the sexes by Judith Sargent Murray, one of Brown's contemporaries, see Appendix A.

Federalist political propaganda, supporting the Alien and Sedition Acts which sought to control the influx of "dangerous" democratic sentiments from Revolutionary Europe by limiting freedom of expression in America; Tompkins calls *Wieland* a "plea for the restoration of civic authority" and a warning of the "dangers of mob rule." However, because the idyll is also savaged from within, by the threat of incest and patriarchal family violence, one can read *Wieland*, as Shirley Samuels has, as a critique of Federalist assumptions that the early Republic was weakened exclusively by foreign contagions – the excesses of the French revolution, uncontrolled immigration, unprotected trade – rather than by dangers both foreign and closer to home.[1]

Brown's apparent ambiguity on these and other matters has been interpreted by some scholars as a deliberate anti-authoritarian strategy. Cathy N. Davidson, for example, has claimed that "Brown employed the dialogue form to explore ideas, not to advance or to substantiate them." According to Davidson, Brown's use of dialogue, debate, and letters in his major fiction – formal elements that led New Critics to accuse Brown of stylistic inferiority – functioned as "an early American version of Bakhtin's 'dialogical' text, a carnivalesque performance in which the author resolutely refuses to delimit his intentions while also allowing his characters their own ambiguities and even a spirit of 'revolt' against any constraining proprieties the text might threaten to impose."[2] Others prefer to follow cultural biographer Stephen Watt's view that Brown "followed a convulsive ideological evolution from youthful utopian to stodgy middle-age conservative." His four major novels are politically ambiguous, according to this argument, because they dramatize Brown's inner turmoil before he solidified his political beliefs and abandoned the writing of novels. Whether one agrees with Watt's claim that Brown's politics changed "on or about April 1800"[3] or with Davidson's assertion that he debated rather than advanced the arguments his fictions

---

1 See Appendices for 1790s American reactions to European political organizations such as the Bavarian Illuminati. Jane Tompkins, *Sensational Designs*, 58; Shirley Samuels, *Romances of the Republic*, 44-56.

2 Cathy N. Davidson, "The Matter and Manner of Charles Brockden Brown's *Alcuin*," in Bernard Rosenthal, ed. *Critical Essays on Charles Brockden Brown*, 82.

3 Stephen Watt, *The Romance of Real Life*, 131.

present, one can recognize a marked change in the material realities of Brown's biography, when he traded his single life as a New York novelist in the late 1790s for the married life of a Philadelphia editor and businessman in the first decade of the nineteenth century.

Brown's Biography

Charles Brockden Brown was born in 1771, five years before the start of the American Revolution, in Philadelphia, the thirteen colonies' intellectual and political centre and the city that later became the infant nation's capital. His childhood therefore coincided with some of the most traumatic years in the history of America. His father was a liberal merchant who, like other colonists, opposed the Stamp Act and supported the goals of the Revolution. However, because Brown's father was a Quaker pacifist, he would not bear arms and refused to take the patriotic oath; as a consequence, he was interned for eight months and the family business was pillaged by patriots during the Revolution.

One could argue that because of his family's experience as pacifist supporters of a revolution that was, by definition, violent, Charles Brockden Brown, from an early age, occupied a contrarian relationship to his culture. At the Philadelphia Friends Latin School, which he attended from age eleven, Brown was taught by Tory sympathizer Robert Proud, who stimulated and challenged Brown's convictions in the Quaker tradition of intellectual dialogue. When he was fifteen, he founded the Belles Lettres club with eight male friends including William Wood Wilkins and Joseph Bringhurst, who met regularly, sometimes at the home of statesman Benjamin Franklin, to debate issues such as the morality of suicide, the imperfections of government, the limits of liberty, and possible rationalizations for lying. When Brown completed his schooling in 1787, the same year the Federal Convention met in Philadelphia to draft the Constitution, he began apprenticing at the law offices of Alexander Wilcocks at the urging of his parents and older brothers.[1]

While apprenticing for the law, Brown also pursued literary interests, noting in his journals ideas for epic poems on the discovery of

---

1   On Brown's legal career, see Robert A. Ferguson, *Law and Letters in American Culture* (Cambridge, MA: Harvard University Press, 1984) 129-49.

America or the conquests of Mexico and Peru, and composing imitations of the Book of Psalms, the Book of Job, and the Ossian poems.[1] On the eve of the French Revolution, when Brown was eighteen, he published his first literary works: the "Rhapsodist" sketches, which appeared anonymously in the *Columbian Magazine*, a distinguished literary journal, and a poem entitled "An Inscription for General Washington's Tomb Stone," published in the *State Gazette of North Carolina*. In these and other early writings, Brown debated the merits of organized religion, gender equality, political utopias, and self-interest, all issues of central concern to the early republic.

Love of debate may have prompted Brown's initial interest in the law, but the young intellectual soon became disillusioned. "[I] was perpetually encumbered with the rubbish of the law," he wrote to a friend, "and waded with laborious steps through its endless tautologies, its impertinent circuities, its lying assertions and hateful artifices."[2] As representations of the law in his later fiction indicate, Brown viewed the law as a "tissue of shreds and remnants of a barbarous antiquity patched by the stupidity of modern workmen into new deformity" (*Ormond* 51). He was especially critical of the ways in which, even after the Revolution had attempted to dismantle the American class system, the Constitution had through its restricted franchise continued to limit women's, non-whites', and the poor's access to power and wealth. In 1793, the same year the French monarchy was abolished and political stability replaced by the Reign of Terror, Brown abandoned the law to attempt a life of letters.

Between 1793 and 1798, Brown wrote prodigiously but published little. Robert Ferguson has described his output during this period as a "series of vague, incoherent projects easily abandoned or interrupted by long periods of malaise."[3] However, this time was crucial for Brown's development as a writer, primarily because of the friendships he made with intellectual men who encouraged him, particularly Elihu Hubbard Smith, whom he met in Philadelphia in 1790. Trained

---

1   Emory Elliott, *Revolutionary Writers: Literature and Authority in the New Republic 1725-1810* (New York: Oxford University Press, 1982) 214.

2   Quoted in Harry R. Warfel, *Charles Brockden Brown: American Gothic Novelist* (Gainesville: University Press of Florida, 1949) 29.

3   Robert A. Ferguson, "Yellow Fever and Charles Brockden Brown: The Context of the Emerging Novelist," *Early American Literature* 14 (1980): 295.

as a medical doctor by noted Philadelphian physician Dr. Benjamin Rush, Smith was also a man of letters, an opera librettist, author of a biography of the Connecticut Wits, and editor of an anthology of American poetry. Although he was a staunch Federalist and Brown was more persuaded at this time by continental writers, philosophers whose writings had inspired the French Revolution, and by the radical positions of English Jacobin writers such as William Godwin, Smith became Brown's closest friend and patron. It was Smith who gave Brown the confidence he needed to evade the pleas of his family to abandon his literary projects and join the family business. When Smith established a medical practice in New York City upon his graduation, Brown left Philadelphia frequently for extended visits with him. There he became involved in the Friendly Club, a society of letters founded by Smith which included a number of Federalist intellectuals such as James Kent (later Chancellor of New York), William Dunlap (playwright and later Brown's first biographer), lawyer William Johnson, and Timothy Dwight (later a conservative minister and Yale College president), who also encouraged Brown to take his writing seriously. Like the Belles Lettres club to which Brown had belonged as a teenager, the Friendly Club met regularly to discuss recent philosophical writings and literature. During 1796 and 1797, the Club's members also listened to Brown read aloud from his works in progress. Early in 1798, Brown began to publish a number of works in quick succession: "The Man At Home," a story published serially in the *Weekly Magazine* beginning in February 1798; *Alcuin*, a dialogue on women's rights published in book form in March 1798 and in revised form, as "The Rights of Women," in the *Weekly Magazine* in March and April 1798. He also published a brief excerpt from a novel *Skywalk*, now lost, in the *Weekly Magazine* in March 1798. In April 1799, when the Friendly Club founded the *Monthly Magazine and American Review*, whose aim was to "extract the quintessence of European wisdom; to review and estimate the labours of all writers, domestic and foreign,"[1] Brown became the editor and a frequent contributor of essays, criticism, and short works of fiction.[2]

---

1 Introduction, Charles Brockden Brown, *Edgar Huntly* (New York, 1928) x.
2 For information on Brown's short fiction, see Alfred Weber, ed. *Somnambulism and Other Stories* (Frankfurt am Main: Verlag Peter Lang, 1987).

After travelling back and forth between Philadelphia and New York for several years, Brown officially moved to New York City in July 1798 to share an apartment with Smith and Johnson, just when a yellow fever epidemic was breaking out there. While tending patients, Smith contracted the disease and died suddenly in September 1798; Brown also fell dangerously ill. Biographers speculate that this was probably the turning point in Brown's career: motivated by the loss of the man who had been his close friend, peer and patron, and struck by the parallel vulnerability of the infant nation during its second experience of yellow fever outbreak, Brown began a frantic period of writing novels, each of which is haunted by violent threats to the personal and political body. Robert A. Ferguson estimates that Brown was at work on all four of the major novels between September (when Smith died) and November 1798.[1] *Wieland* (1798), *Ormond* (1799), *Arthur Mervyn* (Part One, 1799; Part Two, 1800), and *Edgar Huntly* (1799) were all written within an eighteen-month period in 1798 and 1799, during which time Brown reflected on the young Republic's anxious response to the aftermath of the French Revolution – the Reign of Terror in France and the violent slave rebellion on the Caribbean island of St. Domingue (now Haiti). This quartet of novels can be read as revisiting the drama of the American revolution from a vantage point twenty years later.

Late in 1800, after publishing Part Two of *Arthur Mervyn*, Brown returned to Philadelphia to work for the family business, ceased publication of the *Monthly Magazine*, and decided abruptly not to write any more novels. In one issue of a periodical he edited later, he confessed: "I should enjoy a larger share of my own respect at the present moment if nothing had ever flowed from my pen, the production of which could be traced to me."[2] Although he did continue to write novels for a few more months – he published two sentimental novels, *Clara Howard* and *Jane Talbot*, in 1801 – and although he continued to publish fiction and essays anonymously in *The Portfolio* and the magazines he continued to edit, this period, beginning when he returned to Philadelphia to work for the family business and

---

1 Ferguson, "Yellow Fever," 302.

2 Quoted in Alan Axelrod, *Charles Brockden Brown: An American Tale* (Austin: University of Texas Press, 1983) 126.

culminating in his happy marriage to Elizabeth Linn, sister of Presbyterian minister John Linn, in 1803, marks a shift in his career from novelist to editor and journalist. It also marks a change in his philosophical outlook from religious questioner to orthodox Christian. After a turbulent adolescence in which he questioned and appeared to disavow his religious upbringing (reflected in works such as *Wieland*), in 1803, Brown began to edit *The Literary Magazine and American Register*, a semi-annual of book reviews, fiction, government reports, and essays which he vowed would embrace the cause of religion.

Where as a young man Brown had probably been pro-Jeffersonian in his leanings and had served as a sort of devil's advocate within the Federalist-identified Friendly Club, during the final decade of his career, after Jefferson had been elected President in 1800, Brown wrote four unsigned or pseudonymously published political pamphlets critical of Jefferson's administration: "An Address to the Government of the United States, on the Cession of Louisiana to the French" (1803), a work whose author claims to have found evidence of a French plan to expand in North America, thereby promoting American paranoia of French duplicity; "Monroe's Embassy, or, The Conduct of the Government in Relation to Our Claims to the Navigation of the Mississippi" (1803), a dialogic piece, part of which is presented as authored by Jefferson, the other by a merchant impatient with what he perceives to be Jefferson's conciliatory diplomacy vis à vis French belligerence; "The British Treaty of Commerce and Navigation" (1807), which continues to criticize Jefferson's government's attempt to avoid war with Britain through trade restrictions and negotiations; and "An Address to the Congress of the United States on the Utility and Justice of Restrictions upon Foreign Commerce" (1809), which questions the effectiveness of Jefferson's controversial Embargo policy.

During this time Brown also translated and annotated a geographical study of the United States by French author Comte de Volney. When *The Literary Magazine and American Register* ceased publication in 1807, and Brown's family business also dissolved, Brown continued his own small retail business and started a new magazine called *The American Register, or General Repository of History, Politics, and Science,* which published only five issues before his health began to decline. When he died of tuberculosis on February 22, 1810, he was at work on *A Complete System of Geography*.[1]

Ormond

Coinciding with the recent renewal of critical interest in Brown's work has been a desire to explore some of his lesser known writings, for example, his journalistic and editorial contributions to early American periodicals, his letters, his domestic sentimental fiction *Jane Talbot* (1801) and *Clara Howard* (1801), and the least discussed of his four major novels, *Ormond; or, the Secret Witness* (1799). Although Brown's second novel has the distinction of having been the first American novel to be reprinted in England, and was praised by Romantic writers such as Percy Shelley,[2] it was not as popular among Brown's American contemporaries as two of his other major novels, *Edgar Huntly* and *Wieland*, and in twentieth-century scholarship it has suffered from critical neglect.[3]

Set primarily in post-Revolutionary Philadelphia, then the early republic's capital, *Ormond* tells the story of the young chaste Constantia Dudley's attempts to support herself and her family and to preserve her republican virtue, in a community threatened by a yellow fever epidemic, rising tides of immigrant refugees from political crises around the world, and confidence games associated with emergent market capitalism.

---

1 For a detailed discussion of the continuities between Brown's interest in geography, particularly in statistics about American demographics in the 1790s, and his encyclopedic attention to the heterogeneity of American identity in his fiction, see Martin Bruckner, "Literacy, Geography and Domestic Politics in the Writings of Charles Brockden Brown," an unpublished paper delivered at the "Revising Charles Brockden Brown" conference.

2 Kenneth Dauber, *The Idea of Authorship in America: Democratic Poetics from Franklin to Melville* (Madison: University of Wisconsin Press, 1990) 55.

3 Book-length studies of early American literature — such as Jane Tompkins's *Sensational Designs*, Shirley Samuels's *Romances of the Republic*, Elizabeth Barnes's *States of Feeling*, Christopher Looby's *Voicing America* — if they discuss Brown's works at all, tend to focus on the other three of his four major novels. Other than chapters in Julia Stern's *The Plight of Feeling*, and Robert Levine's *Conspiracy and Romance: Studies in Brockden Brown, Cooper, Hawthorne and Melville* (Cambridge: Cambridge University Press, 1989), the only detailed treatments of *Ormond* appear in essays published in periodicals. See Works Cited and Recommended Reading.

Like the geographer he became near the end of his life, Charles Brockden Brown the novelist was obsessed with the risks and benefits of boundaries and borders. In his lifetime, the literal borders of the United States were established by Revolutionary War in 1776 and then redrawn to reflect the acquisition of the Louisiana territory in 1803; during the same period America's diplomatic borders also fluctuated according to the early republic's shifting allegiances to England and France, its major trading partners and ideological parents. Speaking more metaphorically, one could say that the boundaries of late-eighteenth-century American society were also being remapped, when the hierarchies implicit in relationships between imperial nations and colonies, states and subjects, parents and children, husbands and wives, were being challenged by radical new philosophies. As a novelist writing during this volatile period, Brown was interested in documenting the shifting geographies – social, political, familial, sexual – of the early republic.

Featuring gender, racial, and class masquerade, *Ormond* meditates on the blurring of many conventional boundaries – between male and female, foreign and domestic, working-class tenant and property owner, self and other – in the decade following the drafting of the American constitution. The most critical boundary for Brown is that which distinguishes the public from the private. Both concepts are over-determined in *Ormond*: Brown aligns the private with spaces which are bounded, for example, the (feminine) body contained by the limits of personal identity, the home determined by its walls, and the nation defined by its borders; the private, according to Brown, is the site that defines and safeguards virtue, independence, and self-reliance. Conversely he constructs the public as that which exists outside of boundaries, i.e., the streets, the wilderness, the world of free market capitalism. For Brown, the public is initially defined in terms of the threats to the boundaries of the private – to personal identity, female chastity, and homely liberty – it occasions.

In *Ormond*, the critical relation between the public and the private in *fin-de-siècle* America is often represented spatially, by recurring images of literal thresholds, doorways, and keyholes – sites that at once buttress the divisions between the private household and the public sphere at the same time that they acknowledge their permeability. Although Brown's Gothic novel features no Gothic monster, *per se*, the social landscape Brown depicts in *Ormond* is rendered monstrous in moments where the distinctions between private and public suddenly collapse and the vulnerability of the private space – the body, the household, the nation – is exposed. In *Skin Shows: Gothic Horror and the Technology of Monsters* , Judith Halberstam has noted that the "monsters of the nineteenth century metaphorized modern subjectivity as a balancing act between inside/outside, female/male, body/mind, native/foreign, proletarian/aristocrat."[1] Subtitled "The Secret Witness," Brown's baroque tale features many individuals or forces that, undetected, cross thresholds into the private: radical immigrants who challenge the early republic's commitment to democracy; impostors like Craig, who enters the Dudley home and joins the family business, only to defraud it; voyeurs, like Baxter, who spies on the private activities of his neighbours; morally questionable men like Ormond, who penetrates locked chambers, eavesdrops on private conversations, reads minds, and threatens to rape women; and contagions like the yellow fever, a disease that no number of locked doors and windows can keep out of the private home.[2] This furtive movement from the public sphere inward to the private is mirrored by the movement that violently pulls elements of the private – the private woman or private possessions such as Dudley's lute or Constantia's miniature – out into the public, into the marketplace, where they lose their singular meanings and become commodities. Even the family home, traditionally aligned with the private, through the new market culture, has become a piece of real estate exchanged between buyers and sellers, executors and heirs.[3]

Initially Brown depicts the permeability of the boundaries between these spheres as the source of *Ormond's* Gothic horror, where the body is threatened by rape, seduction, or contagion; the house-

---

1 Judith Halberstam, *Skin Shows: Gothic Horror and the Technology of Monsters* (Chapel Hill: Duke University Press, 1995) 1.

2 Ormond's masquerade as a chimney sweep is worth noting here in the sense that this disguise permits him to enter the Dudley home through its chimney, a figural violation that anticipates his later attempted rape of Constantia. Significantly, Ormond's masquerades deny others' access to his private sphere while he gains access to theirs. Brown notes: "No one was more impenetrable than Ormond, though no one's real character seemed more easily discerned" (131).

3 The Dudleys' summer home at Perth Amboy, for example, "modelled by the owner's particular direction" (254) and "painted by Mr. Dudley's own hand," (253)

hold is wracked by deceptive strangers, counterfeit cheques, masquerading visitors; and the nation is straining to incorporate the tens of thousands of new immigrants who come from post-Revolutionary France, incendiary St. Domingue, and elsewhere. But ultimately, Brown's novel questions the naivete of a binary opposition that understands the private realm as a guaranteed site of protection from public threats to the body, household, and nation. Beginning with Dudley's own acknowledgement that "the serpent which had stung him [had been] nurtured in his own bosom" (49), *Ormond* exposes the ways in which the private sphere veils its own unspeakable dangers, in particular, the threat of paternal incest that Brown euphemistically describes as Dudley's "dreadful infatuation[s] and "low debaucher[ies]"(57).

Instead of privileging the private over the public, *Ormond* finally acknowledges the impossibility of keeping the public and the private separate; indeed the necessity of relaxing the boundaries between the public and the private if the Republic is to function as a democracy. In many ways, this erasure of boundaries could be said to enact precisely what is implicit in democratic rhetoric, by interpellating private individuals by drawing them out of the domestic and into the *res publica*, and by allowing individuals to circulate more freely, particularly in terms of gender, class, and nationality.[1] For example, the collapse of a structural opposition between public and private also deconstructs the gendering of those spaces that contain women within the private, domestic sphere. Too great a permeability, however, and individual identity and liberty will be violated, submerged, in the public sphere; too little permeability and the individual will remain isolated and uninterpellated.

Ormond, then, is preoccupied with imagining an ideal relationship

---

symbolizes a sentimental rather than commercial relation to things. When financial ruin forces the Dudleys to sell the home, however, it immediately becomes a commodity to which the owner feels no emotional attachment: the first buyer almost immediately resells the property to Ormond, who then appropriates it to Helena Cleve, who later wills it to Constantia.

1   According to Elizabeth Jane Hinds, "a purely 'private' domain — the home and its domestic activity — could no longer remain separate from a 'public' world of economic activity by the end of the eighteenth century....The private world of private property depends on and, finally, is the model of the public world of commerce." *Private Property: Charles Brockden Brown's Gendered Economics of Virtue* (Newark: University of Delaware Press, 1997) 13, 45.

between the private sphere and the public sphere on three registers: the national, represented by the state; the civic and commercial, represented by the household; and the personal, represented by the body. Composed when the Federalists were drafting the controversial Alien and Sedition Acts, which attempted to restrict the influx of extremist views from France and other sites of democratic revolution, the novel poses questions about the feasibility of achieving absolute independence from other individuals, communities, and nations: How can the United States play a role in international diplomacy while remaining an independent nation? How can one's home economy interact with others while retaining independence? How can one preserve one's personal liberty while simultaneously extending what one Brown scholar has termed "fellow feeling"?[1]

If Brown's central figure for the dangerous collapse of boundaries between the public and the private is the threat of penetration – the nation being overrun by threatening immigrants from France and St. Domingue; the household being penetrated by thieves and murderers; and the body being violated by rape and contagion – then the model antidote for this collapse appears to be romantic union, most conservatively interpreted within the bounds of marriage, an arrangement at once intensely private and significantly political, whereby someone from outside the domestic circle joins the private household. Traditionally the marriage of equals represents the ideal move of the individual from the private domestic but ultimately isolated realm to the public realm. Significantly, it is also the sole means by which the private woman can be made public, if only in the limited sense of being made known sexually to her husband and socially to his kin.

By introducing *Ormond* as a "biographical sketch" (3) of Constantia Dudley, most likely addressed to a prospective husband, Brown frames his novel with a meditation on the intersections between political and sexual virtue. The story begins as a sentimental romance following the young heroine as she moves from youthful reliance on her father's protection and support to independent maturity, when she becomes a young woman capable of choosing her own appropriate marital partner. *Ormond* maps the young republic's attempts to achieve a balance between privacy and publicity onto Constantia's

---

1 Julia Stern, *The Plight of Feeling*, 6.

efforts to retain her "homely liberty" – defined variously as her privacy, her virtue, her self-sufficiency, her independence, her intellectual freedom – while establishing relationships with friends, neighbours, employers, figures of authority, and most significantly, potential husbands. As an unmarried woman, Constantia's participation in the public sphere is most fraught. The Republican woman by definition is expected both to participate in the *res publica* and to retain her virtue, the sexual chastity which served as an index of the privacy achieved by the woman's family. In *Ormond*, Brown particularizes the risks to the private self on the public stage in the case of the woman whose private virtue goes under siege in public.

After her father's business is ruined by Craig, a young man adopted into the family as Dudley's business partner (and possibly his future son-in-law), the Dudleys lose their family home – the seat of privacy, financial self-sufficiency, and family intimacy – and Constantia's blind, depressed father abdicates his role as head of the household. At this point in the novel, the father and daughter exchange their gendered spheres: because Dudley "hate[s] to be seen or known" (121), and makes vain attempts to preserve his privacy by changing the family name, staying indoors, and avoiding "visitants" (61), he becomes the "man at home," to use Brown's phrase, while his chaste teenaged daughter Constantia, who is originally aligned with the domestic and the private, is forced out into the public sphere, to negotiate relations with employers, landlords, and tradespeople as she struggles to preserve the independence of her household.

After rejecting several suitors whom she considers too young or her intellectual inferior, and avoiding the unwanted sexual advances of common men she encounters in the thoroughfares, Constantia meets two individuals who inspire her admiration and love: Ormond, a wealthy intellectual involved in secret international political schemes, and Martinette de Beauvais, a freedom fighter who has cross-dressed to fight for liberty in both Europe and America. In contrast to the transparent Constantia, who is aligned with the home and efforts to maintain the household in the midst of poverty, disease, and fraud, both Martinette and Ormond are allied with masquerade and the public sphere, with contemporary wars, world politics, and masculine military exploits. Born in Europe, employed by various armies across the continent, and temporarily residing in the United States, they are affiliated with no home country, no family nor domestic residence, but rather exist on the international stages they inhabit as public figures.

Although Constantia is intellectually seduced by Ormond and considers marrying him, her romantic passion is also piqued by Martinette, a woman she decides "would prove worthy of her love" (93). This passion prepares the reader for Constantia's similar ardour for her long-lost childhood companion Sophia, who is ultimately identified as the narrator when the friends are reunited late in the novel. With the introduction of these three competing passions, Brown represents both heterosexual marriage and queer romantic union as possible means by which Constantia might preserve her "homely liberty" while participating in the public sphere of the early republic.

However, the climax of the novel seems a cynical surrender to the impossibility of achieving this utopian desire. The heterosexual marriage plot dissolves when the jealous Ormond murders Constantia's father and corners Constantia in a deserted farmhouse at Perth Amboy and threatens her with rape. Similarly, the homosocial sorority that Constantia has enjoyed, first with Martinette, and later with her soulmate Sophia, also seems unsustainable. Sophia's arrival at the house at Perth Amboy recalls her first reunion with Constantia when one woman hears the other's voice through a closed door (241). Brown's image of this second reunion, two women on either side of a locked door neither of them can open, is particularly bleak. The threshold permeated by all of the novel's villains, whether yellow fever, confidence men, or seducers, cannot be spanned by Sophia without the use of violence. Significantly, although Constantia has succeeded in preventing Ormond from raping her by killing him, Brown describes Constantia at this climax to the novel in language associated with the victims of seduction, "hands ... clasped on her breast ..., eyes wildly fixed upon the ceiling, and streaming with tears, and hair unbound and falling confusedly over her bosom and neck" (272) as if to suggest that women's attempts to participate in the public sphere necessitate their violation. And despite her rapturous reunion with her long-lost soulmate, the final scenes of the novel depict Constantia's absolute isolation: with Sophia attending to her new husband, Martinette vanished, her father murdered, and her ex-lover dead by her own hand, Constantia is lost in interiority, in the "erroneous accusations of her conscience" (274).

Brown's ultimate despair regarding the possibility of finding a means of balancing the private and public demands on the self is also reflected in the novel's form. Beginning purportedly as a biographical sketch of the virtuous Republican heroine Constantia Dudley, the novel quickly widens its focus to incorporate digressions, embedded narratives, and biographical sketches of the family, friends, and neighbours through whom Constantia's identity is constituted, as if to suggest that the independent self artificially constructed by biography is ultimately a fiction: that the individual subject is always already part of a larger heterogeneous whole; that the private home is always already penetrated by the public; that the nation must always engage in diplomatic relations with other nations; and that, in order to become part of the *res publica*, women must imagine some sort of participation in the public sphere. It also widens to incorporate the potential suitors who may bring Constantia virtuously into the public sphere through romantic union.

The novel's conclusion, however, reverses this gesture by drawing Constantia into progressively narrower worlds and more private spaces. Whereas the early movement of the novel is epistemologically toward experimentation – new homes, new livelihoods, new foods, new friendships, new suitors – and spatially toward the potential opportunities for fellowship, commerce, and exercise of civic duty in the public sphere, the later scenes of the novel return to known quantities and the private sphere. In the final chapters of the novel, Constantia rejects her third suitor and flees the nation's capital, retreating first to a rural family summer home, later to England, and finally to what Amy Kaplan has termed "the privileged space of the domestic novel – the interiority of the female subject."[1] One could argue that Constantia's flight to the house at Perth Amboy, a site of pastoral immunity from the urban world and its adjacent capitalist market culture, also represents somewhat of a chronological retreat, a nostalgic desire to return to a pre-market, perhaps even pre-Revolutionary Jeffersonian idyll associated with Constantia's (and the nation's) "infantile days" (253), her "innocent and careless youth" (254). The return to England and away from the Republican experiment

---

1   Amy Kaplan, "Manifest Domesticity," *American Literature* 70:3 (1998): 600.

altogether compounds this nostalgic desire for the known values of the pre-Revolutionary world. Given Brown's tendency to spatialize his abstract thoughts, Constantia's final psychological retreat to repeated reviews of the traumatic events preceding her rescue appears to signal her inability or refusal to permit the public to permeate her private world.

Like the form of the Gothic novel, which Maggie Kilgour has compared to Frankenstein's monster, pieced together not altogether seamlessly out of its constituent parts, *Ormond* is concerned with what one could call "crises of relation." Gothic novels often document characters' attempts to negotiate original relationships to larger units so as to exercise individual newfound liberty without forsaking affectional bonds. If *Ormond* depicts a crisis of relation, in the sense that all possible means of interpellating the private individual into the public sphere are foreclosed by the collapse of potential relationships at the novel's end, Brown's vision of the possibilities of intersections between the private world of the individual and the public world of the nation is pessimistic. That said, however, one could find some optimism in Brown's depictions of acts of storytelling. Like the "marriage of speaking and hearing" that Faulkner describes in *Absalom, Absalom!* one hundred and thirty years later, *Ormond* seems to offer storytelling as an alternative union to the marriages and other intimate relationships that ultimately fail in the novel by bringing the isolated individual into the republic of letters through personal narration. Julia Stern has noted that storytelling functions as "a medium of countercontagion in *Ormond*, through which women face loss and attempt to reweave the social fabric their republican brothers have critically weakened."[1] Where confidence men like Craig use their invented autobiographies for self-aggrandizement or refuse to offer tales (Ormond significantly resists all invitations to provide details about his life), women like Martinette, Sophia and Constantia consistently use stories to establish bonds between the private individual and the stranger who listens to her tale. In a novel which rationally debates the value of marriage but offers no models of healthy marriage, storytelling appears to be the most sensual exchange between intimates. Brown scholars, for example, have speculated that

---

1   Stern, *The Plight of Feeling*, 156.

the narrative Sophia tells the mysterious I.E. Rosenberg may function as Sophia's efforts to woo Rosenberg as a husband for her isolated friend. Martinette's sharing of her autobiography with Constantia, beginning in Chapter 19, resembles nothing more than Othello's seduction of Desdemona through a recitation of military exploits; similarly Sophia's and Constantia's joyful exchange of stories at their reunion is described in language far more erotic than any other relationship in the novel: "The appetite for sleep and for food were confounded and lost amidst the impetuosities of a master passion. To look and to talk to each other afforded enchanting occupation for every moment. I would not part from her side, but eat and slept ... with her breath fanning my cheek.... The story of each other's wanderings was told with endless amplification and minuteness.... Henceforth, the stream of our existence was to mix; we were to act and to think in common" (241, 242). Sophia's vision of two independent individuals suddenly acting and thinking in common because of the stories they have shared underlines for the reader the value Brown sees in beginning to write the national narratives that will incorporate the individual American subject into a national imagined community.

If Brown ultimately despairs over the possibility of the public and private spheres safely intersecting through marriage or homosocial union, his own storytelling example in *Ormond* successfully maps the private experiences of his heroine onto the larger political world of America in the first decades after the Revolution. With *Edgar Huntly, Arthur Mervyn,* and *Wieland,* the other novels Brown wrote within the same eighteen-month period, *Ormond* forms a quartet meditating on the historical and social development of the infant nation in a crucial decade of American history.

A Note on the Text

This edition of *Ormond* is based on the 1887 edition published in Philadelphia by David McKay, which, according to Eleanor Tilton, has almost all the emendations accepted by or introduced in the Bicentennial critical edition. Spelling of proper names has been corrected; some spelling and punctuation have been modernized. The goal of this edition is to make available to students an affordable edition of a novel that is currently only available in an expensive scholarly edition. Brief annotations accompany the text to clarify unfamiliar terms. The appendices – Judith Sargent Murray's "On the Equality of the Sexes"; excerpts from John Robison's anti-Illuminati essay, *Proofs of a Conspiracy Against All the Religions and Governments of Europe, Carried on in the Secret Meetings of Free Masons, Illuminati, and Reading Societies*; and excerpts from Reverend Jedidiah Morse's "A Sermon Exhibiting the Present Dangers, and Consequent Duties of the Citizens of the United States" – are intended to provide the reader with historical context for topics raised by the novel.

Charles Brockden Brown: A Brief Chronology

1771   Born January 17 in Philadelphia to merchant Quaker parents.

1781   Began study at the Philadelphia Friends Latin School.

1787   Completed schooling and began studying law at the office of Alexander Wilcocks. Founded the Belles Lettres Club with eight friends.

1789   Contributed the "Rhapsodist" essays to the *Columbian Magazine*.

1790   Met Elihu Hubbard Smith, a medical student and intellectual.

1792   Abandoned the law.

1793   Yellow fever epidemic in Philadelphia.

1794   Wrote poem entitled "Devotion: An Epistle."

1795   Began writing his Philadelphia novel (probably *Arthur Mervyn*).

1796   Moved to New York. Joined the Friendly Club, a group of intellectuals which included Smith, playwright William Dunlap (later his biographer) and others.

1797   Returned to Philadelphia. Completed novel entitled *Sky-Walk* which was never published. Wrote *Alcuin: A Dialogue*, a fictional debate on women's rights.

1798   Published essays and short fiction in the *Philadelphia Weekly Magazine*. *Alcuin* published. Moved to New York in July, where yellow fever epidemic raged. Smith died of yellow fever in September. Brown was seriously infected by yellow fever. His gothic novel *Wieland* published. Drafted "Carwin the Biloquist."

1799   *Ormond*, Part One of *Arthur Mervyn*, and *Edgar Huntly* published. Began to publish and edit *The Monthly Magazine*, and *American Review*.

1800   Part Two of *Arthur Mervyn* published. *The Monthly Magazine* ceased publication in December. Returned to Philadelphia to work with brothers for family mercantile business.

1801   Sentimental novels *Clara Howard* and *Jane Talbot* published.

1803   Began to edit and publish *The Literary Magazine* and *Ameri-*

can Register. Wrote and published political pamphlets: "An Address to the Government of the United States on the Cessation of Louisiana to the French" and "Monroe's Embassy; or, The Conduct of the Government in Relation to Our Claims to the Navigation of the Mississippi."

1804   Married Elizabeth Linn, sister of poet John Blair Linn. Three sons and one daughter. Translation of Volney's *Tableau du climat et du sol des Etats-Unis* published.

1805   Published "Sketch of the Life and Character of John Blair Linn," to accompany Linn's poem, "Valerian."

1806   Family business dissolved. The publication of *The Register* ceased.

1807   Political pamphlet "The British Treaty of Commerce and Navigation" published. Began to publish *The American Register, or General Repository of History, Politics, and Science.* Abandoned *The Literary Magazine.*

1809   Political pamphlet "An Address to the Congress of the United States on the Utility and Justice of Restrictions upon Foreign Commerce" published.

1810   Died of tuberculosis in Philadelphia.

ORMOND;

OR, THE SECRET WITNESS

TO I.E. ROSENBERG

YOU are anxious to obtain some knowledge of the history of Constantia Dudley. I am well acquainted with your motives, and allow that they justify your curiosity. I am willing, to the utmost of my power, to comply with your request, and will now dedicate what leisure I have to the composition of her story.

My narrative will have little of that merit which flows from unity of design. You are desirous of hearing an authentic, and not a fictitious, tale. It will, therefore, be my duty to relate events in no artificial or elaborate order, and without that harmonious congruity and luminous amplification which might justly be displayed in a tale flowing merely from invention. It will be little more than a biographical sketch, in which the facts are distributed and amplified, not as a poetical taste would prescribe, but as the materials afforded me, sometimes abundant and sometimes scanty, would permit.

Constantia, like all the beings made known to us, not by fancy, but experience, has numerous defects. You will readily perceive that her tale is told by her friend; but I hope you will not discover many or glaring proofs of a disposition to extenuate her errors or falsify her character.

Ormond will, perhaps, appear to you a contradictory or unintelligible being. I pretend not to the infallibility of inspiration. He is not a creature of fancy. It was not prudent to unfold *all* the means by which I gained a knowledge of his actions; but these means, though singularly fortunate and accurate, could not be unerring and complete. I have shown him to you as he appeared, on different occasions and at successive periods, to me. This is all that you will demand from a faithful biographer.

If you were not deeply interested in the fate of my friend, yet my undertaking will not be useless, inasmuch as it will introduce you to scenes to which you have been hitherto a stranger. The modes of life, the influence of public events upon the character and happiness of individuals, in America, are new to you. The distinctions of birth, the artificial degrees of esteem or contempt which connect themselves with different professions and ranks in your native country,[1] are but little known among us. Society and manners constitute your favourite study; and I am willing to believe that my relation will supply you with knowledge, on these heads, not to be otherwise obtained. If these details be, in that respect, unsatisfactory, all that I can add is my counsel to go and examine for yourself.

S.C.

---

1 Germany.

CHAPTER I.

STEPHEN DUDLEY was a native of New York. He was educated to the profession of a painter. His father's trade was that of an apothecary. But, his son manifesting an attachment to the pencil, he was resolved that it should be gratified. For this end Stephen was sent at an early age to Europe, and not only enjoyed the instructions of Fuseli and Bartolozzi,[1] but spent a considerable period in Italy in studying the Augustan and Medicean monuments. It was intended that he should practise his art in his native city; but the young man, though reconciled to this scheme by deference to paternal authority, and by a sense of its propriety, was willing as long as possible to postpone it. The liberality of his father relieved him from all pecuniary cares. His whole time was devoted to the improvement of his skill in his favourite art, and the enriching of his mind with every valuable accomplishment. He was endowed with a comprehensive genius and indefatigable industry. His progress was proportionably rapid, and he passed his time without much regard to futurity, being too well satisfied with the present to anticipate a change. A change, however, was unavoidable, and he was obliged at length to pay a reluctant obedience to his father's repeated summons. The death of his wife had rendered his society still more necessary to the old gentleman.

He married before his return. The woman whom he had selected was an unportioned orphan, and was recommended merely by her moral qualities. These, however, were eminent, and secured to her, till the end of her life, the affection of her husband. Though painting was capable of fully gratifying his taste as matter of amusement, he quickly found that in his new situation it would not answer the ends of a profession. His father supported himself by the profits of his shop, but with all his industry he could do no more than procure a subsistence for himself and his son.

Till his father's death young Dudley attached himself to painting.

---

1   Fuseli and Bartolozzi: Influential in the English romantic movement, Henry Fuseli (1741-1825) was a Swiss-born painter known for his melodramatic historical and Gothic paintings. Francesco Bartolozzi (1727-1815) was an engraver who, after studying painting and engraving in Florence and Venice, began his career in Rome. In 1764 Bartolozzi was invited to make engravings for his English patron, King George III.

His gains were slender; but he loved the art, and his father's profession rendered his own exertions in a great degree superfluous. The death of the elder Dudley introduced an important change in his situation. It thenceforth became necessary to strike into some new path, to deny himself the indulgence of his inclinations and regulate his future exertions by a view to nothing but gain. There was little room for choice. His habits had disqualified him for mechanical employments. He could not stoop to the imaginary indignity which attended them, nor spare the time necessary to obtain the requisite degree of skill. His father died in possession of some stock, and a sufficient portion of credit to supply its annual decays. He lived at what they call a *good stand*, and enjoyed a certain quantity of permanent custom. The knowledge that was required was as easily obtained as the elements of any other profession, and was not wholly unallied to the pursuits in which he had sometimes engaged. Hence he could not hesitate long in forming his resolution, but assumed the management of his father's concerns with a cheerful and determined spirit.

The knowledge of his business was acquired in no long time. He was stimulated to the acquisition by a sense of duty, he was inured to habits of industry, and there were few things capable to resist a strenuous exertion of his faculties. Knowledge of whatever kind afforded a compensation to labour; but, the task being finished, that which remained, which in ordinary apprehensions would have been esteemed an easy and smooth path, was to him insupportably disgustful. The drudgery of a shop, where all the faculties were at a stand and one day was an unvaried repetition of the foregoing, was too incongenial to his disposition not to be a source of discontent. This was an evil which it was the tendency of time to increase rather than diminish. The longer he endured it the less tolerable it became. He could not forbear comparing his present situation with his former, and deriving from the contrast perpetual food for melancholy.

The indulgence of his father had contributed to instil into him prejudices, in consequence of which a certain species of disgrace was annexed to every employment of which the only purpose was gain. His present situation not only precluded all those pursuits which exalt and harmonize the feelings, but was detested by him as something humiliating and ignominious. His wife was of a pliant temper, and her condition less influenced by this change than that of her husband. She was qualified to be his comforter; but, instead of dispelling his gloom by judicious arguments or a seasonable example of vivacity, she caught the infection that preyed upon his mind, and augmented his anxieties by partaking in them.

By enlarging in some degree the foundation on which his father had built, he had provided the means of a future secession, and might console himself with the prospect of enjoying his darling ease at some period of his life. This period was necessarily too remote for his wishes; and, had not certain occurrences taken place, by which he was flattered with the immediate possession of ease, it is far from being certain that he would not have fallen a victim to his growing disquietudes.

He was one morning engaged behind his counter as usual, when a youth came into his shop, and, in terms that bespoke the union of fearlessness and frankness, inquired whether he could be engaged as an apprentice. A proposal of this kind could not be suddenly rejected or adopted. He stood in need of assistance: the youth was manly and blooming, and exhibited a modest and ingenuous aspect. It was possible that he was, in every respect, qualified for the post for which he applied, but it was previously necessary to ascertain these qualifications. For this end he requested the youth to call at his house in the evening, when he should be at leisure to converse with him, and furnished him with suitable directions.

The youth came according to appointment. On being questioned as to his birthplace and origin, he stated that he was a native of Wakefield, in Yorkshire; that his family were honest, and his education not mean; that he was the eldest of many children, and, having attained an age at which he conceived it his duty to provide for himself, he had, with the concurrence of his friends, come to America, in search of the means of independent subsistence; that he had just arrived in a ship which he named, and, his scanty stock of money being likely to be speedily consumed, this had been the first effort he had made to procure employment.

His tale was circumstantial and consistent, and his veracity appeared liable to no doubt. He was master of his book and his pen, and had acquired more than the rudiments of Latin. Mr. Dudley did not require much time to deliberate. In a few days the youth was established as a member of his family and as a coadjutor in his shop, nothing but food, clothing, and lodging being stipulated as the reward of his services.

The young man improved daily in the good opinion of his master. His apprehension was quick, his sobriety invariable, and his application incessant. Though by no means presumptuous or arrogant, he was not wanting in a suitable degree of self-confidence. All his propensities appeared to concentre in his occupation and the promotion of his master's interest, from which he was drawn aside by no allurements of sensual or intellectual pleasure. In a short time he was able to relieve his master of most of the toils of his profession; and Mr. Dudley a thousand times congratulated himself on possessing a servant equally qualified by his talents and his probity. He gradually remitted his attention to his own concerns, and placed more absolute reliance on the fidelity of his dependant.

Young Craig (that was the name of the youth) maintained a punctual correspondence with family, and confided to his patron not only copies of all the letters which he himself wrote, but those which, from time to time, he received. He had several correspondents, but the chief of those were his mother and his eldest sister. The sentiments contained in their letters breathed the most appropriate simplicity and tenderness, and flowed, with the nicest propriety, from the different relationships of mother and sister. The style and even the penmanship were distinct and characteristical.

One of the first of these epistles was written by the mother to Mr. Dudley, on being informed by her son of his present engagement. It was dictated by that concern for the welfare of her child befitting the maternal character. Gratitude for the ready acceptance of the youth's services, and for the benignity of his deportment towards him, a just representation of which had been received by her from the boy himself, was expressed with no inconsiderable elegance; as well as her earnest wishes that Mr. Dudley should extend to him not only the indulgence, but the moral superintendence, of a parent.

To this Mr. Dudley conceived it incumbent upon him to return a consenting answer, and letters were in this manner occasionally interchanged between them.

Things remained in this situation for three years, during which period every day enhanced the reputation of Craig for stability and integrity. A sort of provisional engagement had been made between the parents, unattended, however, by any legal or formal act, that things should remain on their present footing for three years. When this period terminated, it seemed as if a new engagement had become necessary. Craig expressed the utmost willingness to renew the former contract, but his master began to think that the services of his pupil merited a higher recompense. He ascribed the prosperity that had hitherto attended him to the disinterested exertions of his apprentice. His social and literary gratifications had been increased by the increase of his leisure. These were capable of being still more enlarged. He had not yet acquired what he deemed a sufficiency, and could not therefore wholly relieve himself from the turmoils and humiliation of a professional life. He concluded that he should at once consult his own interest and perform no more than an act of justice to a faithful servant, by making Craig his partner, and allowing him a share of the profits, on condition of his discharging all the duties of the trade.

When this scheme was proposed to Craig, he professed unbounded gratitude, considered all that he had done as amply rewarded by the pleasure of performance, and as being nothing more than was prescribed by his duty. He promised that this change in his situation should have no other effect than to furnish new incitements to diligence and fidelity in the promotion of an interest which would then become, in a still higher degree than formerly, a common one. Mr. Dudley communicated his intention to Craig's mother, who, in addition to many grateful acknowledgments, stated that a kinsman of her son had enabled him, in case of entering into partnership, to add a small sum to the common stock, and that for this sum Craig was authorized to draw upon a London banker.

The proposed arrangement was speedily effected. Craig was charged with the management of all affairs, and Mr. Dudley retired to the enjoyment of still greater leisure. Two years elapsed, and nothing occurred to interrupt the harmony that subsisted between the partners. Mr. Dudley's condition might be esteemed prosperous. His wealth was constantly accumulating. He had nearly attained all that he wished, and his wishes still aimed at nothing less than splendid opulence. He had annually increased the permanent sources of his revenue. His daughter was the only survivor of many children, who perished in their infancy, before habit and maturity had rendered the parental tie difficult to break. This daughter had already exhibited proofs of a mind susceptible of high improvement, and the loveliness of her person promised to keep pace with her mental acquisitions. He charged himself with the care of her education, and found no weariness or satiety in this task that might not be amply relieved by the recreations of science and literature. He flattered himself that his career, which had hitherto been exempt from any considerable impediment, would terminate in tranquillity. Few men might, with more propriety, have discarded all apprehensions respecting futurity.

Craig had several sisters and one brother, younger than himself. Mr. Dudley, desirous of promoting the happiness of this family, proposed to send for this brother and have him educated to his own profession, insinuating to his partner that, at the time when the boy should have gained sufficient stability and knowledge, he himself might be disposed to relinquish the profession altogether, on terms particularly advantageous to the two brothers, who might thenceforth conduct their business jointly. Craig had been eloquent in praise of this lad, and his testimony had, from time to time, been confirmed by that of his mother and sister. He had often expressed his wishes for the prosperity of the lad, and, when his mother had expressed her doubts as to the best method of disposing of him, modestly requested Mr. Dudley's advice on this head. The proposal, therefore, might be supposed to be particularly acceptable; and yet Craig expressed reluctance to concur with it. This reluctance was accompanied with certain tokens which sufficiently showed whence it arose. Craig appeared unwilling to increase those obligations under which he already laboured. His sense of gratitude was too acute to allow him to heighten it by the reception of new benefits.

It might be imagined that this objection would be easily removed; but the obstinacy of Craig's opposition was invincible. Mr. Dudley could not relinquish a scheme to which no stronger objection could be made. And, since his partner could not be prevailed upon to make this proposal to the friends of the lad, he was determined to do it himself. He maintained an intercourse by letters with several of those friends which he formed in his youth. One of them usually resided in London. From him he received, about this time, a letter, in which, among other information, the writer mentioned his intention of setting out on a tour through Yorkshire and the Scottish Highlands. Mr.

Dudley thought this a suitable opportunity for executing his design in favour of young Craig. He entertained no doubts about the worth and condition of this family, but was still desirous of obtaining some information on this head from one who would pass through the town where they resided, who would examine with his own eyes, and on whose discernment and integrity he could place an implicit reliance. He concealed this intention from his partner, and intrusted his letter to a friend who was just embarking for Europe. In due season he received an answer, confirming, in all respects, Craig's representations, but informing him that the lad had been lately disposed of in a way not equally advantageous with that which Mr. Dudley had proposed, but such as would not admit of change.

If doubts could possibly be entertained respecting the character and views of Craig, this evidence would have dispelled them. But plans, however skilfully contrived, if founded on imposture, cannot fail of being sometimes detected. Craig had occasion to be absent from the city for some weeks. Meanwhile, a letter had been left at his lodgings by one who merely inquired if that were the dwelling of Mr. Dudley, and, being answered by the servant in the affirmative, left the letter without further parley. It was superscribed with a name unknown to any of the family, and in a hand which its badness rendered almost illegible. The servant placed it in a situation to be seen by his master.

Mr. Dudley allowed it to remain unopened for a considerable time. At length, deeming it excusable to discover, by any means, the person to whom it was addressed, he ventured to unseal it. It was dated at Portsmouth in New Hampshire. The signature was Mary Mansfield. It was addressed to her son, and was a curious specimen of illiterateness. Mary herself was unable to write, as she reminds her son, and had therefore procured the assistance of Mrs. Dewitt, for whose family she washed. The amanuensis was but little superior in the arts of penmanship to her principal. The contents of the epistle were made out with some difficulty. This was the substance of it: —

Mary reproaches her son for deserting her and letting five years pass away without allowing her to hear from him. She informed him of her distresses as they flowed from sickness and poverty, and were aggravated by the loss of her son, who was so handsome and promising a lad. She related her marriage with Zekel Hackney, who first brought her tidings of her boy. He was master, it seems, of a fishing-smack,[1] and voyaged sometimes to New York. In one of his visits to this city, he met a mighty spry young man, in whom he thought he recognized his wife's son. He had traced him to the house of Mr. Dudley, and, on inquiry, discovered that the lad resided here. On his return he communicated the tidings to his spouse, who had now written to reproach him for his neglect of his poor old mother, and to entreat his assistance to relieve her from the necessity of drudging for her livelihood.

This letter was capable of an obvious construction. It was, no doubt, founded in mistake, though it was to be acknowledged that the mistake was singular. Such was the conclusion immediately formed by Mr. Dudley. He quietly replaced the letter on the mantel-piece, where it had before stood, and dismissed the affair from his thoughts.

Next day Craig returned from his journey. Mr. Dudley was employed in examining some papers in a desk that stood behind the door in the apartment in which the letter was placed. There was no other person in the room when Craig entered it. He did not perceive Mr. Dudley, who was screened from observation by his silence and by an open door. As soon as he entered, Mr. Dudley looked at him, and made no haste to speak. The letter, whose superscription was turned towards him, immediately attracted Craig's attention. He seized it with some degree of eagerness, and, observing the broken seal, thrust it hastily into his pocket, muttering at the same time, in a tone betokening a mixture of consternation and anger, "Damn it!" He immediately left the room, still uninformed of the presence of Mr. Dudley, who began to muse, with some earnestness, on what he had seen. Soon after he left this room and went into another, in which the family usually sat. In about twenty minutes Craig made his appearance with his usual freedom and plausibility. Complimentary and customary topics were discussed. Mrs. Dudley and her daughter were likewise present. The uneasiness which the incident just mentioned had occasioned in the mind of Mr. Dudley was at first dispelled by the disembarrassed behaviour of his partner; but new matter of suspicion was speedily afforded him. He observed that his partner spoke of his present entrance as of the first since his arrival, and that when the lady

---

1   fishing-smack: single-masted boat.

mentioned that he had been the subject of a curious mistake, a letter being directed to him by a strange name and left there during his absence, he pretended total ignorance of the circumstance. The young lady was immediately directed by her mother to bring the letter, which lay, she said, on the mantel-tree in the next room.

During this scene Mr. Dudley was silent. He anticipated the disappointment of the messenger, believing the letter to have been removed. What then was his surprise when the messenger returned bearing the letter in her hand! Craig examined and read it, and commented, with great mirth, on the contents, acting all the while as if he had never seen it before. These appearances were not qualified to quiet suspicion. The more Dudley brooded over them, the more dissatisfied he became. He, however, concealed his thoughts as well from Craig himself as his family, impatiently waiting for some new occurrence to arise by which he might square his future proceedings.

During Craig's absence, Mrs. Dudley had thought this a proper occasion for cleaning his apartment. The furniture, and, among the rest, a large chest strongly fastened, was removed into an adjoining room, which was otherwise unoccupied and which was usually kept locked. When the cleansing was finished, the furniture was replaced, except this trunk, which its bulk, the indolence of the servant, and her opinion of its uselessness, occasioned her to leave in the closet.

About a week after this, on a Saturday evening, Craig invited to sup with him a friend who was to embark, on the ensuing Monday, for Jamaica. During supper, at which the family were present, the discourse turned on the voyage on which the guest was about to enter. In the course of talk, the stranger expressed how much he stood in need of a strong and commodious chest, in which he might safely deposit his clothes and papers. Not being apprized of the early departure of the vessel, he had deferred, till it was too late, applying to an artisan.

Craig desired him to set himself at rest on that head, for that he had in his possession just such a trunk as he described. It was of no use to him, being long filled with nothing better than refuse and lumber, and that, if he would, he might send for it the next morning. He turned to Mrs. Dudley, and observed that the trunk to which he alluded was in her possession, and he would thank her to direct its removal into his own apartment, that he might empty it of its present contents and prepare it for the service of his friend. To this she readily assented.

There was nothing mysterious in this affair, but the mind of Mr. Dudley was pained with doubts. He was now as prone to suspect as he was formerly disposed to confidence. This evening he put the key of the closet in his own pocket. When inquired for the next day, it was of course missing. It could not be found on the most diligent search. The occasion was not of such moment as to justify breaking the door. Mr. Dudley imagined that he saw, in Craig, more uneasiness at this disappointment than he was willing to express. There was no remedy. The chest remained where it was, and next morning the ship departed on her voyage.

Craig accompanied his friend on board, was prevailed upon to go to sea with him, designing to return with the pilot-boat; but, when the pilot was preparing to leave the vessel, such was this man's complaisance to the wishes of his friend, that he concluded to perform the remainder of the voyage in his company. The consequences are easily seen. Craig had gone with a resolution of never returning. The unhappy Dudley was left to deplore the total ruin of his fortune which had fallen a prey to the arts of a subtle impostor.

The chest was opened, and the part which Craig had been playing for some years with so much success was perfectly explained. It appeared that the sum which Craig had contributed to the common stock, when first admitted into partnership, had been previously purloined from the daily receipts of his shop, of which an exact register was kept. Craig had been so indiscreet as to preserve this accusing record, and it was discovered in this depository. He was the son of Mary Mansfield, and a native of Portsmouth. The history of the Wakefield family, specious and complicated as it was, was entirely fictitious. The letters had been forged, and the correspondence supported by his own dexterity. Here was found the letter which Mr. Dudley had written to his friend requesting him to make certain inquiries at Wakefield, and which he imagined that he had delivered with his own hands to a trusty bearer. Here was the original draught of the answer he received. The manner in which this stratagem had been accomplished came gradually to light. The letter which was written to the Yorkshire traveller had been purloined, and another, with a similar superscription, in which the hand of Dudley was exactly imitated, and containing only brief and general remarks, had been placed in its stead. Craig must have suspected its contents, and by this suspicion have been incited to the theft. The answer which the Englishman had really written, and which sufficiently corresponded with the forged letter, had been intercepted by Craig, and furnished him a model from which he might construct an answer adapted to his own purposes.

This imposture had not been sustained for a trivial purpose. He had embezzled a large share of the stock, and had employed the credit of the house to procure extensive remittances to be made to an agent at a distance, by whom the property was effectually secured. Craig had gone to participate these spoils, while the whole estate of Mr. Dudley was insufficient to pay the demands that were consequently made upon him.

It was his lot to fall into the grasp of men who squared their actions by no other standard than law, and who esteemed every claim to be incontestably just that could plead that sanction. They did not indeed throw him into prison. When they had despoiled him of every remnant of his property, they deemed themselves entitled to his gratitude for leaving his person unmolested.

CHAPTER II.

THUS in a moment was this man thrown from the summit of affluence to the lowest indigence. He had been habituated to independence and ease. This reverse, therefore, was the harder to bear. His present situation was much worse than at his father's death. Then he was sanguine with youth and glowing with health. He possessed a fund on which he could commence his operations. Materials were at hand, and nothing was wanted but skill to use them. Now he had advanced in life. His frame was not exempt from infirmity. He had so long reposed on the bosom of opulence and enjoyed the respect attendant on wealth, that he felt himself totally incapacitated for a new station. His misfortune had not been foreseen. It was embittered by the consciousness of his own imprudence, and by recollecting that the serpent which had stung him was nurtured in his own bosom.

It was not merely frugal fare and an humble dwelling to which he was condemned. The evils to be dreaded were beggary and contempt. Luxury and leisure were not merely denied him. He must bend all his efforts to procure clothing and food, to preserve his family from nakedness and famine. His spirit would not brook dependence. To live upon charity, or to take advantage of the compassion of his friends, was a destiny far worse than any other. To this, therefore, he would not consent. However irksome and painful it might prove, he determined to procure his bread by the labour of his hands.

But to what scene or kind of employment should he betake himself? He could not endure to exhibit this reverse of fortune on the same theatre which had witnessed his prosperity. One of his first measures was to remove from New York to Philadelphia. How should he employ himself in his new abode? Painting, the art in which he was expert, would not afford him the means of subsistence. Though no despicable musician, he did not esteem himself qualified to be a teacher of this art. This profession, besides, was treated by his new neighbours with general though unmerited contempt. There were few things on which he prided himself more than on the facilities and elegancies of his penmanship. He was, besides, well acquainted with arithmetic and accounting. He concluded, therefore, to offer his services as a writer in a public office. This employment demanded little bodily exertion. He had spent much of his time at the book and the desk: his new occupation, therefore, was farther recommended by its resemblance to his ancient modes of life.

The first situation of this kind for which he applied he obtained. The duties were constant, but not otherwise toilsome or arduous. The emoluments were slender; but by contracting, within limits as narrow as possible, his expenses, they could be made subservient to the mere purposes of subsistence. He hired a small house in the suburbs of the city. It consisted of a room above and below, and a kitchen. His wife, daughter, and one girl, composed its inhabitants.

As long as his mind was occupied in projecting and executing these arrangements, it was diverted from uneasy contemplations. When his life became uniform, and day followed day in monotonous succession, and the novelty of his employment had disappeared, his cheerfulness began likewise to fade, and was succeeded by unconquerable melancholy. His present condition was in every respect the contrast of his former. His servitude was intolerable. He was associated with sordid hirelings, gross and uneducated, who treated his age with rude familiarity, and insulted his ears with ribaldry and scurril jests. He was subject to command, and had his portion of daily drudgery allotted to him, to be performed for a pittance no more than would buy the bread which he daily consumed. The task assigned him was technical and formal. He was perpetually encumbered with the rubbish of law, and waded with laborious steps through its endless tautologies, its impertinent circuities, its lying assertions and hateful artifices. Nothing occurred to relieve or diversify the scene. It was one tedious round of scrawling and jargon; a tissue made up of the shreds and remnants of barbarous antiquity, polluted with the rust of ages, and patched, by the stupidity of modern workmen, into new deformity.

When the day's task was finished, jaded spirits, and a body enfeebled by reluctant application, were but little adapted to domestic enjoyments. These indeed were incompatible with a temper like his, to whom the privation of the comforts that attended his former condition was equivalent to the loss of life. These privations were still more painful to his wife, and her death added one more calamity to those under which he already groaned. He had always loved her with the tenderest affection, and he justly regarded this evil as surpassing all his former woes.

But his destiny seemed never weary of persecuting him. It was not enough that he should fall a victim to the most atrocious arts, that he should wear out his days in solitude and drudgery, that he should feel not only the personal restraints and hardships attendant upon indigence, but the keener pangs that result from negligence and contumely. He was imperfectly recovered from the shock occasioned by the death of his wife, when his sight was invaded by a cataract. Its progress was rapid, and terminated in total blindness.

He was now disabled from pursuing his usual occupation. He was shut out from the light of heaven, and debarred of every human comfort. Condemned to eternal dark and worse than the helplessness of infancy, he was dependent for the meanest offices on the kindness of others, and he who had formerly abounded in the gifts of fortune thought only of ending his days in a jail or an almshouse.

His situation, however, was alleviated by one circumstance. He had a daughter, whom I have formerly mentioned as the only survivor of many children. She was sixteen years of age when the storm of adversity fell upon her father's house. It may be thought that one educated as she had been, in the gratification of all her wishes, and at an age of timidity and inexperience, would have been less fitted than her father for encountering misfortune; and yet, when the task of comforter fell upon her, her strength was not found wanting. Her fortitude was immediately put to the test. This reverse did not only affect her obliquely and through the medium of her family, but directly, and in one way usually very distressful to female feelings.

Her fortune and character had attracted many admirers. One of them had some reason to flatter himself with success. Miss Dudley's notions had little in common with those around her. She had learned to square her conduct, in a considerable degree, not by the hasty impulses of inclination, but by the dictates of truth. She yielded nothing to caprice or passion. Not that she was perfectly exempt from intervals of weakness or from the necessity of painful struggles, but these intervals were transient, and these struggles always successful. She was no stranger to the pleadings of love, from the lips of others and in her own bosom; but its tumults were brief, and speedily gave place to quiet thoughts and steadfast purposes.

She had listened to the solicitations of one not unworthy in himself, and amply recommended by the circumstances of family and fortune. He was young, and therefore impetuous. Of the good that he sought, he was not willing to delay the acquisition for a moment. She had been taught a very different lesson. Marriage included vows of irrevocable affection and obedience. It was a contract to endure for life. To form this connection in extreme youth, before time had unfolded and modelled the characters of the parties, was, in her opinion, a proof of pernicious and opprobrious temerity. Not to perceive the propriety of delay in this case, or to be regardless of the motives that would enjoin upon us a deliberate procedure, furnished an unanswerable objection to any man's pretensions. She was sensible, however, that this, like other mistakes, was curable. If her arguments failed to remove it, time, it was likely, would effect the purpose. If she rejected a matrimonial proposal for the present, it was for reasons that might not preclude her future acceptance of it.

Her scruples, in the present case, did not relate to the temper, or person, or understanding of her lover, but to his age, to the imperfections of their acquaintance, and to the want of that permanence of character which can flow only from the progress of time and knowledge. These objections, which so rarely exist, were conclusive with her. There was no danger of her relinquishing them in compliance with the remonstrances of parents and the solicitations of her lover, though the one and the other were urged with all the force of authority and insinuation. The prescriptions of duty were too clear to allow her to hesitate and waver, but the consciousness of rectitude could not secure her from temporary vexations.

Her parents were blemished with some of the frailties of that character. They held themselves entitled to prescribe in this article, but they forbore to exert their power. They condescended to persuade; but it was manifest that they regarded their own conduct as a relaxation of right; and, had not the lover's importunities suddenly ceased, it is not possible to tell how far the happiness of Miss Dudley might have been endangered. The misfortunes of her father were no sooner publicly known, than the youth forbore his visits, and embarked on a voyage which he had long projected, but which had been hitherto delayed by a superior regard to the interests of his passion.

It must be allowed that the lady had not foreseen this event. She had exercised her judgment upon his character, and had not been deceived. Before this desertion, had it been clearly stated to her apprehension, she would have readily admitted it to be probable. She knew the fascination of wealth, and the delusiveness of self-confidence. She was superior to the folly of supposing him exempt from sinister influences, and deaf to the whispers of ambition; and yet the manner in which she was affected by this event convinced her that her heart had a larger share than her reason in dictating her expectations.

Yet it must not be supposed that she suffered any very acute distress on this account. She was grieved less for her own sake than his. She had no design of entering into marriage in less than seven years from this period. Not a single hope, relative to her own condition, had been frustrated. She had only been mistaken in her favourable conceptions of another. He had exhibited less constancy and virtue than her heart had taught her to expect.

With those opinions, she could devote herself, with a single heart, to the alleviation of her parents' sorrows. This change in her condition she treated lightly, and retained her cheerfulness unimpaired. This happened because, in a rational estimate, and so far as it affected herself, the misfortune was slight, and because her dejection would only tend to augment the disconsolateness of her parents, while, on the other hand, her serenity was calculated to infuse the same confidence into them. She indulged herself in no fits of exclamation or moodiness. She listened in silence to their invectives and laments, and seized every opportunity that offered to inspire them with courage, to set before them the good, as well as ill, to which they were reserved, to suggest expedients for improving their condition, and to soften the asperities of his new mode of life, to her father, by every species of blandishment and tenderness.

She refused no personal exertion to the common benefit. She incited her father to diligence, as well by her example as by her exhortations; suggested plans, and superintended or assisted in the execution of them. The infirmities of sex and age vanished before the motives to courage and activity flowing from her new situation. When settled in his new abode and profession, she began to deliberate what conduct was incumbent on herself, how she might participate with her father the burden of the common maintenance, and blunt the edge of this calamity by the resources of a powerful and cultivated mind.

In the first place, she disposed of every superfluous garb and trinket. She reduced her wardrobe to the plainest and cheapest establishment. By this means alone, she supplied her father's necessities with a considerable sum. Her music and even her books were not spared, – not from the slight esteem in which these were held by her, but because she was thenceforth to become an economist of time as well as of money, because musical instruments are not necessary to the practice of this art in its highest perfection, and because books, when she should procure leisure to read or money to purchase them, might be obtained in a cheaper and more commodious form than those costly and splendid volumes with which her father's munificence had formerly supplied her.

To make her expenses as limited as possible was her next care. For this end she assumed the province of cook, the washing of house and clothes, and the cleansing of furniture. Their house was small, the family consisted of no more than four persons, and all formality and expensiveness were studiously discarded; but her strength was unequal to unavoidable tasks. A vigorous constitution could not supply the place of laborious habits, and this part of her plan must have been changed for one less frugal. The aid of a servant must have been hired, if it had not been furnished by gratitude.

Some years before this misfortune, her mother had taken under her protection a girl, the daughter of a poor woman, who subsisted by labour, and who, dying, left this child without friend or protector. This girl possessed no very improvable capacity, and therefore could not benefit by the benevolent exertions of her young mistress as much as the latter desired; but her temper was artless and affection- ate, and she attached herself to Constantia with the most entire devotion. In this change of fortune she would not consent to be separated; and Miss Dudley, influenced by her affection to her Lucy, and reflecting that on the whole it was most to her advantage to share with her at once her kindness and her poverty, retained her as her companion. With this girl she shared the domestic duties, scrupling not to divide with her the meanest and most rugged as well as the lightest offices.

This was not all. She, in the next place, considered whether her ability extended no further than to save. Could she not by the employment of her hands increase the income as well as diminish the expense? Why should she be precluded from all lucrative occupation? She soon came to a resolution. She was mistress of her needle, and this skill she conceived herself bound to employ for her own subsis- tence.

Clothing is one of the necessaries of human existence. The art of the tailor is scarcely of less use than that of the tiller of the ground. There are few the gains of which are better merited, and less injuri- ous to the principles of human society. She resolved therefore to become a workwoman, and to employ in this way the leisure she pos- sessed from household avocations. To this scheme she was obliged to reconcile not only herself but her parents. The conquest of their prej- udices was no easy task, but her patience and skill finally succeeded, and she procured needlework in sufficient quantity to enable her to enhance in no trivial degree the common fund.

It is one thing barely to comply with the urgencies of the case, and to do that which in necessitous circumstances is best. But to conform with grace and cheerfulness, to yield no place to fruitless recriminations and repinings, to contract the evils into as small a compass as possible, and extract from our condition all possible good, is a task of a different kind.

Mr. Dudley's situation required from him frugality and diligence. He was regular and unintermitted in his application to his pen. He was frugal. His slender income was administered agreeably to the maxims of his daughter; but he was unhappy. He experienced in its full extent the bitterness of disappointment.

He gave himself up for the most part to a listless melancholy. Sometimes his impatience would produce effects less excusable, and conjure up an accusing and irascible spirit. His wife and even his daughter he would make the objects of peevish and absurd reproaches. These were moments when her heart drooped indeed, and her tears could not be restrained from flowing. These fits were transitory and rare, and, when they had passed, the father seldom failed to mingle tokens of contrition and repentance with the tears of his daughter. Her arguments and soothings were seldom disappointed of success. Her mother's disposition was soft and pliant, but she could not accommodate herself to the necessity of her husband's affairs. She was obliged to endure the want of some indulgences, but she reserved to herself the liberty of complaining, and to subdue this spirit in her was found utterly impracticable. She died a victim to discontent.

This event deepened the gloom that shrouded the soul of her father, and rendered the task of consolation still more difficult. She did not despair. Her sweetness and patience was invincible by any thing that had already happened, but her fortitude did not exceed the standard of human nature. Evils now began to menace her, to which it is likely she would have yielded, had not their approach been intercepted by an evil of a different kind.

The pressure of grief is sometimes such as to prompt us to seek a refuge in voluntary death. We must lay aside the burden which we cannot sustain. If thought degenerate into a vehicle of pain, what remains but to destroy that vehicle? For this end death is the obvious, but not the only, or, morally speaking, the worst, means. There is one method of obtaining the bliss of forgetfulness, in comparison with which suicide is innocent.

The strongest mind is swayed by circumstances. There is no firmness of integrity, perhaps, able to repel every species of temptation which is produced by the present constitution of human affairs; and yet temptation is successful chiefly by virtue of its gradual and invisible approaches. We rush into danger, because we are not aware of its existence, and have not therefore provided the means of safety, and the demon that seizes us is hourly reinforced by habit. Our opposition grows fainter in proportion as our adversary acquires new strength, and the man becomes enslaved by the most sordid vices, whose fall would, at a former period, have been deemed impossible, or who would have been imagined liable to any species of depravity more than to this.

Mr. Dudley's education had entailed upon him many errors; yet who would have supposed it possible for him to be enslaved by a depraved appetite, to be enamoured of low debauchery, and to grasp at the happiness that intoxication had to bestow? This was a mournful period in Constantia's history. My feelings will not suffer me to dwell upon it. I cannot describe the manner in which she was affected by the first symptoms of this depravity, the struggles which she made to counteract this dreadful infatuation, and the grief which she experienced from the repeated miscarriage of her efforts. I will not detail her various expedients for this end, the appeals which she made to his understanding, to his sense of honour and dread of infamy, to the gratitude to which she was entitled, and to the injunctions of parental duty. I will not detail his fits of remorse, his fruitless penitence and continual relapses, nor depict the heart-breaking scenes of uproar and violence and foul disgrace that accompanied his paroxysms of drunkenness.

The only intellectual amusement which this lady allowed herself was writing. She enjoyed one distant friend, with whom she maintained an uninterrupted correspondence, and to whom she confided a circumstantial and copious relation of all these particulars. That friend is the writer of these memoirs. It is not impossible but that these letters may be communicated to the world at some future period. The picture which they exhibit is hourly exemplified and realized, though, in the many-coloured scenes of human life, none surpasses it in disastrousness and horror. My eyes almost wept themselves dry over this part of her tale.

In this state of things Mr. Dudley's blindness might justly be accounted, even in its immediate effects, a fortunate event. It dissolved the spell by which he was bound, and which, it is probable, would never have been otherwise broken. It restored him to himself, and showed him, with a distinctness which made him shudder, the gulf to which he was hastening. But nothing can compensate to the sufferer the evils of blindness. It was the business of Constantia's life to alleviate those sufferings, to cherish and console her father, and to rescue him, by the labour of her hands, from dependence on public charity. For this end, her industry and solicitude were never at rest. She was able, by that industry, to provide him and herself with necessaries. Their portion was scanty, and, if it sometimes exceeded the standard of their wants, not less frequently fell short of it. For all her toils and disquietudes she esteemed herself fully compensated by the smiles of her father. He indeed could seldom be prompted to smile, or to suppress the dictates of that despair which flowed from his sense of this new calamity, and the aggravations of hardship which his recent insobrieties had occasioned to his daughter.

She purchased what books her scanty stock would allow, and borrowed others. These she read to him when her engagements would permit. At other times she was accustomed to solace herself with her own music. The lute which her father had purchased in Italy, and which had been disposed of, among the rest of his effects, at public sale, had been gratuitously restored to him by the purchaser, on condition of his retaining it in his possession. His blindness and inoccupation now broke the long silence to which this instrument had been condemned, and afforded an accompaniment to the young lady's voice.

Her chief employment was conversation. She resorted to this as the best means of breaking the monotony of the scene; but this purpose was not only accomplished, but other benefits of the highest value accrued from it. The habits of a painter eminently tended to vivify and make exact her father's conceptions and delineations of visible objects. The sphere of his youthful observation comprised more ingredients of the picturesque than any other sphere. The most precious materials of the moral history of mankind are derived from the revolutions of Italy. Italian features and landscape constitute the chosen field of the artist. No one had more carefully explored this field than Mr. Dudley. His time, when abroad, had been divided between residence at Rome, and excursions to Calabria and Tuscany. Few impressions were effaced from his capacious register, and these were now rendered, by his eloquence, nearly as conspicuous to his companion as to himself.

She was imbued with an ardent thirst of knowledge, and, by the acuteness of her remarks and the judiciousness of her inquiries, reflected back upon his understanding as much improvement as she received. These efforts to render his calamity tolerable, and inure him to the profiting by his own resources, were aided by time; and, when reconciled by habit to unrespited gloom, he was sometimes visited by gleams of cheerfulness, and drew advantageous comparisons between his present and former situation. A stillness not unakin to happiness frequently diffused itself over their winter evenings. Constantia enjoyed, in their full extent, the felicities of health and self-approbation. The genius and eloquence of her father, nourished by perpetual exercise, and undiverted from its purpose by the intrusion of visible objects, frequently afforded her a delight in comparison with which all other pleasures were mean.

CHAPTER III.

THIS period of tranquillity was short. Poverty hovered at their threshold, and, in a state precarious as theirs, trials could not be long excluded. The lady was more accustomed to anticipate good than evil, but she was not unconscious that the winter, which was hastening, would bring with it numerous inconveniences. Wants during that season are multiplied, while the means of supplying them either fail or are diminished. Fuel is, alone, a cause of expense equal to all other articles of subsistence. Her dwelling was old, crazy, and full of avenues to air. It was evident that neither fire nor clothing would, in a habitation like that, attemper the chilling blasts. Her scanty gains were equal to their needs during summer, but would probably fall short during the prevalence of cold.

These reflections could not fail sometimes to intrude. She indulged them as long as they served merely to suggest expedients and provisions for the future, but laboured to call away her attention when they merely produced anxiety. This she more easily effected, as some months of summer were still to come, and her knowledge of the vicissitudes to which human life is subject taught her to rely upon the occurrence of some fortunate though unforeseen event.

Accident suggested an expedient of this kind. Passing through an alley in the upper part of the town, her eye was caught by a label on the door of a small house signifying that it was to be let. It was smaller than that she at present occupied, but it had an aspect of much greater comfort and neatness. Its situation near the centre of the city, in a quiet, cleanly, and well-paved alley, was far preferable to that of her present habitation, in the suburbs, scarcely accessible in winter, for pools and gullies, and in a neighbourhood abounding with indigence and profligacy. She likewise considered that the rent of this might be less, and that the proprietor of this might have more forbearance and benignity than she had hitherto met with.

Unconversant as she was with the world, imbued with the timidity of her sex and her youth, many enterprises were arduous to her which would, to age and experience, have been easy. Her reluctances, however, when required by necessity, were overcome, and all the measures which her situation prescribed executed with address and dispatch. One marking her deportment would have perceived nothing but dignity and courage. He would have regarded these as the fruits of habitual independence and exertion, whereas they were merely the results of clear perceptions and inflexible resolves.

The proprietor of this mansion was immediately sought out, and a bargain, favourable as she could reasonably desire, concluded. Possession was to be taken in a week. For this end carters and draymen were to be engaged, household implements to be prepared for removal, and negligence and knavery prevented by scrupulous attention. The duties of superintendence and execution devolved upon her. Her father's blindness rendered him powerless. His personal ease required no small portion of care. Household and professional functions were not to be omitted. She stood alone in the world. There was none whose services or counsel she could claim. Tortured by multiplicity of cares, shrinking from exposure to rude eyes and from contention with refractory and insolent spirits, and overpowered with fatigue and disgust, she was yet compelled to retain a cheerful tone in her father's presence, and to struggle with his regrets and his peevishness.

Oh, my friend, methinks I now see thee, encountering the sneers and obstinacy of the meanest of mankind, subjecting that frame of thine, so exquisitely delicate, and therefore so feeble, to the vilest drudgery. I see thee, leading thy unhappy father to his new dwelling, and stifling the sighs produced by his fruitless repinings and unseasonable scruples. Why was I not partaker of thy cares and labours? Why was I severed from thee by the ocean, and kept in ignorance of thy state? I was not without motives to anxiety, for I was friendless as thou; but how unlike to thine was my condition! I reposed upon down and tissue, never moved but with obsequious attendance and pompous equipage; painting and music were consolations ever at hand, and my cabinet was stored with poetry and science. These, indeed, were insufficient to exclude care, and, with regard to the past, I have no wish but that I had shared with my friend her toilsome and humiliating lot. However an erroneous world might judge, thy life was full of dignity, and thy moments of happiness not few, since happiness is only attendant on the performance of our duty.

A toilsome and sultry week was terminated by a Sabbath of repose. Her new dwelling possessed indisputable advantages over her old. Not the least of these benefits consisted in the vicinity of people peaceable and honest, though poor. She was no longer shocked by the clamours of debauchery, and exposed by her situation to the danger of being mistaken by the profligate of either sex for one of their own class. It was reasonable to consider this change of abode as fortunate; and yet circumstances quickly occurred which suggested a very different conclusion.

She had no intercourse, which necessity did not prescribe, with the rest of the world. She screened herself as much as possible from intercourse with prying and loquacious neighbours. Her father's inclination in this respect coincided with her own, though their love of seclusion was prompted by different motives. Visitants were hated by the father, because his dignity was hurt by communication with the vulgar. The daughter set too much value upon time willingly to waste it upon trifles and triflers. She had no pride to subdue, and therefore never escaped from well-meant importunity at the expense of politeness and good-humour. In her moments of leisure, she betook herself to the poet and the moralist for relief.

She could not at all times suppress the consciousness of the evils which surrounded and threatened her. She could not but rightly estimate the absorbing and brutifying nature of that toil to which she was condemned. Literature had hitherto been regarded as her solace. She knew that meditation and converse, as well as books and the pen, are instruments of knowledge; but her musing thoughts were too often fixed upon her own condition. Her father's soaring moods and luminous intervals grew less frequent. Conversation was too rarely abstracted from personal considerations, and strayed less often than before into the wilds of fancy or the mazes of analysis.

These circumstances led her to reflect whether subsistence might not be obtained by occupations purely intellectual. Instruction was needed by the young of both sexes. Females frequently performed the office of teachers. Was there no branch of her present knowledge which she might claim wages for imparting to others? Was there no art within her reach to acquire, convertible into means of gain? Women are generally limited to what is sensual and ornamental. Music and painting, and the Italian and French languages, are bounds which they seldom pass. In these pursuits it is not possible – nor is it expected – that they should arrive at the skill of adepts. The education of Constantia had been regulated by the peculiar views of her father, who sought to make her, not alluring and voluptuous, but eloquent and wise. He therefore limited her studies to Latin and English. Instead of familiarizing her with the amorous effusions of Petrarch and Racine, he made her thoroughly conversant with Tacitus and Milton. Instead of making her a practical musician or pencilist, he conducted her to the school of Newton and Hartley, unveiled to her the mathematical properties of light and sound, taught her, as a metaphysician and anatomist, the structure and power of the senses, and discussed with her the principles and progress of human society.[1]

---

1   Constantia's father is eager to provide her with an education that avoids the sensuality and ornamental qualities of most women's educations at this time. Petrarch (1304-74) was an Italian poet and humanist best known for his courtly love sonnets. Racine (1639-99) was a neoclassical French tragic dramatist whose characters often acted in ways criticized as excessively passionate. In contrast to their excess, Dudley esteems the works of Tacitus (c.55-117?), a Roman historian known for his history of the Roman empire, and John Milton (1608-1674), poet, writer, and political pamphleteer. Brown might be referring to Milton's *Of Education* (1644) which stresses classical learning as a means of acquiring moral understanding, to Milton's writing on social and political issues, i.e. his defence of civil and religious liberty, or to *Paradise Lost* and *Paradise Regained* whose emphasis on moral behaviour might

These accomplishments tended to render her superior to the rest of women, but in no degree qualified her for the post of a female instructor. She saw and lamented her deficiencies, and gradually formed the resolution of supplying them. Her knowledge of the Latin tongue and of grammatical principles rendered easy the acquisition of Italian and French, these being merely scions from the Roman stock.

Having had occasion, previous to her change of dwelling, to purchase paper at a bookseller's, the man had offered her, at a very low price, a second-hand copy of Veroni's grammar. The offer had been declined, her views at that time being otherwise directed. Now, however, this incident was remembered, and a resolution instantly formed to purchase the book. As soon as the light declined and her daily task at the needle had drawn to a close, she set out to execute this purpose. Arriving at the house of the bookseller, she perceived that the doors and windows were closed. Night having not yet arrived, the conjecture easily occurred that some one had died in the house. She had always dealt with this man for books and paper, and had always been treated with civility. Her heart readily admitted some sympathy with his distress, and, to remove her doubts, she turned to a person who stood at the entrance of the next house, and who held a cloth steeped in vinegar to his nostrils. In reply to her question, the stranger said, in a tone of the deepest consternation, "Mr. Watson do you mean? He is dead; he died last night of the *yellow fever.*"

The name of this disease was not absolutely new to her ears.[1] She had been apprized of its rapid and destructive progress in one quarter of the city, but, hitherto, it had existed, with regard to her, chiefly in

---

give Constantia an antidote to the "amorous effusions" her father fears. Sir Isaac Newton (1643-1727) was an English mathematician and physicist who established modern laws of physical dynamics. David Hartley (1705-1757) was an associationist psychologist who believed that distinctly human qualities, such as imagination, ambition, sympathy, religious affection and morality, are learned rather than innate.

1   In 1793, an epidemic of yellow fever killed over 4,000 citizens of Philadelphia. It was the worst health disaster ever to befall an American city. Believed to have been brought to the young nation's capital aboard a ship from the West Indies, the fever killed one in six citizens who did not flee the city. Despite homemade preventives such as cloth masks soaked in garlic juice, vinegar, or camphor, the city ground to a halt as victims exhibited symptoms ranging from headache, backache and fever to jaundice and vomiting blood. Some, like Brown himself, gained immunity for life from one non-fatal attack.

the form of rumour. She had not realized the nature or probable extent of the evil. She lived at no great distance from the seat of the malady, but her neighbourhood had been hitherto exempt. So wholly unused was she to contemplate pestilence, except at a distance, that its actual existence in the bosom of this city was incredible.

Contagious diseases, she well knew, periodically visited and laid waste the Greek and Egyptian cities. It constituted no small part of that mass of evil, political and physical, by which that portion of the world had been so long afflicted. That a pest equally malignant had assailed the metropolis of her own country – a town famous for the salubrity of its airs and the perfection of its police – had something in it so wild and uncouth, that she could not reconcile herself to the possibility of such an event.

The death of Watson, however, filled her mind with awful reflections. The purpose of her walk was forgotten amidst more momentous considerations. She bent her steps pensively homeward. She had now leisure to remark the symptoms of terror with which all ranks appeared to have been seized. The streets were as much frequented as ever, but there were few passengers whose countenances did not betray alarm, and who did not employ the imaginary antidote to infection, – vinegar.

Having reached home, she quickly discovered in her father an unusual solemnity and thoughtfulness. He had no power to conceal his emotions from his daughter, when her efforts to discover them were earnestly exerted. She learned that during her absence he had been visited by his next neighbour, – a thrifty, sober, and well-meaning, but ignorant and meddling, person, by name Whiston. This person, being equally inquisitive into other men's affairs and communicative of his own, was always an unwelcome visitant. On this occasion, he had come to disburden on Mr. Dudley his fears of disease and death. His tale of the origin and progress of the epidemic, of the number and suddenness of recent deaths, was delivered with endless prolixity. With this account he mingled prognostics of the future, counselled Mr. Dudley to fly from the scene of danger, and stated his own schemes and resolutions. After having thoroughly affrighted and wearied his companion, he took his leave.

Constantia endeavoured to remove the impression which had been thus needlessly made. She urged her doubts as to the truth of

Whiston's representations, and endeavoured, in various ways, to extenuate the danger.

"Nay, my child," said her father, "thou needest not reason on the subject. I am not afraid. At least, on my own account, I fear nothing. What is life to me, that I should dread to lose it? If on any account I should tremble, it is on thine, my angelic girl. Thou dost not deserve thus early to perish; and yet, if my love for thee were rational, perhaps I ought to wish it. An evil destiny will pursue thee to the close of thy life, be it never so long.

"I know that ignorance and folly breed the phantoms by which themselves are perplexed and terrified, and that Whiston is a fool; but here the truth is too plain to be disguised. This malady is pestilential. Havoc and despair will accompany its progress, and its progress will be rapid. The tragedies of Marseilles and Messina[1] will be reacted on this stage.

"For a time, we in this quarter will be exempt; but it will surely reach us at last, and then, whither shall we fly? For the rich, the whole world is a safe asylum; but for us, indigent and wretched, what fate is reserved but to stay and perish? If the disease spare us, we must perish by neglect and famine. Alarm will be far and wide diffused. Fear will hinder those who supply the market from entering the city. The price of food will become exorbitant. Our present source of subsistence, ignominious and scanty as it is, will be cut off. Traffic and labour of every kind will be at an end. We shall die, but not until we have witnessed and endured horrors that surpass thy powers of conception.

"I know full well the enormity of this evil. I have been at Messina, and talked with many who witnessed the state of that city in 1743. I will not freeze thy blood with the recital. Anticipation has a tendency to lessen or prevent some evils, but pestilence is not of that number. Strange untowardness of destiny! That thou and I should be cast upon a scene like this!"

Mr. Dudley joined with uncommon powers of discernment a species of perverseness not easily accounted for. He acted as if the inevitable evils of her lot were not sufficient for the trial of his daugh-

---

1   tragedies of Marseilles and Messina: Marseilles, a city in Southeast France, and Messina, an Italian Mediterranean port, were both the sites of black death outbreaks in the early part of the eighteenth century, which killed almost half their populations.

ter's patience. Instead of comforter and counsellor, he fostered impatience in himself, and endeavoured, with the utmost diligence, to undermine her fortitude and disconcert her schemes. The task was assigned to her, not only of subduing her own fears, but of maintaining the contest with his disastrous eloquence. In most cases she had not failed of success. Hitherto their causes of anxiety her own observation had, in some degree, enabled her to estimate at their just value. The rueful pictures which his imagination was wont to portray affected her for a moment; but deliberate scrutiny commonly enabled her to detect and demonstrate their fallacy. Now, however, the theme was new. Panic and foreboding found their way to her heart in defiance of her struggles. She had no experience by which to counteract this impulse. All that remained was to beguile her own and her father's cares by counterfeiting cheerfulness and introducing new topics.

This panic, stifled for a time, renewed its sway when she retired to her chamber. Never did futurity wear, to her fancy, so dark a hue. Never did her condition appear to her in a light so dreary and forlorn. To fly from the danger was impossible. How should accommodation at a distance be procured? The means of subsistence were indissolubly connected with her present residence, but the progress of this disease would cut off these means, and leave her to be beset not only with pestilence but famine. What provision could she make against an evil like this?

CHAPTER IV.

THE terms on which she had been admitted into this house included the advance of one quarter's rent and the monthly payment of subsequent dues. The requisite sum had been with difficulty collected, the landlord had twice called to remind her of her stipulation, and this day had been fixed for the discharge of this debt. He had omitted, contrary to her expectations and her wishes, to come. It was probable, however, that they should meet on the ensuing day. If he should fail in this respect, it appeared to be her duty to carry the money to his house; and this it had been her resolution to perform.

Now, however, new views were suggested to her thoughts. By the payment of this debt she should leave herself nearly destitute. The flight and terror of the citizens would deprive her of employment. Want of food was an immediate and inevitable evil which the payment of this sum would produce. Was it just to incur this evil? To retain the means of luxurious gratification would be wrong, but to bereave herself and her father of bare subsistence was surely no dictate of duty.

It is true the penalty of nonpayment was always in the landlord's hands. He was empowered by the law to sell their movables and expel them from his house. It was now no time for a penalty like this to be incurred. But from this treatment it was reasonable to hope that his lenity would save them. Was it not right to wait till the alternative of expulsion or payment was imposed? Meanwhile, however, she was subjected to the torments of suspense and to the guilt of a broken promise. These consequences were to be eluded only in one way. By visiting her landlord and stating her true condition, it was possible that his compassion would remit claims which were in themselves unreasonable and uncommon. The tender of the money, accompanied by representations sufficiently earnest and pathetic, might possibly be declined.

These reflections were, next morning, submitted to her father. Her decision in this case was of less importance in his eyes than in those of his daughter. Should the money be retained, it was, in his opinion, a pittance too small to afford them effectual support. Supposing provisions to be had at any price, which was itself improbable, that price would be exorbitant. The general confusion would probably last for months, and thirty dollars would be devoured in a few weeks even in a time of safety. To give or to keep was indifferent for another reason. It was absurd for those to consult about means of subsistence for the next month, when it was fixed that they should die to-morrow. The true proceeding was obvious. The landlord's character was well known to him by means of the plaints and invectives of their neighbours, most of whom were tenants of the same man. If the money were offered, his avarice would receive it, in spite of all the pleas that she should urge. If it were detained without leave, an officer of justice would quickly be despatched to claim it.

This statement was sufficient to take away from Constantia the hope that she had fostered. "What then," said she, after a pause, "is my father's advice? Shall I go forthwith and deliver the money?"

"No," said he; "stay till he sends for it. Have you forgotten that Mathews resides in the very midst of this disease? There is no need to thrust yourself within its fangs. They will reach us time enough. It is likely his messenger will be an agent of the law. No matter. The debt will be merely increased by a few charges. In a state like ours, the miserable remnant is not worth caring for."

This reasoning did not impart conviction to the lady. The danger flowing from a tainted atmosphere was not small; but to incur that danger was wiser than to exasperate their landlord, to augment the debt, and to encounter the disgrace accruing from a constable's visits. The conversation was dropped, and, presently after, she set out on a visit to Mathews.

She fully estimated the importance to her happiness of the sum which she was going to pay. The general panic had already, in some degree, produced the effect she chiefly dreaded – the failure of employment for her needle. Her father had, with his usual diligence at self-torment, supplied her with sufficient proofs of the covetous and obdurate temper of her creditor. Insupportable, however, as the evil of payment was, it was better to incur it spontaneously than by means of legal process. The desperateness of this proceeding, therefore, did not prevent her from adopting it, but it filled her heart with the bitterest sensations. Absorbed, as she passed along, by these, she was nearly insensible to the vacancy which now prevailed in a quarter which formerly resounded with the din of voices and carriages.

As she approached the house to which she was going, her reluctance to proceed increased. Frequently she paused to recollect the motives that had prescribed this task, and to reinforce her purposes. At length she arrived at the house. Now, for the first time, her attention was excited by the silence and desolation that surrounded her. This evidence of fear and of danger struck upon her heart. All appeared to have fled from the presence of this unseen and terrible foe. The temerity of adventuring thus into the jaws of the pest now appeared to her in glaring colours.

Appearances suggested a reflection which had not previously occurred, and which tended to console her. Was it not probable that Mathews had likewise flown? His habits were calculated to endear to him his life; he would scarcely be among the last to shun perils like these; the omission of his promised visit on the preceding day might be owing to his absence from the city, and thus, without subjection to any painful alternative, she might be suffered to retain the money.

To give certainty to this hope, she cast her eye towards the house opposite to which she now stood. Her heart drooped on perceiving proofs that the dwelling was still inhabited. The door was open, and the windows in the second and third storey were raised. Near the entrance, in the street, stood a cart. The horse attached to it, in his form and furniture and attitude, was an emblem of torpor and decay. His gaunt sides, motionless limbs, his gummy and dead eyes, and his head hanging to the ground, were in unison with the craziness of the vehicle to which he belonged, and the paltry and bedusted harness which covered him. No attendant nor any human face was visible. The stillness, though at an hour customarily busy, was uninterrupted except by the sound of wheels moving at an almost indistinguishable distance.

She paused for a moment to contemplate this unwonted spectacle. Her trepidations were mingled with emotions not unakin to sublimity, but the consciousness of danger speedily prevailed, and she hastened to acquit herself of her engagement. She approached the door for this purpose, but before she could draw the bell her motions were attested by sounds from within. The staircase was opposite the door. Two persons were now discovered descending the stair. They lifted between them a heavy mass, which was presently discerned to be a coffin. Shocked by this discovery, and trembling, she withdrew from the entrance.

At this moment a door on the opposite side of the street opened and a female came out. Constantia approached her involuntarily, and, her appearance not being unattractive, adventured, more by gestures than by words, to inquire whose obsequies were thus unceremoniously conducted. The woman informed her that the dead was Mathews, who, two days before, was walking about, indifferent to and braving danger. She cut short the narrative, which her companion seemed willing to prolong and to embellish with all its circumstances, and hastened home with her utmost expedition.

The mind of Constantia was a stranger to pusillanimity. Death, as the common lot of all, was regarded by her without perturbation. The value of life, though not annihilated, was certainly diminished, by adversity. With whatever solemnity contemplated, it excited on her own account no aversion or inquietude. For her father's sake only, death was an evil to be ardently deprecated. The nature of the prevalent disease, the limits and modes of its influence, the risk that is incurred by approaching the sick or the dead, or by breathing the surrounding element, were subjects foreign to her education. She judged like the mass of mankind from the most obvious appearances, and was subject, like them, to impulses which disdained the control of her reason. With all her complacency for death and speculative resignation to the fate that governs the world, disquiet and alarm pervaded her bosom on this occasion.

The deplorable state to which her father would be reduced by her death was seen and lamented; but her tremulous sensations flowed not from this source. They were, in some sort, inexplicable and mechanical. In spite of recollection and reflection, they bewildered and harassed her, and subsided only of their own accord.

The death of Mathews was productive of one desirable consequence. Till the present tumult were passed, and his representatives had leisure to inspect his affairs, his debtors would probably remain unmolested. He, likewise, who should succeed to the inheritance, might possess very different qualities, and be as much distinguished for equity as Mathews had been for extortion. These reflections lightened her footsteps as she hied homeward. The knowledge she had gained, she hoped, would counterpoise, in her father's apprehension, the perils which accompanied the acquisition of it.

She had scarcely passed her own threshold, when she was followed by Whiston. This man pursued the occupation of a cooper. He performed journeywork in a shop, which, unfortunately for him, was situated near the water, and at a small distance from the scene of original infection. This day his employer had dismissed his workmen, and Whiston was at liberty to retire from the city, – a scheme which had been the theme of deliberation and discussion during the preceding fortnight.

Hitherto his apprehensions seemed to have molested others more than himself. The rumours and conjectures industriously collected during the day were, in the evening, copiously detailed to his neighbours, and his own mind appeared to be disburdened of its cares in proportion as he filled others with terror and inquietude. The predictions of physicians, the measures of precaution prescribed by the government, the progress of the malady, and the history of the victims who were hourly destroyed by it, were communicated with tormenting prolixity and terrifying minuteness.

On these accounts as well as on others, no one's visits were more unwelcome than his. As his deportment was sober and honest, and his intentions harmless, he was always treated, by Constantia, with politeness, though his entrance always produced a momentary depression of her spirits. On this evening she was less fitted than ever to repel those anxieties which his conversation was qualified to produce. His entrance, therefore, was observed with sincere regret.

Contrary, however, to her expectation, Whiston brought with him new manners and a new expression of countenance. He was silent and abstracted; his eye was full of inquietude, and wandered with perpetual restlessness. On these tokens being remarked, he expressed, in faltering accents, his belief that he had contracted this disease, and that now it was too late for him to leave the city.

Mr. Dudley's education was somewhat medical. He was so far interested in his guest as to inquire into his sensations. They were such as were commonly the preludes to fever. Mr. Dudley, while he endeavoured, by cheerful tones, to banish his dejection, exhorted him to go home, and to take some hot and wholesome draught, in consequence of which he might rise to-morrow with his usual health. This advice was gratefully received, and Whiston put a period to his visit much sooner than was customary.

Mr. Dudley entertained no doubts that Whiston was seized with the reigning disease, and extinguished the faint hope which his daughter had cherished, that their district would escape. Whiston's habitation was nearly opposite their own; but, as they made no use of their front-room, they had seldom an opportunity of observing the transactions of their neighbours. This distance and seclusion were congenial with her feelings, and she derived pleasure from her father's confession that they contributed to personal security.

Constantia was accustomed to rise with the dawn, and traverse, for an hour, the State-House Mall. As she took her walk the next morning, she pondered with astonishment the present situation of the city. The air was bright and pure, and apparently salubrious. Security and silence seemed to hover over the scene. She was only reminded of the true state of things by the occasional appearance of carriages loaded with household utensils tending toward the country, and by the odour of vinegar by which every passenger was accompanied. The public walk was cool and fragrant as formerly, skirted by verdure as bright and shaded by foliage as luxuriant, but it was no longer frequented by lively steps and cheerful countenances. Its solitude was uninterrupted by any but herself.

This day passed without furnishing any occasion to leave the house. She was less sedulously employed than usual, as the clothes on which she was engaged belonged to a family who had precipitately left the city. She had leisure, therefore, to ruminate. She could not but feel some concern in the fate of Whiston. He was a young man who subsisted on the fruits of his labour, and divided his gains with an only sister who lived with him, and who performed every household office.

This girl was humble and innocent, and of a temper affectionate and mild. Casual intercourse only had taken place between her and Constantia. They were too dissimilar for any pleasure to arise from communication; but the latter was sufficiently disposed to extend to her harmless neighbour the sympathy and succour which she needed. Whiston had come from a distant part of the country, and his sister was the only person in the city with whom he was connected by ties of kindred. In case of his sickness, therefore, their condition would be helpless and deplorable.

Evening arrived, and Whiston failed to pay his customary visit. She mentioned this omission to her father, and expressed her apprehension as to the cause of it. He did not discountenance the inference which she drew from this circumstance, and assented to the justice of the picture which she drew of the calamitous state to which Whiston and his sister would be reduced by the indisposition of either. She then ventured to suggest the propriety of visiting the house, and of thus ascertaining the truth.

To this proposal Mr. Dudley urged the most vehement objections. What purpose could be served by entering their dwelling? What benefit would flow but the gratification of a dangerous curiosity? Constantia was disabled from furnishing pecuniary aid. She could not act the part of physician or nurse. Her father stood in need of a thousand personal services, and the drudgery of cleansing and cooking already exceeded the bounds of her strength. The hazard of contracting the disease by conversing with the sick was imminent. What services was she able to render equivalent to the consequences of her own sickness and death?

These representations had temporary influence. They recalled her, for a moment, from her purpose; but this purpose was speedily re-embraced. She reflected that the evil to herself, formidable as it was, was barely problematical. That converse with the sick would impart this disease was by no means certain. Whiston might at least be visited. Perhaps she should find him well. If sick, his disease might be unepidemical, or curable by seasonable assistance. He might stand in need of a physician, and she was more able than his sister to summon this aid.

Her father listened calmly to her reasonings. After a pause, he gave his consent. In doing this, he was influenced not by the conviction that his daughter's safety would be exposed to no hazard, but from a belief that, though she might shun infection for the present, it would inevitably seize her during some period of the progress of this pest.

CHAPTER V.

IT WAS now dusk, and she hastened to perform this duty. Whiston's dwelling was wooden and of small dimensions. She lifted the latch softly and entered. The lower room was unoccupied. She advanced to the foot of a narrow staircase, and knocked and listened, but no answer was returned to the summons. Hence there was reason to infer that no one was within; but this, from other considerations, was extremely improbable. The truth could be ascertained only be ascending the stair. Some feminine scruples were to be subdued before this proceeding could be adopted.

After some hesitation, she determined to ascend. The staircase was terminated by a door at which she again knocked for admission, but in vain. She listened, and presently heard the motion as of some one in bed. This was succeeded by tokens of vehement exertions to vomit. These signs convincing her that the house was not without a tenant, she could not hesitate to enter the room.

Lying in a tattered bed, she now discovered Mary Whiston. Her face was flushed and swelled, her eyes closed, and some power appeared to have laid a leaden hand upon her faculties. The floor was moistened and stained by the effusion from her stomach. Constantia touched her hand, and endeavoured to rouse her. It was with difficulty that her attention was excited. Her languid eyes were scarcely opened before they again closed and she sunk into forgetfulness.

Repeated efforts, however, at length recalled her to herself, and extorted from her some account of her condition. On the day before, at noon, her stomach became diseased, her head dizzy, and her limbs unable to support her. Her brother was absent, and her drowsiness, interrupted only by paroxysms of vomiting, continued till his return late in the evening. He had then shown himself for a few minutes at her bedside, had made some inquiries and precipitately retired, since when he had not reappeared.

It was natural to imagine that Whiston had gone to procure medical assistance. That he had not returned, during a day and a half, was matter of surprise. His own indisposition was recollected, and his absence could only be accounted for by supposing that sickness had disabled him from regaining his own house. What was his real destiny, it was impossible to conjecture. It was not till some months after this period that satisfactory intelligence was gained upon this head.

It appeared that Whiston had allowed his terrors to overpower the sense of what was due to his sister and to humanity. On discovering the condition of the unhappy girl, he left the house, and, instead of seeking a physician, he turned his steps towards the country. After travelling some hours, being exhausted by want of food, by fatigue, and by mental as well as bodily anguish, he laid himself down under the shelter of a hayrick, in a vacant field. Here he was discovered in the morning by the inhabitants of a neighbouring farm-house. These people had too much regard for their own safety to accommodate him under their roof, or even to approach within fifty paces of his person.

A passenger, whose attention and compassion had been excited by this incident, was endowed with more courage. He lifted the stranger in his arms, and carried him from this unwholesome spot to a barn. This was the only service which the passenger was able to perform. Whiston, deserted by every human creature, burning with fever, tormented into madness by thirst, spent three miserable days in agony. When dead, no one would cover his body with earth, but he was suffered to decay by piecemeal.

The dwelling, being at no great distance from the barn, could not be wholly screened from the malignant vapour which a corpse thus neglected could not fail to produce. The inhabitants were preparing, on this account, to change their abode, but, on the eve of their departure, the master of the family became sick. He was, in a short time, followed to the grave by his mother, his wife, and four children.

They probably imbibed their disease from the tainted atmosphere around them. The life of Whiston and their own lives might have been saved by affording the wanderer an asylum and suitable treatment, or, at least, their own deaths might have been avoided by interring his remains.

Meanwhile, Constantia was occupied with reflecting on the scene before her. Not only a physician, but a nurse, was wanting. The last province it was more easy for her to supply than the former. She was acquainted with the abode of but one physician. He lived at no small distance from this spot. To him she immediately hastened; but he was absent, and his numerous engagements left it wholly uncertain when he would return and whether he would consent to increase the number of his patients. Direction was obtained to the residence of another, who was happily disengaged, and who promised to attend immediately. Satisfied with this assurance, she neglected to request directions, by which she might regulate herself on his failing to come.

During her return her thoughts were painfully employed in considering the mode proper for her to pursue in her present perplexing situation. She was for the most part unacquainted with the character of those who composed her neighbourhood. That any would be willing to undertake the tendance of this girl was by no means probable. As wives and mothers, it would perhaps be unjust to require or permit it. As to herself, there were labours and duties of her own sufficient to engross her faculties; yet, by whatever foreign cares or tasks she was oppressed, she felt that to desert this being was impossible.

In the absence of her friend, Mary's state exhibited no change. Constantia, on regaining the house, lighted the remnant of a candle, and resumed her place by the bedside of the sick girl. She impatiently waited for the arrival of the physician, but hour succeeded hour and he came not. All hope of his coming being extinguished, she bethought herself that her father might be able to inform her of the best manner of proceeding. It was likewise her duty to relieve him from the suspense in which her absence would unavoidably plunge him.

On entering her own apartment, she found a stranger in company with Mr. Dudley. The latter, perceiving that she had returned, speedily acquainted her with the views of their guest. His name was M'Crea; he was the nephew of their landlord and was now become, by reversion, the proprietor of the house which they occupied. Mathews had been buried the preceding day, and M'Crea, being well acquainted with the engagements which subsisted between the deceased and Mr. Dudley, had come, thus unseasonably, to demand the rent. He was not unconscious of the inhumanity and sordidness of this proceeding, and therefore endeavoured to disguise it by the usual pretences. All his funds were exhausted. He came not only in his own name, but in that of Mrs. Mathews, his aunt, who was destitute of money to procure daily and indispensable provision, and who was striving to collect a sufficient sum to enable her and the remains of her family to fly from a spot where their lives were in perpetual danger.

These excuses were abundantly fallacious, but Mr. Dudley was too proud to solicit the forbearance of a man like this. He recollected that the engagement on his part was voluntary and explicit, and he disdained to urge his present exigencies as reasons for retracting it. He expressed the utmost readiness to comply with the demand, and merely desired him to wait till Miss Dudley returned. From the inquietudes with which the unusual duration of her absence had filled him, he was now relieved by her entrance.

With an indignant and desponding heart, she complied with her father's directions, and the money being reluctantly delivered, M'Crea took a hasty leave. She was too deeply interested in the fate of Mary Whiston to allow her thoughts to be diverted for the present into a new channel. She described the desolate condition of the girl to her father, and besought him to think of something suitable to her relief.

Mr. Dudley's humanity would not suffer him to disapprove of his daughter's proceeding. He imagined that the symptoms of the patient portended a fatal issue. There were certain complicated remedies which might possibly be beneficial, but these were too costly, and the application would demand more strength than his daughter could bestow. He was unwilling, however, to leave anything within his power untried. Pharmacy had been his trade, and he had reserved, for domestic use, some of the most powerful evacuants. Constantia was supplied with some of these, and he consented that she should spend the night with her patient and watch their operation.

The unhappy Mary received whatever was offered, but her stomach refused to retain it. The night was passed by Constantia without closing her eyes. As soon as the day dawned, she prepared once more to summon the physician, who had failed to comply with his promise. She had scarcely left the house, however, before she met him. He pleaded his numerous engagements in excuse for his last night's negligence, and desired her to make haste to conduct him to the patient.

Having scrutinized her symptoms, he expressed his hopelessness of her recovery. Being informed of the mode in which she had been treated, he declared his approbation of it, but intimated that, these being unsuccessful, all that remained was to furnish her with any liquid she might choose to demand, and wait patiently for the event. During this interview, the physician surveyed the person and dress of Constantia with an inquisitive eye. His countenance betrayed marks of curiosity and compassion, and had he made any approaches to confidence and friendliness, Constantia would not have repelled them. His air was benevolent and candid, and she estimated highly the usefulness of a counsellor and friend in her present circumstances. Some motive, however, hindered him from tendering his service, and in a few moments he withdrew.

Mary's condition hourly grew worse. A corroded and gangrenous stomach was quickly testified by the dark hue and poisonous malignity of the matter which was frequently ejected from it. Her stupor gave place to some degree of peevishness and restlessness. She drank the water that was held to her lips with unspeakable avidity, and derived from this source a momentary alleviation of her pangs. Fortunately for her attendant, her agonies were not of long duration. Constantia was absent from her bedside as rarely and for periods as short as possible. On the succeeding night, the sufferings of the patient terminated in death.

This event took place at two o'clock in the morning, – an hour whose customary stillness was, if possible, increased tenfold by the desolation of the city. The poverty of Mary and of her nurse had deprived the former of the benefits resulting from the change of bed and clothes. Every thing about her was in a condition noisome and detestable. Her yellowish and haggard visage, conspicuous by a feeble light, an atmosphere freighted with malignant vapours, and reminding Constantia at every instant of the perils which encompassed her, the consciousness of solitude and sensations of deadly sickness in her own frame, were sufficient to intimidate a soul of firmer texture than hers.

She was sinking fast into helplessness, when a new train of reflections showed her the necessity of the perseverance. All that remained was to consign the corpse to the grave. She knew that vehicles for this end were provided at the public expense; that, notice being given of the occasion there was for their attendance, a receptacle and carriage for the dead would be instantly provided. Application at this hour, she imagined, would be unseasonable. It must be deferred till the morning, which was yet at some distance.

Meanwhile, to remain at her present post was equally useless and dangerous. She endeavoured to stifle the conviction that some mortal sickness had seized upon her own frame. Her anxieties of head and stomach she was willing to impute to extraordinary fatigue and watchfulness, and hoped that they would be dissipated by an hour's unmolested repose. She formed the resolution of seeking her own chamber.

At this moment, however, the universal silence underwent a slight interruption. The sound was familiar to her ears. It was a signal frequently repeated at the midnight hour during this season of calamity. It was the slow movement of a hearse, apparently passing along the street in which the alley where Mr. Dudley resided terminated. At first this sound had no other effect than to aggravate the dreariness of all around her. Presently it occurred to her that this vehicle might be disengaged. She conceived herself bound to see the last offices performed for the deceased Mary. The sooner so irksome a duty was discharged, the better. Every hour might augment her incapacity for exertion. Should she be unable, when the morning arrived, to go as far as the City-Hall and give the necessary information, the most shocking consequences would ensue. Whiston's house and her own were opposite each other and not connected with any on the same side. A narrow space divided them, and her own chamber was within the sphere of the contagion which would flow, in consequence of such neglect, from that of her neighbour.

Influenced by these considerations, she passed into the street, and gained the corner of the alley, just as the carriage, whose movements she had heard, arrived at the same spot. It was accompanied by two men, negroes, who listened to her tale with respect. Having already a burden of this kind, they could not immediately comply with this request. They promised that, having disposed of their present charge, they would return forthwith and be ready to execute her orders.

Happily, one of these persons was known to her. At other seasons his occupation was that of *wood-carter*, and as such he had performed some services for Mr. Dudley. His temper was gentle and obliging. The character of Constantia had been viewed by him with reverence, and his kindness had relieved her from many painful offices. His old occupation being laid aside for a time, he had betaken himself, like many others of his colour and rank, to the conveyance and burial of the dead.

At Constantia's request, he accompanied her to Whiston's house, and promised to bring with him such assistance as would render her further exertions and attendance unnecessary. Glad to be absolved from any new task, she now retired to her own chamber. In spite of her distempered frame, she presently sunk into sweet sleep. She awoke not till the day had made considerable progress, and found herself invigorated and refreshed. On re-entering Whiston's house, she discovered that her humble friend had faithfully performed his promise, the dead body having disappeared. She deemed it unsafe, as well as unnecessary, to examine the clothes and other property remaining; but, leaving every thing in the condition in which it had been found, she fastened the windows and doors, and thenceforth kept as distant from the house as possible.

CHAPTER VI.

Constantia had now leisure to ruminate upon her own condition. Every day added to the devastation and confusion of the city. The most populous streets were deserted and silent. The greater number of inhabitants had fled, and those who remained were occupied with no cares but those which related to their own safety. The labours of the artisan and the speculations of the merchant were suspended. All shops but those of the apothecaries were shut. No carriage but the hearse was seen, and this was employed, night and day, in the removal of the dead. The customary sources of subsistence were cut off. Those whose fortunes enabled them to leave the city, but who had deferred till now their retreat, were denied an asylum by the terror which pervaded the adjacent country, and by the cruel prohibitions which the neighbouring towns and cities thought it necessary to adopt. Those who lived by the fruits of their daily labour were subjected, in this total inactivity, to the alternative of starving or of subsisting upon public charity.

The meditations of Constantia suggested no alternative but this. The exactions of M'Crea had reduced her whole fortune to five dollars. This would rapidly decay, and her utmost ingenuity could discover no means of procuring a new supply. All the habits of their life had combined to fill both her father and herself with aversion to the acceptance of charity. Yet this avenue, opprobrious and disgustful as it was, afforded the only means of escaping from the worst extremes of famine.

In this state of mind, it was obvious to consider in what way the sum remaining might be most usefully expended. Every species of provision was not equally nutritious or equally cheap. Her mind, active in the pursuit of knowledge and fertile of resources, had lately been engaged in discussing with her father the best means of retaining health in a time of pestilence. On occasions when the malignity of contagious diseases has been most signal, some individuals have escaped. For their safety, they were doubtless indebted to some peculiarities in their constitution or habits. Their diet, their dress, their kind and degree of exercise, must somewhat have contributed to their exemption from the common destiny. These, perhaps, could be ascertained, and when known it was surely proper to conform to them.

In discussing these ideas, Mr. Dudley introduced the mention of a Benedictine of Messina, who, during the prevalence of the plague in that city, was incessantly engaged in administering assistance to those who needed. Notwithstanding his perpetual hazards, he retained perfect health, and was living thirty years after this event. During this period, he fostered a tranquil, fearless, and benevolent spirit, and restricted his diet to water and polenta.[1] Spices, and meats, and

---

1 polenta: an inexpensive, nutritious dish made from ground corn; also known in America as "hasty pudding."

liquors, and all complexities of cookery, were utterly discarded.

These facts now occurred to Constantia's reflections with new vividness, and led to interesting consequences. Polenta, and hasty-pudding or samp, are preparations of the same substance, – a substance which she needed not the experience of others to convince her was no less grateful than nutritive. Indian meal was procurable at ninety cents per bushel. By recollecting former experiments, she knew that this quantity, with no accompaniment but salt, would supply wholesome and plentiful food for four months to one person.[1] The inference was palpable. Three persons were now to be supplied with food, and this supply could be furnished, during four months, at the trivial expense of three dollars. This expedient was at once so uncommon and so desirable, as to be regarded with temporary disbelief. She was inclined to suspect some latent error in her calculation. That a sum thus applied should suffice for the subsistence of a year, which, in ordinary cases, is expended in a few days, was scarcely credible. The more closely, however, the subject was examined, the more incontestably did this inference flow. The mode of preparation was simple and easy, and productive of the fewest toils and inconveniences. The attention of her Lucy was sufficient to this end, and the drudgery of marketing was wholly precluded.

She easily obtained the concurrence of her father, and the scheme was found as practicable and beneficial as her fondest expectations had predicted. Infallible security was thus provided against hunger. This was the only care that was urgent and immediate. While they had food and were exempt from disease, they could live, and were not without their portion of comfort. Her hands were unemployed, but her mind was kept in continual activity. To seclude herself as much as possible from others was the best means of avoiding infection. Spectacles of misery which she was unable to relieve would merely tend to harass her with useless disquietudes and make her frame more accessible to disease. Her father's instructions were sufficient to give her a competent acquaintance with the Italian and

---

1 See this useful fact explained and demonstrated in Count Rumford's Essays. [C.B.B.] Benjamin Thompson, Count Rumford (1753-1814), an Anglo-American scientist, was made Count of the Holy Roman Empire in 1791. His many accomplishments included introducing sociological reforms in Ireland and England, reorganizing the army in Bavaria, and inventing new techniques of cooking, heating, and lighting influenced by his theory of heat.

French languages. His dreary hours were beguiled by this employment, and her mind was furnished with a species of knowledge which she hoped, in future, to make subservient to a more respectable and plentiful subsistence than she had hitherto enjoyed.

Meanwhile, the season advanced, and the havoc which this fatal malady produced increased with portentous rapidity. In alleys and narrow streets, in which the houses were smaller, the inhabitants more numerous and indigent, and the air pent up with unwholesome limits, it raged with greatest violence. Few of Constantia's neighbours possessed the means of removing from the danger. The inhabitants of this alley consisted of three hundred persons. Of these, eight or ten experienced no interruption of their health. Of the rest, two hundred were destroyed in the course of three weeks. Among so many victims, it may be supposed that this disease assumed every terrific and agonizing shape.

It was impossible for Constantia to shut out every token of a calamity thus enormous and thus near. Night was the season usually selected for the removal of the dead. The sound of wheels thus employed was incessant. This, and the images with which it was sure to be accompanied, bereaved her of repose. The shrieks and laments of survivors, who could not be prevented from attending the remains of a husband or child to the place of interment, frequently struck her senses. Sometimes, urged by a furious delirium, the sick would break from their attendants, rush into the streets, and expire on the pavement, amidst frantic outcries and gestures. By these she was often roused from imperfect sleep, and called to reflect upon the fate which impended over her father and herself.

To preserve health in an atmosphere thus infected, and to ward off terror and dismay in a scene of horrors thus hourly accumulating, was impossible. Constantia found it vain to contend against the inroads of sadness. Amidst so dreadful a mortality, it was irrational to cherish the hope that she or her father would escape. Her sensations, in no long time, seemed to justify her apprehensions. Her appetite forsook her, her strength failed, the thirst and lassitude of fever invaded her, and the grave seemed to open for her reception.

Lucy was assailed by the same symptoms at the same time. Household offices were unavoidably neglected. Mr. Dudley retained his health, but he was able only to prepare his scanty food, and supply the cravings of his child with water from the well. His imagination marked him out for the next victim. He could not be blind to the consequences of his own indisposition at a period so critical. Disabled from contributing to each other's assistance, destitute of medicine and food, and even of water to quench their tormenting thirst, unvisited, unknown, and perishing in frightful solitude! These images had a tendency to prostrate the mind, and generate or ripen the seeds of this fatal malady, which, no doubt, at this period of its progress, every one had imbibed.

Contrary to all his fears, he awoke each morning free from pain, though not without an increase of debility. Abstinence from food, and the liberal use of cold water, seemed to have a medicinal operation on the sick. Their pulse gradually resumed its healthful tenor, their strength and their appetite slowly returned, and in ten days they were able to congratulate each other on their restoration.

I will not recount that series of disastrous thoughts which occupied the mind of Constantia during this period. Her lingering and sleepless hours were regarded by her as preludes to death. Though at so immature an age, she had gained large experience of the evils which are allotted to man. Death, which, in her prosperous state, was peculiarly abhorrent to her feelings, was now disrobed of terror. As an entrance into scenes of lightsome and imperishable being, it was the goal of all her wishes. As a passage to oblivion it was still desirable, since forgetfulness was better than the life which she had hitherto led, and which, should her existence be prolonged, it was likely that she could continue to lead.

These gloomy meditations were deprived from the languors of her frame. When these disappeared, her cheerfulness and fortitude revived. She regarded with astonishment and delight the continuance of her father's health and her own restoration. That trial seemed to have been safely undergone to which the life of every one was subject. The air, which till now had been arid and sultry, was changed into cool and moist. The pestilence had reached its utmost height, and now symptoms of remission and decline began to appear. Its declension was more rapid than its progress, and every day added vigour to hope.

When her strength was somewhat retrieved, Constantia called to mind a good woman who lived in her former neighbourhood, and from whom she had received many proofs of artless affection. This woman's name was Sarah Baxter. She lived within a small distance of Constantia's former dwelling. The trade of her husband was that of porter, and she pursued, in addition to the care of a numerous family, the business of a laundress. The superior knowledge and address of Constantia had enabled her to be serviceable to this woman in certain painful and perplexing circumstances.

This service was repaid with the utmost gratitude. Sarah regarded her benefactress with a species of devotion. She could not endure to behold one whom every accent and gesture proved to have once enjoyed affluence and dignity, performing any servile office. In spite of her own multiplied engagements, she compelled Constantia to accept her assistance on many occasions, and could scarcely be prevailed upon to receive any compensation for her labour. Washing clothes was her trade, and from this task she insisted on relieving her lovely patroness.

Constantia's change of dwelling produced much regret in the kind Sarah. She did not allow it to make any change in their previous arrangements, but punctually visited the Dudleys once a week, and carried home with her whatever stood in need of ablution. When the prevalence of disease disabled Constantia from paying her the usual wages, she would by no means consent to be absolved from this task. Her earnestness on this head was not to be eluded; and Constantia, in consenting that her work should, for the present, be performed gratuitously, solaced herself with the prospect of being able, by some future change of fortune, amply to reward her.

Sarah's abode was distant from danger, and her fears were turbulent. She was, nevertheless, punctual in her visits to the Dudleys, and anxious for their safety. In case of their sickness, she had declared her resolution to be their attendant and nurse. Suddenly, however, her visits ceased. The day on which her usual visit was paid was the same with that on which Constantia sickened, but her coming was expected in vain. Her absence was, on some accounts, regarded with pleasure, as it probably secured her from the danger connected with the office of a nurse; but it added to Constantia's cares, inasmuch as her own sickness, or that of some of her family, was the only cause of her detention.

To remove her doubts, the first use which Constantia made of her recovered strength was to visit her laundress. Sarah's house was a theatre of suffering. Her husband was the first of his family assailed by the reigning disease. Two daughters, nearly grown to womanhood, well-disposed and modest girls, the pride and support of their mother, and who lived at service, returned home, sick, at the same time, and died in a few days. Her husband had struggled for eleven days with his disease, and was seized, just before Constantia's arrival, with the pangs of death.

Baxter was endowed with great robustness and activity. This disease did not vanquish him but with tedious and painful struggles. His muscular force now exhausted itself in ghastly contortions, and the house resounded with his ravings. Sarah's courage had yielded to so rapid a succession of evils. Constantia found her shut up in a chamber distant from that of her dying husband, in a paroxysm of grief, and surrounded by her younger children.

Constantia's entrance was like that of an angelic comforter. Sarah was unqualified for any office but that of complaint. With great difficulty she was made to communicate the knowledge of her situation. Her visitant then passed into Baxter's apartment. She forced herself to endure this tremendous scene long enough to discover that it was hastening to close. She left the house, and, hastening to the proper office, engaged the immediate attendance of a hearse. Before the lapse of an hour Baxter's lifeless remains were thrust into a coffin and conveyed away.

Constantia now exerted herself to comfort and encourage the survivors. Her remonstrances incited Sarah to perform with alacrity the measures which prudence dictates on these occasions. The house was purified by the admission of air and the sprinkling of vinegar. Constantia applied her own hand to these tasks, and set her humble friend an example of forethought and activity. Sarah would not consent to part with her till a late hour in the evening.

These exertions had like to have been fatally injurious to Constantia. Her health was not sufficiently confirmed to sustain offices so arduous. In the course of the night her fatigue terminated in fever. In the present more salubrious state of the atmosphere, it assumed no malignant symptoms, and shortly disappeared. During her indisposition she was attended by Sarah, in whose honest bosom no sentiment was more lively than gratitude. Constantia, having promised to renew her visit the next day, had been impatiently expected, and Sarah had come to her dwelling in the evening, full of foreboding and anxiety, to ascertain the cause of her delay. Having gained the bedside of her patroness, no consideration could induce her to retire from it.

Constantia's curiosity was naturally excited as to the cause of Baxter's disease. The simple-hearted Sarah was prolix and minute in the history of her own affairs. No theme was more congenial to her temper than that which was now proposed. In spite of redundance and obscurity in the style of the narrative, Constantia found it in powerful excitements of her sympathy. The tale, on its own account, as well as from the connection of some of its incidents with a subsequent part of these memoirs, is worthy to be here inserted. However foreign the destiny of Monrose may at present appear to the story of the Dudleys, there will hereafter be discovered an intimate connection between them.

CHAPTER VII.

ADJACENT to the house occupied by Baxter was an antique brick tenement. It was one of the first erections made by the followers of William Penn.[1] It had the honour to be used as the temporary residence of that venerable person. Its moss-grown penthouse, crumbling walls, and ruinous *porch*, made it an interesting and picturesque object. Notwithstanding its age, it was still tenable.

This house was occupied, during the preceding months, by a Frenchman. His dress and demeanour were respectable. His mode of life was frugal almost to penuriousness, and his only companion was a daughter. The lady seemed not much less than thirty years of age, but was of a small and delicate frame. It was she that performed every household office. She brought water from the pump and provisions from the market. Their house had no visitants, and was almost always closed. Duly, as the morning returned, a venerable figure was seen issuing from his door, dressed in the same style of tarnished splendour and old-fashioned preciseness. At the dinner-hour he as regularly returned. For the rest of the day he was invisible.

---

1   William Penn (1644-1718): English Quaker who founded the colony of Pennsylvania in 1681 and served as its first governor. Anywhere he had resided would have been especially honoured.

The habitations in this quarter are few and scattered. The pestilence soon showed itself here, and the flight of most of the inhabitants augmented its desolateness and dreariness. For some time, Monrose (that was his name) made his usual appearance in the morning. At length the neighbours remarked that he no longer came forth as usual. Baxter had a notion that Frenchmen were exempt from this disease. He was, besides, deeply and rancorously prejudiced against that nation. There will be no difficulty in accounting for this, when it is known that he had been an English grenadier at Dettingen and Minden.[1] It must likewise be added, that he was considerably timid, and had sickness in his own family. Hence it was that the disappearance of Monrose excited in him no inquisitiveness as to the cause. He did not even mention this circumstance to others.

The lady was occasionally seen as usual in the street. There were always remarkable peculiarities in her behaviour. In the midst of grave and disconsolate looks, she never laid aside an air of solemn dignity. She seemed to shrink from the observation of others, and her eyes were always fixed upon the ground. One evening Baxter was passing the pump while she was drawing water. The sadness which her looks betokened, and a suspicion that her father might be sick, had a momentary effect upon his feelings. He stopped and asked how her father was. She paid a polite attention to his question, and said something in French. This, and the embarrassment of her air, convinced him that his words were not understood. He said no more, (what, indeed, could he say?) but passed on.

Two or three days after this, on returning in the evening to his family, his wife expressed her surprise in not having seen Miss Monrose in the street that day. She had not been at the pump, nor had gone, as usual, to market. This information gave him some disquiet; yet he could form no resolution. As to entering the house and offering his aid, if aid were needed, he had too much regard for his own safety, and too little for that of a frog-eating Frenchman, to think

---

1 Dettingen and Minden: Dettingen is a village in northwest Bavaria, where, in 1743, English, Dutch and German allies of Austria fighting under George II of England defeated the French in the War of Austrian Succession. Minden, a town in North Rhine-West Phalia, Germany, was the scene of an English Hanoverian victory over the French, Austrian and Russian forces in 1759, during the Seven Years War.

seriously of that expedient. His attention was speedily diverted by other objects, and Monrose was, for the present, forgotten.

Baxter's profession was that of a porter. He was thrown out of employment by the present state of things. The solicitude of the guardians of the city was exerted on this occasion, not only in opposing the progress of disease and furnishing provisions to the destitute, but in the preservation of property. For this end the number of nightly watchmen was increased. Baxter entered himself in this service. From nine till twelve o'clock at night it was his province to occupy a certain post.

On this night he attended his post as usual. Twelve o'clock arrived, and he bent his steps homeward. It was necessary to pass by Monrose's door. On approaching this house, the circumstance mentioned by his wife recurred to him. Something like compassion was conjured up in his heart by the figure of the lady, as he recollected to have lately seen it. It was obvious to conclude that sickness was the cause of her seclusion. The same, it might be, had confined her father. If this were true, how deplorable might be their present condition! Without food, without physician or friends, ignorant of the language of the country, and thence unable to communicate their wants or solicit succour, fugitives from their native land, neglected, solitary and poor.

His heart was softened by these images. He stopped involuntarily when opposite their door. He looked up at the house. The shutters were closed, so that light, if it were within, was invisible. He stepped into the porch, and put his eye to the keyhole. All was darksome and waste. He listened, and imagined that he heard the aspirations of grief. The sound was scarcely articulate, but had an electrical effect upon his feelings. He retired to his home full of mournful reflections.

He was willing to do something for the relief of the sufferers, but nothing could be done that night. Yet succour, if delayed till the morning, might be ineffectual. But how, when the morning came, should he proceed to effectuate his kind intentions? The guardians of the public welfare, at this crisis, were distributed into those who counselled and those who executed. A set of men, self-appointed to the generous office, employed themselves in seeking out the destitute or sick, and imparting relief. With this arrangement Baxter was acquainted. He was resolved to carry tidings of what he had heard and seen to one of those persons early the next day.

Baxter, after taking some refreshment, retired to rest. In no long time, however, he was awakened by his wife, who desired him to notice a certain glimmering on the ceiling. It seemed the feeble and flitting ray of a distant and moving light, coming through the window. It did not proceed from the street, for the chamber was lighted from the side and not from the front of the house. A lamp borne by a passenger, or the attendants of a hearse, could not be discovered in this situation. Besides, in the latter case it would be accompanied by the sound of the vehicle, and, probably, by weeping and exclamations of despair. His employment, as the guardian of property, naturally suggested to him the idea of robbery. He started from his bed, and went to the window.

His house stood at the distance of about fifty paces from that of Monrose. There was annexed to the latter a small garden or yard, bounded by a high wooden fence. Baxter's window overlooked this space. Before he reached the window, the relative situation of the two habitations occurred to him. A conjecture was instantly formed that the glimmering proceeded from this quarter. His eye, therefore, was immediately fixed upon Monrose's back-door. It caught a glimpse of a human figure passing into the house through this door. The person had a candle in his hand. This appeared by the light which streamed after him, and which was perceived, though faintly, through a small window of the dwelling, after the back-door was closed.

The person disappeared too quickly to allow him to say whether it was male or female. This scrutiny confirmed rather than weakened the apprehensions that first occurred. He reflected on the desolate and helpless condition of this family. The father might be sick; and what opposition could be made by the daughter to the stratagems or violence of midnight plunderers? This was an evil which it was his duty, in an extraordinary sense, to obviate. It is true, the hour of watching was past, and this was not the district assigned to him; but Baxter was, on the whole, of a generous and intrepid spirit. In the present case, therefore, he did not hesitate long in forming his resolution. He seized a hanger that hung at his bedside, and which had hewn many a Hungarian and French hussar to pieces. With this he descended to the street. He cautiously approached Monrose's house. He listened at the door, but heard nothing. The lower apartment, as he discovered through the keyhole, was deserted and dark. These appearances could not be accounted for. He was, as yet, unwilling to call or knock. He was solicitous to obtain some information by silent means, and without alarming the persons within, who, if they were robbers, might thus be put upon their guard and enabled to escape. If none but the family were there, they would not understand his signals, and might impute the disturbance to the cause which he was desirous to obviate. What could he do? Must he patiently wait till some incident should happen to regulate his motions?

In this uncertainty, he bethought himself of going round to the back part of the dwelling and watching the door which had been closed. An open space, filled with rubbish and weeds, adjoined the house and garden on one side. Hither he repaired, and, raising his head above the fence, at a point directly opposite the door, waited with considerable impatience for some token or signal by which he might be directed in his choice of measures.

Human life abounds with mysterious appearances. A man perched on a fence at midnight, mute and motionless, and gazing at a dark and dreary dwelling, was an object calculated to rouse curiosity. When the muscular form and rugged visage, scarred and furrowed into something like ferocity, were added, – when the nature of the calamity by which the city was dispeopled was considered, – the motives to plunder, and the insecurity of property, arising from the pressure of new wants on the poor and the flight or disease of the rich, were attended to, – an observer would be apt to admit fearful conjectures.

We know not how long Baxter continued at this post. He remained here, because he could not, as he conceived, change it for a better. Before his patience was exhausted, his attention was called by a noise within the house. It proceeded from the lower room. The sound was that of steps, but this was accompanied with other inexplicable tokens. The kitchen-door at length opened. The figure of Miss Monrose, pale, emaciated, and haggard, presented itself. Within the door stood a candle. It was placed on a chair within sight, and its rays streamed directly against the face of Baxter as it was reared above the top of the fence. This illumination, faint as it was, bestowed a certain air of wildness on features which nature, and the sanguinary habits of a soldier, had previously rendered, in an eminent degree, harsh and stern. He was not aware of the danger of discovery in consequence of this position of the candle. His attention was, for a few seconds, engrossed by the object before him. At length he chanced to notice another object.

At a few yards' distance from the fence, and within it, some one appeared to have been digging. An opening was made in the ground, but it was shallow and irregular. The implement which seemed to have been used was nothing more than a fire-shovel, for one of these he observed lying near the spot. The lady had withdrawn from the door, though without closing it. He had leisure, therefore, to attend to this new circumstance, and to reflect upon the purpose for which this opening might have been designed.

Death is familiar to the apprehensions of a soldier. Baxter had assisted at the hasty interment of thousands, the victims of the sword or of pestilence. Whether it was because this theatre of human calamity was new to him, and death, in order to be viewed with his ancient unconcern, must be accompanied in the ancient manner, with halberds and tents, certain it is that Baxter was irresolute and timid in every thing that respected the yellow fever. The circumstances of the time suggested that this was a grave, to which some victim of this disease was to be consigned. His teeth chattered when he reflected how near he might now be to the source of infection; yet his curiosity retained him at his post.

He fixed his eyes once more upon the door. In a short time the lady again appeared at it. She was in a stooping posture, and appeared to be dragging something along the floor. His blood ran cold at this spectacle. His fear instantly figured to itself a corpse, livid and contagious. Still he had no power to move. The lady's strength, enfeebled as it was by grief, and perhaps by the absence of nourishment, seemed scarcely adequate to the task which she had assigned herself.

Her burden, whatever it was, was closely wrapped in a sheet. She drew it forward a few paces, then desisted, and seated herself on the ground, apparently to recruit her strength and give vent to the agony of her thoughts in sighs. Her tears were either exhausted or refused to flow, for none were shed by her. Presently she resumed her undertaking. Baxter's horror increased in proportion as she drew nearer to the spot where he stood; and yet it seemed as if some fascination had forbidden him to recede.

At length the burden was drawn to the side of the opening in the earth. Here it seemed as if the mournful task was finished. She threw herself once more upon the earth. Her senses seemed for a time to have forsaken her. She sat buried in reverie, her eyes scarcely open, and fixed upon the ground, and every feature set to the genuine expression of sorrow. Some disorder, occasioned by the circumstance of dragging, now took place in the vestment of what he had rightly predicted to be a dead body. The veil by accident was drawn aside, and exhibited to the startled eye of Baxter the pale and ghastly visage of the unhappy Monrose.

This incident determined him. Every joint in his frame trembled, and he hastily withdrew from the fence. His first motion in doing this produced a noise by which the lady was alarmed; she suddenly threw her eyes upward, and gained a full view of Baxter's extraordinary countenance, just before it disappeared. She manifested her terror by a piercing shriek. Baxter did not stay to mark her subsequent conduct, to confirm or to dissipate her fears, but retired, in confusion, to his own house.

Hitherto his caution had availed him. He had carefully avoided all employments and places from which he imagined imminent danger was to be dreaded. Now, through his own inadvertency, he had rushed, as he believed, into the jaws of the pest. His senses had not been assailed by any noisome effluvia. This was no unplausible ground for imagining that this death had some other cause than the yellow fever. This circumstance did not occur to Baxter. He had been told that Frenchmen were not susceptible of this contagion. He had hitherto believed this assertion, but now regarded it as having been fully confuted. He forgot that Frenchmen were undoubtedly mortal, and that there was no impossibility in Monrose's dying, even at this time, of a malady different from that which prevailed.

Before morning he began to feel very unpleasant symptoms. He related his late adventure to his wife. She endeavoured, by what arguments her slender ingenuity suggested, to quiet his apprehensions, but in vain. He hourly grew worse, and, as soon as it was light, despatched his wife for a physician. On interrogating this messenger, the physician obtained information of last night's occurrences; and, this being communicated to one of the dispensers of the public charity, they proceeded, early in the morning, to Monrose's house. It was closed, as usual. They knocked and called, but no one answered. They examined every avenue to the dwelling, but none of them were accessible. They passed into the garden, and observed, on a spot marked out by Baxter, a heap of earth. A very slight exertion was sufficient to remove it and discover the body of the unfortunate exile beneath.

After unsuccessfully trying various expedients for entering the house, they deemed themselves authorized to break the door. They entered, ascended the staircase, and searched every apartment in the house, but no human being was discoverable. The furniture was wretched and scanty, but there was no proof that Monrose had fallen a victim to the reigning disease. It was certain that the lady had disappeared. It was inconceivable whither she had gone.

Baxter suffered a long period of sickness. The prevailing malady appeared upon him in its severest form. His strength of constitution, and the careful attendance of his wife, were insufficient to rescue him from the grave. His case may be quoted as an example of the force of imagination. He had probably already received, through the medium of the air, or by contact of which he was not conscious, the seeds of this disease. They might perhaps have lain dormant, had not this panic occurred to endow them with activity.

CHAPTER VIII.

SUCH were the facts circumstantially communicated by Sarah. They afforded to Constantia a theme of ardent meditation. The similitude between her own destiny and that of this unhappy exile could not fail to be observed. Immersed in poverty, friendless, burdened with the maintenance and nurture of her father, their circumstances were nearly parallel. The catastrophe of her tale was the subject of endless but unsatisfactory conjecture.

She had disappeared between the flight of Baxter and the dawn of the day. What path had she taken? Was she now alive? Was she still an inhabitant of this city? Perhaps there was a coincidence of taste as well as fortunes between them. The only friend that Constantia ever enjoyed, congenial with her in principles, sex, and age, was at a distance that forbade communication. She imagined that Ursula Monrose would prove worthy of her love, and felt unspeakable regret at the improbability of their ever meeting.

Meanwhile, the dominion of cold began to be felt, and the contagious fever entirely disappeared. The return of health was hailed with rapture by all ranks of people. The streets were once more busy and frequented. The sensation of present security seemed to shut out from all hearts the memory of recent disasters. Public entertainments were thronged with auditors. A new theatre had lately been constructed, and a company of English comedians had arrived during the prevalence of the malady. They now began their exhibitions, and their audiences were overflowing.

Such is the motley and ambiguous condition of human society, such is the complexity of all effects, from what cause soever they spring, that none can tell whether this destructive pestilence was, on the whole, productive of most pain or most pleasure. Those who had been sick and had recovered found, in this circumstance, a source of exultation. Others made haste, by new marriages, to supply the place of wives, husbands, and children whom the scarcely-extinguished pestilence had swept away.

Constantia, however, was permitted to take no share in the general festivity. Such was the colour of her fate, that the yellow fever, by affording her a respite from toil, supplying leisure for the acquisition of a useful branch of knowledge, and leading her to the discovery of a cheaper, more simple, and more wholesome method of subsistence, had been friendly, instead of adverse, to her happiness. Its disappearance, instead of relieving her from suffering, was the signal for the approach of new cares.

Of her ancient customers, some were dead, and others were slow in resuming their ancient habitations and their ordinary habits. Meanwhile, two wants were now created and were urgent. The season demanded a supply of fuel, and her rent had accumulated beyond her power to discharge. M'Crea no sooner returned from the country than he applied to her for payment. Some proprietors, guided by humanity, had remitted their dues, but M'Crea was not one of these. According to his own representation, no man was poorer than himself; and the punctual payment of all that was owing to him was no more than sufficient to afford him a scanty subsistence.

He was aware of the indigence of the Dudleys, and was therefore extremely importunate for payment, and could scarcely be prevailed upon to allow them the interval of a day for the discovery of expedients. This day was passed by Constantia in fruitless anxieties. The ensuing evening had been fixed for a repetition of his visit. The hour arrived, but her invention was exhausted in vain. M'Crea was punctual to the minute. Constantia was allowed no option. She merely declared that the money demanded she had not to give, nor could she foresee any period at which her inability would be less than it then was.

These declarations were heard by her visitant with unspeakable vexation. He did not fail to expatiate on the equity of his demands, the moderation and forbearance he had hitherto shown, notwithstanding the extreme urgency of his own wants, and the inflexible rigour with which he had been treated by *his* creditors. This rhetoric was merely the prelude to an intimation that he must avail himself of any lawful means by which he might gain possession of *his own*.

This insinuation was fully comprehended by Constantia, but it was heard without any new emotions. Her knowledge of her landlord's character taught her to expect but one consequence. He paused to observe what effect would be produced by this indirect menace. She answered, without any change of tone, that the loss of habitation and furniture, however inconvenient at this season, must be patiently endured. If it were to be prevented only by the payment of money, its prevention was impossible.

M'Crea renewed his regrets that there should be no other alternative. The law sanctioned his claims, and justice to his family, which was already large, and likely to increase, required that they should not be relinquished; yet such was the mildness of his temper and his aversion to proceed to this extremity, that he was willing to dispense with immediate payment on two conditions. First, that they should leave his house within a week; and secondly, that they should put into his hands some trinket or movable, equal in value to the sum demanded, which should be kept by him as a pledge.

This last hint suggested an expedient for obviating the present distress. The lute with which Mr. Dudley was accustomed to solace in his solitude was, if possible, more essential to his happiness than shelter or food. To his daughter it possessed little direct power to please. It was inestimable merely for her father's sake. Its intrinsic value was at least equal to the sum due, but to part with it was to bereave him of a good which nothing else could supply. Besides, not being a popular and salable instrument, it would probably be contemptuously rejected by the ignorance and avarice of M'Crea.

There was another article in her possession, of some value in traffic, and of a kind which M'Crea was far more likely to accept. It was the miniature portrait of her friend, executed by a German artist, and set in gold. This image was a precious though imperfect substitute for sympathy and intercourse with the original. Habit had made this picture a source of a species of idolatry. Its power over her sensations was similar to that possessed by a beautiful Madonna over the heart of a juvenile enthusiast. It was the mother of the only devotion which her education had taught her to consider as beneficial or true.

She perceived the necessity of parting with it, on this occasion, with the utmost clearness, but this necessity was thought upon with indescribable repugnance. It seemed as if she had not thoroughly conceived the extent of her calamity till now. It seemed as if she could have endured the loss of eyes with less reluctance than the loss of this inestimable relic. Bitter were the tears which she shed over it as she took it from her bosom and consigned it to those rapacious hands that were stretched out to receive it. She derived some little consolation from the promise of this man that he would keep it safely till she was able to redeem it.

The other condition – that of immediate removal from the house – seemed at first sight impracticable. Some reflection, however, showed her that the change might not only be possible but useful. Among other expedients for diminishing expense, that of limiting her furniture and dwelling to the cheapest standard had often occurred. She now remembered that the house occupied by Monrose was tenantless; that its antiquity, its remote and unpleasant situation, and its small dimensions, might induce M'Crea, to whom it belonged, to let it at a much lower price than that which he now exacted. M'Crea would have been better pleased if her choice had fallen on a different house; but he had powerful though sordid reasons for desiring the possession of this tenement. He assented, therefore, to her proposal, provided her removal took place without delay.

In the present state of her funds this removal was impossible. Mere shelter would not suffice during this inclement season. Without fuel, neither cold could be excluded nor hunger relieved. There was nothing convertible into money but her lute. No sacrifice was more painful, but an irresistible necessity demanded it.

Her interview with M'Crea took place while her father was absent from the room. On his return she related what had happened, and urged the necessity of parting with his favourite instrument. He listened to her tale with a sigh. "Yes," said he, "do what thou wilt, my child. It is unlikely that any one will purchase it. It is certain that no one will give for it what I gave; but thou mayest try.

"It has been to me a faithful friend. I know not how I should have lived without it. Its notes have cheered me with the sweet remembrances of old times. It was, in some degree, a substitute for the eyes which I have lost; but now let it go, and perform for me perhaps the dearest of its services. It may help us to sustain the severities of this season."

There was no room for delay. She immediately set out in search of a purchaser. Such a one was most likely to be found in the keeper of a musical repository, who had lately arrived from Europe. She entertained but slight hopes that an instrument scarcely known among her neighbours would be bought at any price, however inconsiderable.

She found the keeper of the shop engaged in conversation with a lady, whose person and face instantly arrested the attention of Constantia. A less sagacious observer would have eyed the stranger with indifference. But Constantia was ever busy in interpreting the language of features and looks.[1] Her sphere of observation had been narrow, but her habits of examining, comparing, and deducing, had thoroughly exhausted that sphere. These habits were eminently strong with relation to the class of objects. She delighted to investigate the human countenance, and treasured up numberless conclusions as to the coincidence between mental and external qualities.

She had often been forcibly struck by forms that were accidentally seen, and which abounded with this species of mute expression. They conveyed at a single glance what could not be imparted by volumes. The features and shape sunk, as it were, into perfect harmony with sentiments and passions. Every atom of the frame was pregnant with significance. In some, nothing was remarkable but this power of the outward figure to exhibit the internal sentiments. In others, the intelligence thus unveiled was remarkable for its heterogeneous or energetic qualities; for its tendency to fill her heart with veneration or abhorrence, or to involve her in endless perplexities.

The accuracy and vividness with which pictures of this kind presented themselves to her imagination resembled the operations of a

---

1   Here Constantia practises physiognomy, the art of judging human character from facial features.

sixth sense. It cannot be doubted, however, that much was owing to the enthusiastic tenor of her own conceptions, and that her conviction of the truth of the picture principally flowed from the distinctness and strength of its hues.

The figure which she now examined was small, but of exquisite proportions. Her complexion testified the influence of a torrid sun; but the darkness veiled, without obscuring, the glowing tints of her cheek. The shade was remarkably deep; but a deeper still was required to become incompatible with beauty. Her features were irregular; but defects of symmetry were amply supplied by eyes that anticipated speech, and positions which conveyed that to which language was inadequate.

It was not the chief tendency of her appearance to seduce or to melt. Hers were the polished cheek and the mutability of muscle which belong to woman, but the genius conspicuous in her aspect was heroic and contemplative. The female was absorbed, so to speak, in the rational creature, and the emotions most apt to be excited in the gazer partook less of love than of reverence.

Such is the portrait of this stranger, delineated by Constantia. I copy it with greater willingness, because, if we substitute a nobler stature, and a complexion less uniform and delicate, it is suited, with the utmost accuracy, to herself. She was probably unconscious of this resemblance; but this circumstance may be supposed to influence her in discovering such attractive properties in a form thus vaguely seen. These impressions, permanent and cogent as they were, were gained at a single glance. The purpose which led her thither was too momentous to be long excluded.

"Why," said the master of the shop, "this is lucky. Here is a lady who has just been inquiring for an instrument of this kind. Perhaps the one you have will suit her. If you will bring it to me, I will examine it, and, if it is complete, will make a bargain with you." He then turned to the lady who had first entered, and a short dialogue in French ensued between them. The man repeated his assurances to Constantia, who, promising to hasten back with the instrument, took her leave. The lute, in its structure and ornaments, has rarely been surpassed. When scrutinized by this artist, it proved to be complete, and the price demanded for it was readily given.

By this means the Dudleys were enabled to change their habitation and to supply themselves with fuel. To obviate future exigencies,

Constantia betook herself once more to the needle. They persisted in the use of their simple fare, and endeavoured to contract their wants and methodize their occupations by a standard as rigid as possible. She had not relinquished her design of adopting a new and more liberal profession, but though, when indistinctly and generally considered, it seemed easily effected, yet the first steps which it would be proper to take did not clearly or readily suggest themselves. For the present she was contented to pursue the beaten track, but was prepared to benefit by any occasion that time might furnish, suitable to the execution of her plan.

CHAPTER IX.

It may be asked if a woman of this character did not attract the notice of the world. Her station, no less than her modes of thinking, excluded her from the concourse of the opulent and the gay. She kept herself in privacy; her engagements confined her to her own fireside; and her neighbours enjoyed no means of penetrating through that obscurity in which she wrapped herself. There were, no doubt, persons of her own sex capable of estimating her worth, and who could have hastened to raise so much merit from the indigence to which it was condemned. She might, at least, have found associates and friends justly entitled to her affection. But whether she were peculiarly unfortunate in this respect, or whether it arose from a jealous and unbending spirit that would remit none of its claims to respect, and was backward in its overtures to kindness and intimacy, it so happened that her hours were, for a long period, enlivened by no companion but her father and her faithful Lucy. The humbleness of her dwelling, her plain garb, and the meanness of her occupation, were no passports to the favour of the rich and vain. These, added to her youth and beauty, frequently exposed her to insults, from which, though productive for a time of mortification and distress, she, for the most part, extricated herself by her spirited carriage and presence of mind.

One incident of this kind it will be necessary to mention. One evening her engagements carried her abroad. She had proposed to return immediately, finding by experience the danger that was to be dreaded by a woman young and unprotected. Somewhat occurred that unavoidably lengthened her stay, and she set out on her return at a late hour. One of the other sex offered her his guardianship; but this she declined, and proceeded homeward alone.

Her way lay through streets but little inhabited, and whose few inhabitants were of the profligate class. She was conscious of the inconveniences to which she was exposed, and therefore tripped along with all possible haste. She had not gone far before she perceived, through the dusk, two men standing near a porch before her. She had gone too far to recede or change her course without exciting observation, and she flattered herself that the persons would behave with decency. Encouraged by these reflections, and somewhat hastening her pace, she went on. As soon as she came opposite the place where they stood, one of them threw himself round, and caught her arm, exclaiming, in a broad tone, "Whither so fast, my love, at this time of night?" The other, at the same time, threw his arms round her waist, crying out, "A pretty prize, by G—— ; just in the nick of time."

They were huge and brawny fellows, in whose grasp her feeble strength was annihilated. Their motions were so sudden that she had not time to escape by flight. Her struggles merely furnished them with a subject of laughter. He that held her waist proceeded to pollute her cheeks with his kisses, and drew her into the porch. He tore her from the grasp of him who first seized her, who seemed to think his property invaded, and said, in a surly tone, "What now, Jemmy? Damn your heart, d'ye think I'll be fobbed? Have done with your slabbering, Jemmy. First come, first served," and seemed disposed to assert his claims by force.

To this brutality Constantia had nothing to oppose but fruitless struggles and shrieks for help. Succour was, fortunately, at hand. Her exclamations were heard by a person across the street, who instantly ran, and with some difficulty disengaged her from the grasp of the ruffians. He accompanied her the rest of the way, bestowed on her every polite attention, and, though pressed to enter the house, declined the invitation. She had no opportunity of examining the appearance of her new friend. This the darkness of the night, and her own panic, prevented.

Next day a person called upon her whom she instantly recognized to be her late protector. He came with some message from his sister. His manners were simple and unostentatious, and breathed the genuine spirit of civility. Having performed his commission, and once more received the thanks which she poured forth with peculiar warmth for his last night's interposition, he took his leave.

The name of this man was Balfour. He was middle-aged, of a figure neither elegant nor ungainly, and an aspect that was mild and placid, but betrayed few marks of intelligence. He was an adventurer from Scotland, whom a strict adherence to the maxims of trade had rendered opulent. He was governed by the principles of mercantile integrity in all his dealings, and was affable and kind, without being generous, in his treatment of inferiors. He was a stranger to violent emotions of any kind, and his intellectual acquisitions were limited to his own profession.

His demeanour was tranquil and uniform. He was sparing of words, and these were uttered in the softest manner. In all his transactions he was sedate and considerate. In his dress and mode of living there were no appearances of parsimony, but there were, likewise, as few traces of profusion.

His sister had shared in his prosperity. As soon as his affairs would permit, he sent for her to Scotland, where she had lived in a state little removed from penury, and had for some years been vested with the superintendence of his household. There was a considerable resemblance between them in person and character. Her profession, or those arts in which her situation had compelled her to acquire skill, had not an equal tendency to enlarge the mind as those of her brother, but the views of each were limited to one set of objects. His superiority was owing, not to any inherent difference, but to accident.

Balfour's life had been a model of chasteness and regularity, – though this was owing more to constitutional coldness and a frugal spirit, than to virtuous forbearance; but, in his schemes for the future, he did not exclude the circumstance of marriage. Having attained a situation secure, as the nature of human affairs will admit, from the chances of poverty, the way was sufficiently prepared for matrimony. His thoughts had been for some time employed in the selection of a suitable companion, when this rencounter happened with Miss Dudley.

Balfour was not destitute of those feelings which are called into play by the sight of youth and beauty in distress. This incident was not speedily forgotten. The emotions produced by it were new to him. He reviewed them oftener, and with more complacency, than any which he had before experienced. They afforded him so much satisfaction, that, in order to preserve them undiminished, he resolved to repeat his visit. Constantia treated him as one from whom she had received a considerable benefit. Her sweetness and gentleness were uniform, and Balfour found that her humble roof promised him more happiness than his own fireside, or the society of his professional brethren.

He could not overlook, in the course of such reflections as these, the question relative to marriage, and speedily determined to solicit the honour of her hand. He had not decided without his usual foresight and deliberation; nor had he been wanting in the accuracy of his observations and inquiries. Those qualifications, indeed, which were of chief value in his eyes, lay upon the surface. He was no judge of her intellectual character, or of the loftiness of her morality. Not even the graces of person, or features, or manners, attracted much of his attention. He remarked her admirable economy of time and money and labour, the simplicity of her dress, her evenness of temper, and her love of seclusion. These were essential requisites of a wife, in his apprehension. The insignificance of his own birth, the lowness of his original fortune, and the efficacy of industry and temperance to confer and maintain wealth, had taught him indifference as to birth or fortune in his spouse. His moderate desires in this respect were gratified, and he was anxious only for a partner that would aid him in preserving rather than in enlarging his property. He esteemed himself eminently fortunate in meeting with one in whom every matrimonial qualification concentred.

He was not deficient in modesty, but he fancied that, on this occasion, there was no possibility of miscarriage. He held her capacity in deep veneration, but this circumstance rendered him more secure of success. He conceived this union to be even more eligible with regard to her than to himself, and confided in the rectitude of her understanding for a decision favourable to his wishes.

Before any express declaration was made, Constantia easily predicted the event from the frequency of his visits and the attentiveness of his manners. It was no difficult task to ascertain this man's character. Her modes of thinking were, in few respects, similar to those of her lover. She was eager to investigate, in the first place, the attributes of his mind. His professional and household maxims were not of inconsiderate importance, but they were subordinate considerations. In the poverty of his discourse and ideas, she quickly found reasons for determining her conduct.

Marriage she had but little considered, as it is in itself. What are the genuine principles of that relation, and what conduct with respect to it is prescribed to rational beings by their duty, she had not hitherto investigated. But she was not backward to inquire what were the precepts of duty in her own particular case. She knew herself to be young; she was sensible of the daily enlargement of her knowledge: every day contributed to rectify some error or confirm some truth. These benefits she owed to her situation, which, whatever were its evils, gave her as much freedom from restraint as is consistent with the state of human affairs. Her poverty fettered her exertions and circumscribed her pleasures. Poverty, therefore, was an evil, and the reverse of poverty to be desired. But riches were not barren of constraint, and its advantages might be purchased at too dear a rate.

Allowing that the wife is enriched by marriage, how humiliating were the conditions annexed to it in the present case! The company of one with whom we have no sympathy, nor sentiments in common, is, of all species of solitude, the most loathsome and dreary. The nuptial life is attended with peculiar aggravations, since the tie is infrangible, and the choice of a more suitable companion, if such a one should offer, is forever precluded. The hardships of wealth are not incompensated by some benefits; but these benefits, false and hollow as they are, cannot be obtained by marriage. Her acceptance of Balfour would merely aggravate her indigence.

Now she was at least mistress of the product of her own labour. Her tasks were toilsome, but the profits, though slender, were sure, and she administered her little property in what manner she pleased. Marriage would annihilate this power. Henceforth she would be bereft even of personal freedom. So far from possessing property, she herself would become the property of another.

She was not unaware of the consequences flowing from differences of capacity, and that power, to whomsoever legally granted, will be exercised by the most addressful; but she derived no encouragement from these considerations. She would not stoop to gain her end by the hateful arts of the sycophant, and was too wise to place an unbounded reliance on the influence of truth. The character, likewise, of this man sufficiently exempted him from either of those influences.

She did not forget the nature of the altar-vows. To abdicate the use of her own understanding was scarcely justifiable in any case; but to vow an affection that was not felt and could not be compelled, and to promise obedience to one whose judgement was glaringly defective, were acts atrociously criminal. Education, besides, had created in her an insurmountable abhorrence of admitting to conjugal privileges the man who had no claim upon her love. It could not be denied that a state of abundant accommodation was better than the contrary; but this consideration, though, in the most rational estimate, of some weight, she was not so depraved and effeminate as to allow to overweigh the opposite evils. Homely liberty was better than splendid servitude.

Her resolution was easily formed, but there were certain impediments in the way of its execution. These chiefly arose from deference to the opinion and compassion for the infirmities of her father. He assumed no control over her actions. His reflections in the present case were rather understood than expressed. When uttered, it was with the mildness of equality and the modesty of persuasion. It was this circumstance that conferred upon them all their force. His decision, on so delicate a topic, was not wanting in sagacity and moderation; but, as a man, he had his portion of defects, and his frame was enfeebled by disease and care; yet he set no higher value on the ease and independence of his former condition than any man of like experience. He could not endure to exist on the fruits of his daughter's labour. He ascribed her decision to a spirit of excessive refinement, and was, of course, disposed to give little quarter to maiden scruples. They were phantoms, he believed, which experience would dispel. His morality, besides, was of a much more flexible kind; and the marriage vows were, in his opinion, formal and unmeaning, and neither in themselves, nor in the apprehension of the world, accompanied with any rigorous obligation. He drew more favourable omens from the known capacity of his daughter and the flexibility of her lover.

She demanded his opinion and advice. She listened to his reasonings, and revolved them with candour and impartiality. She stated her objections with simplicity, but the difference of age and sex was sufficient to preclude agreement. Arguments were of no use but to prolong the debate; but, happily, the magnanimity of Mr. Dudley would admit of no sacrifice. Her opinions, it is true, were erroneous; but he was willing that she should regulate her conduct by her own conceptions of right, and not by those of another. To refuse Balfour's offers was an evil, but an evil inexpressibly exceeded by that of accepting them contrary to her own sense of propriety.

Difficulties, likewise, arose from the consideration of what was due to the man who had already benefited her, and who, in this act, intended to confer upon her further benefit. These, though the source of some embarrassments, were not sufficient to shake her resolution. Balfour could not understand her principal objections. They were of a size altogether disproportioned to his capacity. Her moral speculations were quite beyond the sphere of his reflections. She could not expatiate, without a breach of civility, on the disparity of their minds; and yet this was the only or principal ground on which she had erected her scruples.

Her father loved her too well not to be desirous of relieving her from a painful task, though undertaken without necessity, and contrary to his opinion. "Refer him to me," said he; "I will make the best of the matter, and render your refusal as palatable as possible. But do you authorize me to make it absolute, and without appeal."

"My dear father, how good you are! but that shall be my province. If I err, let the consequences of my mistake be confined to myself. It would be cruel indeed to make you the instrument in a transaction which your judgment disapproves. My reluctance was a weak and foolish thing. Strange, indeed, if the purity of my motives will not bear me out on this, as it has done on many more arduous occasions!"

"Well, be it so; that is best, I believe. Ten to one but I, with my want of eyes, would blunder, while yours will be of no small use in a contest with a lover. They will serve you to watch the transitions in his placid physiognomy, and overpower his discontents."

She was aware of the inconveniences to which this resolution would subject her; but since they were unavoidable, she armed herself with the requisite patience. Her apprehensions were not without reason. More than one conference was necessary to convince him of her meaning, and in order to effect her purpose she was obliged to behave with so much explicitness as to hazard giving him offence. This affair was productive of no small vexation. He had put too much faith in the validity of his pretensions, and the benefits of perseverance, to be easily shaken off.

This decision was not borne by him with as much patience as she wished. He deemed himself unjustly treated, and his resentment exceeded those bounds of moderation which he prescribed to himself on all other occasions. From his anger, however, there was not much to be dreaded; but, unfortunately, his sister partook of his indignation, and indulged her petulance, which was enforced by every gossiping and tattling propensity, to the irreparable disadvantage of Constantia.

She owed her support to her needle. She was dependent, therefore, on the caprice of customers. This caprice was swayable by every breath, and paid a merely subordinate regard, in the choice of workwomen, to the circumstances of skill, cheapness, and diligence. In consequence of this, her usual sources of subsistence began to fail.

Indigence, as well as wealth, is comparative. He indeed must be wretched, whose food, clothing, and shelter are limited, both in kind and quantity, by the standard of mere necessity; who in the choice of food, for example, is governed by no consideration but its cheapness, and its capacity to sustain nature. Yet to this degree of wretchedness was Miss Dudley reduced.

As her means of subsistence began to decay, she reflected on the change of employment that might become necessary. She was mistress of no lucrative art but that which now threatened to be useless. There was but one avenue through which she could hope to escape from the pressure of absolute want. This she regarded with an aversion that nothing but extreme necessity, and the failure of every other expedient, would be able to subdue. This was the hiring of herself as a servant. Even that could not answer all her purposes. If a subsistence were provided by it for herself, whither should her father and her Lucy betake themselves for support?

Hitherto her labour had been sufficient to shut out famine and the cold. It is true she had been cut off from all the direct means of personal or mental gratification; but her constitution had exempted her from the insalutary effects of sedentary application. She could not tell how long she could enjoy this exemption, but it was absurd to anticipate those evils which might never arrive. Meanwhile, her situation was not destitute of comfort. The indirect means of intellectual improvement in conversation and reflection, the inexpensive amusement of singing, and, above all, the consciousness of performing her duty and maintaining her independence inviolate, were still in her possession. Her lodging was humble and her fare frugal; but these, temperance and a due regard to the use of money, would require from the most opulent.

Now, retrenchments must be made even from this penurious provision. Her exertions might somewhat defer, but could not prevent, the ruin of her unhappy family. Their landlord was a severe exactor of his dues. The day of quarterly payment was past, and he had not failed in his usual punctuality. She was unable to satisfy his demands, and Mr. Dudley was officially informed that, unless payment was made before a day fixed, resort would be had to the law in that case made and provided.

This seemed to be the completion of their misfortunes. It was not enough to soften the implacability of their landlord. A respite might possibly be obtained from this harsh sentence. Entreaties might prevail upon him to allow of their remaining under this roof for some time longer; but shelter at this inclement season was not enough. Without fire they must perish with the cold; and fuel could be procured only for money, of which the last shilling was expended. Food was no less indispensable; and, their credit being gone, not a loaf could be extorted from the avarice of the bakers in the neighbourhood.

The sensations produced by this accumulation of distress may be more easily conceived than described. Mr. Dudley sunk into despair when Lucy informed him that the billet of wood she was putting on the fire was the last. "Well," said he, "the game is up. Where is my daughter?" The answer was that she was up-stairs.

"Why, there she has been this hour. Tell her to come down and warm herself. She must needs be cold; and here is a cheerful blaze. I feel it myself. Like the lightning that precedes death, it beams thus brightly, though in a few moments it will be extinguished forever. Let my darling come and partake of its comforts before they expire."

Constantia had retired in order to review her situation and devise some expedients that might alleviate it. It was a sore extremity to which she was reduced. Things had come to a desperate pass, and the remedy required must be no less desperate. It was impossible to see her father perish. She herself would have died before she would have condescended to beg. It was not worth prolonging a life which must subsist upon alms. She would have wandered into the fields at dusk, have seated herself upon an unfrequented bank, and serenely waited the approach of that death which the rigours of the seasons would have rendered sure. But, as it was, it became her to act in a very different manner.

During her father's prosperity, some mercantile intercourse had taken place between him and a merchant of this city. The latter, on some occasion, had spent a few nights at her father's house. She was greatly charmed with the humanity that shone forth in his conversation and behaviour. From that time to this, all intercourse had ceased. She was acquainted with the place of his abode, and knew him to be affluent. To him she determined to apply as a suppliant in behalf of her father. She did not inform Mr. Dudley of this intention, conceiving it best to wait till the event had been ascertained, for fear of exciting fallacious expectations. She was further deterred by the apprehension of awakening his pride and bringing on herself an absolute prohibition.

She arrived at the door of Mr. Melbourne's house, and, inquiring for the master of it, was informed that he had gone out of town, and was not expected to return within a week.

Her scheme, which was by no means unplausible, was thus completely frustrated. There was but one other resource, on which she had already deliberated, and to which she had determined to apply if that should fail. That was to claim assistance from the superintendents of the poor. She was employed in considering to which of them, and in what manner, she should make her application, when she turned the corner of Lombard and Second Streets. That had scarcely been done, when, casting her eyes mournfully round her, she caught a glimpse of a person whom she instantly recognised, passing into the market-place. She followed him with quick steps, and, on a second examination, found that she had not been mistaken. This was no other than Thomas Craig, to whose malignity and cunning all her misfortunes were imputable.

She was at first uncertain what use to make of this discovery. She followed him almost instinctively, and saw him at length enter the Indian Queen Tavern. Here she stopped. She entertained a confused conception that some beneficial consequences might be extracted from this event. In the present hurry of her thoughts she could form no satisfactory conclusion; but it instantly occurred to her that it would at least be proper to ascertain the place of his abode. She stepped into the inn and made the suitable inquiries. She was informed that the gentleman had come from Baltimore a month before, and had since resided at that house. How soon he meant to leave the city her informant was unable to tell.

Having gained this intelligence, she returned home, and once more shut herself in her chamber to meditate on this new posture of affairs.

CHAPTER X.

CRAIG was indebted to her father. He had defrauded him by the most atrocious and illicit arts. On either account he was liable to prosecution; but her heart rejected the thought of being the author of injury to any man. The dread of punishment, however, might induce him to refund, uncoercively, the whole or some part of the stolen property. Money was at this moment necessary to existence, and she conceived herself justly entitled to that of which her father had been perfidiously despoiled.

But the law was formal and circuitous. Money itself was necessary to purchase its assistance. Besides, it could not act with unseen virtue and instantaneous celerity. The co-operation of advocates and officers was required. They must be visited, and harangued, and importuned. Was she adequate to the task? Would the energy of her mind supply the place of experience, and, with a sort of miraculous efficacy, afford her the knowledge of official processes and dues? As little, on this occasion, could be expected from her father as from her. He was infirm and blind. The spirit that animated his former days was flown. His heart's blood was chilled by the rigours of his fortune. He had discarded his indignation and his enmities, and, together with them, hope itself had perished in his bosom. He waited, in tranquil despair, for that stroke which would deliver him from life and all the woes that it inherits.

But these considerations were superfluous. It was enough that justice must be bought, and that she had not the equivalent. Legal proceedings are encumbered with delay, and her necessities were urgent.

Succour, if withheld till the morrow, would be useless. Hunger and cold would not be trifled with. What resource was there left in this her uttermost distress? Must she yield, in imitation of her father, to the cowardly suggestions of despair?

Craig might be rich. His coffers might be stuffed with thousands. All that he had, according to the principles of social equity, was hers; yet he, to whom nothing belonged, rioted in superfluity, while she, the rightful claimant, was driven to the point of utmost need. The proper instrument of her restoration was law; but its arm was powerless, for she had not the means of bribing it into activity. But was law the only instrument?

Craig, perhaps, was accessible. Might she not, with propriety, demand an interview, and lay before him the consequences of his baseness? He was not divested of the last remains of humanity. It was impossible that he should not relent at the picture of those distresses of which he was the author. Menaces of legal prosecution she meant not to use, because she was unalterably resolved against that remedy. She confided in the efficacy of her pleadings to awaken his justice. This interview she was determined immediately to seek. She was aware that by some accident her purpose might be frustrated. Access to his person might, for the present, be impossible, or might be denied. It was proper, therefore, to write him a letter, which might be substituted in place of an interview. It behooved her to be expeditious, for the light was failing, and her strength was nearly exhausted by the hurry of her spirits. Her fingers, likewise, were benumbed with the cold. She performed her task, under these disadvantages, with much difficulty. This was the purport of her letter: —

"THOMAS CRAIG: —

"An hour ago I was in Second Street, and saw you. I followed you till you entered the Indian Queen Tavern. Knowing where you are, I am now preparing to demand an interview. I may be disappointed in this hope, and therefore write you this.

"I do not come to upbraid you, to call you to a legal or any other account for your actions. I presume not to weigh your merits. The God of equity be your judge. May he be as merciful, in the hour of retribution, as I am disposed to be!

"It is only to inform you that my father is on the point of perishing with want. You know who it was that reduced him to this condition. I persuade myself I shall not appeal to your justice in vain. Learn of this justice to afford him instant succour.

"You know who it was that took you in, a houseless wanderer, protected and fostered your youth, and shared with you his confidence and his fortune. It is he who now, blind and indigent, is threatened, by an inexorable landlord, to be thrust into the street, and who is, at this moment, without fire and without bread.

"He once did you some little service; now he looks to be compensated. All the retribution he asks is to be saved from perishing. Surely you will not spurn at his claims. Thomas Craig has done nothing that shows him deaf to the cries of distress. He would relieve a dog from such suffering.

"Forget that you have known my father in any character but that of a suppliant for bread. I promise you that, on this condition, I also will forget it. If you are so far just, you have nothing to fear. Your property and reputation shall both be safe. My father knows not of your being in this city. His enmities are extinct, and, if you comply with this request, he shall know you only as a benefactor.

C. DUDLEY."

Having finished and folded this epistle, she once more returned to the tavern. A waiter informed her that Craig had lately been in, and was now gone out to spend the evening. "Whither had he gone?" she asked.

"How was he to know where gentlemen eat their suppers? Did she take him for a witch? What, in God's name, did she want with him at that hour? Could she not wait, at least, till he had done his supper? He warranted her pretty face would bring him home time enough."

Constantia was not disconcerted at this address. She knew that females are subjected, through their own ignorance and cowardice, to a thousand mortifications. She set its true value on base and low-minded treatment. She disdained to notice this ribaldry, but turned away from the servant to meditate on this disappointment.

A few moments after, a young fellow, smartly dressed, entered the apartment. He was immediately addressed by the other, who said to him, "Well, Tom, where's your master? There's a lady wants him," (pointing to Constantia, and laying a grinning emphasis on the word "lady.") She turned to the newcomer: – "Friend, are you Mr. Craig's servant?"

The fellow seemed somewhat irritated at the bluntness of her interrogatory. The appellation of servant sat uneasily, perhaps, on his pride, especially as coming from a person of her appearance. He put on an air of familiar ridicule, and surveyed her in silence. She resumed in an authoritative tone: – "Where does Mr. Craig spend this evening? I have business with him of the highest importance, and that will not bear delay. I must see him this night." He seemed preparing to make some impertinent answer, but she anticipated it: – "You had better answer me with decency. If you do not, your master shall hear of it."

This menace was not ineffectual. He began to perceive himself in the wrong, and surlily muttered, "Why, if you must know, he is gone to Mr. Ormond's." And where lived Mr. Ormond? In Arch Street; he mentioned the number on her questioning him to that effect.

Being furnished with this information, she left him. Her project was not to be thwarted by slight impediments, and she forthwith proceeded to Ormond's dwelling. "Who was this Ormond?" she inquired of herself as she went along; "whence originated and of what nature is the connection between him and Craig? Are they united by union of designs and sympathy of character, or is this stranger a new subject on whom Craig is practicing his arts? The last supposition is not impossible. Is it not my duty to disconcert his machinations and save a new victim from his treachery? But I ought to be sure before I act. He may now be honest, or tending to honesty, and my interference may cast him backward, or impede his progress."

The house to which she had been directed was spacious and magnificent. She was answered by a servant, whose uniform was extremely singular and fanciful, and whose features and accents bespoke him to be English, with a politeness to which she knew that the simplicity of her garb gave her no title. Craig, he told her, was in the drawing-room above-stairs. He offered to carry him any message, and ushered her, meanwhile, into a parlour. She was surprised at the splendour of the room. The ceiling was painted with a gay design, the walls stuccoed in relief, and the floor covered with a Persian carpet, with suitable accompaniments of mirrors, tables, and sofas.

Craig had been seated at the window above. His suspicions were ever on the watch. He suddenly espied a figure and face on the opposite side of the street, which an alteration of garb and the improvements of time could not conceal from his knowledge. He was startled at this incident, without knowing the extent of its consequences. He saw her cross the way opposite this house, and immediately after heard the bell ring. Still, he was not aware that he himself was the object of this visit, and waited, with some degree of impatience, for the issue of this adventure.

Presently he was summoned to a person below, who wished to see him. The servant shut the door, as soon as he had delivered the message, and retired.

Craig was thrown into considerable perplexity. It was seldom that he was wanting in presence of mind and dexterity, but the unexpectedness of this incident made him pause. He had not forgotten the awful charms of his summoner. He shrunk at the imagination of her rebukes. What purpose could be answered by admitting her? It was, undoubtedly, safest to keep at a distance; but what excuse should be given for refusing this interview? He was roused from his reverie by a second and more urgent summons. The person could not conveniently wait; her business was of the utmost moment, and would detain him but a few minutes.

The anxiety which was thus expressed to see him only augmented his solicitude to remain invisible. He had papers before him which he had been employed in examining. This suggested an excuse: – "Tell her that I am engaged just now, and cannot possibly attend to her. Let her leave her business. If she has any message, you may bring it to me."

It was plain to Constantia that Craig suspected the purpose of her visit. This might have come to his knowledge by means impossible for her to divine. She now perceived the wisdom of the precaution she had taken. She gave her letter to the servant with this message: – "Tell him I shall wait here for an answer, and continue to wait till I receive one."

Her mind was powerfully affected by the criticalness of her situation. She had gone thus far, and saw the necessity of persisting to the end. The goal was within view, and she formed a sort of desperate determination not to relinquish the pursuit. She could not overlook the possibility that he might return no answer, or return an unsatisfactory one. In either case, she was resolved to remain in the house till driven from it by violence. What other resolution could she form? To return to her desolate home penniless was an idea not to be endured.

The letter was received and perused. His conscience was touched, but compunction was a guest whose importunities he had acquired a peculiar facility of eluding. Here was a liberal offer. A price was set upon his impunity. A small sum, perhaps, would secure him from all future molestation. – "She spoke, to-be-sure, in a damned high tone. 'Twas a pity that the old man should be hungry before supper-time. Blind, too! Harder still, when he cannot find his way to his mouth. Rent unpaid, and a flinty-hearted landlord. A pretty pickle, to-be-sure. Instant payment, she says. Won't part without it. Must come down with the stuff. I know this girl. When her heart is once set upon a thing, all the devils will not turn her out of her way. She promises silence. I can't pretend to bargain with her. I'd as lief be ducked as meet her face to face. I know she'll do what she promises. That was always her grand failing. How the little witch talks! Just the dreamer she ever was! Justice! Compassion! Stupid fool! One would think she'd learned something of the world by this time."

He took out his pocket-book. Among the notes it contained, the lowest was fifty dollars. This was too much: yet there was no alternative; something must be given. She had detected his abode, and he knew it was in the power of the Dudleys to ruin his reputation and obstruct his present schemes. It was probable that, if they should exert themselves, their cause would find advocates and patrons. Still, the gratuitous gift of fifty dollars sat uneasily upon his avarice. One idea occurred to reconcile him to the gift. There was a method he conceived of procuring the repayment of it with interest. He enclosed the note in a blank piece of paper and sent it to her.

She received the paper, and opened it with trembling fingers. When she saw what were its contents, her feelings amounted to rapture. A sum like this was affluence to her in her present condition. At least it would purchase present comfort and security. Her heard glowed with exultation, and she seemed to tread with the lightness of air as she hied homeward. The languor of a long fast, the numbness of the cold, were forgotten. It is worthy of remark how much of human accommodation was comprised within this small compass; and how sudden was this transition from the verge of destruction to the summit of security.

Her first business was to call upon her landlord and pay him his demand. On her return she discharged the little debts she had been obliged to contract, and purchased what was immediately necessary. Wood she could borrow from her next neighbour, and this she was willing to do, now that she had the prospect of repaying it.

CHAPTER XI.

ON LEAVING Mr. Ormond's house, Constantia was met by that gentleman. He saw her as she came out, and was charmed with the simplicity of her appearance. On entering, he interrogated the servant as to the business that brought her thither.

"So," said he, as he entered the drawing-room where Craig was seated, "you have had a visitant. She came, it seems, on a pressing occasion, and would be put off with nothing but a letter."

Craig had not expected this address, but it only precipitated the execution of a design that he had formed. Being aware of this or similar accidents, he had constructed and related, on a previous occasion, to Ormond, a story suitable to his purpose.

"Ay," said he, in a tone of affected compassion, "it is a sad affair enough. I am sorry it is not in my power to help the poor girl. She is wrong in imputing her father's misfortunes to me, but I know the source of her mistake. Would to Heaven it was in my power to repair the wrongs they have suffered, not from me, but from one whose relationship is a disgrace to me."

"Perhaps," replied the other, "you are willing to explain this affair."

"Yes, I wish to explain it. I was afraid of some such accident as this. An explanation is due to my character. I have already told you my story. I mentioned to you a brother of mine. There is scarcely thirteen months' difference in our ages. There is a strong resemblance between him and me in our exterior, though I hope there is none at all in our minds. This brother was the partner of a gentleman, the father of this girl, at New York. He was a long time nothing better than an apprentice to Mr. Dudley, but he advanced so much in the good graces of his master that he finally took him into partnership. I did not know, till I arrived on the continent, the whole of his misconduct. It appears that he embezzled the property of the house and fled away with it, and the consequence was that his quondam master was ruined. I am often mistaken for my brother, to my no small inconvenience; but all this I told you formerly. See what a letter I just now received from this girl."

Craig was one of the most plausible of men. His character was a standing proof of the vanity of physiognomy. There were few men who could refuse their confidence to his open and ingenuous aspect. To this circumstance, perhaps, he owed his ruin. His temptations to deceive were stronger than what are incident to most other men. Deception was so easy a task, that the difficulty lay, not in infusing false opinions respecting him, but in preventing them from being spontaneously imbibed. He contracted habits of imposture imperceptibly. In proportion as he deviated from the practice of truth, he discerned the necessity of extending and systematizing his efforts, and of augmenting the original benignity and attractiveness of his looks by studied additions. The further he proceeded, the more difficult it was to return. Experience and habit added daily to his speciousness, till at length the world perhaps might have been searched in vain for his competitor.

He had been introduced to Ormond under the most favourable auspices. He had provided against a danger which he knew to be imminent, by relating his own story as if it were his brother's. He had, however, made various additions to it, serving to aggravate the heinousness of his guilt. This arose partly from policy, and partly from the habit of lying, which was prompted by a fertile invention and rendered inveterate by incessant exercise. He interwove in his tale an intrigue between Miss Dudley and his brother. The former was seduced, and this man had employed his skill in chirographical imitation in composing letters from Miss Dudley to his brother, which sufficiently attested her dishonour. He and his brother he related to have met in Jamaica, where the latter died, by which means his personal property and papers came into his possession.

Ormond read the letter which his companion presented to him on this occasion. The papers which Craig had formerly permitted him to inspect had made him familiar with her handwriting. The penmanship was, indeed, similar, yet this was written in a spirit not quite congenial with that which had dictated her letters to her lover. But he reflected that the emergency was extraordinary, and that the new scenes through which she had passed had, perhaps, enabled her to retrieve her virtue and enforce it. The picture which she drew of her father's distresses affected him and his companion very differently. He pondered on it for some time in silence; he then looked up, and, with his usual abruptness, said, "I suppose you gave her something?"

"No. I was extremely sorry that it was not in my power. I have nothing but a little trifling silver about me. I have no more at home than will barely suffice to pay my board here, and my expenses to Baltimore. Till I reach there I cannot expect a supply. I was less uneasy, I confess, on this account, because I knew you to be equally willing and much more able to afford the relief she asks."

This, Mr. Ormond had predetermined to do. He paused only to deliberate in what manner it could, with most propriety, be done. He was always willing, when he conferred benefits, to conceal the author. He was not displeased when gratitude was misplaced, and readily allowed his instruments to act as if they were principals. He questioned not the veracity of Craig, and was, therefore, desirous to free him from the molestation that was threatened in the way which had been prescribed. He put a note of one hundred dollars into his hand, and enjoined him to send it to the Dudleys that evening, or early the next morning. "I am pleased," he added, "with the style of this letter: it can be of no service to you; leave it in my possession."

Craig would much rather have thrown it into the fire; but he knew the character of his companion, and was afraid to make any objection to his request. He promised to send or carry the note the next morning, before he set out on his intended journey.

This journey was to Baltimore, and was undertaken so soon merely to oblige his friend, who was desirous of remitting to Baltimore a considerable sum in English guineas, and who had been for some time in search of one who might execute this commission with fidelity. The offer of Craig had been joyfully accepted, and the next morning had been the time fixed for his departure, – a period the most opportune for Craig's designs that could be imagined. To return to Miss Dudley.

The sum that remained to her after the discharge of her debts would quickly be expended. It was no argument of wisdom to lose sight of the future in the oblivion of present care. The time would inevitably come when new resources would be necessary. Every hour brought nearer the period without facilitating the discovery of new expedients. She related the recent adventure to her father. He acquiesced in the propriety of her measures, but the succour that she had thus obtained consoled him but little. He saw how speedily it would again be required, and was hopeless of a like fortunate occurrence.

Some days had elapsed, and Constantia had been so fortunate as to procure some employment. She was thus engaged in the evening when they were surprised by a visit from their landlord. This was an occurrence that foreboded them no good. He entered with abruptness, and scarcely noticed the salutations that he received. His bosom swelled with discontent, which seemed ready to be poured out upon his two companions. To the inquiry as to the condition of his health and that of his family, he surlily answered, "Never mind how I am. None the better for my tenants, I think. Never was a man so much plagued as I have been. What with one putting me off from time to time, what with another quarrelling about terms and denying his agreement, and another running away in my debt, I expect nothing but to come to poverty – God help me! – at last. But this was the worst of all. I was never before treated so in all my life. I don't know what or when I shall get to the end of my troubles. To be fobbed out of my rent and twenty-five dollars into the bargain! It is very strange treatment, I assure you, Mr. Dudley."

"What is it you mean?" replied that gentleman. "You have received your dues, and —"

"Received my dues, indeed! High enough, too! I have received none of my dues! I have been imposed upon. I have been put to very great trouble, and expect some compensation. There is no knowing the character of one's tenants. There is nothing but knavery in the world, one would think. I'm sure no man has suffered more by bad tenants than I have. But this is the strangest treatment I ever met with. Very strange, indeed; and, Dudley, I must be paid without delay. To lose my rent and twenty-five dollars into the bargain is too hard. I never met with the equal of it, – not I. Besides, I wouldn't be put to all this trouble for twice the sum."

"What does all this mean, Mr. M'Crea? You seem inclined to scold; but I cannot conceive why you came here for that purpose. This behaviour is improper."

"No, it's very proper, and I want payment of my money. Fifty dollars you owe me. Miss comes to me to pay me my rent, as I thought. She brings me a fifty-dollar note; I changes it for her, for I thought to-be-sure I was quite safe; but, behold, when I sends it to the bank to get the money, they sends me back word that it's forged, and calls on me, before a magistrate, to tell them where I got it from. I'm sure I never was so flustered in my life. I would not have such a thing for ten times the sum."

He proceeded to descant on his loss without any interruption from his auditors, whom this intelligence had struck dumb. Mr. Dudley instantly saw the origin and full extent of this misfortune. He was, nevertheless, calm, and indulged in no invectives against Craig. "It is all of a piece," said he: "our ruin is inevitable. Well, then, let it come."

After M'Crea had railed himself weary, he flung out of the house, warning them the next morning he should distrain for his rent, and, at the same time, sue them for the money that Constantia had received in exchange for her note. Miss Dudley was unable to pursue her task. She laid down her needle, and fixed her eyes upon her father. They had been engaged in earnest discourse when their landlord entered. Now there was a pause of profound silence, till the affectionate Lucy, who sufficiently comprehended this scene, gave vent to her affliction in sobs. Her mistress turned to her: –

"Cheer up, my Lucy. We shall do well enough, my girl. Our state is bad enough, without doubt, but despair will make it worse."

The anxiety that occupied her mind related less to herself than to her father. He indeed, in the present instance, was exposed to prosecution. It was he who was answerable for the debt, and whose person would be thrown into durance by the suit that was menaced. The horrors of prison had not hitherto been experienced or anticipated. The worse evil that she had imagined was inexpressibly inferior to this. The idea had in it something terrific and loathsome. The mere supposition of its being possible was not to be endured. If all other expedients should fail, she thought of nothing less than desperate resistance. No. It was better to die than to go to prison.

For a time she was deserted of her admirable equanimity. This, no doubt, was the result of surprise. She had not yet obtained the calmness necessary to deliberation. During this gloomy interval, she would perhaps have adopted any scheme, however dismal and atrocious, which her father's despair might suggest. She would not refuse to terminate her own and her father's unfortunate existence by poison or the cord.

This confusion of mind could not exist long. It gradually gave place to cheerful prospects. The evil perhaps was not without its timely remedy. The person whom she had set out to visit, when her course was diverted by Craig, she once more resolved to apply to; to lay before him, without reserve, her father's situation, to entreat pecuniary succour, and to offer herself as a servant in his family, or in that of any of his friends who stood in need of one. This resolution in a slight degree consoled her; but her mind had been too thoroughly disturbed to allow her any sleep during that night.

She equipped herself betimes, and proceeded with a doubting heart to the house of Mr. Melbourne. She was informed that he had risen, but was never to be seen at so early an hour. At nine o'clock he would be disengaged, and she would be admitted. In the present state of her affairs, this delay was peculiarly unwelcome. At breakfast, her suspense and anxieties would not allow her to eat a morsel, and, when the hour approached, she prepared herself for a new attempt.

As she went out, she met at the door a person whom she recognised, and whose office she knew to be that of a constable. Constantia had exercised, in her present narrow sphere, that beneficence which she had formerly exerted in a larger. There was nothing, consistent with her slender means, that she did not willingly perform for the service of others. She had not been sparing of consolation and personal aid in many cases of personal distress that had occurred in her neighbourhood. Hence, as far as she was known she was reverenced.

The wife of their present visitant had experienced her succour and sympathy on occasion of the death of a favourite child. The man, notwithstanding his office, was not of a rugged or ungrateful temper. The task that was now imposed upon him he undertook with extreme reluctance. He was somewhat reconciled to it by the reflection that another might not perform it with that gentleness and lenity which he found in himself a disposition to exercise on all occasions, but particularly on the present.

She easily guessed at his business, and, having greeted him with the utmost friendliness, returned with him into the house. She endeavoured to remove the embarrassment that hung about him, but in vain.

Having levied what the law very properly calls a distress, he proceeded, after much hesitation, to inform Dudley that he was charged with a message from a magistrate, summoning him to come forthwith and account for having a forged bank-note in his possession.

M'Crea had given no intimation of this. The painful surprise that it produced soon yielded to a just view of this affair. Temporary inconvenience and vexation was all that could be dreaded from it. Mr. Dudley hated to be seen or known. He usually walked out in the dusk of the evening, but limited his perambulations to a short space. At all other times he was obstinately recluse. He was easily persuaded by his daughter to allow her to perform this unwelcome office in his stead. He had not received nor even seen the note. He would have willingly spared her the mortification of a judicial examination, but he knew that this was unavoidable. Should he comply with this summons himself, his daughter's presence would be equally necessary.

Influenced by these considerations, he was willing that his daughter should accompany the messenger, who was content that they should consult their mutual convenience in this respect. This interview was to her not without its terrors, but she cherished the hope that it might ultimately conduce to good. She did not foresee the means by which this would be effected, but her heart was lightened by a secret and inexplicable faith in the propitiousness of some event that was yet to occur. This faith was powerfully enforced when she reached the magistrate's door, and found that he was no other than Melbourne, whose succour she intended to solicit. She was speedily ushered, not into his office, but into a private apartment, where he received her alone.

He had been favourably prepossessed with regard to her character by the report of the officer, who, on being charged with the message, had accounted for the regret which he manifested, by dwelling on the merits of Miss Dudley. He behaved with great civility, requested her to be seated, and accurately scrutinized her appearance. She found herself not deceived in her preconceptions of this gentleman's character, and drew a favourable omen as to the event of this interview by what had already taken place. He viewed her in silence for some time, and then, in a conciliating tone, said, –

"It seems to me, madam, as if I had seen you before. Your face, indeed, is of that kind which, when once seen, is not easily forgotten.

I know it is a long time since, but I cannot tell when or where. If you will not deem me impertinent, I will venture to ask you to assist my conjectures. You name, as I am informed, is Acworth." (I ought to have mentioned that Mr. Dudley, on his removal from New York, among other expedients to obliterate the memory of his former condition and conceal his poverty from the world, had made this change in his name.)

"That, indeed," said the lady, "is the name which my father at present bears. His real name is Dudley. His abode was formerly in Queen Street, New York. Your conjecture, sir, is not erroneous. This is not the first time we have seen each other. I well recollect your having been at my father's house in the days of his prosperity."

"Is it possible?" exclaimed Mr. Melbourne, starting from his seat in the first impulse of his astonishment. "Are you the daughter of my friend Dudley, by whom I have so often been hospitably entertained? I have heard of his misfortunes, but knew not that he was alive, or in what part of the world he resided.

"You are summoned on a very disagreeable affair; but I doubt not you will easily exculpate your father. I am told that he is blind, and that his situation is by no means as comfortable as might be wished. I am grieved that he did not confide in the friendship of those that knew him. What could prompt him to conceal himself?"

"My father has a proud spirit. It is not yet broken by adversity. He disdains *to beg*, but I must now assume *that office* for his sake. I came hither this morning to lay before you his situation, and to entreat your assistance to save him from a prison. He cannot pay for the poor tenement he occupies, and our few goods are already under distress. He has, likewise, contracted a debt. He is, I suppose, already sued on this account, and must go to jail unless saved by the interposition of some friend."

"It is true," said Melbourne, "I yesterday granted a warrant against him at the suit of Malcolm M'Crea. Little did I think that the defendant was Stephen Dudley; but you may dismiss all apprehensions on that score. That affair shall be settled to your father's satisfaction. Meanwhile, we will, if you please, dispatch this unpleasant business respecting a counterfeit note received in payment from you by this M'Crea."

Miss Dudley satisfactorily explained that affair. She stated the relation in which Craig had formerly stood to her father, and the acts of which he had been guilty. She slightly touched on the distresses which the family had undergone during their abode in this city, and the means by which she had been able to preserve her father from want. She mentioned the circumstances which compelled her to seek his charity as the last resource, and the casual encounter with Craig by which she was for the present diverted from that design. She laid before him a copy of the letter she had written, and explained the result of the gift of the note which now appeared to be counterfeit. She concluded with stating her present views, and soliciting him to receive her into his family in quality of servant, or use his interest with some of his friends to procure a provision of this kind. This tale was calculated deeply to affect a man of Mr. Melbourne's humanity.

"No," said he, "I cannot listen to such a request. My inclination is bounded by my means. These will not allow me to place you in an independent situation; but I will do what I can. With your leave, I will introduce you to my wife, in your true character. Her good sense will teach her to set a just value on your friendship. There is no disgrace in earning your subsistence by your own industry. She and her friends will furnish you with plenty of materials; but if there ever be a deficiency, look to me for a supply."

Constantia's heart overflowed at this declaration. Her silence was more eloquent than any words could have been. She declined an immediate introduction to his wife, and withdrew, but not till her new friend had forced her to accept some money.

"Place it to account," said he. "It is merely paying you beforehand, and discharging a debt at the time when it happens to be most useful to the creditor."

To what entire and incredible reverses is the tenor of human life subject! A short minute shall effect a transition from a state utterly destitute of hope, to a condition where all is serene and abundant. The path which we employ all our exertions to shun is often found, upon trial, to be the true road to prosperity.

Constantia retired from this interview with a heart bounding with exultation. She related to her father all that had happened. He was pleased on her account, but the detection of his poverty by Melbourne was the parent of new mortification. His only remaining hope relative to himself was that he should die in his obscurity, whereas it was probable that his old acquaintance would trace him to his covert. This prognostic filled him with the deepest inquietude, and all the reasonings of his daughter were insufficient to appease him.

Melbourne made his appearance in the afternoon. He was introduced, by Constantia, to her father. Mr. Dudley's figure was emaciated, and his features corroded by his ceaseless melancholy. His blindness produced in them a woeful and wildering expression. His dress betokened his penury, and was in unison with the meanness of his habitation and furniture. The visitant was struck with the melancholy contrast which these appearances exhibited to the joyousness and splendour that he had formerly witnessed.

Mr. Dudley received the salutations of his guest with an air of embarrassment and dejection. He resigned to his daughter the task of sustaining the conversation, and excused himself from complying with the urgent invitations of Melbourne, while, at the same time, he studiously forbore all expressions tending to encourage any kind of intercourse between them.

The guest came with a message from his wife, who entreated Miss Dudley's company to tea with her that evening, adding that she should be entirely alone. It was impossible to refuse compliance with this request. She cheerfully assented, and in the evening was introduced to Mrs. Melbourne by her husband.

Constantia found in this lady nothing that called for reverence or admiration, though she could not deny her some portion of esteem. The impression which her own appearance and conversation made upon her entertainer was much more powerful and favourable. A consciousness of her own worth, and disdain of the malevolence of fortune, perpetually shone forth in her behaviour. It was modelled by a sort of mean between presumption on the one hand and humility on the other. She claimed no more than what was justly due to her, but she claimed no less. She did not soothe our vanity nor fascinate our pity by diffident reserves and flutterings. Neither did she disgust by arrogant negligence and uncircumspect loquacity.

At parting, she received commissions in the way of her profession, which supplied her with abundant and profitable employment. She abridged her visit on her father's account, and parted from her new friend just early enough to avoid meeting with Ormond, who entered the house a few minutes after she had left it.

"What pity," said Melbourne to him, "you did not come a little sooner! You pretend to be a judge of beauty. I should like to have heard your opinion of a face that has just left us."

"Describe it," said the other.

"That is beyond my capacity. Complexion and hair and eyebrows may be painted, but these are of no great value in the present case. It is in the putting them together that nature has here shown her skill, and not in the structure of each of the parts individually considered. Perhaps you may at some time meet each other here. If a lofty fellow like you, now, would mix a little common sense with his science, this girl might hope for a husband, and her father for a natural protector."

"Are they in search of one or the other?"

"I cannot say they are. Nay, I imagine they would bear any imputation with more patience than that; but certain I am they stand in need of them. How much would it be to the honour of a man like you, rioting in wealth, to divide it with one lovely and accomplished as this girl is, and struggling with indigence!"

Melbourne then related the adventure of the morning. It was easy for Ormond to perceive that this was the same person of whom he already had some knowledge; but there were some particulars in the narrative that excited surprise. A note had been received from Craig, at the first visit in the evening, and this note was for no more than fifty dollars. This did not exactly tally with the information received from Craig. But this note was forged. Might not this girl mix a little imposture with her truth? Who knows her temptations to hypocrisy? It might have been a present from another quarter, and accompanied with no very honourable conditions. Exquisite wretch! Those whom honesty will not let live must be knaves. Such is the alternative offered by the wisdom of society.

He listened to the tale with apparent indifference. He speedily shifted the conversation to new topics, and put an end to his visit sooner than ordinary.

CHAPTER XII.

I KNOW no task more arduous than a just delineation of the character of Ormond. To scrutinize and ascertain our own principles are abundantly difficult. To exhibit these principles to the world with absolute sincerity can scarcely be expected. We are prompted to conceal and to feign by a thousand motives; but truly to portray the motives and relate the actions of another appears utterly impossible. The attempt, however, if made with fidelity and diligence, is not without its use.

To comprehend the whole truth, with regard to the character and conduct of another, may be denied to any human being; but different observers will have, in their pictures, a greater or less portion of this truth. No representation will be wholly false, and some, though not perfectly, may yet be considerably, exempt from error.

Ormond was, of all mankind, the being most difficult and most deserving to be studied. A fortunate concurrence of incidents has unveiled his actions to me with more distinctness than to any other. My knowledge is far from being absolute; but I am conscious of a kind of duty, first to my friend, and secondly to mankind, to impart the knowledge I possess.

I shall omit to mention the means by which I became acquainted with his character, nor shall I enter, at this time, into every part of it. His political projects are likely to possess an extensive influence on the future condition of this Western World.[1] I do not conceive myself

 1   Ormond's "political projects" link him with the Bavarian Illuminati, a celebrated secret society, founded in 1776, by law Professor Adam Weishaupt, who was in conflict with the Jesuit administrators of the University of Ingolstadt. When they refused to pay him and spread word that he was a dangerous freethinker, he founded a society of intellectuals who taught in seclusion and turned susceptible youths away from the teachings of the church to embrace deistic and republican principles, in an organization akin to freemasonry; hence the term has been applied to other thinkers regarded as atheistic or free-thinking, such as the French Encyclopaedists. The main characteristic of the group was "the propriety of employing, for a good purpose, the means which the wicked employed for evil purposes; and it was taught that the preponderancy of good in the ultimate result consecrated every mean employed; and that wisdom and virtue consisted in properly determining this balance." From John Robison's *Proofs of a Conspiracy against All the Religions and governments of Europe, Carried on in the Secret Meetings of Free Masons, Illuminati and Reading Societies* (see Appendix B, p. 290). Although the society was small, starting with only 5 members, under Baron Adolf Friedrich Knigge's direction the society grew to more than 2000 members by 1784 including professionals, students, artists and intellectuals such as Herder and Goethe. By 1787 the Order of the Illuminati had been demolished by Bavarian officials; however, the legend of the Order continued to be powerful in Europe and abroad. When the French Revolution broke out in 1789, many blamed the Illuminati; in the late 1790s American preachers began to spread rumours of connections between the Illuminati and the Reign of Terror.

authorized to communicate a knowledge of his schemes, which I gained in some sort surreptitiously, or, at least, by means of which he was not apprized. I shall merely explain the maxims by which he was accustomed to regulate his private deportment.

No one could entertain loftier conceptions of human capacity than Ormond, but he carefully distinguished between men in the abstract, and men as they are. The former were beings to be impelled, by the breath of accident, in a right or a wrong road; but, whatever direction they should receive, it was the property of their nature to persist in it. Now, this impulse had been given. No single being could rectify the error. It was the business of the wise man to form a just estimate of things, but not to attempt, by individual efforts, so chimerical an enterprise as that of promoting the happiness of mankind. Their condition was out of the reach of a member of a corrupt society to control. A mortal poison pervaded the whole system, by means of which every thing received was converted into bane and purulence. Efforts designed to ameliorate the condition of an individual were sure of answering a contrary purpose. The principles of the social machine must be rectified, before men can be beneficially active. Our motives may be neutral or beneficent, but our actions tend merely to the production of evil.

The idea of total forbearance was not less delusive. Man could not be otherwise than a cause of perpetual operation and efficacy. He was part of a machine, and as such had not power to withhold his agency. Contiguousness to other parts – that is, to other men – was all that was necessary to render him a powerful concurrent. What, then, was the conduct incumbent on him? Whether he went forward or stood still, whether his motives were malignant, or kind, or indifferent, the mass of evils was equally and necessarily augmented. It did not follow from these preliminaries that virtue and duty were

Brown's friend Yale President and Reverend Timothy Dwight, for example, claimed, in a sermon he preached to the 1798 graduating class at Yale College, that this "infidel philosophy" would make the home a "brothel", wives and daughters "bawd[s] and ... strumpets" and bury the "purity, the happiness, and the hopes, of mankind, ... under a promiscuous and universal concubinage." Timothy Dwight, *Nature, and Danger, of Infidel Philosophy, exhibited in Two Discourses, Addressed to the Candidates for the Baccalaureate, in Yale College.* (New Haven: 1798; 79).

In 1800, American novelist Sarah Sayward Barrell Keating Wood published a novel, *Julia and the Illuminated Baron*, which featured a French Illuminatus who attempts to seduce the heroine.

terms without a meaning, but they require us to promote our own, happiness, and not the happiness of others. Not because the former end is intrinsically preferable, not because the happiness of others is unworthy of primary consideration, but because it is not to be attained. Our power in the present state of things is subjected to certain limits. A man may reasonably hope to accomplish his end, when he proposes nothing but his own good. Any other point is inaccessible.

He must not part with benevolent desire: this is a constituent of happiness. He sees the value of general and particular felicity; he sometimes paints it to his fancy; but, if this be rarely done, it is in consequence of virtuous sensibility, which is afflicted on observing that his pictures are reversed in the real state of mankind. A wise man will relinquish the pursuit of general benefit, but not the desire of that benefit, or the perception of that in which this benefit consists, because these are among the ingredients of virtue and the sources of his happiness.

Principles, in the looser sense of that term, have little influence on practice. Ormond was, for the most part, governed, like others, by the influences of education and present circumstances. It required a vigilant discernment to distinguish whether the stream of his actions flowed from one or the other. His income was large, and he managed it nearly on the same principles as other men. He thought himself entitled to all the splendour and ease which it would purchase; but his taste was elaborate and correct. He gratified his love of the beautiful, because the sensations it afforded were pleasing, but made no sacrifices to the love of distinction. He gave no expensive entertainments for the sake of exciting the admiration of stupid gazers, or the flattery or envy of those who shared them. Pompous equipage and retinue were modes of appropriating the esteem of mankind which he held in profound contempt. The garb of his attendants was fashioned after the model suggested by his imagination, and not in compliance with the dictates of custom.

He treated with systematic negligence the etiquette that regulates the intercourse of persons of a certain class. He everywhere acted, in this respect, as if he were alone, or among familiar associates. The very appellations of Sir, and Madam, and Mister, were, in his apprehension, servile and ridiculous; and, as custom or law had annexed no penalty to the neglect of these, he conformed to his own opinions. It was easier for him to reduce his notions of equality to practice than for most others. To level himself with others was an act of condescension and not of arrogance. It was requisite to descend rather than to rise, – a task the most easy, if we regard the obstacles flowing from the prejudice of mankind, but far most difficult, if the motives of the agent be considered.

That in which he chiefly placed his boast was his sincerity. To this he refused no sacrifice. In consequence of this, his deportment was disgusting to weak minds, by a certain air of ferocity and haughty negligence. He was without the attractions of candour, because he regarded not the happiness of others but in subservience to his sincerity. Hence it was natural to suppose that the character of this man was easily understood. He affected to conceal nothing. No one appeared more exempt from the instigations of vanity. He set light by the good opinions of others, had no compassion for their prejudices, and hazarded assertions in their presence which he knew would be, in the highest degree, shocking to their previous notions. They might take it, he would say, as they list. Such were his conceptions, and the last thing he would give up was the use of his tongue. It was his way to give utterance to the suggestions of his understanding. If they were disadvantageous to him in the opinions of others, it was well. He did not wish to be regarded in any light but the true one. He was contented to be rated by the world at his just value. If they esteemed him for qualities he did not possess, was he wrong in rectifying their mistake? but, in reality, if they valued him for that to which he had no claim, and which he himself considered as contemptible, he must naturally desire to show them their error, and forfeit that praise which, in his own opinion, was a badge of infamy.

In listening to his discourse, no one's claim to sincerity appeared less questionable. A somewhat different conclusion would be suggested by a survey of his actions. In early youth he discovered in himself a remarkable facility in imitating the voice and gestures of others. His memory was eminently retentive, and these qualities would have rendered his career, in the theatrical profession, illustrious, had not his condition raised him above it. His talents were occasionally exerted for the entertainment of convivial parties and private circles, but he gradually withdrew from such scenes, as he advanced in age, and devoted his abilities to higher purposes.

His aversion to duplicity had flowed from experience of its evils.

He had frequently been made its victim: in consequence of this his temper had become suspicious, and he was apt to impute deceit on occasions when others, of no inconsiderable sagacity, were abundantly disposed to confidence. One transaction had occurred in his life, in which the consequences of being misled by false appearances were of the utmost moment to his honour and safety. The usual mode of solving his doubts he deemed insufficient, and the eagerness of his curiosity tempted him, for the first time, to employ, for this end, his talents at imitation. He therefore assumed a borrowed character and guise, and performed his part with so much skill as fully to accomplish his design. He whose mask would have secured him from all other attempts was thus taken through an avenue which his caution had overlooked, and the hypocrisy of his pretensions unquestionably ascertained.

Perhaps, in a comprehensive view, the success of this expedient was unfortunate. It served to recommend this method of encountering deceit, and informed him of the extent of those powers which are so liable to be abused. A subtlety much inferior to Ormond's would suffice to recommend this mode of action. It was defensible on no other principle than necessity. The treachery of mankind compelled him to resort to it. If they should deal in a manner as upright and explicit as himself, it would be superfluous. But since they were in the perpetual use of stratagems and artifices, it was allowable, he thought, to wield the same arms.

It was easy to perceive, however, that this practice was recommended to him by other considerations. He was delighted with the power it conferred. It enabled him to gain access, as if by supernatural means, to the privacy of others, and baffle their profoundest contrivances to hide themselves from his view. It flattered him with the possession of something like omniscience. It was, besides, an art in which, as in others, every accession of skill was a source of new gratification. Compared with this, the performance of the actor is the sport of children. This profession he was accustomed to treat with merciless ridicule, and no doubt some of his contempt arose from a secret comparison between the theatrical species of imitation and his own. He blended in his own person the functions of poet and actor, and his dramas were not fictitious but real. The end that he proposed was not the amusement of a playhouse mob. His were scenes in which hope and fear exercised a genuine influence, and in which was maintained that resemblance to truth so audaciously and grossly violated on the stage.

It is obvious how many singular conjectures must have grown out of this propensity. A mind of uncommon energy like Ormond's, which had occupied a wide sphere of action, and which could not fail of confederating its efforts with those of minds like itself, must have given birth to innumerable incidents, not unworthy to be exhibited by the most eloquent historian. It is not my business to relate any of these. The fate of Miss Dudley is intimately connected with his. What influence he obtained over her destiny, in consequence of this dexterity, will appear in the sequel.

It arose from these circumstances that no one was more impenetrable than Ormond, though no one's real character seemed more easily discerned. The projects that occupied his attention were diffused over an ample space; and his instruments and coadjutors were culled from a field whose bounds were those of the civilized world. To the vulgar eye, therefore, he appeared a man of speculation and seclusion, and was equally inscrutable in his real and assumed characters. In his real, his intents were too lofty and comprehensive, as well as too assiduously shrouded from profane inspection, for them to scan. In the latter, appearances were merely calculated to mislead and not to enlighten.

In his youth he had been guilty of the usual excesses incident to his age and character. These had disappeared and yielded place to a more regular and circumspect system of action. In the choice of his pleasures he still exposed himself to the censure of the world. Yet there was more of grossness and licentiousness in the expression of his tenets, than in the tenets themselves. So far as temperance regards the maintenance of health, no man adhered to its precepts with more fidelity; but he esteemed some species of connection with the other sex as venial, which mankind in general are vehement in condemning.

In his intercourse with women he deemed himself superior to the allurements of what is called love. His inferences were drawn from a consideration of the physical propensities of a human being. In his scale of enjoyments, the gratifications which belonged to these were placed at the bottom. Yet he did not entirely disdain them, and, when they could be purchased without the sacrifice of superior advantages, they were sufficiently acceptable.

His mistake on this head was the result of his ignorance. He had not hitherto met with a female worthy of his confidence. Their views were limited and superficial, or their understandings were betrayed by the tenderness of their hearts. He found in them no intellectual energy, no superiority to what he accounted vulgar prejudice, and no affinity with the sentiments which he cherished with most devotion. Their presence had been capable of exciting no emotion which he did not quickly discover to be vague and sensual; and the uniformity of his experience at length instilled into him a belief that the intellectual constitution of females was essentially defective. He denied the reality of that passion which claimed a similitude or sympathy of minds as one of its ingredients.

CHAPTER XIII.

HE RESIDED in New York some time before he took up his abode in Philadelphia. He had some pecuniary concerns with a merchant of that place. He occasionally frequented his house, finding, in the society which it afforded him, scope for amusing speculation, and opportunities of gaining a species of knowledge of which at that time he stood in need. There was one daughter of the family who of course constituted a member of the domestic circle.

Helena Cleves was endowed with every feminine and fascinating quality. Her features were modified by the most transient sentiments, and were the seat of a softness at all times blushful and bewitching. All those graces of symmetry, smoothness, and lustre, which assemble in the imagination of the painter when he calls from the bosom of her natal deep the Paphian divinity,[1] blended their perfections in the shade, complexion, and hair of this lady. Her voice was naturally thrilling and melodious, and her utterance clear and distinct. A musical education had added to all these advantages the improvements of art, and no one could swim in the dance with such airy and transporting elegance.

---

1 Paphian divinity: Aphrodite, goddess of love.

It is obvious to inquire whether her mental were, in any degree, on a level with her exterior accomplishments. Should you listen to her talk, you would be liable to be deceived in this respect. Her utterance was so just, her phrases so happy, and her language so copious and correct, that the hearer was apt to be impressed with an ardent veneration of her abilities; but the truth is, she was calculated to excite emotions more voluptuous than dignified. Her presence produced a trance of the senses rather than an illumination of the soul. It was a topic of wonder how she should have so carefully separated the husk from the kernel, and be so absolute a mistress of the vehicle of knowledge with so slender means of supplying it; yet it is difficult to judge but from comparison. To say that Helena Cleves was silly or ignorant would be hatefully unjust. Her understanding bore no disadvantageous comparison with that of the majority of her sex; but, when placed in competition with that of some eminent females or of Ormond, it was exposed to the risk of contempt.

This lady and Ormond were exposed to mutual examination. The latter was not unaffected by the radiance that environed this girl, but her true character was easily discovered, and he was accustomed to regard her merely as an object charming to the senses. His attention to her was dictated by this principle. When she sang or talked, it was not unworthy of the strongest mind to be captivated with her music and her elocution; but these were the limits which he set to his gratifications. That sensations of a different kind never ruffled his tranquillity must not be supposed, but he too accurately estimated their consequences to permit himself to indulge them.

Unhappily, the lady did not exercise equal fortitude. During a certain interval Ormond's visits were frequent, and she insensibly contracted for him somewhat more than reverence. The tenor of his discourse was little adapted to cherish her hopes. In the declaration of his opinions he was never withheld by scruples of decorum or a selfish regard to his own interest. His matrimonial tenets were harsh and repulsive. A woman of keener penetration would have predicted, from them, the disappointment of her wishes; but Helena's mind was uninured to the discussion of logical points and the tracing of remote consequences. His presence inspired feelings which would not permit her to bestow an impartial attention on his arguments. It is not enough to say that his reasonings failed to convince her: the combined influence of passion and an unenlightened understanding hindered her from fully comprehending them. All she gathered was a vague conception of something magnificent and vast in his character.

Helena was destined to experience the vicissitudes of fortune. Her father died suddenly and left her without provision. She was compelled to accept the invitations of a kinswoman, and live, in some sort, a life of dependence. She was not qualified to sustain this reverse of fortune in a graceful manner. She could not bear the diminution of her customary indulgences, and to these privations were added the inquietudes of a passion which now began to look with an aspect of hopelessness.

These events happened in the absence of Ormond. On his return he made himself acquainted with them. He saw the extent of this misfortune to a woman of Helena's character, but knew not in what manner it might be effectually obviated. He esteemed it incumbent on him to pay her a visit in her new abode. This token at least of respect or remembrance his duty appeared to prescribe.

This visit was unexpected by the lady. Surprise is the enemy of concealment. She was oppressed with a sense of her desolate situation. She was sitting in her own apartment in a museful posture. Her fancy was occupied with the image of Ormond, and her tears were flowing at the thought of their eternal separation, when he entered softly and unperceived by her. A tap upon the shoulder was the first signal of his presence. So critical an interview could not fail of unveiling the true state of the lady's heart. Ormond's suspicions were excited, and these suspicions speedily led to an explanation.

Ormond retired to ruminate on this discovery. I have already mentioned his sentiments respecting love. His feelings relative to Helena did not contradict his principles, yet the image which had formerly been exquisite in loveliness had now suddenly gained unspeakable attractions. This discovery had set the question in a new light. It was of sufficient importance to make him deliberate. He reasoned somewhat in the following manner: –

"Marriage is absurd. This flows from the general and incurable imperfection of the female character. No woman can possess that worth which would induce me to enter into this contract, and bind myself, without power of revoking the decree, to her society. This opinion may possibly be erroneous; but it is undoubtedly true with respect to Helena, and the uncertainty of the position in general will increase the necessity of caution in the present case. That woman may exist whom I should not fear to espouse. This is not her. Some accident may cause our meeting. Shall I then disable myself, by an irrevocable obligation, from profiting by so auspicious an occurrence?"

This girl's society was to be enjoyed in one of two ways. Should he consult his inclination, there was little room for doubt. He had never met with one more highly qualified for that species of intercourse which he esteemed rational. No man more abhorred the votaries of licentiousness. Nothing was more detestable to him than a mercenary alliance. Personal fidelity, and the existence of that passion of which he had, in the present case, the good fortune to be the object, were indispensable in his scheme. The union was indebted for its value on the voluntariness with which it was formed, and the entire acquiescence of the judgment of both parties in its rectitude. Dissimulation and artifice were wholly foreign to the success of his project. If the lady thought proper to assent to his proposal it was well. She did so because assent was more eligible than refusal.

She would, no doubt, prefer marriage. She would deem it more conducive to happiness. This was an error. This was an opinion, his reasons for which he was at liberty to state to her; at least it was justifiable in refusing to subject himself to loathsome and impracticable obligations. Certain inconveniences attended women who set aside, on these occasions, the sanction of law; but these were imaginary. They owed their force to the errors of the sufferer. To annihilate them, it was only necessary to reason justly; but, allowing these inconveniences their full weight and an indestructible existence, it was but a choice of evils. Were they worse in this lady's apprehension than an eternal and hopeless separation? Perhaps they were. If so, she would make her election accordingly. He did nothing but lay the conditions before her. If his scheme should obtain the concurrence of her unbiassed judgment, he should rejoice. If not, her conduct should be uninfluenced by him. Whatever way she should decide, he would assist her in adhering to her decision, but would, meanwhile, furnish her with the materials of a right decision.

This determination was singular. Many will regard it as incredible. No man, it will be thought, can put this deception on himself, and imagine that there was genuine beneficence in a scheme like this.

Would the lady more consult her happiness by adopting than by rejecting it? There can be but one answer. It cannot be supposed that Ormond, in stating his proposal, acted with all the impartiality that he pretended; that he did not employ fallacious exaggerations and ambiguous expedients; that he did not seize every opportunity of triumphing over her weakness, and building his success rather on the illusions of her heart than the convictions of her understanding. His conclusions were specious but delusive, and were not uninfluenced by improper biasses; but of this he himself was scarcely conscious, and it must be at least admitted that he acted with scrupulous sincerity.

An uncommon degree of skill was required to introduce this topic so as to avoid the imputation of an insult. This scheme was little in unison with all her preconceived notions. No doubt, the irksomeness of her present situation, the allurements of luxury and ease which Ormond had to bestow, and the revival of her ancient independence and security, had some share in dictating her assent.

Her concurrence was by no means cordial and unhesitating. Remorse and the sense of dishonour pursued her to her retreat, though chosen with a view of shunning their intrusions; and it was only when the reasonings and blandishments of her lover were exhibited, that she was lulled into temporary tranquillity.

She removed to Philadelphia. Here she enjoyed all the consolation of opulence. She was mistress of a small but elegant mansion. She possessed all the means of solitary amusement, and frequently enjoyed the company of Ormond. These, however, were insufficient to render her happy. Certain reflections might, for a time, be repressed or divested of their string, but they insinuated themselves at every interval, and imparted to her mind a hue of dejection from which she could not entirely relieve herself.

She endeavoured to acquire a relish for the pursuits of literature, by which her lonely hours might be cheered; but of this, even in the blithesomeness and serenity of her former days, she was incapable, – much more so now when she was the prey of perpetual inquietude. Ormond perceived this change, not without uneasiness. All his efforts to reconcile her to her present situation were fruitless. They produced a momentary effect upon her. The softness of her temper and her attachment to him would, at his bidding, restore her to vivacity and ease, but the illumination seldom endured longer than his presence and the novelty of some amusement which he had furnished her.

At his next visit, perhaps, he would find that a new task awaited him. She indulged herself in no recriminations or invectives. She could not complain that her lover had deceived her. She had voluntarily and deliberately accepted the conditions prescribed. She regarded her own disposition to repine as a species of injustice. She laid no claim to an increase of tenderness. She hinted not a wish for a change of situation; yet she was unhappy. Tears stole into her eyes, and her thoughts wandered into gloomy reverie, at moments when least aware of their approach, and least willing to indulge them.

Was a change to be desired? Yes; provided that change was equally agreeable to Ormond, and should be seriously proposed by him. Of this she had no hope. As long as his accents rung in her ears, she even doubted whether it were to be wished. At any rate, it was impossible to gain his approbation to it. Her destiny was fixed. It was better than the cessation of all intercourse, yet her heart was a stranger to all permanent tranquillity.

Her manners were artless and ingenuous. In company with Ormond her heart was perfectly unveiled. He was her divinity, to whom every sentiment was visible, and to whom she spontaneously uttered what she thought, because the employment was pleasing, because he listened with apparent satisfaction, and because, in fine, it was the same thing to speak and to think in his presence. There was no inducement to conceal from him the most evanescent and fugitive ideas.

Ormond was not an inattentive or indifferent spectator of those appearances. His friend was unhappy. She shrunk aghast from her own reproaches and the contumelies of the world. This morbid sensibility he had endeavoured to cure, but hitherto in vain. What was the amount of her unhappiness? Her spirits had formerly been gay; but her gayety was capable of yielding place to soul-ravishing and solemn tenderness. Her sedateness was, at those times, the offspring not of reflection but of passion. There still remained much of her former self. He was seldom permitted to witness more than the traces of sorrow. In answer to his inquiries, she, for the most part, described sensations that were gone, and which she flattered herself and him would never return; but this hope was always doomed to disappointment.

Solitude infallibly conjured up the ghost which had been laid, and it was plain that argument was no adequate remedy for this disease.

How far would time alleviate its evils? When the novelty of her condition should disappear, would she not regard it with other eyes? By being familiar with contempt, it will lose its sting; but is that to be wished? Must not the character be thoroughly depraved before the scorn of our neighbours shall become indifferent? Indifference, flowing from a sense of justice, and a persuasion that our treatment is unmerited, is characteristic of the noblest minds; but indifference to obloquy, because we are habituated to it, is a token of peculiar baseness. This, therefore, was a remedy to be ardently deprecated.

He had egregiously overrated the influence of truth and his own influence. He had hoped that his victory was permanent. In order to the success of truth, he was apt to imagine that nothing was needful but opportunities for a complete exhibition of it. They that inquire and reason with sufficient deliberateness and caution must inevitably accomplish their end. These maxims were confuted in the present case. He had formed no advantageous conceptions of Helena's capacity. His aversion to matrimony arose from those conceptions; but experience had shown him that his conclusions, unfavourable as they were, had fallen short of the truth. Convictions which he had conceived her mind to be sufficiently strong to receive and retain were proved to have made no other than momentary impression. Hence his objections to ally himself to a mind inferior to his own were strengthened rather than diminished. But he could not endure the thought of being instrumental to her misery.

Marriage was an efficacious remedy, but he could not as yet bring himself to regard the aptitude of this cure as a subject of doubt. The idea of separation sometimes occurred to him. He was not unapprehensive of the influence of time and absence incurring the most vehement passion, but to this expedient the lady could not be reconciled. He knew her too well to believe that she would willingly adopt it. But the only obstacle to this scheme did not flow from the lady's opposition. He would probably have found upon experiment as strong an aversion to adopt it in himself as in her.

It was easy to see the motives by which he would be likely to be swayed into a change of principles. If marriage were the only remedy, the frequent repetition of this truth must bring him insensibly to doubt the rectitude of his determinations against it. He deeply reflected on the consequence which marriage involves. He scrutinized with the utmost accuracy the character of his friend, and surveyed it in all its parts. Inclination could not fail of having some influence on his opinions. The charms of this favourite object tended to impair the clearness of his view and extenuate or conceal her defects. He entered on the enumeration of her errors with reluctance. Her happiness, had it been wholly disconnected with his own, might have had less weight in the balance; but now, every time the scales were suspended, this consideration acquired new weight.

Most men are influenced, in the formation of this contract, by regards purely physical. They are incapable of higher views. They regard with indifference every tie that binds them to their contemporaries or to posterity. Mind has no part in the motives that guide them. They choose a wife as they choose any household movable, and when the irritation of the senses has subsided, the attachment that remains is the offspring of habit.

Such were not Ormond's modes of thinking. His creed was of too extraordinary a kind not to merit explication. The terms of this contract were, in his eyes, iniquitous and absurd. He could not think with patience of a promise which no time could annul, which pretended to ascertain contingencies and regulate the future. To forego the liberty of choosing his companion, and bind himself to associate with one whom he despised; to raise to his own level one whom nature had irretrievably degraded; to avow, and persist in his adherence to, a falsehood, palpable and loathsome to his understanding; to affirm that he was blind, when in full possession of his senses; to shut his eyes and grope in the dark, and call upon the compassion of mankind on his infirmity, when his organs were in no degree impaired, and the scene around him was luminous and beautiful, – was a height of infatuation that he could never attain. And why should he be thus self-degraded? Why should he take a laborious circuit to reach a point which, when attained, was trivial, and to which reason had pointed out a road short and direct?

A wife is generally nothing more than a household superintendent. This function could not be more wisely vested than it was at present. Every thing in his domestic system was fashioned on strict and inflexible principles. He wanted instruments and not partakers of his authority, – one whose mind was equal and not superior to the cogent apprehension and punctual performance of his will; one whose character was squared, with mathematical exactness, to his situation. Helena, with all her faults, did not merit to be regarded in this light. Her introduction would destroy the harmony of his scheme, and be, with respect to herself, a genuine debasement. A genuine evil would thus be substituted for one that was purely imaginary.

Helena's intellectual deficiencies could not be concealed. She was a proficient in the elements of no science. The doctrine of lines and surfaces was as disproportionate with her intellects as with those of the mock-bird. She had not reasoned on the principles of human action, nor examined the structure of society. She was ignorant of the past or present condition of mankind. History had not informed her of the one, nor the narratives of voyages nor the deductions of geography of the other. The heights of eloquence and poetry were shut out from her view. She could not commune, in their native dialect, with the sages of Rome and Athens. To her those perennial fountains of wisdom and refinement were sealed. The constitution of nature, the attributes of its Author, the arrangement of the parts of the external universe, and the substance, modes of operation, and ultimate destiny of human intelligence, were enigmas unsolved and insoluble by her.

But this was not all. The superstructure could for the present be spared. Nay, it was desirable that the province of rearing it should be reserved for him. All he wanted was a suitable foundation; but this Helena did not possess. He had not hitherto been able to create in her the inclination or the power. She had listened to his precepts with docility. She had diligently conned the lessons which he had prescribed, but the impressions were as fleeting as if they had been made on water. Nature seemed to have set impassable limits to her attainments.

This, indeed, was an unwelcome belief. He struggled to invalidate it. He reflected on the immaturity of her age. What but crude and hasty views was it reasonable to expect at so early a period? If her mind had not been awakened, it had proceeded, perhaps, from the injudiciousness of his plans, or merely from their not having been persisted in. What was wanting but the ornaments of mind to render this being all that poets have feigned of angelic nature? When he indulged himself in imaging the union of capacious understanding with her personal loveliness, his conceptions swelled to a pitch of enthusiasm, and it seemed as if no labour was too great to be employed in the production of such a creature. And yet, in the midst of his glowings, he would sink into sudden dejection at the recollection of that which passion had, for a time, excluded. To make her wise it would be requisite to change her sex. He had forgotten that his pupil was a female, and her capacity therefore limited by nature. This mortifying thought was outbalanced by another. Her attainments, indeed, were suitable to the imbecility of her sex; but did she not surpass, in those attainments, the ordinary rate of women? They must not be condemned because they are outshone by qualities that are necessarily male births.

Her accomplishments formed a much more attractive theme. He overlooked no article in the catalogue. He was confounded at one time, and encouraged at another, on remarking the contradictions that seemed to be included in her character. It was difficult to conceive the impossibility of passing that barrier which yet she was able to touch. She was no poet. She listened to the rehearsal without emotion, or was moved, not by the substance of the passage, by the dazzling image or the magic sympathy, but by something adscititious;[1] yet usher her upon the stage, and no poet would wish for a more powerful organ of his conceptions. In assuming this office, she appeared to have drank in the very soul of the dramatist. What was wanting in judgment was supplied by memory, in the tenaciousness of which she has seldom been rivalled.

Her sentiments were trite and undigested, but were decorated with all the fluences and melodies of elocution. Her musical instructor had been a Sicilian, who had formed her style after the Italian model. This man had likewise taught her his own language. He had supplied her chiefly with Sicilian compositions, both in poetry and melody, and was content to be unclassical for the sake of the feminine and voluptuous graces of his native dialect.

Ormond was an accurate judge of the proficiency of Helena, and of the felicity with which these accomplishments were suited to her character. When his pupil personated the victims of anger and grief, and poured forth the fiery indignation of Calista, or the maternal

---

1 adscititious: not inherent or essential; derived from something outside.

despair of Constance, or the self-contentions of Ipsipile,[1] he could not deny the homage which her talents might claim.

Her Sicilian tutor had found her no less tractable as a votary of painting. She needed only the education of Angelica[2] to exercise as potent and prolific a pencil. This was incompatible with her condition, which limited her attainments to the elements of this art. It was otherwise with music. Here there was no obstacle to skill, and here the assiduities of many years, in addition to a prompt and ardent genius, set her beyond the hopes of rivalship.

Ormond had often amused his fancy with calling up images of excellence in this art. He saw no bounds to the influence of habit in augmenting the speed and multiplying the divisions of muscular motion. The fingers, by their form and size, were qualified to outrun and elude the most vigilant eye. The sensibility of keys and wires had limits; but these limits depended on the structure of the instrument, and the perfection of its structure was proportioned to the skill of the artist. On well-constructed keys and strings, was it possible to carry diversities of movement and pressure too far? How far they could be carried was mere theme of conjecture, until it was his fate to listen to the magical performances of Helena, whose volant finger seemed to be self-impelled. Her touches were creative of a thousand forms of *piano*, and of numberless transitions from grave to quick, perceptible only to ears like her own.

In the selection and arrangement of notes there are no limits to luxuriance and celerity. Helena had long relinquished the drudgery of imitation. She never played but when there were motives to fervour, and when she was likely to ascend without impediment, and to maintain for a suitable period her elevation, to the element of new ideas. The lyrics of Milton and of Metastasio[3] she sung with accompaniments that never tired, because they were never repeated. Her harp

---

1 Calista, Constance and Ipsipile: Calista, heroine of Nicholas Rowe's "she-tragedy" *The Fair Penitent* (1703), is betrothed to Altamont but discovered embracing Lothario. Constance is the mother of Arthur in Shakespeare's *The Life and Death of King John* (1591). Nursemaid in the house of Lycurgus, Ipsipile assists the Argive army but accidentally allows her ward Opheltes to be fatally bitten by a snake.

2 Angelica Kauffmann (1741-1807), Swiss-born artist known for her historical and allegorical paintings and her portraits of contemporaries. In 1769, she helped found the British Royal Academy of Arts and was its first female member.

3 Pietro Metastasio (1698-1782), Italian poet and librettist.

and clavichord supplied her with endless combinations; and these, in the opinion of Ormond, were not inferior to the happiest exertions of Handel and Arne.

Chess was his favourite amusement. This was the only game which he allowed himself to play. He had studied it with so much zeal and success, that there were few with whom he deigned to contend. He was prone to consider it as a sort of criterion of human capacity. He who had acquired skill in this *science* could not be infirm in mind; and yet he found in Helena a competitor not unworthy of all his energies. Many hours were consumed in this employment, and here the lady was sedate, considerate, extensive in foresight, and fertile in expedients.

Her deportment was graceful, inasmuch as it flowed from a consciousness of her defects. She was devoid of arrogance and vanity, neither imagining herself better than she was, and setting light by those qualifications which she unquestionably possessed. Such was the mixed character of this woman.

Ormond was occupied with schemes of a rugged and arduous nature. His intimate associates and the partakers of his confidence were imbued with the same zeal and ardent in the same pursuits. Helena could lay no claim to be exalted to this rank. That one destitute of this claim should enjoy the privileges of his wife was still a supposition truly monstrous. Yet the image of Helena, fondly loving him, and a model, as he conceived, of tenderness and constancy, devoured by secret remorse, and pursued by the scorn of mankind, – a mark for slander to shoot at, and an outcast of society, – did not visit his meditations in vain. The rigour of his principles began now to relent.

He considered that various occupations are incident to every man. He cannot be invariably employed in the promotion of one purpose. He must occasionally unbend, if he desires that the springs of his mind should retain their due vigour. Suppose his life were divided between business and amusement: this was a necessary distribution, and sufficiently congenial with his temper. It became him to select with skill his sources of amusement. It is true that Helena was unable to participate in his graver occupations: what then? In whom were blended so many pleasurable attributes? In her were assembled an exquisite and delicious variety. As it was, he was daily in her company.

He should scarcely be more so if marriage should take place. In that case, no change in their mode of life would be necessary. There was no need of dwelling under the same roof. His revenue was equal to the support of many household establishments. His personal independence would remain equally inviolable. No time, he thought, would diminish his influence over the mind of Helena, and it was not to be forgotten that the transition would to her be happy. It would reinstate her in the esteem of the world, and dispel those phantoms of remorse and shame by which she was at present persecuted.

These were plausible considerations. They tended at least to shake his resolutions. Time would probably have completed the conquest of his pride, had not a new incident set the question in a new light.

CHAPTER XIV.

THE narrative of Melbourne made a deeper impression on the mind of his guest than was at first apparent. This man's conduct was directed by the present impulse; and, however elaborate his abstract notions, he seldom stopped to settle the agreement between his principles and actions. The use of money was a science, like every other branch of benevolence, not reducible to any fixed principles. No man, in the disbursement of money, could say whether he was conferring a benefit or injury. The visible and immediate effects might be good, but evil was its ultimate and general tendency. To be governed by a view to the present rather than to the future was a human infirmity from which he did not pretend to be exempt. This, though an insufficient apology for the conduct of a rational being, was suitable to his indolence, and he was content in all cases to employ it. It was thus that he reconciled himself to beneficent acts and humorously held himself up as an object of censure on occasions when most entitled to applause.

He easily procured information as to the character and situation of the Dudleys. Neighbours are always inquisitive, and happily, in this case, were enabled to make no unfavourable report. He resolved, without hesitation, to supply their wants. This he performed in a manner truly characteristic. There was a method of gaining access to families, and marking them in their unguarded attitudes, more easy and effectual than any other: it required least preparation and cost least pains; the disguise, also, was of the most impenetrable kind. He had served a sort of occasional apprenticeship to the art, and executed its functions with perfect ease. It was the most entire and grotesque metamorphosis imaginable. It was stepping from the highest to the lowest rank in society, and shifting himself into a form as remote from his own as those recorded by Ovid.[1] In a word, it was sometimes his practice to exchange his complexion and habiliments for those of a negro and a chimney-sweep, and to call at certain doors for employment. This he generally secured by importunity and the cheapness of his services.

When the loftiness of his port and the punctiliousness of his nicety were considered, we should never have believed – what yet could be truly asserted – that he had frequently swept his own chimneys, without the knowledge of his own servants.[2] It was likewise true, though equally incredible, that he had played at romps with his scullion, and listened with patience to a thousand slanders on his own character.

In this disguise he visited the house of Mr. Dudley. It was nine o'clock in the morning. He remarked, with critical eyes, the minutest circumstance in the appearance and demeanour of his customers, and glanced curiously at the house and furniture. Every thing was new and every thing pleased. The walls, though broken into roughness by carelessness or time, were adorned with glistening white. The floor, though loose and uneven, and with gaping seams, had received all the improvements which cloth and brush could give. The pine tables, rush chairs, and uncurtained bed, had been purchased at half price, at vendue, and exhibited various tokens of decay; but care and neatness and order were displayed in their condition and arrangement.

The lower apartment was the eating and sitting room. It was likewise Mr. Dudley's bedchamber. The upper room was occupied

---

1 Ovid (43 BC-AD 17). Roman poet known for his *Metamorphoses*, which concerns transformation.

2 Similar exploits are related of Count de la Lippe and Wortley Montagu. [C.B.B.] Edward Wortley Montagu (1713-1776), author and traveller, son of Lady Mary Wortley Montagu and Edward Wortley Montagu. For a time, this roguish adventurer, nicknamed the "British Don Juan," used false names and wore disguises, including Turkish robes.

by Constantia and her Lucy. Ormond viewed every thing with the accuracy of an artist, and carried away with him a catalogue of every thing visible. The faded form of Mr. Dudley, that still retained its dignity, the sedateness, graceful condescension, and personal elegance of Constantia, were new to the apprehension of Ormond. The contrast between the house and its inhabitants rendered the appearance more striking. When he had finished his task, he retired; but, returning in a quarter of an hour, he presented a letter to the young lady. He behaved as if by no means desirous of eluding her interrogatories, and, when she desired him to stay, readily complied. The letter, unsigned and unsuperscribed, was to this effect: –

"The writer of this is acquainted with the transaction between Thomas Craig and Mr. Dudley. The former is debtor to Mr. Dudley in a large sum. I have undertaken to pay as much of this debt, and at such times, as suits my convenience. I have had pecuniary engagements with Craig. I hold myself, in the sum enclosed, discharging so much of his debt. The future payments are uncertain, but I hope they will contribute to relieve the necessities of Mr. Dudley."

Ormond had calculated the amount of what would be necessary for the annual subsistence of this family on the present frugal plan. He had regulated his disbursements accordingly.

It was natural to feel curiosity as to the writer of this epistle. The bearer displayed a prompt and talkative disposition. He had a staring eye and a grin of vivacity forever at command. When questioned by Constantia, he answered that the gentleman had forbidden him to mention his name or the place where he lived. Had he ever met with the same person before? Oh, yes. He had lived with him from a child. His mother lived with him still, and his brothers. His master had nothing for him to do at home, so he sent him out sweeping chimneys, taking from him only half the money that he earned that way. He was a very good master.

"Then the gentleman had been a long time in the city?"

"Oh, yes. All his life, he reckoned. He used to live in Walnut Street, but now he's moved down town." Here he checked himself, and added, – "But I forgets. I must not tell where he lives. He told me I mustn't."

"He has a family and children, I suppose?"

"Oh, yes. Why, don't you know Miss Hetty and Miss Betsy? There again! I was going to tell the name, that he said I must not tell."

Constantia saw that the secret might be easily discovered, but she forbore. She disdained to take advantage of this messenger's imagined simplicity. She dismissed him with some small addition to his demand and with a promise always to employ him in this way.

By this mode Ormond had effectually concealed himself. The lady's conjectures, founded on this delusive information, necessarily wandered widely from the truth. The observations that he had made during this visit afforded his mind considerable employment. The manner in which this lady had sustained so cruel a reverse of fortune, the cheerfulness with which she appeared to forego all the gratifications of affluence, the skill with which she selected her path of humble industry, and the steadiness with which she pursued it, were proofs of a moral constitution from which he supposed the female sex to be debarred. The comparison was obvious between Constantia and Helena, and the result was by no means advantageous to the latter. Was it possible that such a one descended to the level of her father's apprentice? that she sacrificed her honour to a wretch like that? This reflection tended to repress the inclination he would otherwise have felt for cultivating her society, but it did not indispose him to benefit her in a certain way.

On his next visit to his "bella Siciliana," as he called her, he questioned her as to the need in which she might stand of the services of a seamstress; and being informed that they were sometimes wanted, he recommended Miss Acworth to her patronage. He said that he had heard her spoken of in favourable terms by the gossips at Melbourne's. They represented her as a good girl, slenderly provided for, and he wished that Helena would prefer her to all others.

His recommendation was sufficient. The wishes of Ormond, as soon as they became known, became hers. Her temper made her always diligent in search of novelty. It was easy to make work for the needle. In short, she resolved to send for her the next day. The interview accordingly took place on the ensuing morning, not without mutual surprise, and, on the part of the fair Sicilian, not without considerable embarrassment.

This circumstance arose from their having changed their respective names, though from motives of a very different kind. They were not strangers to each other, though no intimacy had ever subsisted between them. Each was merely acquainted with the name, person, and general character of the other. No circumstance in Constantia's situation tended to embarrass her. Her mind had attained a state of serene composure, incapable of being ruffled by an incident of this kind. She merely derived pleasure from the sight of her old acquaintance. The aspect of things around her was splendid and gay. She seemed the mistress of the mansion, and her name was changed. Hence it was unavoidable to conclude that she was married.

Helena was conscious that appearances were calculated to suggest this conclusion. The idea was a painful one. She sorrowed to think that this conclusion was fallacious. The consciousness that her true condition was unknown to her visitant, and the ignominiousness of that truth, gave an air of constraint to her behaviour which Constantia ascribed to a principle of delicacy.

In the midst of reflections relative to herself, she admitted some share of surprise at the discovery of Constantia in a situation so inferior to that in which she had formerly known her. She had heard, in general terms, of the misfortunes of Mr. Dudley, but was unacquainted with particulars; but this surprise, and the difficulty of adapting her behaviour to circumstances, was only in part the source of her embarrassment, though by her companion it was wholly attributed to this cause. Constantia thought it her duty to remove it by open and unaffected manners. She therefore said, in a sedate and cheerful tone, "You see me, madam, in a situation somewhat unlike that in which I was formerly placed. You will probably regard the change as an unhappy one; but, I assure you, I have found it far less so than I expected. I am thus reduced not by my own fault. It is this reflection that enables me to conform to it without a murmur. I shall rejoice to know that Mrs. Eden is as happy as I am."

Helena was pleased with this address, and returned an answer full of sweetness. She had not, in her compassion for the fallen, a particle of pride. She thought of nothing but the contrast between the former situation of her visitant and the present. The fame of her great qualities had formerly excited veneration, and that reverence was by no means diminished by a nearer scrutiny. The consciousness of her own frailty, meanwhile, diffused over the behaviour of Helena a timidity and dubiousness uncommonly fascinating. She solicited Constantia's friendship in a manner than showed she was afraid of nothing but

denial. An assent was eagerly given, and thenceforth a cordial intercourse was established between them.

The real situation of Helena was easily discovered. The officious
person who communicated this information at the same time cau-
tioned Constantia against associating with one of tainted reputation.
This information threw some light upon appearances. It accounted
for that melancholy which Helena was unable to conceal. It
explained that solitude in which she lived, and which Constantia had
ascribed to the death or absence of her husband. It justified the solicitous silence she had hitherto maintained respecting her own affairs,
and which her friend's good sense forbade her to employ any sinister
means of eluding.

No long time was necessary to make her mistress of Helena's character. She loved her with uncommon warmth, though by no means
blind to her defects. She found no expectations from the knowledge
of her character, to which this intelligence operated as a disappointment. It merely excited her pity, and made her thoughtful how she
might assist her in repairing this deplorable error.

This design was of no ordinary magnitude. She saw that it was previously necessary to obtain the confidence of Helena. This was a task
of easy performance. She knew the purity of her own motives and
the extent of her powers, and embarked in this undertaking with full
confidence of success. She had only to profit by a private interview, to
acquaint her friend with what she knew, to solicit a complete and satisfactory disclosure, to explain the impressions which her intelligence
produced, and to offer her disinterested advice. No one knew better
how to couch her ideas in words suitable to the end proposed by her
in imparting them.

Helena was at first terrified; but the benevolence of her friend
quickly entitled her to confidence and gratitude that knew no limits.
She had been deterred from unveiling her heart by the fear of exciting contempt or abhorrence; but when she found that all due
allowances were made, – that her conduct was treated as erroneous in
no atrocious or inexpiable degree, and as far from being insusceptible
of remedy, – that the obloquy with which she had been treated found
no vindicator or participator in her friend, – her heart was considerably relieved. She had been long a stranger to the sympathy and intercourse of her own sex. Now this good, in its most precious form, was

conferred upon her, and she experienced an increase rather than diminution of tenderness, in consequence of her true situation being known.

She made no secret of any part of her history. She did full justice to the integrity of her lover, and explained the unforced conditions on which she had consented to live with him. This relation exhibited the character of Ormond in a very uncommon light. His asperities wounded, and his sternness chilled. What unauthorized conceptions of matrimonial and political equality did he entertain! He had fashioned his treatment of Helena on sullen and ferocious principles. Yet he was able, it seemed, to mould her, by means of them, nearly into the creature that he wished. She knew too little of the man justly to estimate his character. It remained to be ascertained whether his purposes were consistent and upright, or were those of a villain and betrayer.

Meanwhile, what was to be done by Helena? Marriage had been refused on plausible pretences. Her unenlightened understanding made her no match for her lover. She would never maintain her claim to nuptial privileges in his presence, or, if she did, she would never convince him of their validity.

Were they indeed valid? Was not the disparity between them incurable? A marriage of minds so dissimilar could only be productive of misery immediately to him, and, by a reflex operation, to herself. She could not be happy in a union that was the source of regret to her husband. Marriage, therefore, was not possible, or, if possible, was not, perhaps, to be wished. But what was the choice that remained?

To continue in her present situation was not to be endured. Disgrace was a demon that would blast every hope of happiness. She was excluded from all society but that of the depraved. Her situation was eminently critical. It depended, perhaps, on the resolution she should now form whether she should be enrolled among the worst of mankind. Infamy is the worst of evils. It creates innumerable obstructions in the path of virtue. It manacles the hand and entangles the feet that are active only to good. To the weak it is an evil of much greater magnitude. It determines their destiny; and they hasten to merit that reproach which at first, it may be, they did not deserve.

This connection is intrinsically flagitious. Helena is subjected by it to the worst ills that are incident to humanity, the general contempt of mankind, and the reproaches of her own conscience. From these there is but one method from which she can hope to be relieved. The intercourse must cease.

It was easier to see the propriety of separation than to project means for accomplishing it. It was true that Helena loved; but what quarter was due to this passion when divorced from integrity? Is it not in every bosom a perishable sentiment? Whatever be her warmth, absence will congeal it. Place her in new scenes and supply her with new associates. Her accomplishments will not fail to attract votaries. From these she may select a conjugal companion suitable to her mediocrity of talents.

But, alas! what power on earth can prevail on her to renounce Ormond? Others may justly entertain this prospect, but it must be invisible to her. Besides, is it absolutely certain that either her peace of mind or her reputation will be restored by this means? In the opinion of the world her offences cannot, by any perseverance in penitence, be expiated. She will never believe that separation will exterminate her passion. Certain it is that it will avail nothing to the re-establishment of her fame. But, if it were conducive to these ends, how chimerical to suppose that she will ever voluntarily adopt it! If Ormond refuse his concurrence, there is absolutely an end to hope. And what power on earth is able to sway his determinations? At least, what influence was it possible for her to obtain over them?

Should they separate, whither should she retire? What mode of subsistence should she adopt? She has never been accustomed to think beyond the day. She has eaten and drank, but another has provided the means. She scarcely comprehends the principle that governs the world, and in consequence of which nothing can be gained but by giving something in exchange for it. She is ignorant and helpless as a child, on every topic that relates to the procuring of subsistence. Her education has disabled her from standing alone.

But this was not all. She must not only be supplied by others, but sustained in the enjoyment of a luxurious existence. Would you bereave her of the gratifications of opulence? You had better take away her life. Nay, it would ultimately amount to this. She can live but in one way.

At present she is lovely, and, to a certain degree, innocent; but expose her to the urgencies and temptations of want, let personal pollution be the price set upon the voluptuous affluences of her present condition, and it is to be feared there is nothing in the contexture of her mind to hinder her from making the purchase. In every respect, therefore, the prospect was a hopeless one, – so hopeless that her mind insensibly returned to the question which she had at first dismissed with very slight examination, – the question relative to the advantages and probabilities of marriage. A more accurate review convinced her that this was the most eligible alternative. It was, likewise, most easily effected. The lady, of course, would be its fervent advocate. There did not want reasons why Ormond should finally embrace it. In what manner appeals to his reason or his passion might most effectually be made, she knew not.

Helena was ill qualified to be her own advocate. Her unhappiness could not but be visible to Ormond. He had shown himself attentive and affectionate. Was it impossible that, in time, he should reason himself into a spontaneous adoption of this scheme? This, indeed, was a slender foundation for hope, but there was no other on which she could build.

Such were the meditations of Constantia on this topic. She was deeply solicitous for the happiness of her friend. They spent much of their time together. The consolations of her society were earnestly sought by Helena; but, to enjoy them, she was for the most part obliged to visit the former at her own dwelling. For this arrangement Constantia apologized by saying, "You will pardon my requesting you to favour me with your visits rather than allowing you mine. Every thing is airy and brilliant within these walls. There is, besides, an air of seclusion and security about you that is delightful. In comparison, my dwelling is bleak, comfortless, and unretired. But my father is entitled to all my care. His infirmity prevents him from amusing himself, and his heart is cheered by the mere sound of my voice, though not addressed to him. The mere belief of my presence seems to operate as an antidote to the dreariness of solitude; and, now you know my motives, I am sure you will not only forgive but approve of my request."

CHAPTER XV.

WHEN once the subject had been introduced, Helena was prone to descant upon her own situation, and listened with deference to the remarks and admonitions of her companion. Constantia did not conceal from her any of her sentiments. She enabled her to view her own condition in its true light, and set before her the indispensable advantages of marriage, while she, at the same time, afforded her the best directions as to the conduct she ought to pursue in order to effect her purpose.

The mind of Helena was thus kept in a state of perpetual and uneasy fluctuation. While absent from Ormond, or listening to her friend's remonstrances, the deplorableness of her condition arose in its most disastrous hues before her imagination. But the spectre seldom failed to vanish at the approach of Ormond. His voice dissipated every inquietude.

She was not insensible of this inconstancy. She perceived and lamented her own weakness. She was destitute of all confidence in her own exertions. She could not be in the perpetual enjoyment of his company. Her intervals of tranquillity, therefore, were short, while those of anxiety and dejection were insupportably tedious. She revered, but believed herself incapable to emulate, the magnanimity of her monitor. The consciousness of inferiority, especially in a case like this, in which her happiness so much depended on her own exertions, excited in her the most humiliating sensations.

While indulging in fruitless melancholy, the thought one day occurred to her, "Why may not Constantia be prevailed upon to plead my cause? Her capacity and courage are equal to any undertaking. The reasonings that are so powerful in my eyes, would they be trivial and futile in those of Ormond? I cannot have a more pathetic and disinterested advocate."

This idea was cherished with uncommon ardour. She seized the first opportunity that offered itself to impart it to her friend. It was a wild and singular proposal, and was rejected at the first glance. This scheme, romantic and impracticable as it at first seemed, appeared to Helena in the most plausible colours. She could not bear to relinquish her new-born hopes. She saw no valid objection to it. Every thing was easy to her friend, provided her sense of duty and her zeal could be awakened. The subject was frequently suggested to Constantia's reflections. Perceiving the sanguineness of her friend's confidence, and fully impressed with the value of the end to be accomplished, she insensibly veered to the same opinion. At least the scheme was worthy of a candid discussion before it was rejected.

Ormond was a stranger to her. His manners were repulsive and austere. She was a mere girl. Her personal attachment to Helena was all that she could plead in excuse for taking part in her concerns. The subject was delicate. A blunt and irregular character like Ormond's might throw an air of ridicule over the scene. She shrunk from the encounter of a boisterous and man-like spirit.

But were not these scruples effeminate and puerile? Had she studied so long in the school of adversity, without conviction of the duty of a virtuous independence? Was she not a rational being, fully imbued with the justice of her cause? Was it not ignoble to refuse the province of a vindicator of the injured, before any tribunal, however tremendous or unjust? And who was Ormond, that his eye should inspire terror?

The father or brother of Helena might assume the office without indecorum. Nay, a mother or sister might not be debarred from it. Why then should she, who was actuated by equal zeal, and was engaged, by ties stronger than consanguinity, in the promotion of her friend's happiness? It is true she did not view the subject in the light in which it was commonly viewed by brothers and parents. It was not a gust of rage that should transport her into his presence. She did not go to awaken his slumbering conscience and abash him in the pride of guilty triumph, but to rectify deliberate errors and change his course by the change of his principles. It was her business to point out to him the road of duty and happiness, from which he had strayed with no sinister intentions. This was to be done without raving and fury, but with amicable soberness, and in the way of calm and rational remonstrance. Yet there were scruples that would not be shut out, and continually whispered [to] her, "What an office is this for a girl and a stranger to assume!"

In what manner should it be performed? Should an interview be sought, and her ideas be explained without confusion or faltering, undismayed by ludicrous airs or insolent frowns? But this was a point to be examined. Was Ormond capable of such behaviour? If he were, it would be useless to attempt the reformation of his errors. Such a man is incurable and obdurate. Such a man is not to be sought as the husband of Helena; but this, surely, is a different being.

The medium through which she had viewed his character was an ample one, but might not be very accurate. The treatment which Helena had received from him, exclusive of his fundamental error, betokened a mind to which she did not disdain to be allied. In spite of his defects, she saw that their elements were more congenial, and the points of contact between this person and herself more numerous than between her and Helena, whose voluptuous sweetness of temper and mediocrity of understanding excited in her bosom no genuine sympathy.

Every thing is progressive in the human mind. When there is leisure to reflect, ideas will succeed each other in a long train, before the ultimate point be gained. The attention must shift from one side to the other of a given question many times before it settles. Constantia did not form her resolutions in haste; but, when once formed, they were exempt from fluctuation. She reflected before she acted, and therefore acted with consistency and vigour. She did not apprize her friend of her intention. She was willing that she should benefit by her interposition before she knew it was employed.

She sent her Lucy with a note to Ormond's house. It was couched in these terms: —

"Constantia Dudley requests an interview with Mr. Ormond. Her business being of some moment, she wishes him to name an hour when most disengaged."

An answer was immediately returned, that at three o'clock in the afternoon he should be glad to see her.

This message produced no small surprise in Ormond. He had not withdrawn his notice from Constantia, and had marked, with curiosity and approbation, the progress of the connection between the two women. The impressions which he had received from the report of Helena were not dissimilar to those which Constantia had imbibed, from the same quarter, respecting himself; but he gathered from them no suspicion of the purpose of a visit. He recollected his connection with Craig. This lady had had an opportunity of knowing that some connection subsisted between them. He concluded that some information or inquiry respecting Craig might occasion this event. As it was, it gave him considerable satisfaction. It would enable him more closely to examine one with respect to whom he entertained great curiosity.

Ormond's conjecture was partly right. Constantia did not forget her having traced Craig to this habitation. She designed to profit by the occasion which this circumstance afforded her of making some inquiry respecting Craig, in order to introduce, by suitable degrees, a more important subject.

The appointed hour having arrived, he received her in his drawing-room. He knew what was due to his guest. He loved to mortify, by his negligence, the pride of his equals and superiors; but a lower class had nothing to fear from his insolence. Constantia took the seat that was offered to her, without speaking. She had made suitable preparations for this interview, and her composure was invincible. The manners of her host were by no means calculated to disconcert her. His air was conciliating and attentive.

She began with naming Craig, as one known to Ormond, and desired to be informed of his place of abode. She was proceeding to apologize for this request, by explaining, in general terms, that her father's infirmities prevented him from acting for himself; that Craig was his debtor to a large amount; that he stood in need of all that justly belonged to him, and was in pursuit of some means for tracing Craig to his retreat. Ormond interrupted her, examining, at the same time, with a vigilance somewhat too unsparing, the effects which his words should produce upon her: –

"You may spare yourself the trouble of explaining. I am acquainted with the whole affair between Craig and your family. He has concealed from me nothing. I know *all* that has passed between you."

In saying this, Ormond intended that his looks and emphasis should convey his full meaning. In the style of her comments he saw none of those corroborating symptoms that he expected: –

"Indeed! He has been very liberal of his confidence, confession is a token of penitence; but, alas! I fear he has deceived you. To be sincere was doubtless his true interest, but he is too much in the habit of judging superficially. If he has told you all, there is, indeed, no need of explanation. This visit is, in that case, sufficiently accounted for. Is it in your power, sir, to inform us whither he has gone?"

"For what end should I tell you? I promise you you will not follow him. Take my word for it, he is totally unworthy of you. Let the past be no precedent for the future. If you have not made that discovery yourself, I have made it for you. I expect, at least, to be thanked for my trouble."

This speech was unintelligible to Constantia. Her looks betokened a perplexity unmingled with fear or shame.

"It is my way," continued he, "to say what I think. I care little for consequences. I have said that I know *all*. This will excuse me for being perfectly explicit. That I am mistaken is very possible; but I am inclined to place that matter beyond the reach of a doubt. Listen to me, and confirm me in the opinion I have already formed of your good sense, by viewing, in a just light, the unreservedness with which you are treated. I have something to tell, which, if you are wise, you will not be offended at my telling so roundly. On the contrary, you will thank me, and perceive that my conduct is a proof of my respect for you. The person whom you met here is named Craig, but, as he tells me, is not the man you look for. This man's brother – the partner of your father, and, as he assured me, your own accepted and illicitly-gratified lover – is dead."

These words were uttered without any extenuating hesitation or depression of tone. On the contrary, the most offensive terms were drawn out in the most deliberate and emphatic manner. Constantia's cheeks glowed and her eyes sparkled with indignation, but she forbore to interrupt. The looks with which she listened to the remainder of the speech showed that she fully comprehended the scene, and enabled him to comprehend it. He proceeded: –

"This man is a brother of that. Their resemblance in figure occasioned your mistake. Your father's debtor died, it seems, on his arrival at Jamaica. There he met with this brother, and bequeathed to him his property and papers. Some of these papers are in my possession. They are letters from Constantia Dudley, and are parts of an intrigue which, considering the character of the man, was not much to her honour. Such was this man's narrative, told to me some time before your meeting with him at this house. I have a right to judge in this affair; that is, I have a right to my opinion. If I mistake, (and I half suspect myself,) you are able, perhaps, to rectify my error; and, in a case like this, doubtless you will not want the inclination."

Perhaps if the countenance of this man had not been characterized by the keenest intelligence, and a sort of careless and overflowing good-will, this speech might have produced different effects. She was prepared, though imperfectly, for entering into his character. He waited for an answer, which she gave without emotion: –

"You are deceived. I am sorry, for your own sake, that you are. He must have had some end in view, in imposing these falsehoods upon you, which perhaps they have enabled him to accomplish. As to myself, this man can do me no injury. I willingly make you my judge. The letters you speak of will alone suffice to my vindication. They never were received from me, and are forgeries. That man always persisted till he made himself the dupe of his own artifices. That incident in his plot, on the introduction of which he probably the most applauded himself, will most powerfully operate to defeat it.

"Those letters never were received from me, and are forgeries. His skill in imitation extended no further in the present case than my handwriting. My modes of thinking and expression were beyond the reach of his mimicry."

When she had finished, Ormond spent a moment in ruminating. "I perceive you are right," said he. "I suppose he has purloined from me two hundred guineas, which I intrusted to his fidelity. And yet I received a letter; but that may likewise be a forgery. By my soul," continued he, in a tone that had more of satisfaction than disappointment in it, "this fellow was an adept at his trade. I do not repine. I have bought the exhibition at a cheap rate. The pains that he took did not merit a less recompense. I am glad that he was contented with so little. Had he persisted, he might have raised the price far above its value. 'Twill be lamentable if he receive more than he stipulated for, – if, in his last purchase, the gallows should be thrown into the bargain. May he have the wisdom to see that a halter, though not included in his terms, is only a new instance of his good fortune! but his cunning will hardly carry him thus far. His stupidity will, no doubt, prefer a lingering to a sudden exit.

"But this man and his destiny are trifles. Let us leave them to themselves. Your name is Constantia. 'Twas given you, I suppose, that you might be known by it. Pr'ythee, Constantia, was this the only purpose that brought you hither? If it were, it has received as ample a discussion as it merits. You *came* for this end, but will remain, I hope, for a better one. Having dismissed Craig and his plots, let us now talk of each other."

"I confess," said the lady, with a hesitation she could not subdue, "this was not my only purpose. One much more important has produced this visit."

"Indeed! pray, let me know it. I am glad that so trivial an object as Craig did not occupy the first place in your thoughts. Proceed, I beseech you."

"It is a subject on which I cannot enter without hesitation, – a hesitation unworthy of me."

"Stop," cried Ormond, rising and touching the bell; "nothing like time to make a conquest of embarrassment. We will defer this conference six minutes, just while we eat our dinner."

At the same moment a servant entered, with two plates and the usual apparatus for dinner. On seeing this she rose, in some hurry, to depart: – "I thought, sir, you were disengaged. I will call at some other hour."

He seized her hand, and held her from going, but with an air by no means disrespectful. "Nay," said he; "what is it that scares you away? Are you terrified at the mention of victuals? You must have fasted long when it comes to that. I told you true. I am disengaged, but not from the obligation of eating and drinking. No doubt *you* have dined. No reason why *I* should go without my dinner. If you do not choose to partake with me, so much the better. Your temperance ought to dispense with two meals in an hour. Be a looker-on; or, if that will not do, retire into my library, where in six minutes, I will be with you, and lend you my aid in the arduous task of telling me what you came with an intention of telling."

This singular address disconcerted and abashed her. She was contented to follow the servant silently into an adjoining apartment. Here she reflected with no small surprise on the behaviour of this man. Though ruffled, she was not heartily displeased with it. She had scarcely time to recollect herself, when he entered. He immediately seated her, and himself opposite to her. He fixed his eyes without scruple on her face. His gaze was steadfast, but not insolent or oppressive. He surveyed her with the looks with which he would have eyed a charming portrait. His attention was occupied with what he saw, as that of an artist is occupied when viewing a Madonna of Rafaello. At length he broke the silence: –

"At dinner I was busy thinking what it was you had to disclose. I will not fatigue you with my guesses. They would be impertinent, as long as the truth is going to be disclosed." He paused, and then continued: – "But I see you cannot dispense with my aid. Perhaps your business relates to Helena. She has done wrong, and you wish me to rebuke the girl."

Constantia profited by this opening, and said, "Yes; she has done wrong. It is true my business relates to her. I came hither as a suppliant in her behalf. Will you not assist her in recovering the path from which she has deviated? She left it from confiding more in the judgment of her guide than her own. There is one method of repairing the evil. It lies with you to repair that evil."

During this address the gayety of Ormond disappeared. He fixed his eyes on Constantia with new and even pathetic earnestness. "I guessed as much," said he. "I have often been deceived in my judgment of characters. Perhaps I do not comprehend yours. Yet it is not little that I have heard respecting you. Something I have seen. I begin to suspect a material error in my theory of human nature. Happy will it be for Helena if my suspicions be groundless.

"You are Helena's friend. Be mine also, and advise me. Shall I marry this girl, or not? You know on what terms we live. Are they suitable to our respective characters? Shall I wed this girl, or shall things remain as they are?

"I have an irreconcilable aversion to a sad brow and a sick-bed. Helena is grieved, because her neighbours sneer and point at her. So far she is a fool; but that is a folly of which she never will be cured. Marriage, it seems, will set all right. Answer me, Constantia: shall I marry?"

There was something in the tone, but more in the tenor, of this address that startled her. There was nothing in this man but what came upon her unaware. This sudden effusion of confidence was particularly unexpected and embarrassing. She scarcely knew whether to regard it as serious or a jest. On observing her indisposed to speak, he continued: –

"Away with these impertinent circuities and scruples! I know your meaning. Why should I pretend ignorance, and put you to the trouble of explanation? You came hither with no other view than to exact this question and furnish an answer. Why should not we come at once to the point? I have for some time been dubious on this head. There is something wanting to determine the balance. If you have that something, throw it into the proper scale.

"You err if you think this manner of addressing you is wild or improper. This girl is the subject of discourse. If she was not to be so, why did you favour me with this visit? You have sought me, and introduced yourself. I have, in like manner, overlooked ordinary forms, – a negligence that has been systematic with me, but, in the present case, particularly justifiable by your example. Shame on you, presumptuous girl, to suppose yourself the only rational being among mankind. And yet, if you thought so, why did you thus unceremoniously intrude upon my retirements? This act is of a piece with the rest. It shows you to be one whose existence I did not believe possible.

"Take care. You know not what you have done. You came hither as Helena's friend. Perhaps time may show that in this visit you have performed the behest of her bitterest enemy. But that is out of season. This girl is our mutual property. You are her friend; I am her lover. Her happiness is precious in my eyes and in yours. To the rest of mankind she is a noisome weed, that cannot be shunned too cautiously, nor trampled on too much. If we forsake her, infamy, that is now kept at bay, will seize upon her, and, while it mangles her form, will tear from her her innocence. She has no arms with which to contend against that foe. Marriage will place her at once in security. Shall it be? You have an exact knowledge of her strength and her weakness. Of me you know little. Perhaps, before that question can be satisfactorily answered, it is requisite to know the qualities of her husband. Be my character henceforth the subject of your study. I will furnish you with all the light in my power. Be not hasty in deciding; but when your decision is formed, let me know it." He waited for an answer, which she at length summoned resolution enough to give: –

"You have come to the chief point which I had in view in making this visit. To say truth, I came hither to remonstrate with you on withholding that which Helena may justly claim from you. Her happiness will be unquestionably restored and increased by it. Yours will not be impaired. Matrimony will not produce any essential change in your situation. It will produce no greater or different intercourse than now exists. Helena is on the brink of a gulf which I shudder to look upon. I believe that you will not injure yourself by snatching her from it. I am sure that you will confer an inexpressible benefit upon her. Let me, then, persuade you to do her and yourself justice."

"No persuasion," said Ormond, after recovering from a fit of thoughtfulness, "is needful for this end: I only want to be convinced. You have decided, but, I fear, hastily. By what inscrutable influences are our steps guided! Come; proceed in your exhortations. Argue with the utmost clearness and cogency. Arm yourself with all the irresistibles of eloquence. Yet you are building nothing. You are only demolishing. Your argument is one thing. Its tendency is another; and is the reverse of all you expect and desire. My assent will be refused with an obstinacy proportioned to the force that you exert to obtain it, and to the just application of that force."

"I see," replied the lady, smiling, and leaving her seat, "you can talk in riddles as well as other people. This visit has been too long. I shall indeed be sorry if my interference, instead of serving my friend, has injured her. I have acted an uncommon and, as it may seem, an ambiguous part. I shall be contented with construing my motives in my own way. I wish you a good evening."

"'Tis false!" cried he, sternly; "you do not wish it!"

"How?" exclaimed the astonished Constantia.

"I will put your sincerity to the test. Allow me to spend this evening in your company; then it will be well spent, and I shall believe your wishes sincere. Else," continued he, changing his affected austerity into a smile, "Constantia is a liar."

"You are a singular man. I hardly know how to understand you."

"Well, words are made to carry meanings. You shall have them in abundance. Your house is your citadel. I will not enter it without leave. Permit me to visit you when I please. But that is too much. It is more than I would allow you. When will you permit me to visit you?"

"I cannot answer when I do not understand. You clothe your thoughts in a garb so uncouth, that I know not in what light they are to be viewed."

"Well, now, I thought you understood my language, and were an Englishwoman; but I will use another. Shall I have the honour" (bowing with a courtly air of supplication) "of occasionally paying my respects to you at your own dwelling? It would be cruel to condemn those who have the happiness of knowing Miss Dudley, to fashionable restraints. At what hour will she be least incommoded by a visitant?"

"I am as little pleased with formalities," replied the lady, "as you are. My friends I cannot see too often. They need to consult merely their own convenience. Those who are not my friends I cannot see too seldom. You have only to establish your title to that name, and your welcome at all times is sure. Till then you must not look for it."

CHAPTER XVI.

HERE ended this conference. She had by no means suspected the manner in which it would be conducted. All punctilios were trampled under foot by the impetuosity of Ormond. Things were at once, and without delay, placed upon a certain footing. The point which ordinary persons would have employed months in attaining was reached in a moment. While these incidents were fresh in her memory, they were accompanied with a sort of trepidation, the offspring at once of pleasure and surprise.

Ormond had not deceived her expectations; but hearsay and personal examination, however uniform their testimony may be, produce a very different impression. In her present reflections, Helena and her lover approached to the front of the stage and were viewed with equal perspicuity. One consequence of this was, that their characters were more powerfully contrasted with each other, and the ineligibility of marriage appeared not quite so incontestable as before.

Was not equality implied in this compact? Marriage is an instrument of pleasure or pain in proportion as this equality is more or less. What but the fascination of his senses is it that ties Ormond to Helena? Is this a basis on which marriage may properly be built?

If things had not gone thus far, the impropriety of marriage could not be doubted; but, at present, there is a choice of evils, and that may now be desirable which at a former period, and in different circumstances, would have been clearly otherwise.

The evils of the present connection are known; those of marriage are future and contingent: Helena cannot be the object of a genuine and lasting passion; another may: this is not merely possible; nothing is more likely to happen. This event, therefore, ought to be included in our calculation. There would be a material deficiency without it. What was the amount of the misery that would, in this case, ensue?

Constantia was qualified, beyond most others, to form an adequate conception of this misery. One of the ingredients in her character was a mild and steadfast enthusiasm. Her sensibilities to social pleasure, and her conceptions of the benefits to flow from the conformity and concurrence of intentions and wishes heightening and refining the sensual passion, were exquisite.

There, indeed, were evils, the foresight of which tended to prevent them; but was there wisdom in creating obstacles in the way of a suitable alliance? Before we act, we must consider not only the misery produced, but the happiness precluded, by our measures.

In no case, perhaps, is the decision of a human being impartial, or totally uninfluenced by sinister and selfish motives. If Constantia surpassed others, it was not because her motives were pure, but because they possessed more of purity than those of others. Sinister considerations flow in upon us through imperceptible channels, and modify our thoughts in numberless ways, without our being truly conscious of their presence. Constantia was young, and her heart was open at a thousand pores to the love of excellence. The image of Ormond occupied the chief place in her fancy, and was endowed with attractive and venerable qualities. A bias was hence created that swayed her thoughts, though she knew not that they were swayed. To this might justly be imputed some part of that reluctance which she now felt to give Ormond to Helena. But this was not sufficient to turn the scale. That which had previously mounted was indeed heavier than before, but this addition did not enable it to outweigh its opposite. Marriage was still the best, upon the whole; but her heart was tortured to think that, best as it was, it abounded with so many evils.

On the evening of the next day, Ormond entered, with careless abruptness, Constantia's sitting-apartment. He was introduced to her father. A general and unrestrained conversation immediately took place. Ormond addressed Mr. Dudley with the familiarity of an old acquaintance. In three minutes all embarrassment was discarded. The lady and her visitant were accurate observers of each other. In the remarks of the latter (and his vein was an abundant one) there was a freedom and originality altogether new to his hearers. In his easiest and sprightliest sallies were tokens of a mind habituated to profound and extensive views. His associations were formed on a comprehensive scale.

He pretended to nothing, and studied the concealments of ambiguity more in reality than in appearance. Constantia, however, discovered a sufficient resemblance between their theories of virtue and duty. The difference between them lay in the inferences arbitrarily deduced, and in which two persons may vary without end and yet never be repugnant. Constantia delighted her companion by the facility with which she entered into his meaning, the sagacity she displayed in drawing out his hints, circumscribing his conjectures, and thwarting or qualifying his maxims. The scene was generally replete with ardour and contention, and yet the impression left on the mind of Ormond was full of harmony. Her discourse tended to rouse him from his lethargy, to furnish him with powerful excitements; and the time spent in her company seemed like a doubling of existence.

The comparison could not but suggest itself between this scene and that exhibited by Helena. With the latter, voluptuous blandishments, musical prattle, and silent but expressive homage, composed a banquet delicious for a while, but whose sweetness now began to pall upon his taste. It supplied him with no new ideas, and hindered him, by the lulling sensations it inspired, from profiting by his former acquisitions. Helena was beautiful. Apply the scale, and not a member was found inelegantly disposed or negligently moulded, not a curve that was blemished by an angle or ruffled by asperities. The irradiations of her eyes were able to dissolve the knottiest fibres, and their azure was serene beyond any that nature had elsewhere exhibited. Over the rest of her form the glistening and rosy hues were diffused with prodigal luxuriance and mingled in endless and wanton variety. Yet this image had fewer attractions even to the senses than that of Constantia. So great is the difference between forms animated by different degrees of intelligence.

The interviews of Ormond and Constantia grew more frequent. The progress which they made in the knowledge of each other was rapid. Two positions, that were favourite ones with him, were quickly subverted. He was suddenly changed, from being one of the calumniators of the female sex, to one of its warmest eulogists. This was a point on which Constantia had ever been a vigorous disputant; but her arguments, in their direct tendency, would never have made a convert of this man. Their force, intrinsically considered, was nothing. He drew his conclusions from incidental circumstances. Her reasonings might be fallacious or valid, but they were so composed, arranged, and delivered, were drawn from such sources, and accompanied with such illustrations, as plainly testified a manlike energy in the reasoner. In this indirect and circuitous way, her point was unanswerably established.

"Your reasoning is bad," he would say; "every one of your conclusions is false. Not a single allegation but may be easily confuted: and yet I allow that your position is incontrovertibly proved by them. How bewildered is that man who never thinks for himself! who rejects a principle merely because the arguments brought in support of it are insufficient! I must not reject the truth because another has unjustifiably adopted it. I want to reach a certain hill-top. Another has reached it before me, but the ladder he used is too weak to bear me. What then? Am I to stay below on that account? No; I have only to construct one suitable to the purpose, and of strength sufficient."

A second maxim had never been confuted till now. It inculcated the insignificance and hollowness of love. No pleasure, he thought, was to be despised for its own sake. Every thing was good in its place, but amorous gratifications were to be degraded to the bottom of the catalogue. The enjoyments of music and landscape were of a much higher order. Epicurism itself was entitled to more respect.[1] Love, in itself, was, in his opinion, of little worth, and only of importance as the source of the most terrible of intellectual maladies. Sexual sensations associating themselves, in a certain way, with our ideas, beget a disease which has, indeed, found no place in the catalogue, but is a case of more entire subversion and confusion of mind than any other. The victim is callous to the sentiments of honour and shame, insensible to the most palpable distinctions of right and wrong, a systematic opponent of testimony and obstinate perverter of truth.

Ormond was partly right. Madness like death can be averted by no foresight or previous contrivance. This probably is one of its characteristics. He that witnesses its influence on another with most

Ormond's opinion on sex

---

1   Epicurism: system of philosophy based on teachings of Greek philosopher Epicurus that pleasure is the best good and life's primary goal, and that intellectual pleasures are preferable to sensual pleasures.

horror, and most fervently deprecates its ravages, is not therefore more safe. This circumstance was realized in the history of Ormond.

This infatuation, if it may so be called, was gradual in its progress. The sensations which Helena was now able to excite were of a new kind. Her power was not merely weakened, but her endeavours counteracted their own end. Her fondness was rejected with disdain, or borne with reluctance. The lady was not slow in perceiving this change. The stroke of death would have been more acceptable. His own reflections were too tormenting to make him willing to discuss them in words. He was not aware of the effects produced by this change in his demeanor, till informed of it by herself.

One evening he displayed symptoms of uncommon dissatisfaction. Her tenderness was unable to dispel it. He complained of want of sleep. This afforded a hint, which she drew forth into one of her enchanting ditties. Habit had almost conferred upon her the power of spontaneous poesy, and, while she pressed his forehead to her bosom, she warbled forth a strain airy and exuberant in numbers, tender and ecstatic in its imagery: –

> Sleep, extend thy downy pinion;
> Hasten from my cell with speed;
>   Spread around thy soft dominion;
> Much those brows thy balmy presence need.
>
> Wave thy wand of slumberous power,
> Moistened in Lethean dews,
>   To charm the busy spirits of the hour,
> And brighten memory's malignant hues.
>
> Thy mantle, dark and starless, cast
> Over my selected youth;
>   Bury in thy womb the mournful past,
> And soften with thy dreams th' asperities of truth.
>
> The changeful hues of his impassion'd sleep
> My office it shall be to watch the while;
>   With thee, my love, when fancy prompts, to weep,
> And, when thou smil'st, to smile.

But, sleep! I charge thee, visit not these eyes,
   Nor raise thy dark pavilion here,
      Till morrow from the cave of ocean rise,
   And whisper tuneful joy in nature's ear.

      But mutely let me lie, and sateless gaze
   At all the soul that in his visage sits,
      While spirits of harmonious air —

Here her voice sunk, and the line terminated in a sigh. Her muse-ful ardours were chilled by the looks of Ormond. Absorbed in his own thoughts, he appeared scarcely to attend to this strain. His stern-ness was proof against her accustomed fascinations. At length she pathetically complained of his coldness, and insinuated her suspicions that his affection was transferred to another object. He started from her embrace, and, after two or three turns across the room, he stood before her. His large eyes were steadfastly fixed upon her face.

"Ay," said he; "thou hast guessed right. The love, poor as it was, that I had for thee, is gone. Henceforth thou art desolate indeed. Would to God thou wert wise! Thy woes are but beginning; I fear they will ter-minate fatally: if so, the catastrophe cannot come too quickly.

"I disdain to appeal to thy justice, Helena, to remind thee of con-ditions solemnly and explicitly assumed. Shall thy blood be upon thy own head? No. I will bear it myself. Though the load would crush a mountain, I will bear it.

"I cannot help it; I make not myself; I am moulded by circum-stances; whether I shall love thee or not is no longer in my own choice. Marriage is, indeed, still in my power. I may give thee my name and share with thee my fortune. Will these content thee? Thou canst not partake of my love. Thou canst have no part in my tender-ness. These are reserved for another more worthy than thou.

"But no. Thy state is, to the last degree, forlorn. Even marriage is denied thee. Thou wast contented to take me without it, – to dispense with the name of wife; but the being who has displaced thy image in my heart is of a different class. She will be to me a wife, or nothing; and I must be her husband, or perish.

"Do not deceive thyself, Helena. I know what it is in which thou hast placed thy felicity. Life is worth retaining by thee but on one condition. I know the incurableness of thy infirmity; but be not deceived. Thy happiness is ravished from thee. The condition on which thou consentedst to live is annulled. I love thee no longer.

"No truth was every more delicious; none was ever more detestable. I fight against conviction, and I cling to it. That I love thee no longer is at once a subject of joy and of mourning. I struggle to believe thee superior to this shock; that thou wilt be happy, though deserted by me. Whatever be thy destiny, my reason will not allow me to be miserable on that account. Yet I would give the world – I would forfeit every claim but that which I hope upon the heart of Constantia – to be sure that thy tranquillity will survive this stroke.

"But, let come what will, look no longer to me for offices of love. Henceforth, all intercourse of tenderness ceases, – perhaps all personal intercourse whatever. But, though this good be refused, thou art sure of independence. I will guard thy ease and thy honour with a father's scrupulousness. Would to Heaven a sister could be created by adoption! I am willing, for thy sake, to be an impostor. I will own thee to the world for my sister, and carry thee whither the cheat shall never be detected. I would devote my whole life to prevarication and falsehood for thy sake, if that would suffice to make thee happy."

To this speech Helena had nothing to answer. Her sobs and tears choked all utterance. She hid her face with her handkerchief, and sat powerless and overwhelmed with despair. Ormond traversed the room uneasily, sometimes moving to and fro with quick steps, sometimes standing and eyeing her with looks of compassion. At length he spoke: –

"It is time to leave you. This is the first night that you will spend in dreary solitude. I know it will be sleepless and full of agony; but the sentence cannot be recalled. Henceforth regard me as a brother. I will prove myself one. All other claims are swallowed up in a superior affection." In saying this, he left the house, and, almost without intending it, found himself in a few minutes at Mr. Dudley's door.

CHAPTER XVII.

THE POLITENESS of Melbourne had somewhat abated Mr. Dudley's aversion to society. He allowed himself sometimes to comply with urgent invitations. On this evening he happened to be at the house of that gentleman. Ormond entered, and found Constantia alone. An interview of this kind was seldom enjoyed, though earnestly wished for, by Constantia, who was eager to renew the subject of her first conversation with Ormond. I have already explained the situation of her mind. All her wishes were concentred in the marriage of Helena. The eligibility of this scheme, in every view which she took of it, appeared in a stronger light. She was not aware that any new obstacle had arisen. She was free from the consciousness of any secret bias. Much less did her modesty suspect that she herself would prove an unsuperable impediment to this plan.

There was more than usual solemnity in Ormond's demeanour. After he was seated, he continued, contrary to his custom, to be silent. These singularities were not unobserved by Constantia. They did not, however, divert her from her purpose.

"I am glad to see you," said she; "we so seldom enjoy the advantage of a private interview. I have much to say to you. You authorize me to deliberate on your actions, and, in some measure, to prescribe to you. This is a province which I hope to discharge with integrity and diligence. I am convinced that Helena's happiness and your own can be secured in one way only. I will emulate your candour, and come at once to the point. Why have you delayed so long the justice that is due to this helpless and lovely girl? There are a thousand reasons why you should think of no other alternative. You have been pleased to repose some degree of confidence in my judgment. Hear my full and deliberate opinion. Make Helena your wife. This is the unequivocal prescription of your duty."

This address was heard by Ormond without surprise; but his countenance betrayed the acuteness of his feelings. The bitterness that overflowed his heart was perceptible in his tone when he spoke: –

"Most egregiously are you deceived. Such is the line with which human capacity presumes to fathom futurity. With all your discernment, you do not see that marriage would effectually destroy me. You do not see that, whether beneficial or otherwise in its effects, marriage is impossible. You are merely prompting me to suicide: but how shall I inflict the wound? Where is the weapon? See you not that I am powerless? Leap, say you, into the flames. See you not that I am fettered? Will a mountain move at your bidding, sooner than I in the path which you prescribe to me?"

This speech was inexplicable. She pressed him to speak less enigmatically. Had he formed his resolution? If so, arguments and remonstrances were superfluous. Without noticing her interrogatories, he continued: –

"I am too hasty in condemning you. You judge, not against, but without, knowledge. When sufficiently informed, your decision will be right. Yet how can you be ignorant? Can you for a moment contemplate yourself and me, and not perceive an insuperable bar to this union?"

"You place me," said Constantia, "in a very disagreeable predicament. I have not deserved this treatment from you. This is an unjustifiable deviation from plain dealing. Of what impediment do you speak? I can safely say that I know of none."

"Well," resumed he, with augmented eagerness, "I must supply you with knowledge. I repeat, that I perfectly rely on the rectitude of your judgment. Summon all your sagacity and disinterestedness, and choose for me. You know in what light Helena has been viewed by me. I have ceased to view her in this light. She has become an object of indifference. Nay, I am not certain that I do not hate her, – not, indeed, for her own sake, but because I love another. Shall I marry her whom I hate, when there exists one whom I love with unconquerable ardour?"

Constantia was thunderstruck with this intelligence. She looked at him with some expression of doubt. "How is this?" said she. "Why did you not tell me this before?"

"When I last talked with you on this subject, I knew it not myself. It has occurred since. I have seized the first occasion that has offered to inform you of it. Say now, since such is my condition, ought Helena to be my wife?"

Constantia was silent. Her heart bled for what she foresaw would be the sufferings and forlorn destiny of Helena. She had not courage to inquire further into this new engagement.

"I wait for your answer, Constantia. Shall I defraud myself of all the happiness which would accrue from a match of inclination? Shall I put fetters on my usefulness? This is the style in which you speak. Shall I preclude all the good to others that would flow from a suitable alliance? Shall I abjure the woman I love, and marry her whom I hate?"

"Hatred," replied the lady, "is a harsh word. Helena has not deserved that you should hate her. I own this is a perplexing circumstance. It would be wrong to determine hastily. Suppose you give yourself to Helena: will more than yourself be injured by it? Who is this lady? Will she be rendered unhappy by a determination in favour of another? This is a point of the utmost importance."

At these words, Ormond forsook his seat and advanced close up to Constantia: – "You say true. This is a point of inexpressible importance. It would be presumption in me to decide. That is the lady's own province. And now, say truly, are you willing to accept Ormond with all his faults? Who but yourself could be mistress of all the springs of my soul? I know the sternness of your probity. This discovery will only make you more strenuously the friend of Helena. Yet why should you not shun either extreme? Lay yourself out of view. And yet, perhaps, the happiness of Constantia is not unconcerned in this question. Is there no part of me in which you discover your own likeness? Am I deceived, or is it an incontrollable destiny that unites us?"

This declaration was truly unexpected by Constantia. She gathered from it nothing but excitements of grief. After some pause, she said, "This appeal to me has made no change in my opinion. I still think that justice requires you to become the husband of Helena. As to me, do you think my happiness rests upon so slight a foundation? I cannot love but when my understanding points out to me the propriety of love. Ever since I have known you, I have looked upon you as rightfully belonging to another. Love could not take place in my circumstances. Yet I will not conceal from you my sentiments. I am not sure that, in different circumstances, I should not have loved. I am acquainted with your worth. I do not look for a faultless man. I have met with none whose blemishes were fewer.

"It matters not, however, what I should have been. I cannot interfere, in this case, with the claims of my friend. I have no passion to struggle with. I hope, in every vicissitude, to enjoy your esteem, and nothing more. There is but one way in which mine can be secured, and that is by espousing this unhappy girl."

"No!" exclaimed Ormond. "Require not impossibilities. Helena can never be any thing to me. I should, with unspeakably more willingness, assail my own life."

"What," said the lady, "will Helena think of this sudden and dreadful change? I cannot bear to think upon the feelings that this information will excite."

"She knows it already. I have this moment left her. I explained to her, in few words, my motives, and assured her of my unalterable resolution. I have vowed never to see her more but as a brother; and this vow she has just heard."

Constantia could not suppress her astonishment and compassion at this intelligence: – "No, surely; you could not be so cruel! And this was done with your usual abruptness, I suppose. Precipitate and implacable man! Cannot you foresee the effects of this madness? You have planted a dagger in her heart. You have disappointed me. I did not think you could act so inhumanly."

"Nay, beloved Constantia, be not so liberal of your reproaches. Would you have me deceive her? She must shortly have known it. Could the truth be told too soon?"

"Much too soon," replied the lady, fervently. "I have always condemned the maxims by which you act. Your scheme is headlong and barbarous. Could you not regard with some little compassion that love which sacrificed, for your unworthy sake, honest fame and the peace of virtue? Is she not a poor outcast, goaded by compunction, and hooted at by a malignant and misjudging world? And who was it that reduced her to this deplorable condition? For whose sake did she willingly consent to brave evils by which the stoutest heart is appalled? Did this argue no greatness of mind? Who ever surpassed her in fidelity and tenderness? But thus has she been rewarded. I shudder to think what may be the event. Her courage cannot possibly support her against treatment so harsh, so perversely and wantonly cruel. Heaven grant that you are not shortly made bitterly to lament this rashness!"

Ormond was penetrated with these reproaches. They persuaded him for a moment that his deed was wrong; that he had not unfolded his intentions to Helena with a suitable degree of gentleness and caution. Little more was said on this occasion. Constantia exhorted him, in the most earnest and pathetic manner, to return and recant, or extenuate, his former declarations. He could not be brought to promise compliance. When he parted from her, however, he was half resolved to act as she advised. Solitary reflection made him change this resolution, and he returned to his own house.

During the night he did little else than ruminate on the events of the preceding evening. He entertained little doubt of his ultimate success with Constantia. She gratified him in nothing, but left him every thing to hope. She had hitherto, it seems, regarded him with indifference; but this had been sufficiently explained. That conduct would be pursued, and that passion be entertained, which her judgment should previously approve. What then was the obstacle? It originated in the claims of Helena. But what were these claims? It was fully ascertained that he should never be united to this girl. If so, the end contemplated by Constantia, and for the sake of which only his application was rejected, could never be obtained. Unless her rejection of him could procure a husband for her friend, it would, on her own principles, be improper and superfluous.

What was to be done with Helena? It was a terrible alternative to which he was reduced: – to marry her or see her perish. But was this alternative quite sure? Could not she, by time or by judicious treatment, be reconciled to her lot? It was to be feared that he had not made a suitable beginning; and yet, perhaps, it was most expedient that a hasty and abrupt sentence should be succeeded by forbearance and lenity. He regretted his precipitation; and, though used to the melting mood, tears were wrung from him by the idea of the misery which he had probably occasioned. He was determined to repair his misconduct as speedily as possible, and to pay her a conciliating visit the next morning.

He went early to her house. He was informed by the servant that her mistress had not yet risen. "Was it usual," he asked, "for her to lie so late?" "No," he was answered: "she never knew it happen before, but she supposed her mistress was not well. She was just going into her chamber to see what was the matter."

"Why," said Ormond, "do you suppose that she is sick?"

"She was poorly last night. About nine o'clock she sent out for some physic to make her sleep."

"To make her sleep?" exclaimed Ormond, in a faltering and affrighted accent.

"Yes: she said she wanted it for that. So I went to the 'pothecary's. When I come back, she was very poorly indeed. I asked her if I mightn't set up with her. 'No,' she says; 'I do not want anybody. You may go to bed as soon as you please, and tell Fabian to do the same. I shall not want you again.'"

"What did you buy?"

"Some kind of water, – laud'num I think they call it. She wrote it down, and I carried the paper to Mr. Eckhart's; and he gave it to me in a bottle, and I gave it to my mistress."

"'Tis well. Retire. I will see how she is myself."

Ormond had conceived himself fortified against every disaster. He looked for nothing but evil, and therefore, in ordinary cases, regarded its approach without fear or surprise. Now, however, he found that his tremors would not be stilled. His perturbations increased with every step that brought him nearer to her chamber. He knocked, but no answer was returned. He opened, advanced to the bedside, and drew back the curtains. He shrunk from the spectacle that presented itself. Was this the Helena that, a few hours before, was blithesome with health and radiant with beauty? Her visage was serene, but sunken and pale. Death was in every line of it. To his tremulous and hurried scrutiny every limb was rigid and cold.

The habits of Ormond tended to obscure the appearances, if not to deaden the emotions, of sorrow. He was so much accustomed to the frustration of well-intended efforts, and confided so much in his own integrity, that he was not easily disconcerted. He had merely to advert, on this occasion, to the tumultuous state of his feelings, in order to banish their confusion and restore himself to calm. "Well," said he, as he dropped the curtain and turned towards another part of the room, "this, without doubt, is a rueful spectacle. Can it be helped? Is there in man the power of recalling her? There is none such in me.

"She is gone. Well, then, she *is* gone. If she were fool enough to die, I am not fool enough to follow her. I am determined to live and be happy notwithstanding. Why not?

"Yet this is a piteous sight. What is impossible to undo might be easily prevented. A piteous spectacle! But what else, on an ampler scale, is the universe? Nature is a theatre of suffering. What corner is unvisited by calamity and pain? I have chosen as became me. I would rather precede thee to the grave than live to be thy husband.

"Thou hast done my work for me. Thou hast saved thyself and me from a thousand evils. Thou hast acted as seemed to thee best, and I am satisfied.

"Hast thou decided erroneously? They that know thee need not marvel at that. Endless have been the proofs of thy frailty. In favour of this last act something may be said. It is the last thou wilt ever commit. Others only will experience its effects; thou hast, at least, provided for thy own safety.

"But what is here? A letter for me? Had thy understanding been as prompt as thy fingers, I could have borne with thee. I can easily divine the contents of this epistle."

He opened it, and found the tenor to be as follows: —

"You did not use, my dear friend, to part with me in this manner. You never before treated me so roughly. I am sorry, indeed I am, that I ever offended you. Could you suppose that I intended it? And if you knew that I meant not offence, why did you take offence?

"I am very unhappy, for I have lost you, my friend. You will never see me more, you say. That is very hard. I have deserved it, to-be-sure, but I do not know how it has happened. Nobody more desired to please than I have done. Morning, noon, and night, it was my only study: but you will love me no more; you will see me no more. Forgive me, my friend, but I must say, it is very hard.

"You said rightly; I do not wish to live without my friend. I have spent my life happily heretofore. 'Tis true, there have been transient uneasinesses, but your love was a reward and a cure for every thing. I desired nothing better in this world. Did you ever hear me murmur? No; I was not so unjust. My lot was happy, infinitely beyond my deserving. I merited not to be loved by you. Oh that I had suitable words to express my gratitude for your kindness! but this last meeting, — how different from that which went before? Yet even then there was something on your brow like discontent, which I could not warble nor whisper away as I used to do. But, sad as this was, it was nothing like the last.

"Could Ormond be so stern and so terrible? You knew that I would die, but you need not have talked as if I were in the way, and as if you had rather I should die than live. But one thing I rejoice at; I am a poor silly girl, but Constantia is a noble and accomplished one. Most joyfully do I resign you to her, my dear friend. You say you love her. She need not be afraid of accepting you. There will be no danger of your preferring another to her. It was very natural and very right for you to prefer her to me. She and you will be happy in each other. It is this that sweetens the cup I am going to drink. Never did I go to sleep with more good-will than I now go to death. Fare you well, my dear friend."

This letter was calculated to make a deeper impression on Ormond than even the sight of Helena's corpse. It was in vain, for some time, that he endeavoured to reconcile himself to this event. It was seldom that he was able to forget it. He was obliged to exert all his energies to enable him to support the remembrance. The task was, of course, rendered easier by time.

It was immediately requisite to attend to the disposal of the corpse. He felt himself unfit for this mournful office. He was willing to relieve himself from it by any expedient. Helena's next neighbour was an old lady, whose scruples made her shun all direct intercourse with this unhappy girl; yet she had performed many acts of neighbourly kindness. She readily obeyed the summons of Ormond, on this occasion, to take charge of affairs, till another should assume it. Ormond returned home, and sent the following note to Constantia: –

"You have predicted aright. Helena is dead. In a mind like yours every grief will be suspended, and every regard absorbed in the attention due to the remains of this unfortunate girl. *I* cannot attend to them."

Constantia was extremely shocked by this intelligence, but she was not unmindful of her duty. She prepared herself, with mournful alacrity, for the performance of it. Every thing that the occasion demanded was done with diligence and care. Till this was accomplished, Ormond could not prevail upon himself to appear upon the stage. He was informed of this by a note from Constantia, who requested him to take possession of the unoccupied dwelling and its furniture.

Among the terms of his contract with Helena, Ormond had voluntarily inserted the exclusive property of a house and its furniture in this city, with funds adequate to her plentiful maintenance. These he had purchased and transferred to her. To this he had afterwards added a rural retreat, in the midst of spacious and well-cultivated fields, three miles from Perth-Amboy, and seated on the right bank of the Sound. It is proper to mention that this farm was formerly the property of Mr. Dudley, – had been fitted up by him and used as his summer-abode during his prosperity. In the division of his property it had fallen to one of his creditors, from whom it had been purchased by Ormond. This circumstance, in conjunction with the love which she bore to Constantia, had suggested to Helena a scheme, which her want of foresight would, in different circumstances, have occasioned her to overlook. It was that of making her testament, by which she bequeathed all that she possessed to her friend. This was not done without the knowledge and cheerful concurrence of Ormond, who, together with Melbourne and another respectable citizen, were named executors. Melbourne and his friend were induced, by their respect for Constantia, to consent to this nomination.

This had taken place before Ormond and Constantia had been introduced to each other. After this event, Ormond had sometimes been employed in contriving means for securing to his new friend and her father a subsistence more certain than the will of Helena could afford. Her death he considered as an event equally remote and undesirable. This event, however unexpectedly, had now happened, and precluded the necessity of further consideration on this head.

Constantia could not but accept this bequest. Had it been her wish to decline, it was not in her power; but she justly regarded the leisure and independence thus conferred upon her as inestimable benefits. It was a source of unbounded satisfaction on her father's account, who was once more seated in the bosom of affluence. Perhaps, in a rational estimate, one of the most fortunate events that could have befallen those persons was that period of adversity through which they had been doomed to pass. Most of the defects that adhered to the character of Mr. Dudley had, by this means, been exterminated. He was now cured of those prejudices which his early prosperity had instilled, and which had flowed from luxurious indulgences. He had learned to estimate himself at his true value, and to sympathize with sufferings which he himself had partaken.

It was easy to perceive in what light Constantia was regarded by her father. He never reflected on his relation to her without rapture. Her qualities were the objects of his adoration. He resigned himself with pleasure to her guidance. The chain of subordination and duties was reversed. By the ascendency of her genius and wisdom, the province of protection and the tribute of homage had devolved upon her. This had resulted from incessant experience of the wisdom of her measures, and the spectacle of her fortitude and skill in every emergency.

It seemed as if but one evil adhered to the condition of this man. His blindness was an impediment to knowledge and enjoyment, of which the utmost to be hoped was, that he should regard it without pungent regret, and that he should sometimes forget it; that his mind should occasionally stray into foreign paths, and lose itself in sprightly conversations or benign reveries. This evil, however, was by no means remediless.

A surgeon of uncommon skill had lately arrived from Europe. He was one of the numerous agents and dependants of Ormond, and had been engaged to abdicate his native country for purposes widely remote from his profession. The first use that was made of him was to introduce him to Mr. Dudley. The diseased organs were critically examined, and the patient was, with considerable difficulty, prevailed upon to undergo the necessary operation. His success corresponded with Constantia's wishes, and her father was once more restored to the enjoyment of light.

These were auspicious events. Constantia held herself amply repaid by them for all that she had suffered. These sufferings had indeed been light, when compared with the effects usually experienced by others in a similar condition. Her wisdom had extracted its sting from adversity, and, without allowing herself to feel much of the evils of its reign, had employed it as an instrument by which the sum of her present happiness was increased. Few suffered less, in the midst of poverty, than she. No one ever extracted more felicity from the prosperous reverse.

CHAPTER XVIII.

WHEN time had somewhat mitigated the memory of the late disaster, the intercourse between Ormond and Constantia was renewed. The lady did not overlook her obligations to her friend. It was to him that she was indebted for her father's restoration to sight, and to whom both owed, essentially, though indirectly, their present affluence. In her mind, gratitude was no perverse or ignoble principle. She viewed this man as the author of extensive benefits, of which her situation enabled her to judge more accurately than others. It created no bias on her judgment, or, at least, none of which she was sensible. Her equity was perfectly unfettered; and she decided in a way contrary to his inclination, with as little scruple as if the benefits had been received not by herself, but by him. She indeed intended his benefit, though she thwarted his inclinations.

She had few visitants beside himself. Their interviews were daily and unformal. The fate of Helena never produced any reproaches on her part. She saw the uselessness of recrimination, not only because she desired to produce emotions different from those which invective is adapted to excite, but because it was more just to soothe than to exasperate the inquietudes which haunted him.

She now enjoyed leisure. She had always been solicitous for mental improvement. Any means subservient to this end were valuable. The conversation of Ormond was an inexhaustible fund. By the variety of topics and the excitements to reflection it supplied, a more plenteous influx of knowledge was produced than could have flowed from any other source. There was no end to the detailing of facts and the canvassing of theories.

I have already said that Ormond was engaged in schemes of an arduous and elevated nature. These were the topics of epistolary discussion between him and a certain number of coadjutors in different parts of the world. In general discourse, it was proper to maintain a uniform silence respecting these, not only because they involved principles and views remote from vulgar apprehension, but because their success, in some measure, depended on their secrecy. He could not give a stronger proof of his confidence in the sagacity and steadiness of Constantia than he now gave, by imparting to her his schemes and requesting her advice and assistance in the progress of them.

His disclosures, however, were imperfect. What knowledge was imparted, instead of appeasing, only tended to inflame, her curiosity. His answers to her inquiries were prompt, and, at first sight, sufficiently explicit; but, upon reconsideration, an obscurity seemed to gather round them, to be dispelled by new interrogatories. These, in like manner, effected a momentary purpose, but were sure speedily to lead into new conjectures and reimmerse her in doubts. The task was always new, was always in the point of being finished, and always to be recommenced.

Ormond aspired to nothing more ardently than to hold the reins of opinion, – to exercise absolute power over the conduct of others, not by constraining their limbs or by exacting obedience to his authority, but in a way of which his subjects should be scarcely conscious. He desired that his guidance should control their steps, but that his agency, when most effectual, should be least suspected.

If he were solicitous to govern the thoughts of Constantia, or to regulate her condition, the mode which he pursued had hitherto been admirably conducive to that end. To have found her friendless and indigent accorded, with the most fortunate exactness, with his views. That she should have descended to this depth, from a prosperous height, and therefore be a stranger to the torpor which attends hereditary poverty, and be qualified rightly to estimate and use the competence to which, by his means, she was now restored, was all that his providence would have prescribed.

Her thoughts were equally obsequious to his direction. The novelty and grandeur of his schemes could not fail to transport a mind ardent and capacious as that of Constantia. Here his fortune had been no less propitious. He did not fail to discover, and was not slow to seize, the advantages flowing thence. By explaining his plans, opportunity was furnished to lead and to confine her meditations to the desirable track. By adding fictitious embellishments, he adapted it with more exactness to his purpose. By piecemeal and imperfect disclosures her curiosity was kept alive.

I have described Ormond as having contracted a passion for Constantia. This passion certainly existed in his heart, but it must not be conceived to be immutable, or to operate independently of all those impulses and habits which time had interwoven in his character. The person and affections of this woman were the objects sought by him, and which it was the dearest purpose of his existence to gain. This was his supreme good, though the motives to which it was indebted for its pre-eminence in his imagination were numerous and complex.

I have enumerated his opinions on the subject of wedlock. The question will obviously occur, whether Constantia was sought by him with upright or flagitious views. His sentiments and resolutions, on this head, had for a time fluctuated, but were now steadfast. Marriage was, in his eyes, hateful and absurd as ever. Constantia was to be obtained by any means. If other terms were rejected, he was willing, for the sake of this good, to accept her as a wife; but this was a choice to be made only when every expedient was exhausted for reconciling her to a compact of a different kind.

For this end, he prescribed to himself a path suited to the character of this lady. He made no secret of his sentiments and views. He avowed his love, and described, without scruple, the scope of his wishes. He challenged her to confute his principles, and promised a candid audience and profound consideration to her arguments. Her present opinions he knew to be adverse to his own, but he hoped to change them by subtlety and perseverance. His further hopes and designs he concealed from her. She was unaware that, if he were unable to effect a change in her creed, he was determined to adopt a system of imposture, – to assume the guise of a convert to her doctrines, and appear as devout as herself in his notions of the sanctity of marriage.

Perhaps it was not difficult to have foreseen the consequence of these projects. Constantia's peril was imminent. This arose not only from the talents and address of Ormond, but from the community of sentiment which already existed between them. She was unguarded in a point where, if not her whole yet doubtless her principal security and strongest bulwark would have existed. She was unacquainted with religion. She was unhabituated to conform herself to any standard but that connected with the present life. Matrimonial as well as every other human duty was disconnected in her mind with any awful or divine sanction. She formed her estimate of good and evil on nothing but terrestrial and visible consequences.

This defect in her character she owed to her father's system of education. Mr. Dudley was an adherent to what he conceived to be true religion. No man was more passionate in his eulogy of his own form of devotion and belief, or in his invectives against atheistical dogmas; but he reflected that religion assumed many forms, one only of which is salutary or true, and that truth in this respect is incompatible with infantile and premature instruction.

To this subject it was requisite to apply the force of a mature and unfettered understanding. For this end he laboured to lead away the juvenile reflections of Constantia from religious topics, to detain them in the paths of history and eloquence, – to accustom her to the accuracy of geometrical deduction, and to the view of those evils that have flowed, in all ages, from mistaken piety.

In consequence of this scheme, her habits rather than her opinions were undevout. Religion was regarded by her, not with disbelief, but with absolute indifference. Her good sense forbade her to decide before inquiry, but her modes of study and reflection were foreign to, and unfitted her for, this species of discussion. Her mind was seldom called to meditate on this subject, and, when it occurred, her perceptions were vague and obscure. No objects in the sphere which she occupied were calculated to suggest to her the importance of investigation and certainty.

It becomes me to confess, however reluctantly, thus much concerning my friend. However abundantly endowed in other respects, she was a stranger to the felicity and excellence flowing from religion. In her struggles with misfortune, she was supported and cheered by the sense of no approbation but her own. A defect of this nature will perhaps be regarded as of less moment, when her extreme youth is remembered. All opinions in her mind were mutable, inasmuch as the progress of her understanding was incessant.

It was otherwise with Ormond. His disbelief was at once unchangeable and strenuous. The universe was to him a series of events connected by an undesigning and inscrutable necessity, and an assemblage of forms to which no beginning or end can be conceived. Instead of transient views and vague ideas, his meditations, on religious points, had been intense. Enthusiasm was added to disbelief, and he not only dissented but abhorred.

He deemed it prudent, however, to disguise sentiments which, if unfolded in their full force, would wear to her the appearance of insanity. But he saw and was eager to improve the advantage which his anti-nuptial creed derived from the unsettled state of her opinions. He was not unaware, likewise, of the auspicious and indispensable co-operation of love. If this advocate were wanting in her bosom, all his efforts would be in vain. If this pleader were engaged in his behalf, he entertained no doubts of his ultimate success. He conceived that her present situation, all whose comforts were the fruits of his beneficence, and which afforded her no other subject of contemplation than himself, was as favourable as possible to the growth of this passion.

Constantia was acquainted with his wishes. She could not fail to see that she might speedily be called upon to determine a momentous question. Her own sensations and the character of Ormond were, therefore, scrutinized with suspicious attention. Marriage could be justified in her eyes only by community of affections and opinions. She might love without the sanction of her judgment; but while destitute of that sanction, she would never suffer it to sway her conduct.

Ormond was imperfectly known. What knowledge she had gained

flowed chiefly from his own lips, and was therefore unattended with certainty. What portion of deceit or disguise was mixed with his conversation could be known only by witnessing his actions with her own eyes and comparing his testimony with that of others. He had embraced a multitude of opinions which appeared to her erroneous. Till these were rectified, and their conclusions were made to correspond, wedlock was improper. Some of these obscurities might be dispelled, and some of these discords be resolved into harmony, by time. Meanwhile, it was proper to guard the avenues to her heart and screen herself from self-delusion.

There was no motive to conceal her reflections on this topic from her father. Mr. Dudley discovered, without her assistance, the views of Ormond. His daughter's happiness was blended with his own. He lived but in the consciousness of her tranquillity. Her image was seldom absent from his eyes, and never from his thoughts. The emotions which it excited sprung but in part from the relationship of father. It was gratitude and veneration which she claimed from him, and which filled him with rapture.

He ruminated deeply on the character of Ormond. The political and anti-theological tenets of this man were regarded not merely with disapprobation, but antipathy. He was not ungrateful for the benefits which had been conferred upon him. Ormond's peculiarities of sentiment excited no impatience, as long as he was regarded merely as a visitant. It was only as one claiming to possess his daughter that his presence excited, in Mr. Dudley, trepidation and loathing.

Ormond was unacquainted with what was passing in the mind of Mr. Dudley. The latter conceived his own benefactor and his daughter's friend to be entitled to the most scrupulous and affable urbanity. His objections to a nearer alliance were urged with frequent and pathetic vehemence, only in his private interviews with Constantia. Ormond and he seldom met; Mr. Dudley, as soon as his sight was perfectly retrieved, betook himself with eagerness to painting, – an amusement which his late privations had only contributed to endear to him.

Things remained nearly on their present footing for some months. At the end of this period, some engagement obliged Ormond to leave the city. He promised to return with as much speed as circumstances would admit. Meanwhile, his letters supplied her with topics of reflection. These were frequently received, and were models of that energy of style which results from simplicity of structure, from picturesque epithets, and from the compression of much meaning into few words. His arguments seldom imparted conviction, but delight never failed to flow from their lucid order and cogent brevity. His narratives were unequalled for rapidity and comprehensiveness. Every sentence was a treasury to moralists and painters.

CHAPTER XIX.

DOMESTIC and studious occupations did not wholly engross the attention of Constantia. Social pleasures were precious to her heart, and she was not backward to form fellowships and friendships with those around her. Hitherto she had met with no one entitled to an uncommon portion of regard, or worthy to supply the place of the friend of her infancy. Her visits were rare, and, as yet, chiefly confined to the family of Mr. Melbourne. Here she was treated with flattering distinctions, and enjoyed opportunities of extending, as far as she pleased, her connections with the gay and opulent. To this she felt herself by no means inclined, and her life was still eminently distinguished by love of privacy and habits of seclusion.

One morning, feeling an indisposition to abstraction, she determined to drop in, for an hour, on Mrs. Melbourne. Finding Mrs. Melbourne's parlor unoccupied, she proceeded unceremoniously to an apartment on the second floor, where that lady was accustomed to sit. She entered, but this room was likewise empty. Here she cast her eyes on a collection of prints, copied from the Farnese collection, and employed herself, for some minutes, in comparing the forms of Titiano and the Caracchi.[1]

Suddenly, notes of peculiar sweetness were wafted to her ear from without. She listened with surprise, for the tones of her father's lute

---

1 Farnese, Titiano, the Caracchi: Allessandro Farnese, or Pope Paul III (1468-1549), was a patron of the arts. Tiziano Vecellio (1477-1576), also known as Titian, was a Venetian painter who deployed vibrant colours, dynamic scenes and golden light. The Carracci were a family of sixteenth-century Bolognese artists — brothers Annibale and Agostino, and cousin Ludovico — known for the Mannerist artificiality of their painting.

were distinctly recognised. She hied to the window, which chanced to look into a back-court. The music was perceived to come from the window of the next house. She recollected her interview with the purchaser of her instrument at the music-shop, and the powerful impression which the stranger's countenance had made upon her.

The first use she had made of her recent change of fortune was to endeavour the recovery of this instrument. The music-dealer, when reminded of the purchase, and interrogated as to the practicability of regaining the lute, for which she was willing to give treble the price, answered that he had no knowledge of the foreign lady beyond what was gained at the interview which took place in Constantia's presence. Of her name, residence, and condition, he knew nothing, and had endeavoured in vain to acquire knowledge.

Now, this incident seemed to have furnished her with the information she so earnestly sought. This performer was probably the stranger herself. Her residence, so near the Melbournes and in a house which was the property of the magistrate, might be means of information as to her condition, and perhaps of introduction to a personal acquaintance.

While engaged in these reflections, Mrs. Melbourne entered the apartment. Constantia related this incident to her friend, and stated the motives of her present curiosity. Her friend willingly imparted what knowledge she possessed relative to this subject. This was the sum.

This house had been hired, previously to the appearance of yellow fever, by an English family, who left their native soil with a view to a permanent abode in the New World. They had scarcely taken possession of the dwelling, when they were terrified by the progress of the epidemic. They had fled from the danger; but this circumstance, in addition to some others, induced them to change their scheme. An evil so unwonted as pestilence impressed them with a belief of perpetual danger as long as they remained on this side of the ocean. They prepared for an immediate return to England.

For this end their house was relinquished, and their splendid furniture destined to be sold by auction. Before this event could take place, application was made to Mr. Melbourne by a lady whom his wife's description showed to be the same with her of whom Constantia was in search. She not only rented the house, but negotiated, by means of her landlord, the purchase of the furniture.

Her servants were blacks, and all but one, who officiated as steward, unacquainted with the English language. Some accident had proved her name to be Beauvais. She had no visitants, very rarely walked abroad, and then only in the evening with a female servant in attendance. Her hours appeared to be divided between the lute and the pen. As to her previous history or her present sources of subsistence, Mrs. Melbourne's curiosity had not been idle; but no consistent information was obtainable. Some incident had given birth to the conjecture that she was wife, or daughter, or sister, of Beauvais, the partisan of Brissot,[1] whom the faction of Marat had lately consigned to the scaffold; but this conjecture was unsupported by suitable evidence.

This tale by no means diminished Constantia's desire of personal intercourse. She saw no means of effecting her purpose. Mrs. Melbourne was unqualified to introduce her, having been discouraged in all the advances she had made towards a more friendly intercourse. Constantia reflected that her motives to seclusion would probably induce this lady to treat others as her friend had been treated.

It was possible, however, to gain access to her, if not as a friend, yet as the original proprietor of the lute. She determined to employ the agency of Roseveldt, the music shopman, for the purpose of rebuying this instrument. To enforce her application, she commissioned this person, whose obliging temper entitled him to confidence, to state her inducements for originally offering it for sale, and her motives for desiring the repossession on any terms which the lady thought proper to dictate.

Roseveldt fixed an hour in which it was convenient for him to execute her commission. This hour having passed, Constantia, who was anxious respecting his success, hastened to his house. Roseveldt delivered the instrument, which the lady, having listened to his pleas

---

1 Bertrand Poivier de Beauvais (1755-1827): organizer of the Armée Vendéenne, a group of tens of thousands of peasants from the northwest of France who opposed the Revolution, killed republicans and attempted to assist a British invasion. It is unclear how Martinette assumes this surname (through a second marriage?) or why, since Beauvais would have been associated with royalist restoration rather than with democratic revolutions in which Martinette claims to have participated.
Jacques Pierre Brissot de Warville (1754-93): French revolutionary and pamphleteer, leader of the Girondists. Envisioned radical reforms to regender roles in family and nation.

and offers, directed to be gratuitously restored to Constantia. At first, she had expressed her resolution to part with it on no account and at no price. Its music was her only recreation, and this instrument surpassed any she had ever before seen, in the costliness and delicacy of its workmanship. But Roseveldt's representations produced an instant change of resolution, and she not only eagerly consented to restore it, but refused to receive any thing in payment.

Constantia was deeply affected by this unexpected generosity. It was not her custom to be outstripped in this career. She now condemned herself for her eagerness to regain this instrument. During her father's blindness, it was a powerful, because the only, solace of his melancholy. Now he had no longer the same anxieties to encounter, and books and the pencil were means of gratification always at hand. The lute, therefore, she imagined, could be easily dispensed with by Mr. Dudley, whereas its power of consoling might be as useful to the unknown lady as it had formerly been to her father. She readily perceived in what manner it became her to act. Roseveldt was commissioned to redeliver the lute, and to entreat the lady's acceptance of it. The tender was received without hesitation, and Roseveldt dismissed without any inquiry relative to Constantia.

These transactions were reflected on by Constantia with considerable earnestness. The conduct of the stranger, her affluent and lonely state, her conjectural relationship to the actors in the great theatre of Europe, were mingled together in the fancy of Constantia, and embellished with the conceptions of her beauty derived from their casual meeting at Roseveldt's. She forgot not their similitude in age and sex, and delighted to prolong the dream of future confidence and friendship to take place between them. Her heart sighed for a companion fitted to partake in all her sympathies.

This strain, by being connected with the image of a being like herself, who had grown up with her from childhood, who had been entwined with her earliest affections, but from whom she had been severed from the period at which her father's misfortunes commenced, and of whose present condition she was wholly ignorant, was productive of the deepest melancholy. It filled her with excruciating and, for a time, irremediable sadness. It formed a kind of paroxysm, which, like some febrile affections, approached and retired without warning, and against the most vehement struggles.

In this mood, her fancy was thronged with recollections of scenes in which her friend had sustained a part. Their last interview was commonly revived in her remembrance so forcibly as almost to produce a lunatic conception of its reality. A ditty which they had sung together on that occasion flowed to her lips. If ever human tones were qualified to convey the whole soul, they were those of Constantia when she sang: –

> "The breeze awakes; the bark prepares
>   To waft me to a distant shore;
> But far beyond this world of cares,
>   We meet again to part no more."

These fits were accustomed to approach and to vanish by degrees. They were transitory, but not infrequent, and were pregnant with such agonizing tenderness, such heart-breaking sighs, and a flow of such bitter yet delicious tears, that it were not easily decided whether the pleasure or the pain surmounted. When symptoms of their coming were felt, she hastened into solitude, that the progress of her feelings might endure no restraint.

On the evening of the day on which the lute had been sent to the foreign lady, Constantia was alone in her chamber, immersed in desponding thoughts. From these she was recalled by Fabian, her black servant, who announced a guest. She was loath to break off the thread of her present meditations, and inquired, with a tone of some impatience, who was the guest. The servant was unable to tell; it was a young lady whom he had never before seen; she had opened for herself, and entered the parlour without previous notice.

Constantia paused at this relation. Her thoughts had recently been fixed upon Sophia Westwyn. Since their parting four years before, she had heard no tidings of this woman. Her fears imagined no more probable cause of her friend's silence than her death. This, however, was uncertain. The question now occurred, and brought with it sensations that left her no power to move: – was this the guest?

Her doubts were quickly dispelled, for the stranger, taking a light from the table, and not brooking the servant's delay, followed Fabian to the chamber of his mistress. She entered with careless freedom, and presented, to the astonished eyes of Constantia, the figure she had met at Roseveldt's, and the purchaser of her lute.

The stranger advanced towards her with quick steps, and, mingling tones of benignity and sprightliness, said: —

"I have come to perform a duty. I have received from you to-day a lute, that I valued almost as my best friend. To find another in America would not, perhaps, be possible; but, certainly, none equally superb and exquisite as this can be found. To show how highly I esteem the gift, I have come in person to thank you for it." There she stopped.

Constantia could not suddenly recover from the extreme surprise into which the unexpectedness of this meeting had thrown her. She could scarcely sufficiently suppress this confusion to enable her to reply to these rapid effusions of her visitant, who resumed with augmented freedom: —

"I came, as I said, to thank you; but, to say the truth, that was not all. I came likewise to see you. Having done my errand, I suppose I must go. I would fain stay longer and talk to you a little: will you give me leave?"

Constantia, scarcely retrieving her composure, stammered out a polite assent. They seated themselves, and the visitant, pressing the hand which she had taken, proceeded in a strain so smooth, so flowing, sliding from grave to gay, blending vivacity with tenderness, interpreting Constantia's silence with so keen sagacity, and accounting for the singularities of her own deportment in a way so respectful to her companion, and so worthy of a steadfast and pure mind in herself, that every embarrassment and scruple were quickly banished from their interview.

In an hour the guest took her leave. No promise of repeating her visit, and no request that Constantia would repay it, was made. Their parting seemed to be the last; whatever purpose having been contemplated, appeared to be accomplished by this transient meeting. It was of a nature deeply to interest the mind of Constantia. This was the lady who talked with Roseveldt and bargained with Melbourne, and they had been induced, by appearances, to suppose her ignorant of any language but French; but her discourse, on the present occasion, was in English, and was distinguished by unrivalled fluency. Her phrases and habits of pronouncing were untinctured with any foreign mixture, and bespoke the perfect knowledge of a native of America.

On the next evening, while Constantia was reviewing this transaction, calling up and weighing the sentiments which the stranger had uttered, and indulging some regret at the unlikelihood of their again meeting, Martinette (for I shall henceforth call her by her true name), entered the apartment as abruptly as before. She accounted for the visit merely by the pleasure it afforded her, and proceeded in a strain even more versatile and brilliant than before. This interview ended, like the first, without any tokens, on the part of the guest, of resolution or desire to renew it; but a third interview took place on the ensuing day.

Henceforth Martinette became a frequent but hasty visitant, and Constantia became daily more enamoured of her new acquaintance. She did not overlook peculiarities in the conversation and deportment of this woman. These exhibited no tendencies to confidence, or traces of sympathy. They merely denoted large experience, vigorous faculties, and masculine attainments. Herself was never introduced, except as an observer; but her observations on government and manners were profound and critical.

Her education seemed not widely different from that which Constantia had received. It was classical and mathematical; but to this was added a knowledge of political and military transactions in Europe during the present age, which implied the possession of better means of information than books. She depicted scenes and characters with the accuracy of one who had partaken and witnessed them herself.

Constantia's attention had been chiefly occupied by personal concerns. Her youth had passed in contention with misfortune, or in the quietudes of study. She could not be unapprized of contemporary revolutions and wars, but her ideas respecting them were indefinite and vague. Her views and her inferences on this head were general and speculative. Her acquaintance with history was exact and circumstantial in proportion as she retired backward from her own age. She knew more of the siege of Mutina than of that of Lille; more of the machinations of Catiline and the tumults of Claudius, than of the prostration of the Bastille and the proscriptions of Marat.[1]

---

1 Mutina: another name for Modena, a community in northern Italy, southwest of Venice.

Lille, a city in Northern France captured by the English Duke of Marlborough in 1708 and not restored to France until the Treaty of Utrecht in 1713. Democrats during the Belgian revolution fled Belgian provinces for exile in Lille. Catiline (c.108 BC–62 BC) was a Roman politician and conspirator barred from candidacy for the consulship because of accusations of misconduct in office, charges that later

She listened, therefore, with unspeakable eagerness to this reciter, who detailed to her, as the occasion suggested, the progress of action and opinion on the theatre of France and Poland. Conceived and rehearsed as this was, with the energy and copiousness of one who sustained a part in the scene, the mind of Constantia was always kept at the pitch of curiosity and wonder.

But, while this historian described the features, personal deportment, and domestic character of Antoinette, Mirabeau, and Robespierre,[1] an impenetrable veil was drawn over her own condition. There was a warmth and freedom in her details, which bespoke her own co-agency in these events, but was unattended by transports of indignation or sorrow, or by pauses of abstraction, such as were likely to occur in one whose hopes and fears had been intimately blended with public events.

Constantia could not but derive humiliation from comparing her own slender acquirements with those of her companion. She was sensible that all the differences between them arose from diversities of situation. She was eager to discover in what particulars this diversity consisted. She was for a time withheld, by scruples not easily explained, from disclosing her wishes. An accident, however, occurred, to remove these impediments. One evening, this unceremo-

---

proved false. Catiline, feeling cheated, concocted a plot to murder the consuls. He and his conspirators were acquitted in 65 BC. When he ran again in 63 BC, Cicero, the incumbent, and the conservative party were keen to prevent his election at any cost and Catiline was defeated. Claudius I (10 BC-AD 54) was Roman emperor from AD 41-54.

The Bastille, fortress and prison in Paris, was a hated symbol of absolutism during the French Revolution because it housed political prisoners. On July 14, 1789, a mob stormed the prison, marking the start of lower-class participation in the French Revolution.

Jean Paul Marat (1743-93) was a French doctor turned revolutionary/journalist who founded the radical journal *L'Ami du peuple* which bitterly attacked those in power. He was elected in 1792 to the Convention.

1 Marie Antoinette (1755-93) was Queen consort of Louis XVI, King of France. Unpopular because of her extravagance and insensitivity toward the masses, she was tried by the Revolutionary Tribunal during the French Revolution and executed. Mirabeau, Comte de. Title of Honoré Gabriel Victor Riqueti (1749-91). A French revolutionary elected President of the National Assembly. Robespierre, Maximilien François Marie Isidore de (1758-94) was a dogmatic French revolutionary, leader of the Jacobins and the fanatic architect of the Reign of Terror, which permitted the confiscation of property and arrest of suspected traitors (primarily Girondists), many of whom were guillotined. His strict adherence to principle led democrats around the world to fear the excesses of democracy.

nious visitant discovered Constantia busily surveying a chart of the Mediterranean Sea. This circumstance led the discourse to the present state of Syria and Cyprus. Martinette was copious in her details. Constantia listened for a time; and, when a pause ensued, questioned her companion as to the means she possessed of acquiring so much knowledge. This question was proposed with diffidence, and prefaced by apologies.

"Instead of being offended by your question," replied the guest, "I only wonder that it never before occurred to you. Travellers tell us much. Volney and Mariti[1] would have told you nearly all that I have told. With these I have conversed personally, as well as read their books; but my knowledge is, in truth, a species of patrimony. I inherit it."

"Will you be good enough," said Constantia, "to explain yourself?"

"My mother was a Greek of Cyprus. My father was a Slavonian of Ragusa, and I was born in a garden at Aleppo."[2]

"That was a singular concurrence."

"How singular? That a nautical vagrant like my father should sometimes anchor in the Bay of Naples; that a Cyprian merchant should carry his property and daughter beyond the reach of a Turkish sanjack,[3] and seek an asylum so commodious as Napoli; that my father should have dealings with this merchant, see, love, and marry his daughter, and afterwards procure, from the French Government, a consular commission at Aleppo; that the union should, in due time, be productive of a son and daughter, – are events far from being singular. They happen daily."

---

1 Volney: Constantin François de Chasse-boeuf, comte de (1757-1820), a French historian and travel writer, author of *Les Ruines, ou Méditations sur les révolutions des empires* (1791). Volney's work on the ruins of Palmyra, inspired by Enlightenment philosophy, attributed the rise and fall of civilizations to human greed, ignorance, and resistance to natural law, but asserted that Nature and Reason could lead humanity to freedom. When the American Government passed the Alien and Sedition Laws in 1798, Volney, who had been staying in Philadelphia, left the city, fearing that his support of the Republicans would be interpreted by Federalists as sedition. Giovanni Mariti (1736-1806) was an Italian and, like Volney, a travel writer. Most notably, he wrote *Travels in the Islands of Cyprus*.

2 Ragusa: a city of southeast Sicily, Italy, south-southwest of Messina. Aleppo is a city of northwest Syria near the Turkish border. Aleppo prospered under the Ottoman Turks (from 1517).

3 sanjack: in the Turkish Empire, an administrative district.

"And may I venture to ask if this be your history?"

"The history of my parents. I hope you do not consider the place my birth as the sole or the most important circumstance of my life."

"Nothing would please me more than to be enabled to compare it with other incidents. I am apt to think that your life is a tissue of surprising events. That the daughter of a Ragusan and Greek should have seen and known so much; that she should talk English with equal fluency and more correctness than a native; that I should now be conversing with her in a corner so remote from Cyprus and Sicily, are events more wonderful than any which I have known."

"Wonderful! Pish! Thy ignorance, thy miscalculation of probabilities, is far more so. My father talked to me in Slavonic. My mother and her maids talked to me in Greek. My neighbours talked to me in a medley of Arabic, Syriac, and Turkish. My father's secretary was a scholar. He was as well versed in Lysias and Xenophon as any of their contemporaries.[1] He laboured for ten years to enable me to read a language essentially the same with that I used daily to my nurse and mother. Is it wonderful, then, that I should be skilful in Slavonic, Greek, and the jargon of Aleppo? To have refrained from learning was impossible. Suppose a girl, prompt, diligent, inquisitive, to spend ten years of her life partly in Spain, partly in Tuscany, partly in France, and partly in England. With her versatile curiosity and flexible organs, would it be possible for her to remain ignorant of each of these languages? Latin is the mother of them all, and presents itself, of course, to her studious attention."

"I cannot easily conceive motives which should lead you, before the age of twenty, through so many scenes."

"Can you not? You grew and flourished, like a frail mimosa, in the spot where destiny had planted you. Thank my stars, I am somewhat better than a vegetable. Necessity, it is true, and not choice, set me in motion; but I am not sorry for the consequences."

"Is it too much," said Constantia, with some hesitation, "to request a detail of your youthful adventures?"

"Too much to give, perhaps, at a short notice. To such as you, my tale might abound with novelty, while to others, more acquainted

---

1   Lysias (*c.* 459-380 BC): Greek orator and one of the best classical Greek prose writers. Xenophon (430?-355? BC): Greek soldier and writer.

with vicissitudes, it would be tedious and flat. I must be gone in a few minutes. For that and for better reasons, I must not be minute. A summary, at present, will enable you to judge how far a more copious narrative is suited to instruct or to please you.

CHAPTER XX.

"MY father, in proportion as he grew old and rich, became weary of Aleppo. His natal soil, had it been the haunt of Calmucks or Bedouins, his fancy would have transformed into Paradise. No wonder that the equitable aristocracy and the peaceful husbandmen of Ragusa should be endeared to his heart by comparison with Egyptian plagues and Turkish tyranny. Besides, he lived for his children as well as himself. Their education and future lot required him to seek a permanent home.

"He embarked, with his wife and offspring, at Scanderoon.[1] No immediate conveyance to Ragusa offering, the appearance of the plague in Syria induced him to hasten his departure. He entered a French vessel for Marseilles. After being three days at sea, one of the crew was seized by the fatal disease, which had depopulated all the towns upon the coast. The voyage was made with more than usual despatch; but, before we reached our port, my mother and half the crew perished. My father died in the Lazaretto,[2] more through grief than disease.

"My brother and I were children and helpless. My father's fortune was on board this vessel, and was left by his death to the mercy of the captain. This man was honest, and consigned us and our property to the merchant with whom he dealt. Happily for us, our protector was childless and of scrupulous integrity. We henceforth became his adopted children. My brother's education and my own were conducted on the justest principles.

"At the end of four years, our protector found it expedient to make a voyage to Cayenne.[3] His brother was an extensive proprietor

---

1 Scanderoon: formerly Alexandretta, in southern Turkey, the chief port for Aleppo.
2 Lazaretto: a hospital treating contagious diseases.
3 Cayenne: the capital of French Guiana, on Cayenne Island at the mouth of the Cayenne River.

in that colony, but his sudden death made way for the succession of our friend. To establish his claims, his presence was necessary on the spot. He was little qualified for arduous enterprises, and his age demanded repose; but his own acquisitions having been small, and being desirous of leaving us in possession of competence, he cheerfully embarked.

"Meanwhile, my brother was placed at a celebrated seminary in the Pays de Vaud,[1] and I was sent to a sister who resided at Verona. I was at this time fourteen years old, – one year younger than my brother, whom, since that period, I have neither heard of nor seen.

"I was now a woman, and qualified to judge and act for myself. The character of my new friend was austere and devout, and there were so many incongenial points between us that but little tranquillity was enjoyed under her control. The priest who discharged the office of her confessor thought proper to entertain views with regard to me, grossly inconsistent with the sanctity of his profession. He was a man of profound dissimulation and masterly address. His efforts, however, were repelled with disdain. My security against his attempts lay in the uncouthness and deformity which nature had bestowed upon his person and visage, rather than in the firmness of my own principles.

"The courtship of Father Bartoli, the austerities of Madame Roselli, the disgustful or insipid occupations to which I was condemned, made me impatiently wish for a change; but my father (so I will call him) had decreed that I should remain under his sister's guardianship till his return from Guiana. When this would happen was uncertain. Events unforeseen might protract it for years, but it could not arrive in less than a twelvemonth.

"I was incessantly preyed upon by discontent. My solitude was loathsome. I panted after liberty and friendship, and the want of these were not recompensed by luxury and quiet, and by the instructions in useful science which I received from Bartoli, who, though detested as a hypocrite and lover, was venerable as a scholar. He would fain have been an Abelard, but it was not his fate to meet with an Eloisa.[2]

---

1   Pays de Vaud: canton in southwest Switzerland.
2   Abelard and Eloisa: famous pair of lovers. Peter Abelard (1079-1142?) was a French philosopher, theologian and priest who fell in love with his student Eloisa.

"Two years passed away in this durance. My miseries were exquisite. I am almost at a loss to account for the unhappiness of that time, for, looking back upon it, I perceive that an equal period could not have been spent with more benefit. For the sake of being near me, Bartoli importunately offered his instructions. He had nothing to communicate but metaphysics and geometry. These were little to my taste, but I could not keep him at a distance. I had no other alternative than to endure him as a lover or a teacher. His passion for science was at least equal to that which he entertained for me, and both these passions combined to make him a sedulous instructor. He was a disciple of the newest doctrines respecting matter and mind. He denied the impenetrability of the first, and the immateriality of the second. These he endeavoured to inculcate upon me, as well as to subvert my religious tenets, because he delighted, like all men, in transfusing his opinions, and because he regarded my piety as the only obstacle to his designs. He succeeded in dissolving the spell of ignorance, but not in producing that kind of acquiescence he wished. He had, in this respect, to struggle not only with my principles, but my weaknesses. He might have overcome every obstacle but my abhorrence of deformity and age. To cure me of this aversion was beyond his power. My servitude grew daily more painful. I grew tired of chasing a comet to its aphelion,[1] and of untying the knot of an infinite series. A change in my condition became indispensable to my very existence. Languor and sadness, and unwillingness to eat or to move, were at last my perpetual attendants.

"Madame Roselli was alarmed at my condition. The sources of my inquietude were incomprehensible to her. The truth was, that I scarcely understood them myself, and my endeavours to explain them to my friend merely instilled into her an opinion that I was either lunatic or deceitful. She complained and admonished; but my disinclination to my usual employments would not be conquered, and my health rapidly declined. A physician, who was called, confessed that my case was beyond his power to understand, but recommended, as a sort of desperate expedient, a change of scene. A succession and variety of objects might possibly contribute to my cure.

"At this time there arrived, at Verona, Lady D'Arcy, – an English-

---

1 aphelion: that point of a planet's or a comet's orbit farthest from the sun.

woman of fortune and rank, and a strenuous Catholic. Her husband had lately died; and, in order to divert her grief, as well as to gratify her curiosity in viewing the great seat of her religion, she had come to Italy. Intercourse took place between her and Madame Roselli. By this means she gained a knowledge of my person and condition, and kindly offered to take me under her protection. She meant to traverse every part of Italy, and was willing that I should accompany her in all her wanderings.

"This offer was gratefully accepted, in spite of the artifices and remonstrances of Bartoli. My companion speedily contracted for me the affection of a mother. She was without kindred of her own religion, having acquired her faith, not by inheritance, but conversion. She desired to abjure her native country, and to bind herself, by every social tie, to a people who adhered to the same faith. Me she promised to adopt as her daughter, provided her first impressions in my favour were not belied by my future deportment.

"My principles were opposite to hers; but habit, an aversion to displease my friend, my passion for knowledge, which my new condition enabled me to gratify, all combined to make me a deceiver. But my imposture was merely of a negative kind; I deceived her rather by forbearance to contradict, and by acting as she acted, than by open assent and zealous concurrence. My new state was, on this account, not devoid of inconvenience. The general deportment and sentiments of Lady D'Arcy testified a vigorous and pure mind. New avenues to knowledge, by converse with mankind and with books, and by the survey of new scenes, were open for my use. Gratitude and veneration attached me to my friend, and made the task of pleasing her, by a seeming conformity of sentiments, less irksome.

"During this interval, no tidings were received by his sister, at Verona, respecting the fate of Sebastian Roselli. The supposition of his death was too plausible not to be adopted. What influence this disaster possessed over my brother's destiny, I know not. The generosity of Lady D'Arcy hindered me from experiencing any disadvantage from this circumstance. Fortune seemed to have decreed that I should not be reduced to the condition of an orphan.

"At an age and in a situation like mine, I could not long remain unacquainted with love. My abode at Rome introduced me to the knowledge of a youth from England, who had every property which I regarded as worthy of esteem. He was a kinsman of Lady D'Arcy, and as such admitted at her house on the most familiar footing. His patrimony was extremely slender, but was in his own possession. He had no intention of increasing it by any professional pursuit, but was contented with the frugal provision it afforded. He proposed no other end of his existence than the acquisition of virtue and knowledge.

"The property of Lady D'Arcy was subject to her own disposal, but, on the failure of a testament, this youth was, in legal succession, the next heir. He was well acquainted with her temper and views, but, in the midst of urbanity and gentleness, studied none of those concealments of opinion which would have secured him her favour. That he was not of her own faith was an insuperable, but the only, obstacle to the admission of his claims.

"If conformity of age and opinions, and the mutual fascination of love, be a suitable basis for marriage, Wentworth and I were destined for each other. Mutual disclosure added sanctity to our affection; but, the happiness of Lady D'Arcy being made to depend upon the dissolution of our compact, the heroism of Wentworth made him hasten to dissolve it. As soon as she discovered our attachment, she displayed symptoms of the deepest anguish. In addition to religious motives, her fondness for me forbade her to exist but in my society and in the belief of the purity of my faith. The contention, on my part, was vehement between the regards due to her felicity and to my own. Had Wentworth left me the power to decide, my decision would doubtless have evinced the frailty of my fortitude and the strength of my passion; but, having informed me fully of the reasons of his conduct, he precipitately retired from Rome. He left me no means of tracing his footsteps and of assailing his weakness by expostulation and entreaty.

"Lady D'Arcy was no less eager to abandon a spot where her happiness had been so imminently endangered. Our next residence was Palermo. I will not dwell upon the sensations produced by this disappointment in me. I review them with astonishment and self-compassion. If I thought it possible for me to sink again into imbecility so ignominious, I should be disposed to kill myself.

"There was no end to vows of fondness and tokens of gratitude in Lady D'Arcy. Her future life should be devoted to compensate me for this sacrifice. Nothing could console her in that single state in which she intended to live, but the consolations of my fellowship. Her conduct coincided for some time with these professions, and my anguish was allayed by the contemplation of the happiness conferred upon one whom I revered.

"My friend could not be charged with dissimulation and artifice. Her character had been mistaken by herself as well as by me. Devout affections seemed to have filled her heart, to the exclusion of any object besides myself. She cherished with romantic tenderness the memory of her husband, and imagined that a single state was indispensably enjoined upon her by religious duty. This persuasion, however, was subverted by the arts of a Spanish cavalier, young, opulent, and romantic as herself in devotion. An event like this might, indeed, have been easily predicted, by those who reflected that the lady was still in the bloom of life, ardent in her temper, and bewitching in her manners.

"The fondness she had lavished upon me was now, in some degree, transferred to a new object; but I still received the treatment due to a beloved daughter. She was solicitous as ever to promote my gratification, and a diminution of kindness would not have been suspected by those who had not witnessed the excesses of her former passion. Her marriage with the Spaniard removed the obstacle to union with Wentworth. This man, however, had set himself beyond the reach of my inquiries. Had there been the shadow of a clue afforded me, I should certainly have sought him to the ends of the world.

"I continued to reside with my friend, and accompanied her and her husband to Spain. Antonio de Leyva was a man of probity. His mind was enlightened by knowledge and his actions dictated by humanity. Though but little older than myself, and young enough to be the son of his spouse, his deportment to me was a model of rectitude and delicacy. I spent a year in Spain, partly in the mountains of Castile and partly at Segovia. New manners and a new language occupied my attention for a time; but these, losing their novelty, lost their power to please. I betook myself to books, to beguile the tediousness and diversify the tenor of my life.

"This would not have long availed; but I was relieved from new repinings, by the appointment of Antonio de Leyva to a diplomatic office at Vienna. Thither we accordingly repaired. A coincidence of circumstances had led me wide from the path of ambition and study usually allotted to my sex and age. From the computation of eclipses, I now betook myself to the study of man. My proficiency, when I allowed it to be seen, attracted great attention. Instead of adulation and gallantry, I was engaged in watching the conduct of states and revolving the theories of politicians.

"Superficial observers were either incredulous with regard to my character, or connected a stupid wonder with their belief. My attainments and habits they did not see to be perfectly consonant with the principles of human nature. They unavoidably flowed from the illicit attachment of Bartoli, and the erring magnanimity of Wentworth. Aversion to the priest was the grand inciter of my former studies; the love of Wentworth, whom I hoped once more to meet, made me labour to exclude the importunities of others, and to qualify myself for securing his affections.

"Since our parting in Italy, Wentworth had traversed Syria and Egypt, and arrived some months after me at Vienna. He was on the point of leaving the city, when accident informed me of his being there. An interview was effected, and, our former sentiments respecting each other having undergone no change, we were united. Madam de Leyva reluctantly concurred with our wishes, and, at parting, forced upon me a considerable sum of money.

"Wentworth's was a character not frequently met with in the world. He was a political enthusiast, who esteemed nothing more graceful or glorious than to die for the liberties of mankind. He had traversed Greece with an imagination full of the exploits of ancient times, and derived, from contemplating Thermoplyae and Marathon, an enthusiasm that bordered upon frenzy.

"It was now the third year of the Revolutionary War in America, and, previous to our meeting at Vienna, he had formed the resolution of repairing thither and tendering his service to the Congress as a volunteer. Our marriage made no change in his plans. My soul was engrossed by two passions, – a wild spirit of adventure, and a boundless devotion to him. I vowed to accompany him in every danger, to vie with him in military ardour, to combat and to die by his side.

"I delighted to assume the male dress, to acquire skill at the sword, and dexterity in every boisterous exercise. The timidity that commonly attends women gradually vanished. I felt as if imbued by a soul that was a stranger to the sexual distinction. We embarked at Brest, in a frigate destined for St. Domingo.[1] A desperate conflict with an English ship in the Bay of Biscay was my first introduction to a scene of tumult and danger of whose true nature I had formed no previous conception. At first I was spiritless and full of dismay. Experience, however, gradually reconciled me to the life that I had chosen.

"A fortunate shot, by dismasting the enemy, allowed us to prosecute our voyage unmolested. At Cap François[2] we found a ship which transported us, after various perils, to Richmond, in Virginia. I will not carry you through the adventures of four years. You, sitting all your life in peaceful corners, can scarcely imagine that variety of hardship and turmoil which attends the female who lives in a camp.

"Few would sustain these hardships with better grace than I did. I could seldom be prevailed on to remain at distance, and inactive, when my husband was in battle, and more than once rescued him from death by the seasonable destruction of his adversary.

"At the repulse of the Americans at Germantown,[3] Wentworth was wounded and taken prisoner. I obtained permission to attend his sickbed and supply that care without which he would assuredly have died. Being imperfectly recovered, he was sent to England and subjected to a rigorous imprisonment. Milder treatment might have permitted his complete restoration to health; but, as it was, he died.

"His kindred were noble, and rich, and powerful; but it was difficult to make them acquainted with Wentworth's situation. Their assistance, when demanded, was readily afforded; but it came too late to prevent his death. Me they snatched from my voluntary prison, and employed every friendly art to efface from my mind the images of recent calamity.

---

1   Brest: a port city of northwest France on an inlet of the Atlantic Ocean. The Bay of
    Biscay is an arm of the Atlantic near Brittany, France.
    St. Domingo: former Spanish colony discovered by Columbus in 1492. The west
    side of the island was ceded to the French in 1697; the remainder in 1795. French
    planters grew sugar cane there in the second half of the eighteenth century using
    slave labour. Slaves, led by Toussaint L'ouverture, rebelled in 1791, inspired by
    French revolutionary philosophy.
2   Cap François: important port and capital of St. Domingue.
3   Germantown: a residential section of Philadelphia, Pennsylvania, settled in 1683. In
    1777, it was the site of a Revolutionary battle in which Washington's troops unsuc-
    cessfully attacked the British encampment.

"Wentworth's singularities of conduct and opinion had estranged him at an early age from his family. They felt little regret at his fate, but every motive concurred to secure their affection and succour to me. My character was known to many officers, returned from America, whose report, joined with the influence of my conversation, rendered me an object to be gazed at by thousands. Strange vicissitude! Now immersed in the infection of a military hospital, the sport of a wayward fortune, struggling with cold and hunger, with negligence and contumely. A month after, passing into scenes of gayety and luxury, exhibited at operas and masquerades, made the theme of inquiry and encomium at every place of resort, and caressed by the most illustrious among the votaries of science and the advocates of the American cause.

"Here I again met Madame de Leyva. This woman was perpetually assuming new forms. She was a sincere convert to the Catholic religion, but she was open to every new impression. She was the dupe of every powerful reasoner, and assumed with equal facility the most opposite shapes. She had again reverted to the Protestant religion, and, governed by a headlong zeal in whatever cause she engaged, she had sacrificed her husband and child to a new conviction.

"The instrument of this change was a man who passed, at that time, for a Frenchman. He was young, accomplished, and addressful, but was not suspected of having been prompted by illicit views, or of having seduced the lady from allegiance to her husband as well as to her God. De Leyva, however, who was sincere in his religion as well as his love, was hasty to avenge this injury, and, in a contest with the Frenchman, was killed. His wife adopted at once her ancient religion and country, and was once more an Englishwoman.

"At our meeting her affection for me seemed to be revived, and the most passionate entreaties were used to detain me in England. My previous arrangements would not suffer it. I foresaw restraints and inconveniences from the violence and caprice of her passions, and intended henceforth to keep my liberty inviolate by any species of engagement, either of friendship or marriage. My habits were French, and I proposed henceforward to take up my abode at Paris. Since his voyage to Guiana, I had heard no tidings of Sebastian Roselli. This man's image was cherished with filial emotions, and I conceived that the sight of him would amply reward a longer journey than from London to Marseilles.

"Beyond my hopes, I found him in his ancient abode. The voyage, and a residence of three years at Cayenne, had been beneficial to his appearance and health. He greeted me with paternal tenderness, and admitted me to a full participation of his fortune, which the sale of his American property had greatly enhanced. He was a stranger to the fate of my brother. On his return home he had gone to Switzerland, with a view of ascertaining his destiny. The youth, a few months after his arrival at Lausanne, had eloped with a companion, and had hither-to eluded all Roselli's searches and inquiries. My father was easily prevailed upon to transfer his residence from Provence to Paris."

Here Martinette paused, and, marking the clock, "It is time," resumed she, "to begone. Are you not weary of my tale? On the day I entered France, I entered my twenty-third year of my age, so that my promise of detailing my youthful adventures is fulfilled. I must away. Till we meet again, farewell."

CHAPTER XXI.

SUCH was the wild series of Martinette's adventures. Each incident fastened on the memory of Constantia, and gave birth to numberless reflections. Her prospect of mankind seemed to be enlarged, on a sud-den, to double its ancient dimensions. Ormond's narratives had car-ried her beyond the Mississippi, and into the deserts of Siberia. He had recounted the perils of a Russian war, and painted the manners of Mongols and Naudowessies.[1] Her new friend had led her back to the civilized world and portrayed the other half of the species. Men, in their two forms of savage and refined, had been scrutinized by these observers; and what was wanting in the delineations of the one was liberally supplied by the other.

Eleven years in the life of Martinette was unrelated. Her conversa-tion suggested the opinion that this interval had been spent in France. It was obvious to suppose that a woman thus fearless and sagacious

---

1   Nadouessioux: an Ojibwa word for themselves, rendered into French, then short-ened to Sioux. Important tribal confederacy of the North American plains.

had not been inactive at a period like the present, which called forth talents and courage without distinction of sex, and had been particularly distinguished by female enterprise and heroism. Her name easily led to the suspicion of concurrence with the subverters of monarchy, and of participation in their fall. Her flight from the merciless tribunals of the faction that now reigned would explain present appearances.

Martinette brought to their next interview an air of uncommon exultation. On this being remarked, she communicated the tidings of the fall of the sanguinary tyranny of Robespierre.[1] Her eyes sparkled, and every feature was pregnant with delight, while she unfolded, with her accustomed energy, the particulars of this tremendous revolution. The blood which it occasioned to flow was mentioned without any symptoms of disgust or horror.

Constantia ventured to ask if this incident was likely to influence her own condition.

"Yes. It will open the way for my return."

"Then you think of returning to a scene of so much danger?"

"Danger, my girl? It is my element. I am an adorer of liberty, and liberty without peril can never exist."

"But so much bloodshed and injustice! Does not your heart shrink from the view of a scene of massacre and tumult, such as Paris has lately exhibited and will probably continue to exhibit?"

"Thou talkest, Constantia, in a way scarcely worthy of thy good sense. Have I not been three years in a camp? What are bleeding wounds and mangled corpses, when accustomed to the daily sight of them for years? Am I not a lover of liberty? and must I not exult in the fall of tyrants, and regret only that my hand had no share in their destruction?"

"But a woman – how can the heart of women be inured to the shedding of blood?"

"Have women, I beseech thee, no capacity to reason and infer? Are they less open than men to the influence of habit? My hand never faltered when liberty demanded the victim. If thou wert with me at Paris, I could show thee a fusil of two barrels, which is precious

---

1 Robespierre: French statesman tried and guillotined in 1794 for his role in the Reign of Terror following the French Revolution.

beyond any other relic, merely because it enabled me to kill thirteen officers at Jemappes.[1] Two of these were emigrant nobles, whom I knew and loved before the Revolution, but the cause they had since espoused cancelled their claims to mercy."

"What!" said the startled Constantia; "have you fought in the ranks?"

"Certainly. Hundreds of my sex have done the same. Some were impelled by the enthusiasm of love, and some by a mere passion for war; some by the contagion of example; and some – with whom I myself must be ranked, – by a generous devotion to liberty. Brunswick and Saxe-Coburg had to contend with whole regiments of women, – regiments they would have formed, if they had been collected into separate bodies.[2]

"I will tell thee a secret. Thou wouldst never have seen Martinette de Beauvais, if Brunswick had deferred one day longer his orders for retreating into Germany."

"How so?"

"She would have died by her own hand."

"What could lead to such an outrage?"

"The love of liberty."

"I cannot comprehend how that love should prompt you to suicide."

"I will tell thee. The plan was formed, and could not miscarry. A woman was to play the part of a banished Royalist, was to repair to the Prussian camp, and to gain admission to the general. This would have easily been granted to a female and an ex-noble. There she was to assassinate the enemy of her country, and to attest her magnanimity by slaughtering herself. I was weak enough to regret the ignominious retreat of the Prussians, because it precluded the necessity of such a sacrifice."

This was related with accents and looks that sufficiently attested its truth. Constantia shuddered, and drew back, to contemplate more

---

1 Jemappes: a town in West Belgium where, in 1792, the French defeated the Austrians in one of the first important battles of the French Revolutionary Wars.

2 Brunswick and Saxe-Coburg: Charles William Ferdinand, Duke of Brunswick (1735-1806), a Prussian field marshal in the French Revolutionary and Napoleonic War campaigns. Fredrick Augustus I, Saxe-Coburg (1750-1827) aided Frederick II, King of Prussia, against Austria in 1778-79 during the War of the Bavarian Succession.

deliberately the features of her guest. Hitherto she had read in them nothing that bespoke the desperate courage of a martyr and the deep designing of an assassin. The image which her mind had reflected from the deportment of this woman was changed. The likeness which she had feigned to herself was no longer seen. She felt that antipathy was preparing to displace love. These sentiments, however, she concealed, and suffered the conversation to proceed.

Their discourse now turned upon the exploits of several women who mingled in the tumults of the capital and in the armies on the frontiers. Instances were mentioned of ferocity in some, and magnanimity in others, which almost surpassed belief. Constantia listened greedily, though not with approbation, and acquired, at every sentence, new desire to be acquainted with the personal history of Martinette. On mentioning this wish, her friend said that she endeavoured to amuse her exile by composing her own memoirs, and that, on her next visit, she would bring with her the volume, which she would suffer Constantia to read.

A separation of a week elapsed. She felt some impatience for the renewal of their intercourse, and for the perusal of the volume that had been mentioned. One evening Sarah Baxter, whom Constantia had placed in her own occasional service, entered the room with marks of great joy and surprise, and informed her that she at length had discovered Miss Monrose. From her abrupt and prolix account, it appeared that Sarah had overtaken Miss Monrose in the street, and, guided by her own curiosity, as well as by the wish to gratify her mistress, she had followed the stranger. To her utter astonishment, the lady had paused at Mr. Dudley's door, with a seeming resolution to enter it, but presently resumed her way. Instead of pursuing her steps further, Sarah had stopped to communicate this intelligence to Constantia. Having delivered her news, she hastened away, but, returning, in a moment, with a countenance of new surprise, she informed her mistress that on leaving the house she had met Miss Monrose at the door, on the point of entering. She added that the stranger had inquired for Constantia, and was now waiting below.

Constantia took no time to reflect upon an incident so unexpected and so strange, but proceeded forthwith to the parlour. Martinette only was there. It did not instantly occur to her that this lady and Mademoiselle Monrose might possibly be the same. The inquiries she made speedily removed her doubts, and it now appeared that the woman about whose destiny she had formed so many conjectures and fostered so much anxiety was no other than the daughter of Roselli.

Having readily answered her questions, Martinette inquired, in her turn, into the motives of her friend's curiosity. These were explained by a succinct account of the transactions to which the deceased Baxter had been a witness. Constantia concluded with mentioning her own reflections on the tale, and intimating her wish to be informed how Martinette had extricated herself from a situation so calamitous.

"Is there any room for wonder on that head?" replied the guest. "It was absurd to stay longer in the house. Having finished the interment of Roselli, (soldier-fashion,) for he was the man who suffered his foolish regrets to destroy him, I forsook the house. Roselli was by no means poor, but he could not consent to live at ease, or to live at all, while his country endured such horrible oppressions, and when so many of his friends had perished. I complied with his humour, because it could not be changed, and I revered him too much to desert him."

"But whither," said Constantia, "could you seek shelter at a time like that? The city was desolate, and a wandering female could scarcely be received under any roof. All inhabited houses were closed at that hour, and the fear of infection would have shut them against you if they had not been already so."

"Hast thou forgotten that there were at that time at least ten thousand French in this city, fugitives from Marat and from St. Domingo? That they lived in utter fearlessness of the reigning disease, – sung and loitered in the public walks, and prattled at their doors, with all their customary unconcern? Supposest thou that there were none among these who would receive a countrywoman, even if her name had not been Martinette de Beauvais? Thy fancy has depicted strange things; but believe me that, without a farthing and without a name, I should not have incurred the slightest inconvenience. The death of Roselli I foresaw, because it was gradual in its approach, and was sought by him as a good. My grief, therefore, was exhausted before it came, and I rejoiced at his death, because it was the close of all his sorrows. The rueful pictures of my distress and weakness which were given by Baxter existed only in his own fancy."

Martinette pleaded an engagement, and took her leave, professing to have come merely to leave with her the promised manuscript. This interview, though short, was productive of many reflections on the deceitfulness of appearances, and on the variety of maxims by which the conduct of human beings is regulated. She was accustomed to impart all her thoughts and relate every new incident to her father. With this view she now hied to his apartment. This hour it was her custom, when disengaged, always to spend with him.

She found Mr. Dudley busy in revolving a scheme which various circumstances had suggested and gradually conducted to maturity. No period of his life had been equally delightful with that portion of his youth which he had spent in Italy. The climate, the language, the manners of the people, and the sources of intellectual gratification in painting and music, were congenial to his taste. He had reluctantly forsaken these enchanting seats, at the summons of his father, but, on his return to his native country, had encountered nothing but ignominy and pain. Poverty and blindness had beset his path, and it seemed as if it were impossible to fly too far from the scene of his disasters. His misfortunes could not be concealed from others, and every thing around him seemed to renew the memory of all that he had suffered. All the events of his youth served to entice him to Italy, while all the incidents of his subsequent life concurred to render disgustful his present abode.

His daughter's happiness was not to be forgotten. This he imagined would be eminently promoted by the scheme. It would open to her new avenues to knowledge. It would snatch her from the odious pursuit of Ormond, and, by a variety of objects and adventures, efface from her mind any impression which his dangerous artifices might have made upon it.

This project was now communicated to Constantia. Every argument adapted to influence her choice was employed. He justly conceived that the only obstacle to her adoption of it related to Ormond. He expatiated on the dubious character of this man, the wildness of his schemes, and the magnitude of his errors. What could be expected from a man, half of whose life had been spent at the head of a band of Cossacks, spreading devastation in the regions of the Danube, and supporting by flagitious intrigues the tyranny of Catherine,[1] and the

---

1   In 1773-75 the Cossacks revolted and their leaders became loyal supporters of Catherine the Great (1729-96), who was popular with powerful groups opposed to her eccentric husband Peter. In June 1762, conspirators headed by Grigori Orlov,

other half in traversing inhospitable countries, and extinguishing what remained of clemency and justice by intercourse with savages?

It was admitted that his energies were great, but misdirected, and that to restore them to the guidance of truth was not in itself impossible; but it was so with relation to any power that she possessed. Conformity would flow from their marriage, but this conformity was not to be expected from him. It was not his custom to abjure any of his doctrines or recede from any of his claims. She knew likewise the conditions of their union. She must go with him to some corner of the world where his boasted system was established. What was the road to it he had carefully concealed, but it was evident that it lay beyond the precincts of civilized existence.

Whatever were her ultimate decision, it was at least proper to delay it. Six years were yet wanting of that period at which only she formerly considered marriage as proper. To all the general motives for deferring her choice, the conduct of Ormond superadded the weightiest. Their correspondence might continue, but her residence in Europe and converse with mankind might enlighten her judgment and qualify her for a more rational decision.

Constantia was not uninfluenced by these reasonings. Instead of reluctantly admitting them, she somewhat wondered that they had not been suggested by her own reflections. Her imagination anticipated her entrance on that mighty scene with emotions little less than rapturous. Her studies had conferred a thousand ideal charms on a theatre where Scipio and Caesar had performed their parts. Her wishes were no less importunate to gaze upon the Alps and Pyrenees, and to vivify and chasten the images collected from books, by comparing them with their real prototypes.

No social ties existed to hold her to America. Her only kinsman and friend would be the companion of her journeys. This project was likewise recommended by advantages of which she only was qualified

---

her lover, deposed Peter and proclaimed her ruler; shortly afterward Peter was murdered. Catherine's rule began with projects of reform, but after the peasant uprising and the French Revolution, she strengthened serfdom and increased the privileges of the nobility. Her foreign policy was imperialistic: she increased Russian control of the Baltic provinces and Ukraine; began colonization of Alaska; annexed the Crimea; in two wars with Turkey made Russia dominant in southwestern Asia; and secured for Russia the major share in the partitions of Poland in 1772, 1793, and 1795.

to judge. Sophia Westwyn had embarked, four years previous to this date, for England, in company with an English lady and her husband. The arrangements that were made forbade either of the friends to hope for a future meeting. Yet now, by virtue of this project, this meeting seemed no longer to be hopeless.

This burst of new ideas and new hopes on the mind of Constantia took place in the course of a single hour. No change in her external situation had been wrought, and yet her mind had undergone the most signal revolution. The novelty as well as greatness of the prospect kept her in a state of elevation and awe, more ravishing than any she had ever experienced. Anticipations of intercourse with nature in her most august forms, with men in diversified states of society, with the posterity of Greeks and Romans, and with the actors that were now upon the stage, and, above all, with the being whom absence and the want of other attachments had, in some sort, contributed to deify, made this night pass away upon the wings of transport.

The hesitation which existed on parting with her father speedily gave place to an ardour impatient of the least delay. She saw no impediments to the immediate commencement of the voyage. To delay it a month, or even a week, seemed to be unprofitable tardiness. In this ferment of her thoughts, she was neither able nor willing to sleep. In arranging the means of departure and anticipating the events that would successively arise, there was abundant food for contemplation.

She marked the first dawnings of the day, and rose. She felt reluctant to break upon her father's morning slumbers, but considered that her motives were extremely urgent, and that the pleasure afforded him by her zealous approbation of his scheme would amply compensate him for this unseasonable intrusion on his rest. She hastened therefore to his chamber. She entered with blithesome steps, and softly drew aside the curtain.

CHAPTER XXII.

UNHAPPY Constantia! At the moment when thy dearest hopes had budded afresh, when the clouds of insecurity and disquiet had retired from thy vision, wast thou assailed by the great subverter of human schemes. Thou sawest nothing in futurity but an eternal variation and succession of delights. Thou wast hastening to forget dangers and sorrows which thou fondly imaginedst were never to return. This day was to be the outset of a new career; existence was henceforth to be embellished with enjoyments hitherto scarcely within the reach of hope.

Alas! thy predictions of calamity seldom failed to be verified. Not so thy prognostics of pleasure. These, though fortified by every calculation of contingencies, were edifices grounded upon nothing. Thy life was a struggle with malignant destiny, – a contest for happiness in which thou wast fated to be overcome.

She stooped to kiss the venerable cheek of her father, and, by whispering, to break his slumber. Her eye was no sooner fixed upon his countenance, than she started back and shrieked. She had no power to forbear. Her outcries were piercing and vehement. They ceased only with the cessation of breath. She sunk upon a chair in a state partaking more of death than of life, mechanically prompted to give vent to her agonies in shrieks, but incapable of uttering a sound.

The alarm called her servants to the spot. They beheld her dumb, wildly gazing, and gesticulating in a way that indicated frenzy. She made no resistance to their efforts, but permitted them to carry her back to her own chamber. Sarah called upon her to speak, and to explain the cause of these appearances; but the shock which she had endured seemed to have irretrievably destroyed her powers of utterance.

The terrors of the affectionate Sarah were increased. She kneeled by the bedside of her mistress, and, with streaming eyes, besought the unhappy lady to compose herself. Perhaps the sight of weeping in another possessed a sympathetic influence, or nature had made provision for this salutary change. However that be, a torrent of tears now came to her succour, and rescued her from a paroxysm of insanity which its longer continuance might have set beyond the reach of cure.

Meanwhile, a glance at his master's countenance made Fabian fully acquainted with the nature of the scene. The ghastly visage of Mr. Dudley showed that he was dead, and that he had died in some terrific and mysterious manner. As soon as this faithful servant recovered from surprise, the first expedient which his ingenuity suggested was to fly with tidings of this event to Mr. Melbourne. That gentle-man instantly obeyed the summons. With the power of weeping, Constantia recovered the power of reflection. This, for a time, served her only as a medium of anguish. Melbourne mingled his tears with hers, and endeavoured, by suitable remonstrances, to revive her fortitude.

The filial passion is perhaps instinctive to man; but its energy is modified by various circumstances. Every event in the life of Constantia contributed to heighten this passion beyond customary bounds. In the habit of perpetual attendance on her father, of deriv-ing from him her knowledge, and sharing with him the hourly fruits of observation and reflection, his existence seemed blended with her own. There was no other whose concurrence and council she could claim, with whom a domestic and uninterrupted alliance could be maintained. The only bond of consanguinity was loosened, the only prop of friendship was taken away.

Others, perhaps, would have observed that her father's existence had been merely a source of obstruction and perplexity; that she had hitherto acted by her own wisdom, and would find, hereafter, less difficulty in her choice of schemes, and fewer impediments to the execution. These reflections occurred not to her. This disaster had increased, to an insupportable degree, the vacancy and dreariness of her existence. The face she was habituated to behold had disappeared forever; the voice whose mild and affecting tones had so long been familiar to her ears was hushed into eternal silence. The felicity to which she clung was ravished away; nothing remained to hinder her from sinking into utter despair.

The first transports of grief having subsided, a source of consola-tion seemed to be opened in the belief that her father had only changed one form of being for another; that he still lived to be the guardian of her peace and honour, to enter the recesses of her thought, to forewarn her of evil and invite her to good. She grasped at these images with eagerness, and fostered them as the only solaces of her calamity. They were not adapted to inspire her with cheerful-ness, but they sublimed her sensations, and added an inexplicable fas-cination to sorrow.

It was unavoidable sometimes to reflect upon the nature of that death which had occurred. Tokens were sufficiently apparent that outward violence had been the cause. Who could be the performer of so black a deed, by what motives he was guided, were topics of fruitless conjecture. She mused upon this subject, not from the thirst of vengeance, but from a mournful curiosity. Had the perpetrator stood before her and challenged retribution, she would not have lifted a finger to accuse or to punish. The evil already endured left her no power to concert and execute projects for extending that evil to others. Her mind was unnerved, and recoiled with loathing from considerations of abstract justice, or political utility, when they prompted to the prosecution of the murderer.

Melbourne was actuated by different views, but on this subject he was painfully bewildered. Mr. Dudley's deportment to his servants and neighbours was gentle and humane. He had no dealings with the trafficking or labouring part of mankind. The fund which supplied his cravings of necessity or habit was his daughter's. His recreations and employments were harmless and lonely. The evil purpose was limited to his death, for his chamber was exactly in the same state in which negligent security had left it. No midnight footstep or voice, no unbarred door or lifted window, afforded tokens of the presence or traces of the entrance or flight of the assassin.

The meditations of Constantia, however, could not fail in some of their circuities to encounter the image of Craig. His agency in the impoverishment of her father, and in the scheme by which she had like to have been loaded with the penalties of forgery, was of an impervious and unprecedented kind. Motives were unveiled by time, in some degree accounting for his treacherous proceeding; but there was room to suppose an inborn propensity to mischief. Was he not the author of this new evil? His motives and his means were equally inscrutable, but their inscrutability might flow from her own defects in discernment and knowledge, and time might supply her defects in this as in former instances.

These images were casual. The causes of evil were seldom contemplated. Her mind was rarely at liberty to wander from reflection on her irremediable loss. Frequently, when confused by distressful recollections, she would detect herself going to her father's chamber. Often his well-known accents would ring in her ears, and the momentary impulse would be to answer his calls. Her reluctance to sit down to her meals without her usual companion could scarcely be surmounted.

In this state of mind, the image of the only friend who survived, or whose destiny, at least, was doubtful, occurred to her. She sunk into fits of deeper abstraction and dissolved away in tears of more agonizing tenderness. A week after her father's interment, she shut herself up in her chamber, to torment herself with fruitless remembrances. The name of Sophia Westwyn was pronounced, and the ditty that solemnized their parting was sung. Now, more than formerly, she became sensible of the loss of that portrait which had been deposited in the hands of M'Crea as a pledge. As soon as her change of fortune had supplied her with the means of redeeming it, she hastened to M'Crea for that end. To her unspeakable disappointment, he was absent from the city; he had taken a long journey, and the exact period of his return could not be ascertained. His clerks refused to deliver the picture, or even, by searching, to discover whether it was still in their master's possession. This application had frequently and lately been repeated, but without success; M'Crea had not yet returned, and his family were equally in the dark as to the day on which his return might be expected.

She determined, on this occasion, to renew her visit. Her incessant disappointments had almost extinguished hope, and she made inquiries at his door, with a faltering accent and sinking heart. These emotions were changed into surprise and delight, when answer was made that he had just arrived. She was instantly conducted into his presence.

The countenance of M'Crea easily denoted that his visitant was by no means acceptable. There was a mixture of embarrassment and sullenness in his air, which was far from being diminished when the purpose of this visit was explained. Constantia reminded him of the offer and acceptance of this pledge, and of the conditions with which the transaction was accompanied.

He acknowledged, with some hesitation, that a promise had been given to retain the pledge until it were in her power to redeem it; but the long delay, the urgency of his own wants, and particularly the ill treatment which he conceived himself to have suffered in the transaction respecting the forged note, had, in his own opinion, absolved him from this promise. He had therefore sold the picture to a goldsmith, for as much as the gold about it was worth.

This information produced, in the heart of Constantia, a contest between indignation and sorrow, that for a time debarred her from speech. She stifled the anger that was, at length, rising to her lips, and calmly inquired to whom the picture had been sold.

M'Crea answered that for his part he had little dealings in gold and silver, but every thing of that kind which fell to his share he transacted with Mr. D——. This person was one of the most eminent of his profession. His character and place of abode were universally known. The only expedient that remained was to apply to him, and to ascertain, forthwith, the destiny of the picture. It was too probable that, when separated from its case, the portrait was thrown away or destroyed, as a mere encumbrance, but the truth was too momentous to be made the sport of mere probability. She left the house of M'Crea, and hastened to that of the goldsmith.

The circumstance was easily recalled to his remembrance. It was true that such a picture had been offered for sale, and that he had purchased it. The workmanship was curious, and he felt unwilling to destroy it. He therefore hung it up in his shop and indulged the hope that a purchaser would some time be attracted by the mere beauty of the toy.

Constantia's hopes were revived by these tidings, and she earnestly inquired if it were still in his possession.

"No. A young gentleman had entered his shop some months before: the picture had caught his fancy, and he had given a price which the artist owned he should not have demanded, had he not been encouraged by the eagerness which the gentleman betrayed to possess it."

"Who was this gentleman? Had there been any previous acquaintance between them? What was his name, his profession, and where was he to be found?"

"Really," the goldsmith answered, "he was ignorant respecting all those particulars. Previously to this purchase, the gentleman had sometimes entered his shop; but he did not recollect to have since seen him. He was unacquainted with his name and his residence."

"What appeared to be his motives for purchasing this picture?"

"The customer appeared highly pleased with it. Pleasure, rather than surprise, seemed to be produced by the sight of it. If I were permitted to judge," continued the artist, "I should imagine that the young man was acquainted with the original. To say the truth, I hinted as much at the time, and I did not see that he discouraged the supposition. Indeed, I cannot conceive how the picture could otherwise have gained any value in his eyes."

This only heightened the eagerness of Constantia to trace the footsteps of the youth. It was obvious to suppose some communication or connection between her friend and this purchaser. She repeated her inquiries, and the goldsmith, after some consideration, said, "Why, on second-thoughts, I seem to have some notion of having seen a figure like that of my customer go into a lodging-house in Front Street, some time before I met with him at my shop."

The situation of this house being satisfactorily described, and the artist being able to afford her no further information, except as to stature and guise, she took her leave. There were two motives impelling her to prosecute her search after this person, — the desire of regaining this portrait and of procuring tidings of her friend. Involved as she was in ignorance, it was impossible to conjecture how far this incident would be subservient to these inestimable purposes. To procure an interview with this stranger was the first measure which prudence suggested.

She knew not his name or his person. He was once seen entering a lodging-house. Thither she must immediately repair; but how to introduce herself, how to describe the person of whom she was in search, she knew not. She was beset with embarrassments and difficulties. While her attention was entangled by these, she proceeded unconsciously on her way, and stopped not until she reached the mansion that had been described. Here she paused to collect her thoughts.

She found no relief in deliberation. Every moment added to her perplexity and indecision. Irresistibly impelled by her wishes, she at length, in a mood that partook of desperate, advanced to the door and knocked. The summons was immediately obeyed by a woman of decent appearance. A pause ensued, which Constantia at length terminated by a request to see the mistress of the house.

The lady courteously answered that she was the person, and immediately ushered her visitant into an apartment. Constantia being seated, the lady waited for the disclosure of her message. To prolong the silence was only to multiply embarrassments. She reverted to the state of her feelings, and saw that they flowed from inconsistency and folly. One vigorous effort was sufficient to restore her to composure and self-command.

She began with apologizing for a visit unpreceded by an introduction. The object of her inquiries was a person with whom it was of the utmost moment that she should procure a meeting, but whom, by an unfortunate concurrence of circumstances, she was unable to describe by the usual incidents of name and profession. Her knowledge was confined to his external appearance, and to the probability of his being an inmate of this house at the beginning of the year. She then proceeded to describe his person and dress.

"It is true," said the lady; "such a one as you describe has boarded in this house. His name was Martynne. I have good reason to remember him, for he lived with me three months, and then left the country without paying for his board."

"He has gone, then?" said Constantia, greatly discouraged by these tidings.

"Yes. He was a man of specious manners and loud pretensions. He came from England, bringing with him forged recommendatory letters, and, after passing from one end of the country to the other, contracting debts which he never paid and making bargains which he never fulfilled, he suddenly disappeared. It is likely that he has returned to Europe."

"Had he no kindred, no friends, no companions?"

"He found none here. He made pretences to alliances in England, which better information has, I believe, since shown to be false."

This was the sum of the information procurable from this source. Constantia was unable to conceal her chagrin. These symptoms were observed by the lady, whose curiosity was awakened in turn. Questions were obliquely started, inviting Constantia to a disclosure of her thoughts. No advantage would arise from confidence, and the guest, after a few minutes of abstraction and silence, rose to take her leave.

During this conference, some one appeared to be negligently sporting with the keys of a harpsichord, in the next apartment. The notes were too irregular and faint to make a forcible impression on the ear. In the present state of her mind, Constantia was merely conscious of the sound, in the intervals of conversation. Having arisen from her seat, her anxiety to obtain some information that might lead to the point she wished made her again pause. She endeavoured to invent some new interrogatory better suited to her purpose than those which had already been employed. A silence on both sides ensued.

During this interval, the unseen musician suddenly refrained from rambling, and glided into notes of some refinement and complexity. The cadence was aerial; but a thunderbolt, falling at her feet, would not have communicated a more visible shock to the senses of Constantia. A glance that denoted a tumult of soul bordering on distraction was now fixed upon the door that led into the room from whence the harmony proceeded. Instantly the cadence was revived, and some accompanying voice was heard to warble, –

> "Ah! far beyond this world of woes
> We meet to part, – to part no more."

Joy and grief, in their sudden onset and their violent extremes, approached so nearly in their influence on human beings as scarce to be distinguished. Constantia's frame was still enfeebled by her recent distresses. The torrent of emotion was too abrupt and too vehement. Her faculties were overwhelmed, and she sunk upon the floor motionless and without sense, but not till she had faintly articulated, –

"My God! My God! This is a joy unmerited and too great."

CHAPTER XXIII.

I MUST be forgiven if I now introduce myself on the stage. Sophia Westwyn is the friend of Constantia, and the writer of this narrative. So far as my fate was connected with that of my friend, it is worthy to be known. That connection has constituted the joy and misery of my existence, and has prompted me to undertake this task.

I assume no merit from the desire of knowledge and superiority to temptation. There is little of which I can boast; but that little I derived, instrumentally, from Constantia. Poor as my attainments are, it is to her that I am indebted for them all. Life itself was the gift of her father, but my virtue and felicity are her gifts. That I am neither indigent nor profligate, flows from her bounty.

I am not unaware of the divine superintendence, – of the claims upon my gratitude and service which pertain to my God. I know that all physical and moral agents are merely instrumental to the purpose that he wills; but, though the great Author of being and felicity must not be forgotten, it is neither possible nor just to overlook the claims upon our love with which our fellow-beings are invested.

The supreme love does not absorb, but chastens and enforces, all subordinate affections. In proportion to the rectitude of my perceptions and the ardour of my piety, must I clearly discern and fervently love the excellence discovered in my fellow-beings, and industriously promote their improvement and felicity.

From my infancy to my seventeenth year, I lived in the house of Mr. Dudley. On the day of my birth I was deserted by my mother. Her temper was more akin to that of tigress than woman. Yet that is unjust; for beasts cherish their offspring. No natures but human are capable of that depravity which makes insensible to the claims of innocence and helplessness.

But let me not recall her to memory. Have I not enough of sorrow? Yet to omit my causes of disquiet, the unprecedented forlornness of my condition, and the persecutions of an unnatural parent, would be to leave my character a problem, and the sources of my love of Miss Dudley unexplored. Yet I must not dwell upon that complication of iniquities, that savage ferocity and inextinguishable hatred of me, which characterized my unhappy mother.

I was not safe under the protection of Mr. Dudley, nor happy in the caresses of his daughter. My mother asserted the privilege of that relation: she laboured for years to obtain the control of my person and actions, to snatch me from a peaceful and chaste asylum, and detain me in her own house, where, indeed, I should not have been in want of raiment and food, but where ——

O my mother! Let me not dishonour thy name! Yet it is not in my power to enhance thy infamy. Thy crimes, unequalled as they were, were perhaps expiated by thy penitence. Thy offences are too well known; but perhaps they who witnessed thy freaks of intoxication, thy defiance of public shame, the enormity of thy pollutions, the infatuation that made thee glory in the pursuit of a loathsome and detestable trade, may be strangers to the remorse and the abstinence which accompanied the close of thy ignominious life.

For ten years was my peace incessantly molested by the menaces or machinations of my mother. The longer she meditated my destruction, the more tenacious of her purpose and indefatigable in her efforts she became. That my mind was harassed with perpetual alarms was not enough. The fame and tranquillity of Mr. Dudley and his daughter were hourly assailed. My mother resigned herself to the impulses of malignity and rage. Headlong passions, and a vigorous though perverted understanding, were hers. Hence, her stratagems to undermine the reputation of my protector, and to bereave him of domestic comfort, were subtle and profound. Had she not herself been careless of that good which she endeavoured to wrest from others, her artifices could scarcely have been frustrated.

In proportion to the hazard which accrued to my protector and friend, the more ardent their zeal in my defence and their affection for my person became. They watched over me with ineffable solicitude. At all hours and in every occupation, I was the companion of Constantia. All my wants were supplied in the same proportion as hers. The tenderness of Mr. Dudley seemed equally divided between us. I partook of his instructions, and the means of every intellectual and personal gratification were lavished upon me.

The speed of my mother's career in infamy was at length slackened. She left New York, which had long been the theatre of her vices. Actuated by a new caprice, she determined to travel through the Southern States. Early indulgence was the cause of her ruin, but her parents had given her the embellishments of a fashionable education. She delighted to assume all parts, and personate the most opposite characters. She now resolved to carry a new name, and the mask of virtue, into scenes hitherto unvisited.

She journeyed as far as Charleston. Here she met an inexperienced youth, lately arrived from England, and in possession of an ample fortune. Her speciousness and artifices seduced him into a precipitate marriage. Her true character, however, could not be long concealed by herself, and her vices had been too conspicuous for her long to escape recognition. Her husband was infatuated by her blandishments. To abandon her, or to contemplate her depravity with unconcern, were equally beyond his power. Romantic in his sentiments, his fortitude was unequal to his disappointments, and he speedily sunk into the grave. By a similar refinement in generosity, he bequeathed to her his property.

With this accession of wealth, she returned to her ancient abode. The mask lately worn seemed preparing to be thrown aside, and her profligate habits to be resumed with more eagerness than ever; but an unexpected and total revolution was effected, by the exhortations of a Methodist divine. Her heart seemed, on a sudden, to be remoulded, her vices and the abettors of them were abjured, she shut out the intrusions of society, and prepared to expiate, by the rigours of abstinence and the bitterness of tears, the offences of her past life.

In this, as in her former career, she was unacquainted with restraint and moderation. Her remorses gained strength in proportion as she cherished them. She brooded over the images of her guilt, till the possibility of forgiveness and remission disappeared. Her treatment of her daughter and her husband constituted the chief source of her torment. Her awakened conscience refused her a momentary respite from its persecutions. Her thoughts became, by rapid degrees, tempestuous and gloomy, and it was at length evident that her condition was maniacal.

In this state, she was to me an object, no longer of terror, but compassion. She was surrounded by hirelings, devoid of personal attachment, and anxious only to convert her misfortunes to their own advantage. This evil it was my duty to obviate. My presence, for a time, only enhanced the vehemence of her malady; but at length it was only by my attendance and soothing that she was diverted from the fellest purposes. Shocking execrations and outrages, resolutions and efforts to destroy herself and those around her, were sure to take place in my absence. The moment I appeared before her, her fury abated, her gesticulations were becalmed, and her voice exerted only in incoherent and pathetic lamentations.

These scenes, though so different from those which I had formerly been condemned to witness, were scarcely less excruciating. The friendship of Constantia Dudley was my only consolation. She took up her abode with me, and shared with me every disgustful and perilous office which my mother's insanity prescribed.

Of this consolation, however, it was my fate to be bereaved. My mother's state was deplorable, and no remedy hitherto employed was effacious. A voyage to England was conceived likely to benefit, by change of temperature and scenes, and by the opportunity it would afford of trying the superior skill of English physicians. This scheme, after various struggles on my part, was adopted. It was detestable to my imagination, because it severed me from that friend in whose existence mine was involved, and without whose participation knowledge lost its attractions and society became a torment.

The prescriptions of my duty could not be disguised or disobeyed, and we parted. A mutual engagement was formed to record every sentiment and relate every event that happened in the life of either, and no opportunity of communicating information was to be omitted. This engagement was punctually performed on my part. I sought out every method of conveyance to my friend, and took infinite pains to procure tidings from her; but all were ineffectual.

My mother's malady declined, but was succeeded by a pulmonary disease, which threatened her speedy destruction. By the restoration of her understanding, the purpose of her voyage was obtained, and my impatience to return, which the inexplicable and ominous silence of my friend daily increased, prompted me to exert all my powers of persuasion to induce her to revisit America.

My mother's frenzy was a salutary crisis in her moral history. She looked back upon her past conduct with unspeakable loathing, but this retrospect only invigorated her devotion and her virtue; but the thought of returning to the scene of her unhappiness and infamy could not be endured. Besides, life, in her eyes, possessed considerable attractions, and her physicians flattered her with recovery from her present disease, if she would change the atmosphere of England for that of Languedoc and Naples.

I followed her with murmurs and reluctance. To desert her in her present critical state would have been inhuman. My mother's aversions and attachments, habits and views, were dissonant with my own. Conformity of sentiments and impressions of maternal tenderness did not exist to bind us to each other. My attendance was assiduous, but it was the sense of duty that rendered my attendance a supportable task.

Her decay was eminently gradual. No time seemed to diminish her appetite for novelty and change. During three years we traversed every part of France, Switzerland, and Italy. I could not but attend to surrounding scenes, and mark the progress of the mighty revolution, whose effects, like agitation in a fluid, gradually spread from Paris, the centre, over the face of the neighbouring kingdoms; but there passed not a day or an hour in which the image of Constantia was not recalled, in which the most pungent regrets were not felt at the inexplicable silence which had been observed by her, and the most vehement longings indulged to return to my native country. My exertions to ascertain her condition by indirect means, by interrogating natives of America with whom I chanced to meet, were unwearied, but, for a long period, ineffectual.

During this pilgrimage, Rome was thrice visited. My mother's indisposition was hastening to a crisis, and she formed the resolution of closing her life at the bottom of Vesuvius. We stopped, for the sake of a few days' repose, at Rome. On the morning after our arrival, I accompanied some friends to view the public edifices. Casting my eyes over the vast and ruinous interior of the Coliseum, my attention was fixed by the figure of a young man whom, after a moment's pause, I recollected to have seen in the streets of New York. At a distance from home, mere community of country is no inconsiderable bond of affection. The social spirit prompts us to cling even to inanimate objects, when they remind us of ancient fellowships and juvenile attachments.

A servant was dispatched to summon this stranger, who recognized a countrywoman with a pleasure equal to that which I had received. On nearer view, this person, whose name was Courtland, did not belie my favourable prepossessions. Our intercourse was soon established on a footing of confidence and intimacy.

The destiny of Constantia was always uppermost in my thoughts. This person's acquaintance was originally sought chiefly in the hope of obtaining from him some information respecting my friend. On inquiry, I discovered that he had left his native city seven months after me. Having tasked his recollection and compared a number of facts, the name of Dudley at length recurred to him. He had casually heard the history of Craig's imposture and its consequences. These were now related as circumstantially as a memory occupied by subsequent incidents enabled him. The tale had been told to him, in a domestic circle which he was accustomed to frequent, by the person who purchased Mr. Dudley's lute and restored it to its previous owner on the conditions formerly mentioned.

This tale filled me with anguish and doubt. My impatience to search out this unfortunate girl, and share with her her sorrows or relieve them, was anew excited by this mournful intelligence. That

Constantia Dudley was reduced to beggary was too abhorrent to my feelings to receive credit; yet the sale of her father's property, comprising even his furniture and clothing, seemed to prove that she had fallen even to this depth. This enabled me in some degree to account for her silence. Her generous spirit would induce her to conceal misfortunes from her friend which no communication would alleviate. It was possible that she had selected some new abode, and that, in consequence, the letters I had written, and which amounted to volumes, had never reached her hands.

My mother's state would not suffer me to obey the impulse of my heart. Her frame was verging towards dissolution. Courtland's engagements allowed him to accompany us to Naples, and here the long series of my mother's pilgrimages closed in death. Her obsequies were no sooner performed, than I determined to set out on my long-projected voyage. My mother's property, which, in consequence of her decease, devolved upon me, was not inconsiderable. There is scarcely any good so dear to a rational being as competence. I was not unacquainted with its benefits, but this acquisition was valuable to me chiefly as it enabled me to reunite my fate to that of Constantia.

Courtland was my countryman and friend. He was destitute of fortune, and had been led to Europe by the spirit of adventure, and partly on a mercantile project. He had made sale of his property on advantageous terms, in the ports of France, and resolved to consume the produce in examining this scene of heroic exploits and memorable revolutions. His slender stock, though frugally and even parsimoniously administered, was nearly exhausted; and, at the time of our meeting at Rome, he was making reluctant preparations to return.

Sufficient opportunity was afforded us, in an unrestrained and domestic intercourse of three months, which succeeded our Roman interview, to gain a knowledge of each other. There was that conformity of tastes and views between us which could scarcely fail, at an age and in a situation like ours, to give birth to tenderness. My resolution to hasten to America was peculiarly unwelcome to my friend. He had offered to be my companion, but this offer my regard to his interest obliged me to decline; but I was willing to compensate him for this denial, as well as to gratify my own heart, by an immediate marriage.

So long a residence in England and Italy had given birth to friendships and connections of the dearest kind. I had no view but to spend my life with Courtland, in the midst of my maternal kindred, who were English. A voyage to America and reunion with Constantia were previously indispensable; but I hoped that my friend might be prevailed upon, and that her disconnected situation would permit her to return with me to Europe. If this end could not be accomplished, it was my inflexible purpose to live and to die with her. Suitably to this arrangement, Courtland was to repair to London, and wait patiently till I should be able to rejoin him there, or to summon him to meet me in America.

A week after my mother's death, I became a wife, and embarked the next day, at Naples, in a Ragusan ship, destined for New York. The voyage was tempestuous and tedious. The vessel was necessitated to make a short stay at Toulon. The state of that city, however, then in possession of the English and besieged by the revolutionary forces, was adverse to commercial views. Happily, we resumed our voyage on the day previous to that on which the place was evacuated by the British. Our seasonable departure rescued us from witnessing a scene of horrors of which the history of former wars furnishes us with few examples.

A cold and boisterous navigation awaited us. My palpitations and inquietudes augmented as we approached the American coast. I shall not forget the sensations which I experienced at the sight of the Beacon at Sandy Hook. It was first seen at midnight, in a stormy and beclouded atmosphere, emerging from the waves, whose fluctuation allowed it, for some time, to be visible only by fits. This token of approaching land affected me as much as if I had reached the threshold of my friend's dwelling.

At length we entered the port, and I viewed, with high-raised but inexplicable feelings, objects with which I had been from infancy familiar. The flagstaff erected on the Battery recalled to my imagination the pleasures of the evening and morning walks which I had taken on that spot with the lost Constantia. The dream was fondly cherished, that the figure which I saw loitering along the terrace was hers.

On disembarking, I gazed at every female passenger, in hope that it was she whom I sought. An absence of three years had obliterated from my memory none of the images which attended me on my departure.

CHAPTER XXIV.

AFTER a night of repose rather than sleep, I began the search after my friend. I went to the house which the Dudleys formerly inhabited, and which had been the asylum of my infancy. It was now occupied by strangers, by whom no account could be given of its former tenants. I obtained directions to the owner of the house. He was equally unable to satisfy my curiosity. The purchase had been made at a public sale, and terms had been settled, not with Dudley, but with the sheriff.

It is needless to say that the history of Craig's imposture and its consequences were confirmed by every one who resided at that period in New York. The Dudleys were well remembered, and their disappearance, immediately after their fall, had been generally noticed; but whither they had retired was a problem which no one was able to solve.

This evasion was strange. By what motives the Dudleys were induced to change their ancient abode could be vaguely guessed. My friend's grandfather was a native of the West Indies. Descendants of the same stock still resided in Tobago. They might be affluent, and to them it was possible that Mr. Dudley, in this change of fortune, had betaken himself for relief. This was a mournful expedient, since it would raise a barrier between my friend and myself scarcely to be surmounted.

Constantia's mother was stolen by Mr. Dudley from a convent at Amiens. There were no affinities, therefore, to draw them to France. Her grandmother was a native of Baltimore, of a family of some note, by name Ridgeley. This family might still exist, and have either afforded an asylum to the Dudleys, or, at least, be apprized of their destiny. It was obvious to conclude that they no longer existed within the precincts of New York. A journey to Baltimore was the next expedient.

This journey was made in the depth of winter, and by the speediest conveyance. I made no more than a day's sojourn in Philadelphia.

The epidemic by which that city had been lately ravaged, I had not heard of till my arrival in America. Its devastations were then painted to my fancy in the most formidable colours. A few months only had elapsed since its extinction, and I expected to see numerous marks of misery and depopulation.

To my no small surprise, however, no vestiges of this calamity were to be discerned. All houses were open, all streets thronged, and all faces thoughtless or busy. The arts and the amusements of life seemed as sedulously cultivated as ever. Little did I then think what had been, and what at that moment was, the condition of my friend. I stopped for the sake of respite from fatigue, and did not, therefore, pass much time in the streets. Perhaps, had I walked seasonably abroad, we might have encountered each other, and thus have saved ourselves from a thousand anxieties.

At Baltimore I made myself known, without the formality of introduction, to the Ridgeleys. They acknowledged their relationship to Mr. Dudley, but professed absolute ignorance of his fate. Indirect intercourse only had been maintained, formerly, by Dudley with his mother's kindred. They had heard of his misfortune a twelvemonth after it happened; but what measures had been subsequently pursued, their kinsman had not thought proper to inform them.

The failure of this expedient almost bereft me of hope. Neither my own imagination nor the Ridgeleys could suggest any new mode by which my purpose was likely to be accomplished. To leave America without obtaining the end of my visit could not be thought of without agony; and yet the continuance of my stay promised me no relief from my uncertainties.

On this theme I ruminated without ceasing. I recalled every conversation and incident of former times, and sought in them a clue by which my present conjectures might be guided. One night, immersed alone in my chamber, my thoughts were thus employed. My train of meditation was, on this occasion, new. From the review of particulars from which no satisfaction had hitherto been gained, I passed to a vague and comprehensive retrospect.

Mr. Dudley's early life, his profession of a painter, his zeal in this pursuit, and his reluctance to quit it, were remembered. Would he not revert to this profession when other means of subsistence were gone? It is true, similar obstacles with those which had formerly occasioned his resort to a different path existed at present, and no painter of his name was to be found in Philadelphia, Baltimore, or New York. But would it not occur to him, that the patronage denied to his skill by the frugal and unpolished habits of his countrymen might, with more probability of success, be sought from the opulence and luxury of London? Nay, had he not once affirmed, in my hearing, that, if he ever were reduced to poverty, this was the method he would pursue?

This conjecture was too bewitching to be easily dismissed. Every new reflection augmented its force. I was suddenly raised by it from the deepest melancholy to the region of lofty and gay hopes. Happiness, of which I had begun to imagine myself irretrievably bereft, seemed once more to approach within my reach. Constantia would not only be found, but be met in the midst of those comforts which her father's skill could not fail to procure, and on that very stage where I most desired to encounter her. Mr. Dudley had many friends and associates of his youth in London. Filial duty had repelled their importunities to fix his abode in Europe, when summoned home by his father. On his father's death these solicitations had been renewed, but were disregarded for reasons which he, afterwards, himself confessed were fallacious. That they would a third time be preferred, and would regulate his conduct, seemed to me incontestable.

I regarded with wonder and deep regret the infatuation that had hitherto excluded these images from my understanding and my memory. How many dangers and toils had I endured since my embarkation at Naples, to the present moment! How many lingering minutes had I told since my first interview with Courtland! All were owing to my own stupidity. Had my present thoughts been seasonably suggested, I might long since have been restored to the embraces of my friend, without the necessity of an hour's separation from my husband.

These were evils to be repaired as far as it was possible. Nothing now remained but to procure a passage to Europe. For this end diligent inquiries were immediately set on foot. A vessel was found, which, in a few weeks, would set out upon the voyage. Having bespoken a conveyance, it was incumbent on me to sustain with patience the unwelcome delay.

Meanwhile, my mind, delivered from the dejection and perplexities that lately haunted it, was capable of some attention to surrounding objects. I marked the peculiarities of manners and language in my new abode, and studied the effects which a political and religious system so opposite to that with which I had conversed in Italy and Switzerland had produced. I found that the difference between Europe and America lay chiefly in this: – that, in the former, all things tended to extremes, whereas, in the latter, all things tended to the same level. Genius, and virtue, and happiness, on these shores, were distinguished by a sort of mediocrity. Conditions were less unequal, and men were strangers to the heights of enjoyment and the depths of misery to which the inhabitants of Europe are accustomed.

I received friendly notice and hospitable treatment from the Ridgeleys. These people were mercantile and plodding in their habits. I found in their social circle little exercise for the sympathies of my heart, and willingly accepted their aid to enlarge the sphere of my observation.

About a week before my intended embarkation, and when suitable preparation had been made for that event, a lady arrived in town, who was cousin to my Constantia. She had frequently been mentioned in favourable terms in my hearing. She had passed her life in a rural abode with her father, who cultivated his own domain, lying forty miles from Baltimore.

On an offer being made to introduce us to each other, I consented to know one whose chief recommendation in my eyes consisted in her affinity to Constantia Dudley. I found an artless and attractive female, unpolished and undepraved by much intercourse with mankind. At first sight, I was powerfully struck by the resemblances of her features to those of my friend, which sufficiently denoted their connection with a common stock.

The first interview afforded mutual satisfaction. On our second meeting, discourse insensibly led to the mention of Miss Dudley, and of the design which had brought me to America. She was deeply affected by the earnestness with which I expatiated on her cousin's merits, and by the proofs which my conduct had given of unlimited attachment.

I dwelt immediately on the measures which I had hitherto ineffectually pursued to trace her footsteps, and detailed the grounds of my present belief that we should meet in London. During this recital, my companion sighed and wept. When I finished my tale, her tears, instead of ceasing, flowed with new vehemence. This appearance excited some surprise, and I ventured to ask the cause of her grief.

"Alas!" she replied, "I am personally a stranger to my cousin, but her character has been amply displayed to me by one who knew her well. I weep to think how much she has suffered. How much excellence we have lost!"

"Nay," said I, "all her sufferings will, I hope, be compensated, and I by no means consider her as lost. If my search in London be unsuccessful, then shall I indeed despair."

"Despair, then, already," said my sobbing companion, "for your search will be unsuccessful. How I feel for your disappointment! but it cannot be known too soon. My cousin is dead!"

These tidings were communicated with tokens of sincerity and sorrow that left me no room to doubt that they were believed by the relater. My own emotions were suspended till interrogations had obtained a knowledge of her reasons for crediting this fatal event, and till she had explained the time and manner of her death. A friend of Miss Ridgeley's father had witnessed the devastations of the yellow fever in Philadelphia. He was apprized of the relationship that subsisted between his friend and the Dudleys. He gave a minute and circumstantial account of the arts of Craig. He mentioned the removal of my friends to Philadelphia, their obscure and indigent life, and, finally, their falling victims to the pestilence.

He related the means by which he became apprized of their fate, and drew a picture of their death, surpassing all that imagination can conceive of shocking and deplorable. The quarter where they lived was nearly desolate. Their house was shut up, and, for a time, imagined to be uninhabited. Some suspicions being awakened in those who superintended the burial of the dead, the house was entered, and the father and child discovered to be dead. The former was stretched upon his wretched pallet, while the daughter was found on the floor of the lower room, in a state that denoted the sufferance not only of disease, but of famine.

This tale was false. Subsequent discoveries proved this to be a detestable artifice of Craig, who, stimulated by incurable habits, had invented these disasters, for the purpose of enhancing the opinion of his humanity, and of furthering his views on the fortune and daughter of Mr. Ridgeley.

Its falsehood, however, I had as yet no means of ascertaining. I received it as true, and at once dismissed all my claims upon futurity. All hope of happiness, in this mutable and sublunary scene, was fled. Nothing remained but to join my friend in a world where woes are at an end and virtue finds its recompense. "Surely," said I, "there will some time be a close to calamity and discord. To those whose lives have been blameless, but harassed by inquietudes to which not their own but the errors of others have given birth, a fortress will hereafter be assigned unassailable by change, impregnable to sorrow.

"O my ill-fated Constantia! I will live to cherish thy remembrance, and to emulate thy virtue. I will endure the privation of thy friendship and the vicissitudes that shall befall me, and draw my consolation and courage from the foresight of no distant close to this terrestrial scene, and of ultimate and everlasting union with thee."

This consideration, though it kept me from confusion and despair, could not, but with the healing aid of time, render me tranquil or strenuous. My strength was unequal to the struggle of my passions. The ship in which I engaged to embark could not wait for my restoration to health, and I was left behind.

Mary Ridgeley was artless and affectionate. She saw that her society was dearer to me than that of any other, and was therefore seldom willing to leave my chamber. Her presence, less on her own account than by reason of her personal resemblance and her affinity by birth to Constantia, was a powerful solace.

I had nothing to detain me longer in America. I was anxious to change my present lonely state, for the communion of those friends in England, and the performance of those duties, which were left to me. I was informed that a British packet would shortly sail from New York. My frame was sunk into greater weakness than I had felt at any former period; and I conceived that to return to New York by water was more commodious than to perform the journey by land.

This arrangement was likewise destined to be disappointed. One morning I visited, according to my custom, Mary Ridgeley. I found her in a temper somewhat inclined to gayety. She rallied me, with great archness, on the care with which I had concealed from her a tender engagement into which I had lately entered.

I supposed myself to comprehend her allusion, and therefore answered that accident, rather than design, had made me silent on the subject of marriage. She had hitherto known me by no appellation but Sophia Courtland. I had thought it needless to inform her that I was indebted for my name to my husband, Courtland being his name.

"All that," said my friend, "I know already. And so you sagely think that my knowledge goes no farther than that? We are not bound to love our husbands longer than their lives. There is no crime, I believe, in preferring the living to the dead; and most heartily do I congratulate you on your present choice."

"What mean you? I confess, your discourse surpasses my comprehension."

At that moment the bell at the door rung a loud peal. Miss Ridgeley hastened down at this signal, saying, with much significance, –

"I am a poor hand at solving a riddle. Here comes one who, if I mistake it not, will find no difficulty in clearing up your doubts."

Presently she came up, and said, with a smile of still greater archness, "Here is a young gentleman, a friend of mine, to whom I must have the pleasure of introducing you. He has come for the special purpose of solving my riddle." I attended her to the parlour without hesitation.

She presented me, with great formality, to a youth, whose appearance did not greatly prepossess me in favour of his judgment. He approached me with an air supercilious and ceremonious; but the moment he caught a glance at my face, he shrunk back, visibly confounded and embarrassed. A pause ensued, in which Miss Ridgeley had opportunity to detect the error into which she had been led by the vanity of this young man.

"How now, Mr. Martynne!" said my friend, in a tone of ridicule; "is it possible you do not know the lady who is the queen of your affections, the tender and indulgent fair one whose portrait you carry in your bosom, and whose image you daily and nightly bedew with your tears and kisses?"

Mr. Martynne's confusion, instead of being subdued by his struggle, only grew more conspicuous; and, after a few incoherent speeches and apologies, during which he carefully avoided encountering my eyes, he hastily departed.

I applied to my friend, with great earnestness, for an explanation of this scene. It seems that, in the course of conversation with him on the preceding day, he had suffered a portrait which hung at his breast to catch Miss Ridgeley's eye. On her betraying a desire to inspect it more nearly, he readily produced it. My image had been too well copied by the artist not to be instantly recognised.

She concealed her knowledge of the original, and, by questions well adapted to the purpose, easily drew from him confessions that this was the portrait of his mistress. He let fall sundry innuendoes and surmises, tending to impress her with a notion of the rank, fortune, and intellectual accomplishments of the nymph, and particularly of the doting fondness and measureless confidence with which she regarded him.

Her imperfect knowledge of my situation left her in some doubts as to the truth of these pretensions, and she was willing to ascertain the truth by bringing about an interview. To guard against evasions and artifice in the lover, she carefully concealed from him her knowledge of the original, and merely pretended that a friend of hers was far more beautiful than her whom this picture represented. She added, that she expected a visit from her friend the next morning, and was willing, by showing her to Mr. Martynne, to convince him how much he was mistaken in supposing the perfections of his mistress unrivalled.

CHAPTER XXV.

MARTYNNE, while he expressed his confidence that the experiment would only confirm his triumph, readily assented to the proposal, and the interview above described took place, accordingly, the next morning. Had he not been taken by surprise, it is likely the address of a man who possessed no contemptible powers would have extricated him from some of his embarrassment.

That my portrait should be in the possession of one whom I had never before seen, and whose character and manners entitled him to no respect, was a source of some surprise. This mode of multiplying faces is extremely prevalent in this age, and was eminently characteristic of those with whom I had associated in different parts of Europe. The nature of my thoughts had modified my features into an expression which my friends were pleased to consider as a model for those who desired to personify the genius of suffering and resignation.

Hence, among those whose religion permitted their devotion to a picture of a female, the symbols of their chosen deity were added to features and shape that resembled mine. My own caprice, as well as that of others, always dictated a symbolical, and, in every new instance, a different accompaniment of this kind. Hence was offered the means of tracing the history of that picture which Martynne possessed.

It had been accurately examined by Miss Ridgeley, and her description of the frame in which it was placed instantly informed me that it was the same which, at our parting, I left in the possession of Constantia. My friend and myself were desirous of employing the skill of a Saxon painter, by name Eckstein. Each of us were drawn by him, she with the cincture of Venus, and I with the crescent of Dian. This symbol was still conspicuous on the brow of that image which Miss Ridgeley had examined, and served to identify the original proprietor.

This circumstance tended to confirm my fears that Constantia was dead, since that she would part with this picture during her life was not to be believed. It was of little moment to discover how it came into the hands of the present possessor. Those who carried her remains to the grave had probably torn it from her neck and afterwards disposed of it for money.

By whatever means, honest or illicit, it had been acquired by Martynne, it was proper that it should be restored to me. It was valuable to me, because it had been the property of one whom I loved, and it might prove highly injurious to my fame and my happiness, as the tool of this man's vanity and the attestor of his falsehood. I therefore wrote him a letter, acquainting him with my reasons for desiring the repossession of this picture, and offering a price for it at least double its value as a mere article of traffic. Martynne accepted the terms. He transmitted the picture, and with it a note, apologizing for the artifice of which he had been guilty, and mentioning, in order to justify his acceptance of the price which I had offered, that he had lately purchased it for an equal sum, of a goldsmith in Philadelphia.

This information suggested a new reflection. Constantia had engaged to preserve, for the use of her friend, copious and accurate memorials of her life. Copies of these were, on suitable occasions, to be transmitted to me during my residence abroad. These I had never received, but it was highly probably that her punctuality, in the performance of the first part of her engagement, had been equal to my own.

What, I asked, had become of these precious memorials? In the wreck of her property were these irretrievably engulfed? It was not probable that they had been wantonly destroyed. They had fallen, perhaps, into hands careless or unconscious of their value, or still lay, unknown and neglected, at the bottom of some closet or chest. Their recovery might be effected by vehement exertions, or by some miraculous accident. Suitable inquiries, carried on among those who were active in those scenes of calamity, might afford some clue by which the fate of the Dudleys, and the disposition of their property, might come into fuller light. These inquiries could be made only in Philadelphia, and thither, for that purpose, I now resolved to repair. There was still an interval of some weeks before the departure of the packet in which I proposed to embark.

Having returned to the capital, I devoted all my zeal to my darling project. My efforts, however, were without success. Those who administered charity and succour during that memorable season, and who survived, could remove none of my doubts, nor answer any of my inquiries. Innumerable tales, equally disastrous with those which Miss Ridgeley had heard, were related; but, for a considerable period, none of their circumstances were sufficiently accordant with the history of the Dudleys.

It is worthy of remark, in how many ways, and by what complexity of motives, human curiosity is awakened and knowledge obtained. By its connection with my darling purpose, every event in this history of the memorable pest was earnestly sought and deeply pondered. The powerful considerations which governed me made me slight those punctilious impediments which, in other circumstances, would have debarred me from intercourse with the immediate actors and observers. I found none who were unwilling to expatiate on this topic, or to communicate the knowledge they possessed. Their details were copious in particulars and vivid in minuteness. They exhibited the state of manners, the diversified effects of evil or heroic passions, and the endless forms which sickness and poverty assume in the obscure recesses of a commercial and populous city.

Some of these details are too precious to be lost. It is above all things necessary that we should be thoroughly acquainted with the condition of our fellow-beings. Justice and compassion are the fruit of knowledge. The misery that overspreads so large a part of mankind exists chiefly because those who are able to relieve it do not know that it exists. Forcibly to paint the evil, seldom fails to excite the virtue of the spectator and seduce him into wishes, at least, if not into exertions, of beneficence.

The circumstances in which I was placed were, perhaps, wholly singular. Hence, the knowledge I obtained was more comprehensive and authentic than was possessed by any one, even of the immediate actors or sufferers. This knowledge will not be useless to myself or to the world. The motives which dictated the present narrative will hinder me from relinquishing the pen till my fund of observation and experience be exhausted. Meanwhile, let me resume the thread of my tale.

The period allowed me before my departure was nearly expired, and my purpose seemed to be as far from its accomplishment as ever. One evening I visited a lady who was the widow of a physician whose disinterested exertions had cost him his life. She dwelt with pathetic earnestness on the particulars of her own distress, and listened with deep attention to the inquiries and doubts which I laid before her.

After a pause of consideration, she said that an incident like that related by me she had previously heard from one of her friends, whose name she mentioned. This person was one of those whose office consisted in searching out the sufferers, and affording them unsought and unsolicited relief. She was offering to introduce me to this person, when he entered the apartment.

After the usual compliments, my friend led the conversation as I wished. Between Mr. Thompson's tale and that related to Miss Ridgeley there was an obvious resemblance. The sufferers resided in an obscure alley. They had shut themselves up from all intercourse with their neighbours, and had died, neglected and unknown. Mr. Thompson was vested with the superintendence of this district, and had passed the house frequently without suspicion of its being tenanted.

He was at length informed, by one of those who conducted a hearse, that he had seen the window in the upper story of this house lifted and a female show herself. It was night, and the hearseman chanced to be passing the door. He immediately supposed that the person stood in need of his services, and stopped.

This procedure was comprehended by the person at the window, who, leaning out, addressed him in a broken and feeble voice. She asked him why he had not taken a different route, and upbraided him for inhumanity in leading his noisy vehicle past her door. She wanted repose, but the ceaseless rumbling of his wheels would not allow her the sweet respite of a moment.

This invective was singular, and uttered in a voice which united the utmost degree of earnestness with a feebleness that rendered it almost inarticulate. The man was at a loss for a suitable answer. His pause only increased the impatience of the person at the window, who called upon him, in a still more anxious tone, to proceed, and entreated him to avoid this alley for the future.

He answered that he must come whenever the occasion called him; that three persons now lay dead in this alley, and that he must be expeditious in their removal; but that he would return as seldom and make as little noise as possible.

He was interrupted by new exclamations and upbraidings. These terminated in a burst of tears, and assertions that God and man were her enemies, – that they were determined to destroy her; but she trusted that the time would come when their own experience would avenge her wrongs, and teach them some compassion for the misery of others. Saying this, she shut the window with violence, and retired from it, sobbing with a vehemence that could be distinctly overheard by him in the street.

He paused for some time, listening when this passion should cease. The habitation was slight, and he imagined that he heard her traversing the floor. While he stayed, she continued to vent her anguish in exclamations and sighs and passionate weeping. It did not appear that any other person was within.

Mr. Thompson, being next day informed of these incidents, endeavoured to enter the house; but his signals, though loud and frequently repeated, being unnoticed, he was obliged to gain admission by violence. An old man, and a female lovely in the midst of emaciation and decay, were discovered without signs of life. The death of the latter appeared to have been very recent.

In examining the house, no traces of other inhabitants were to be found. Nothing serviceable as food was discovered, but the remnants of mouldy bread scattered on a table. No information could be gathered from neighbours respecting the condition and name of these unfortunate people. They had taken possession of this house during the rage of this malady, and refrained from all communication with their neighbours.

There was too much resemblance between this and the story formerly heard, not to produce the belief that they related to the same persons. All that remained was to obtain directions to the proprietor of this dwelling, and exact from him all that he knew respecting his tenants.

I found in him a man of worth and affability. He readily related, that a man applied to him for the use of this house, and that the application was received. At the beginning of the pestilence, a numerous family inhabited this tenement, but had died in rapid succession. This new applicant was the first to apprize him of this circumstance, and appeared extremely anxious to enter on immediate possession.

It was intimated to him that danger would arise from the pestilential condition of the house. Unless cleansed and purified, disease would be unavoidably contracted. The inconvenience and hazard this applicant was willing to encounter, and, at length, hinted that no alternative was allowed him by his present landlord but to lie in the street or to procure some other abode.

"What was the external appearance of this person?"

"He was infirm, past the middle age, of melancholy aspect and indigent garb. A year had since elapsed, and more characteristic particulars had not been remarked, or were forgotten. The name had been mentioned, but, in the midst of more recent and momentous transactions, had vanished from remembrance. Dudley, or Dolby, or Hadley, seemed to approach more nearly than any other sounds."

Permission to inspect the house was readily granted. It had remained, since that period, unoccupied. The furniture and goods were scanty and wretched, and he did not care to endanger his safety by meddling with them. He believed that they had not been removed or touched.

I was insensible of any hazard which attended my visit, and, with the guidance of a servant, who felt as little apprehension as myself, hastened to the spot. I found nothing but tables and chairs. Clothing was nowhere to be seen. An earthen pot, without handle, and broken, stood upon the kitchen-hearth. No other implement or vessel for the preparation of food appeared.

These forlorn appearances were accounted for by the servant, by supposing the house to have been long since rifled of every thing worth the trouble of removal, by the villains who occupied the neighbouring houses, – this alley, it seems, being noted for the profligacy of its inhabitants.

When I reflected that a wretched hovel like this had been, probably, the last retreat of the Dudleys, when I painted their sufferings, of which the numberless tales of distress of which I had lately been an auditor enabled me to form an adequate conception, I felt as if to lie down and expire on the very spot where Constantia had fallen was the only sacrifice to friendship which time had left to me.

From this house I wandered to the field where the dead had been, promiscuously and by hundreds, interred. I counted the long series of graves, which were closely ranged, and, being recently levelled, exhibited the appearance of a harrowed field. Methought I could have given thousands to know in what spot the body of my friend lay, that I might moisten the sacred earth with my tears. Boards hastily nailed together formed the best receptacle which the exigencies of the time could grant to the dead. Many corpses were thrown into a single excavation, and all distinctions founded on merit and rank were obliterated. The father and child had been placed in the same cart and thrown into the same hole.

Despairing, by any longer stay in the city, to effect my purpose, and the period of my embarkation being near, I prepared to resume my journey. I should have set out the next day, but, a family with whom I had made acquaintance expecting to proceed to New York within a week, I consented to be their companion, and, for that end, to delay my departure.

Meanwhile, I shut myself up in my apartment, and pursued avocations that were adapted to the melancholy tenor of my thoughts. The day preceding that appointed for my journey arrived. It was necessary to complete my arrangements with the family with whom I was to travel, and to settle with the lady whose apartments I occupied.

On how slender threads does our destiny hang! Had not a momentary impulse tempted me to sing my favourite ditty to the harpsichord, to beguile the short interval during which my hostess was conversing with her visitor in the next apartment, I should have speeded to New York, have embarked for Europe, and been eternally severed from my friend, whom I believed to have died in frenzy and beggary, but who was alive and affluent, and who sought me with a diligence scarcely inferior to my own. We imagined ourselves severed from each other by death or by impassable seas; but, at the moment when our hopes had sunk to the lowest ebb, a mysterious destiny conducted our footsteps to the same spot.

I heard a murmuring exclamation; I heard my hostess call, in a voice of terror, for help; I rushed into the room; I saw one stretched on the floor, in the attitude of death; I sprung forward and fixed my eyes upon her countenance; I clasped my hands and articulated, "Constantia!"

She speedily recovered from her swoon. Her eyes opened; she moved, she spoke. Still methought it was an illusion of the senses that created the phantom. I could not bear to withdraw my eyes from her countenance. If they wandered for a moment, I fell into doubt and perplexity, and again fixed them upon her, to assure myself of her existence.

The succeeding three days were spent in a state of dizziness and intoxication. The ordinary functions of nature were disturbed. The appetite for sleep and for food were confounded and lost amidst the impetuosities of a master-passion. To look and to talk to each other afforded enchanting occupation for every moment. I would not part from her side, but eat and slept, walked and mused and read, with my arm locked in hers, and with her breath fanning my cheek.

I have indeed much to learn. Sophia Courtland has never been wise. Her affections disdain the cold dictates of discretion, and spurn at every limit that contending duties and mixed obligations prescribe.

And yet, O precious inebriation of the heart! O pre-eminent love! what pleasure of reason or of sense can stand in competition with those attendant upon thee? Whether thou hiest to the fanes[1] of a benevolent deity, or layest all thy homage at the feet of one who most visibly resembles the perfections of our Maker, surely thy sanction is divine, thy boon is happiness!

---

1   fanes: temples

CHAPTER XXVI.

THE tumults of curiosity and pleasure did not speedily subside. The story of each other's wanderings was told with endless amplification and minuteness. Henceforth, the stream of our existence was to mix; we were to act and to think in common; casual witnesses and written testimony should become superfluous. Eyes and ears were to be eternally employed upon the conduct of each other; death, when it should come, was not to be deplored, because it was an unavoidable and brief privation to her that should survive. Being, under any modification, is dear; but that state to which death is a passage is all-desirable to virtue and all-compensating to grief.

Meanwhile, precedent events were made the themes of endless conversation. Every incident and passion in the course of four years was revived and exhibited. The name of Ormond was, of course, frequently repeated by my friend. His features and deportment were described; her meditations and resolutions, with regard to him, fully disclosed. My counsel was asked, in what manner it became her to act.

I could not but harbour aversion to a scheme which should tend to sever me from Constantia, or to give me a competitor in her affections. Besides this, the properties of Ormond were of too mysterious a nature to make him worthy of acceptance. Little more was known concerning him than what he himself had disclosed to the Dudleys, but this knowledge would suffice to invalidate his claims.

He had dwelt, in his conversations with Constantia, sparingly on his own concerns. Yet he did not hide from her that he had been left in early youth to his own guidance; that he had embraced, when almost a child, the trade of arms; that he had found service and promotion in the armies of Potemkin and Romanov;[1] that he had executed secret and diplomatic functions at Constantinople and Berlin; that in the latter city he had met with schemers and reasoners who aimed at the new-modelling of the world, and the subversion of all that has hitherto been conceived elementary and fundamental in the

---

1   Grigory Aleksandrovich Potemkin (1739-1791) was a Russian field marshal, states-
    man, and the lover/collaborator of Catherine the Great. Pyotr Aleksandrovich,
    Count Romanov, was a Russian Army officer who distinguished himself in the
    Seven Years War (1756-63) and the Russo-Turkish War (1768-74).

constitution of man and of government; that some of those reformers had secretly united to break down the military and monarchical fabric of German policy; that others, more wisely, had devoted their secret efforts, not to overturn, but to build; that, for this end, they embraced an exploring and colonizing project; that he had allied himself to these, and for the promotion of their projects had spent six years of his life in journeys by sea and land, in tracts unfrequented till then by any European.

What were the moral or political maxims which this adventurous and visionary sect had adopted, and what was the seat of their new-born empire, – whether on the shore of an *austral* continent, or in the heart of desert America, – he carefully concealed. These were exhibited or hidden, or shifted, according to his purpose. Not to reveal too much, and not to tire curiosity or overtask belief, was his daily labour. He talked of alliance with the family whose name he bore, and who had lost their honours and estates by the Hanoverian succession to the crown of England.

I had seen too much of innovation and imposture, in France and Italy, not to regard a man like this with aversion and fear. The mind of my friend was wavering and unsuspicious. She had lived at a distance from scenes where principles are hourly put to the test of experiment; where all extremes of fortitude and pusillanimity are accustomed to meet; where recluse virtue and speculative heroism give place, as if by magic, to the last excesses of debauchery and wickedness; where pillage and murder are engrafted on systems of all-embracing and self-oblivious benevolence, and the good of mankind is professed to be pursued with bonds of association and covenants of secrecy. Hence, my friend had decided without the sanction of experience, had allowed herself to wander into untried paths, and had hearkened to positions pregnant with destruction and ignominy.

It was not difficult to exhibit, in their true light the enormous errors of this man, and the danger of prolonging their intercourse. Her assent to accompany me to England was readily obtained. Too much despatch could not be used; but the disposal of her property must first take place. This was necessarily productive of some delay.

I had been made, contrary to inclination, expert in the management of all affairs relative to property. My mother's lunacy, subsequent disease, and death, had imposed upon me obligations and cares little suitable to my sex and age. They could not be eluded or transferred to others; and, by degrees, experience enlarged my knowledge and familiarized my tasks.

It was agreed that I should visit and inspect my friend's estate in Jersey, while she remained in her present abode, to put an end to the views and expectations of Ormond, and to make preparation for her voyage. We were reconciled to a temporary separation by the necessity that prescribed it.

During our residence together, the mind of Constantia was kept in perpetual ferment. The second day after my departure, the turbulence of her feelings began to subside, and she found herself at leisure to pursue those measures which her present situation prescribed.

The time prefixed by Ormond for the termination of his absence had nearly arrived. Her resolutions respecting this man, lately formed, now occurred to her. Her heart drooped as she revolved the necessity of disuniting their fates; but that this disunion was proper could not admit of doubt. How information of her present views might be most satisfactorily imparted to him, was a question not instantly decided. She reflected on the impetuosity of his character, and conceived that her intentions might be most conveniently unfolded in a letter. This letter she immediately sat down to write. Just then the door opened, and Ormond entered the apartment.

She was somewhat, and for a moment, startled by this abrupt and unlooked-for entrance. Yet she greeted him with pleasure. Her greeting was received with coldness. A second glance at his countenance informed her that his mind was somewhat discomposed.

Folding his hands on his breast, he stalked to the window and looked up at the moon. Presently he withdrew his gaze from this object, and fixed it upon Constantia. He spoke, but his words were produced by a kind of effort:

"Fit emblem," he exclaimed, "of human versatility! One impediment is gone. I hoped it was the only one. But no! the removal of that merely made room for another. Let this be removed. Well, fate will interplace a third. All our toils will thus be frustrated, and the ruin will finally redound upon our heads." There he stopped.

This strain could not be interpreted by Constantia. She smiled, and, without noticing his incoherences, proceeded to inquire into his adventures during their separation. He listened to her, but his eyes, fixed upon hers, and his solemnity of aspect, were immovable. When she paused, he seated himself close to her, and, grasping her hand with a vehemence that almost pained her, said, –

"Look at me; steadfastly. Can you read my thoughts? Can your discernment reach the bounds of my knowledge and the bottom of my purposes? Catch you not a view of the monsters that are starting into birth *here*? " (and he put his left hand to his forehead.) "But you cannot. Should I paint them to you verbally, you would call me jester or deceiver. What pity that you have not instruments for piercing into thoughts!"

"I presume," said Constantia, affecting cheerfulness which she did not feel, "such instruments would be useless to me. You never scruple to say what you think. Your designs are no sooner conceived than they are expressed. All you know, all you wish, and all you purpose, are known to others as soon as to yourself. No scruples of decorum, no foresight of consequences, are obstacles in your way."

"True," replied he; "all obstacles are trampled under foot but one."

"What is the insuperable one?"

"Incredulity in him that hears. I must not say what will not be credited. I must not relate feats and avow schemes, when my hearer will say, 'Those feats were never performed; these schemes are not yours.' I care not if the truth of my tenets and the practicability of my purposes be denied. Still, I will openly maintain them; but when my assertions will themselves be disbelieved, when it is denied that I adopt the creed and project the plans which I affirm to be adopted and projected by me, it is needless to affirm.

"To-morrow I mean to ascertain the height of the lunar mountains by travelling to the top of them. Then I will station myself in the track of the last comet, and wait till its circumvolution suffers me to leap upon it; then, by walking on its surface, I will ascertain whether it be hot enough to burn my soles. Do you believe that this can be done?"

"No."

"Do you believe, in consequence of my assertion, that I design to do this, and that, in my apprehension, it is easy to be done?"

"Not unless I previously believe you to be lunatic."

"Then why should I assert my purposes? Why speak, when the hearer will infer nothing from my speech but that I am either lunatic or liar?"

"In that predicament, silence is best."

"In that predicament I now stand. I am not going to unfold myself. Just now, I pitied thee for want of eyes. 'Twas a foolish compassion. Thou art happy, because thou seest not an inch before thee or behind." Here he was for a moment buried in thought; then breaking from his reverie, he said, "So your father is dead?"

"True," said Constantia, endeavouring to suppress her rising emotions; "he is no more. It is so recent an event that I imagined you a stranger to it."

"False imagination! Thinkest thou I would refrain from knowing what so nearly concerns us both? Perhaps your opinion of my ignorance extends beyond this. Perhaps I know not your fruitless search for a picture. Perhaps I neither followed you nor led you to a being called Sophia Courtland. I was not present at the meeting. I am unapprized of the effects of your romantic passion for each other. I did not witness the rapturous effusions and inexorable counsels of the newcomer. I know not the contents of the letter which you are preparing to write."

As he spoke this, the accents of Ormond gradually augmented in vehemence. His countenance bespoke a deepening inquietude and growing passion. He stopped at the mention of the letter, because his voice was overpowered by emotion. This pause afforded room for the astonishment of Constantia. Her interviews and conversations with me took place at seasons of general repose, when all doors were fast and avenues shut, in the midst of silence, and in the bosom of retirement. The theme of our discourse was, commonly, too sacred for any ears but our own; disclosures were of too intimate and delicate a nature for any but a female audience; they were too injurious to the fame and peace of Ormond for him to be admitted to partake of them: yet his words implied a full acquaintance with recent events, and with purposes and deliberations shrouded, as we imagined, in impenetrable secrecy.

As soon as Constantia recovered from the confusion of these thoughts, she eagerly questioned him: – "What do you know? How do you know what has happened, or what is intended?"

"Poor Constantia!" he explained, in a tone bitter and sarcastic. "How hopeless is thy ignorance! To enlighten thee is past my power. What do I know? Everything. Not a tittle has escaped me. Thy letter is superfluous; I know its contents before they are written. I was to be told that a soldier and a traveller, a man who refused his faith to dreams, and his homage to shadows, merited only scorn and forget-fulness. That thy affections and person were due to another; that intercourse between us was henceforth to cease; that preparation was making for a voyage to Britain, and that Ormond was to walk to his grave alone!"

In spite of harsh tones and inflexible features, these words were accompanied with somewhat that betrayed a mind full of discord and agony. Constantia's astonishment was mingled with dejection. The discovery of a passion deeper and less curable than she suspected – the perception of embarrassments and difficulties in the path which she had chosen, that had not previously occurred to her – threw her mind into anxious suspense.

The measures she had previously concerted were still approved. To part from Ormond was enjoined by every dictate of discretion and duty. An explanation of her motives and views could not take place more seasonably than at present. Every consideration of justice to herself and humanity to Ormond made it desirable that this interview should be the last. By inexplicable means, he had gained a knowledge of her intentions. It was expedient, therefore, to state them with clear-ness and force. In what words this was to be done, was the subject of momentary deliberation.

Her thoughts were discerned, and her speech anticipated, by her companion: – "Why droopest thou, and why thus silent, Constantia? The secret of thy fate will never be detected. Till thy destiny be finished, it will not be the topic of a single fear. But not for thyself, but me, art thou concerned. Thou dreadest, yet determinest, to con-firm my predictions of thy voyage to Europe and thy severance from me.

"Dismiss thy inquietudes on that score. What misery thy scorn and thy rejection are able to inflict is inflicted already. Thy decision was known to me as soon as it was formed. Thy motives were known. Not an argument or plea of thy counsellor, not a syllable of her invective, not a sound of her persuasive rhetoric, escaped my hearing. I know thy decree to be immutable. As my doubts, so my wishes have taken their flight. Perhaps, in the depth of thy ignorance, it was supposed that I should struggle to reverse thy purpose by menaces or supplica-tions; that I should boast of the cruelty with which I should avenge an imaginary wrong upon myself. No. All is very well. Go. Not a whisper of objection or reluctance shalt thou hear from me."

"If I could think," said Constantia, with tremulous hesitation, "that you part from me without anger; that you see the rectitude of my proceeding – "

"Anger! Rectitude! I pr'ythee, peace. I know thou art going. I know that all objection to thy purpose would be vain. Thinkest thou that thy stay, undictated by love, the mere fruit of compassion, would afford me pleasure or crown my wishes? No. I am not so dastardly a wretch. There was something in thy power to bestow, but thy will accords not with thy power. I merit not the boon, and thou refusest it. I am content."

Here Ormond fixed more significant eyes upon her. "Poor Constantia!" he continued. "Shall I warn thee of the danger that awaits thee? For what end? To elude it is impossible. It will come, and thou, perhaps, wilt be unhappy. Foresight that enables not to shun, only precreates, the evil.

"Come it will. Though future, it knows not the empire of contingency. An inexorable and immutable decree enjoins it. Perhaps it is thy nature to meet with calmness what cannot be shunned. Perhaps, when it is past, thy reason will perceive its irrevocable nature, and restore thee to peace. Such is the conduct of the wise; but such, I fear, the education of Constantia Dudley will debar her from pursuing.

"Fain would I regard it as the test of thy wisdom. I look upon thy past life. All the forms of genuine adversity have beset thy youth. Poverty, disease, servile labour, a criminal and hapless parent, have been evils which thou hast not ungracefully sustained. An absent friend and murdered father were added to thy list of woes, and here thy courage was deficient. Thy soul was proof against substantial misery, but sunk into helpless cowardice at the sight of phantoms.

"One more disaster remains. To call it by its true name would be useless or pernicious. Useless, because thou wouldst pronounce its occurrence impossible; pernicious, because, if its possibility were granted, the omen would distract thee with fear. How shall I describe it? Is it loss of fame? No. The deed will be unwitnessed by a human creature. Thy reputation will be spotless, for nothing will be done by thee unsuitable to the tenor of thy past life. Calumny will not be heard to whisper. All that know thee will be lavish of their eulogies as ever. Their eulogies will be as justly merited. Of this merit thou wilt entertain as just and as adequate conceptions as now.

"It is no repetition of the evils thou hast already endured; it is neither drudgery, nor sickness, nor privation of friends. Strange perverseness of human reason! It is an evil; it will be thought upon with agony; it will close up all the sources of pleasurable recollection; it will exterminate hope; it will endear oblivion, and push thee into an untimely grave. Yet to grasp it is impossible. The moment we inspect it nearly, it vanishes. Thy claims to human approbation and divine applause will be undiminished and unaltered by it. The testimony of approving conscience will have lost none of its explicitness and energy. Yet thou wilt feed upon sighs; thy tears will flow without remission; thou wilt grow enamoured of death, and perhaps wilt anticipate the stroke of disease.

"Yet perhaps my prediction is groundless as my knowledge. Perhaps thy discernment will avail to make thee wise and happy. Perhaps thou wilt perceive thy privilege of sympathetic and intellectual activity to be untouched. Heaven grant the non-fulfilment of my prophecy, thy disenthralment from error, and the perpetuation of thy happiness."

Saying this, Ormond withdrew. His words were always accompanied with gestures and looks and tones that fastened the attention of the hearer; but the terms of his present discourse afforded, independently of gesticulation and utterance, sufficient motives to attention and remembrance. He was gone, but his image was contemplated by Constantia; his words still rung in her ears.

The letter she designed to compose was rendered, by this interview, unnecessary. Meanings of which she and her friend alone were conscious were discovered by Ormond, through some other medium than words; yet that was impossible. A being unendowed with preternatural attributes could gain the information which this man possessed, only by the exertion of his senses.

All human precautions had been used to baffle the attempts of any secret witness. She recalled to mind the circumstances in which conversations with her friend had taken place. All had been retirement, secrecy, and silence. The hours usually dedicated to sleep had been devoted to this better purpose. Much had been said, in a voice low and scarcely louder than a whisper. To have overheard it at the distance of a few feet was apparently impossible.

Their conversations had not been recorded by her. It could not be believed that this had been done by Sophia Courtland. Had Ormond and her friend met during the interval that had elapsed between her separation from the latter and her meeting with the former? Human events are conjoined by links imperceptible to keenest eyes. Of Ormond's means of information she was wholly unapprized. Perhaps accident would sometime unfold them. One thing was incontestable: – that her schemes and her reasons for adopting them were known to him.

What unforeseen effects had that knowledge produced! In what ambiguous terms had he couched his prognostics of some mighty evil that awaited her! He had given a terrible but contradictory description of her destiny. An event was to happen, akin to no calamity which she had already endured, disconnected with all which the imagination of man is accustomed to deprecate, capable of urging her to suicide, and yet a kind which left it undecided whether she would regard it with indifference.

What reliance should she place upon prophetic incoherencies thus wild? What precautions should she take against a danger thus inscrutable and imminent?

CHAPTER XXVII.

THESE incidents and reflections were speedily transmitted to me. I had always believed the character and machinations of Ormond to be worthy of caution and fear. His means of information I did not pretend, and thought it useless, to investigate. We cannot hide our actions and thoughts from one of powerful sagacity, whom the detection sufficiently interests to make him use all the methods of detection in his power. The study of concealment is, in all cases, fruitless or hurtful. All that duty enjoins is to design and to execute nothing which may not be approved by a divine and omniscient Observer. Human scrutiny is neither to be solicited nor shunned. Human approbation or censure can never be exempt from injustice, because our limited perceptions debar us from a thorough knowledge of any actions and motives but our own.

On reviewing what had passed between Constantia and me, I recollected nothing incompatible with purity and rectitude. That Ormond was apprized of all that had passed, I by no means inferred from the tenor of his conversation with Constantia; nor, if this had been incontestably proved, should I have experienced any trepidation or anxiety on that account.

His obscure and indirect menaces of evil were of more importance. His discourse on this topic seemed susceptible only of two constructions. Either he intended some fatal mischief, and was willing to torment her by fears, while he concealed from her the nature of her danger, that he might hinder her from guarding her safety by suitable precautions; or, being hopeless of rendering her propitious to his wishes, his malice was satisfied with leaving her a legacy of apprehension and doubt.

Constantia's unacquaintance with the doctrines of that school in which Ormond was probably instructed led her to regard the conduct of this man with more curiosity and wonder than fear. She saw nothing but a disposition to sport with her ignorance and bewilder her with doubts.

I do not believe myself destitute of courage. Rightly to estimate the danger and encounter it with firmness are worthy of a rational being; but to place our security in thoughtlessness and blindness is only less ignoble than cowardice. I could not forget the proofs of violence which accompanied the death of Mr. Dudley. I could not overlook, in the recent conversation with Constantia, Ormond's allusion to her murdered father. It was possible that the nature of this death had been accidentally imparted to him; but it was likewise possible that his was the knowledge of one who performed the act.

The enormity of this deed appeared by no means incongruous with the sentiments of Ormond. Human life is momentous or trivial in our eyes, according to the course which our habits and opinions have taken. Passion greedily accepts, and habit readily offers, the sacrifice of another's life, and reason obeys the impulse of education and desire.

A youth of eighteen, a volunteer in a Russian army encamped in Bessarabia, made prey of a Tartar girl, found in the field of a recent battle. Conducting her to his quarters, he met a friend, who, on some pretence, claimed the victim. From angry words they betook themselves to swords. A combat ensued, in which the first claimant ran his antagonist through the body. He then bore his prize unmolested away, and having exercised brutality of one kind upon the helpless victim, stabbed her to the heart, as an offering to the manes[1] of Sarsefield, the friend whom he had slain. Next morning, willing more signally to expiate his guilt, he rushed alone upon a troop of Turkish foragers, and brought away five heads, suspended, by their gory locks, to his horse's mane. These he cast upon the grave of Sarsefield, and conceived himself fully to have expiated yesterday's offence. In reward for his prowess, the general gave him a commission in the Cossack troops. This youth was Ormond; and such is a specimen of his exploits during a military career of eight years, in a warfare the most savage and implacable, and, at the same time, the most iniquitous and wanton, which history records.

With passions and habits like these, the life of another was a trifling sacrifice to vengeance or impatience. How Mr. Dudley had excited the resentment of Ormond, by what means the assassin had accomplished his intention without awakening alarm or incurring suspicion, it was not for me to discover. The inextricability of human events, the imperviousness of cunning, and the obduracy of malice, I had frequent occasions to remark.

I did not labour to vanquish the security of my friend. As to precautions, they were useless. There was no fortress, guarded by barriers of stone and iron and watched by sentinels that never slept, to which she might retire from his stratagems. If there were such a retreat, it would scarcely avail her against a foe circumspect and subtle as Ormond.

I pondered on the condition of my friend. I reviewed the incidents of her life. I compared her lot with that of others. I could not but discover a sort of incurable malignity in her fate. I felt as if it were denied to her to enjoy a long life or permanent tranquillity. I asked myself what she had done, entitling her to this incessant persecution. Impatience and murmuring took place of sorrow and fear in my heart. When I reflected that all human agency was merely subservient to a divine purpose, I fell into fits of accusation and impiety.

This injustice was transient, and soberer views convinced me that

---

1   *manes:* the spirits of the dead, regarded as minor supernatural powers in ancient Roman religion; the revered spirits of those who have died.

every scheme, comprising the whole, must be productive of partial and temporary evil. The sufferings of Constantia were limited to a moment; they were the unavoidable appendages of terrestrial existence; they formed the only avenue to wisdom, and the only claim to uninterrupted fruition and eternal repose in an after-scene.

The course of my reflections, and the issue to which they led, were unforeseen by myself. Fondly as I doted upon this woman, methought I could resign her to the grave without a murmur or a tear. While my thoughts were calmed by resignation, and my fancy occupied with nothing but the briefness of that space and evanescence of that time which severs the living from the dead, I contemplated, almost with complacency, a violent or untimely close to her existence.

This loftiness of mind could not always be accomplished or constantly maintained. One effect of my fears was to hasten my departure to Europe. There existed no impediment but the want of a suitable conveyance. In the first packet that should leave America, it was determined to secure a passage. Mr. Melbourne consented to take charge of Constantia's property, and, after the sale of it, to transmit to her the money that should thence arise.

Meanwhile, I was anxious that Constantia should leave her present abode and join me in New York. She willingly adopted this arrangement, but conceived it necessary to spend a few days at her house in Jersey. She could reach the latter place without much deviation from the straight road, and she was desirous of resurveying a spot where many of her infantile days had been spent.

This house and domain I have already mentioned to have once belonged to Mr. Dudley. It was selected with the judgment and adorned with the taste of a disciple of the schools of Florence and Vicenza. In his view, cultivation was subservient to the picturesque, and a mansion was erected, eminent for nothing but chastity of ornaments and simplicity of structure. The massive parts were of stone; the outer surfaces were smooth, snow-white, and diversified by apertures and cornices, in which a cement uncommonly tenacious was wrought into proportions the most correct and forms the most graceful. The floors, walls, and ceilings, consisted of a still more exquisitely-tempered substance, and were painted by Mr. Dudley's own hand. All appendages of this building, as seats, tables, and cabinets, were modelled by the owner's particular direction, and in a manner scrupulously classical.

He had scarcely entered on the enjoyment of this splendid possession, when it was ravished away. No privation was endured with more impatience that this; but, happily, it was purchased by one who left Mr. Dudley's arrangements unmolested, and who shortly after conveyed it entire to Ormond. By him it was finally appropriated to the use of Helena Cleves, and now, by a singular contexture of events, it had reverted to those hands in which the death of the original proprietor, if no other change had been made in his condition, would have left it. The farm still remained in the tenure of a German emigrant, who held it partly on condition of preserving the garden and mansion in safety and in perfect order.

This retreat was now revisited by Constantia, after an interval of four years. Autumn had made some progress, but the aspect of nature was, so to speak, more significant than at any other season. She was agreeably accommodated under the tenant's roof, and found a nameless pleasure in traversing spaces in which every object prompted an endless train of recollections.

Her sensations were not foreseen. They led to a state of mind inconsistent, in some degree, with the projects adopted in obedience to the suggestions of a friend. Every thing in this scene had been created and modelled by the genius of a father. It was a kind of fane, sanctified by his imaginary presence.

To consign the fruits of his industry and invention to foreign and unsparing hands seemed a kind of sacrilege, for which she almost feared that the dead would rise to upbraid her. Those images which bind us to our natal soil, to the abode of our innocent and careless youth, were recalled to her fancy by the scenes which she now beheld. These were enforced by considerations of the dangers which attended her voyage from storms and from enemies, and from the tendency to revolution and war which seemed to actuate all the nations of Europe. Her native country was by no means exempt from similar tendencies, but these evils were less imminent, and its manners and government, in their present modifications, were unspeakably more favourable to the dignity and improvement of the human race than those which prevailed in any part of the ancient world.

My solicitations and my obligation to repair to England overweighed her objections, but her new reflections led her to form new determinations with regard to this part of her property. She concluded to retain possession, and hoped that some future event would allow her to return to this favourite spot without forfeiture of my society. An abode of some years in Europe would more eminently qualify her for the enjoyment of retirement and safety in her native country. The time that should elapse before her embarkation, she was desirous of passing among the shades of this romantic retreat.

I was by no means reconciled to this proceeding. I loved my friend too well to endure any needless separation without repining. In addition to this, the image of Ormond haunted my thoughts, and gave birth to incessant but indefinable fears. I believed that her safety would very little depend on the nature of her abode, or the number or watchfulness of her companions. My nearness to her person would frustrate no stratagem, nor promote any other end than my own entanglement in the same fold. Still, that I was not apprized each hour of her condition, that her state was lonely and sequestered, were sources of disquiet, the obvious remedy to which was her coming to New York. Preparations for departure were assigned to me, and these required my continuance in the city.

Once a week, Laffert, her tenant, visited, for purposes of traffic, the city. He was the medium of our correspondence. To him I entrusted a letter, in which my dissatisfaction at her absence, and the causes which gave it birth, were freely confessed.

The confidence of safety seldom deserted my friend. Since her mysterious conversation with Ormond, he had utterly vanished. Previously to that interview, his visits or his letters were incessant and punctual; but since, no token was given that he existed. Two months had elapsed. He gave her no reason to expect a cessation of intercourse. He had parted from her with his usual abruptness and informality. She did not conceive it incumbent on her to search him out, but she would not have been displeased with an opportunity to discuss with him more fully the motives of her conduct. This opportunity had been hitherto denied.

Her occupations in her present retreat were, for the most part, dictated by caprice or by chance. The mildness of autumn permitted her to ramble, during the day, from one rock and one grove to another. There was a luxury in musing, and in the sensations which the scenery and silence produced, which, in consequence of her long estrangement from them, were accompanied with all the attractions of novelty, and from which she would not consent to withdraw.

In the evening she usually retired to the mansion, and shut herself up in that apartment which, in the original structure of the house, had been designed for study, and no part of whose furniture had been removed or displaced. It was a kind of closet on the second floor, illuminated by a spacious window, through which a landscape of uncommon amplitude and beauty was presented to the view. Here the pleasures of the day were revived, by recalling and enumerating them in letters to her friend. She always quitted this recess with reluctance, and seldom till the night was half spent.

One evening she retired hither when the sun had just dipped beneath the horizon. Her implements of writing were prepared; but before the pen was assumed, her eyes rested for a moment on the variegated hues which were poured out upon the western sky and upon the scene of intermingled waters, copses, and fields. The view comprised a part of the road which led to this dwelling. It was partially and distantly seen, and the passage of horses or men was betokened chiefly by the dust which was raised by their footsteps.

A token of this kind now caught her attention. It fixed her eye chiefly by the picturesque effect produced by interposing its obscurity between her and the splendours which the sun had left. Presently she gained a faint view of a man and horse. This circumstance laid no claim to attention, and she was withdrawing her eye, when the traveller's stopping and dismounting at the gate made her renew her scrutiny. This was reinforced by something in the figure and movements of the horseman which reminded her of Ormond.

She started from her seat with some degree of palpitation. Whence this arose, whether from fear or from joy, or from intermixed emotions, it would not be easy to ascertain. Having entered the gate, the visitant, remounting his horse, set the animal on full speed. Every moment brought him nearer, and added to her first belief. He stopped not till he reached the mansion. The person of Ormond was distinctly recognised.

An interview at this dusky and lonely hour, in circumstances so abrupt and unexpected, could not fail to surprise, and, in some degree, to alarm. The substance of his last conversation was recalled.

The evils which were darkly and ambiguously predicted thronged to her memory. It seemed as if the present moment was to be, in some way, decisive of her fate. This visit she did not hesitate to suppose designed for her, but somewhat uncommonly momentous must have prompted him to take so long a journey.

The rooms on the lower floor were dark, the windows and doors being fastened. She had entered the house by the principal door, and this was the only one at present unlocked. The room in which she sat was over the hall, and the massive door beneath could not be opened without noisy signals. The question that occurred to her, by what means Ormond would gain admittance to her presence, she supposed would be instantly decided. She listened to hear his footsteps on the pavement, or the creaking of hinges. The silence, however, continued profound as before.

After a minute's pause, she approached the window more nearly and endeavoured to gain a view of the space before the house. She saw nothing but the horse, whose bridle was thrown over his neck, and who was left at liberty to pick up what scanty herbage the lawn afforded to his hunger. The rider had disappeared.

It now occurred to her that this visit had a purpose different from that which she at first conjectured. It was easily conceived that Ormond was unacquainted with her residence at this spot. The knowledge could only be imparted to him by indirect or illicit means. That these means had been employed by him, she was by no means authorized to infer from the silence and distance he had lately maintained. But if an interview with her were not the purpose of his coming, how should she interpret it?

CHAPTER XXVIII.

While occupied with these reflections, the light hastily disappeared, and darkness, rendered, by a cloudy atmosphere, uncommonly intense, succeeded. She had the means of lighting a lamp that hung against the wall, but had been too much immersed in thought to notice the deepening of the gloom. Recovering from her reverie, she looked around her with some degree of trepidation, and prepared to strike a spark that would enable her to light her lamp.

She had hitherto indulged an habitual indifference to danger. Now the presence of Ormond, the unknown purpose that led him hither, and the defencelessness of her condition, inspired her with apprehensions to which she had hitherto been a stranger. She had been accustomed to pass many nocturnal hours in this closet. Till now, nothing had occurred that made her enter it with circumspection or continue in it with reluctance.

Her sensations were no longer tranquil. Each minute that she spent in this recess appeared to multiply her hazards. To linger here appeared to her the height of culpable temerity. She hastily resolved to return to the farmer's dwelling, and, on the morrow, to repair to New York. For this end she was desirous to produce a light. The materials were at hand.

She lifted her hand to strike the flint, when her ear caught a sound which betokened the opening of the door that led into the next apartment. Her motion was suspended, and she listened as well as a throbbing heart would permit. That Ormond's was the hand that opened, was the first suggestion of her fears. The motives of this unseasonable entrance could not be reconciled with her safety. He had given no warning of his approach, and the door was opened with tardiness and seeming caution.

Sounds continued, of which no distinct conception could be obtained, or the cause that produced them assigned. The floors of every apartment being composed, like the walls and ceiling, of cement, footsteps were rendered almost undistinguishable. It was plain, however, that some one approached her own door.

The panic and confusion that now invaded her was owing to surprise, and to the singularity of her situation. The mansion was desolate and lonely. It was night. She was immersed in darkness. She had not the means, and was unaccustomed to the office, of repelling personal injuries. What injuries she had reason to dread, who was the agent, and what were his motives, were subjects of vague and incoherent meditation.

Meanwhile, low and imperfect sounds, that had in them more of inanimate than human, assailed her ear. Presently they ceased. An inexplicable fear deterred her from calling. Light would have exercised a friendly influence. This it was in her power to produce, but not without motion and noise; and these, by occasioning the discovery of her being in the closet, might possibly enhance her danger.

Conceptions like these were unworthy of the mind of Constantia. An interval of silence succeeded, interrupted only by the whistling of the blast without. It was sufficient for the restoration of her courage. She blushed at the cowardice which had trembled at a sound. She considered that Ormond might, indeed, be near, but that he was probably unconscious of her situation. His coming was not with the circumspection of an enemy. He might be acquainted with the place of her retreat, and had come to obtain an interview, with no clandestine or mysterious purposes. The noises she had heard had, doubtless, proceeded from the next apartment, but might be produced by some harmless or vagrant creature.

These considerations restored her tranquillity. They enabled her, deliberately, to create a light, but they did not dissuade her from leaving the house. Omens of evil seemed to be connected with this solitary and darksome abode. Besides, Ormond had unquestionably entered upon this scene. It could not be doubted that she was the object of his visit. The farm-house was a place of meeting more suitable and safe than any other. Thither, therefore, she determined immediately to return.

The closet had but one door, and this led into the chamber where the sounds had arisen. Through this chamber, therefore, she was obliged to pass, in order to reach the staircase, which terminated in the hall below.

Bearing the light in her left hand, she withdrew the bolt of the door and opened. In spite of courageous efforts, she opened with unwillingness, and shuddered to throw a glance forward or advance a step into the room. This was not needed, to reveal to her the cause of her late disturbance. Her eye instantly lighted on the body of a man, supine, motionless, stretched on the floor, close to the door through which she was about to pass.

A spectacle like this was qualified to startle her. She shrunk back, and fixed a more steadfast eye upon the prostrate person. There was no mark of blood or of wounds, but there was something in the attitude more significant of death than of sleep. His face rested on the floor, and his ragged locks concealed what part of his visage was not hidden by his posture. His garb was characterized by fashionable elegance, but was polluted with dust.

The image that first occurred to her was that of Ormond. This instantly gave place to another, which was familiar to her apprehension. It was at first too indistinctly seen to suggest a name. She continued to gaze and to be lost in fearful astonishment. Was this the person whose entrance had been overheard, and who had dragged himself hither to die at her door? Yet, in that case, would not groans and expiring efforts have testified his condition and invoked her succour? Was he not brought hither in the arms of his assassin? She mused upon the possible motives that induced some one thus to act, and upon the connection that might subsist between her destiny and that of the dead.

Her meditations, however fruitless in other respects, could not fail to show her the propriety of hastening from this spot. To scrutinize the form or face of the dead was a task to which her courage was unequal. Suitably accompanied and guarded, she would not scruple to return and ascertain, by the most sedulous examination, the cause of this ominous event.

She stepped over the breathless corpse, and hurried to the staircase. It became her to maintain the command of her muscles and joints, and to proceed without faltering or hesitation. Scarcely had she reached the entrance of the hall, when, casting anxious looks forward, she beheld a human figure. No scrutiny was requisite to inform her that this was Ormond.

She stopped. He approached her with looks and gestures placid but solemn. There was nothing in his countenance rugged or malignant. On the contrary, there were tokens of compassion.

"So," said he, "I expected to meet you. A light, gleaming from the window, marked you out. This and Laffert's directions have guided me."

"What," said Constantia, with discomposure in her accent, "was your motive for seeking me?"

"Have you forgotten," said Ormond, "what passed at our last interview? The evil that I then predicted is at hand. Perhaps you were incredulous; you accounted me a madman or deceiver; now I am come to witness the fulfilment of my words and the completion of your destiny. To rescue you I have not come: that is not within the compass of human powers.

"Poor Constantia," he continued, in tones that manifested genuine sympathy, "look upon thyself as lost. The toils that beset thee are inextricable. Summon up thy patience to endure the evil. Now will the last and heaviest trial betide thy fortitude. I could weep for thee, if my manly nature would permit. This is the scene of thy calamity, and this the hour."

These words were adapted to excite curiosity mingled with terror. Ormond's deportment was of an unexampled tenor, as well as that evil which he had so ambiguously predicted. He offered no protection from danger, and yet gave no proof of being himself an agent or auxiliary. After a minute's pause, Constantia, recovering a firm tone, said, –

"Mr. Ormond, your recent deportment but ill accords with your professions of sincerity and plain dealing. What your purpose is, or whether you have any purpose, I am at a loss to conjecture. Whether you most deserve censure or ridicule, is a point which you afford me not the means of deciding, and to which, unless on your own account, I am indifferent. If you are willing to be more explicit, or if there be any topic on which you wish further to converse, I will not refuse your company to Laffert's dwelling. Longer to remain here would be indiscreet and absurd."

So saying, she motioned towards the door. Ormond was passive, and seemed indisposed to prevent her departure, till she laid her hand upon the lock. He then, without moving from his place, exclaimed, –

"Stay! Must this meeting, which fate ordains to be the last, be so short? Must a time and place so suitable for what remains to be said and done be neglected or misused? No. You charge me with duplicity, and deem my conduct either ridiculous or criminal. I have stated my reasons for concealment, but these have failed to convince you. Well, here is now an end to doubt. All ambiguities are appearing to vanish."

When Ormond began to speak, Constantia paused to hearken to him. His vehemence was not of that nature which threatened to obstruct her passage. It was by entreaty that he apparently endeavoured to detain her steps, and not by violence. Hence arose her patience to listen. He continued: –

"Constantia! thy father is dead. Art thou not desirous of detecting the author of his fate? Will it afford thee no consolation to know that the deed is punished? Wilt thou suffer me to drag the murderer to thy feet? Thy justice will be gratified by this sacrifice. Somewhat will be due to him who avenged thy wrong in the blood of the perpetrator. What sayest thou? Grant me thy permission, and in a moment I will drag him hither."

These words called up the image of the person whose corpse she had lately seen. It was readily conceived that to him Ormond alluded; but this was the assassin of her father, and his crime had been detected and punished by Ormond! These images had no other effect than to urge her departure: she again applied her hand to the lock, and said, –

"This scene must not be prolonged. My father's death I desire not to hear explained or to see revenged, but whatever information you are willing or able to communicate must be deferred."

"Nay," interrupted Ormond, with augmented vehemence, "art thou equally devoid of curiosity and justice? Thinkest thou that the enmity which bereft thy father of life will not seek thy own? There are evils which I cannot prevent thee from enduring, but there are, likewise, ills which my counsel will enable thee and thy friend to shun. Save me from witnessing thy death. Thy father's destiny is sealed; all that remained was to punish his assassin; but thou and thy Sophia still live. Why should ye perish by a like stroke?"

This intimation was sufficient to arrest the steps of Constantia. She withdrew her hand from the door, and fixed eyes of the deepest anxiety on Ormond: – "What mean you? How am I to understand —"

"Ah!" said Ormond, "I see thou wilt consent to stay. Thy detention shall not be long. Remain where thou art during one moment, – merely while I drag hither thy enemy and show thee a visage which thou wilt not be slow to recognise." Saying this, he hastily ascended the staircase, and quickly passed beyond her sight.

Deportment thus mysterious could not fail of bewildering her thoughts. There was somewhat in the looks and accents of Ormond, different from former appearances; tokens of a hidden purpose and a smothered meaning were perceptible, – a mixture of the inoffensive and the lawless, which, added to the loneliness and silence that encompassed her, produced a faltering emotion. Her curiosity was overpowered by her fear, and the resolution was suddenly conceived of seizing this opportunity to escape.

A third time she put her hand to the lock and attempted to open. The effort was ineffectual. The door that was accustomed to obey the gentlest touch was now immovable. She had lately unlocked and passed through it. Her eager inspection convinced her that the principal bolt was still withdrawn, but a small one was now perceived, of whose existence she had not been apprized, and over which her key had no power.

Now did she first harbour a fear that was intelligible in its dictates. Now did she first perceive herself sinking in the toils of some lurking enemy. Hope whispered that this foe was not Ormond. His conduct had bespoken no willingness to put constraint upon her steps. He talked not as if he were aware of this obstruction, and yet his seeming acquiescence might have flowed from a knowledge that she had no power to remove beyond his reach.

He warned her of danger to her life, of which he was her self-appointed rescuer. His counsel was to arm her with sufficient caution; the peril that awaited her was imminent; this was the time and place of its occurrence, and here she was compelled to remain, till the power that fastened would condescend to loose the door. There were other avenues to the hall. These were accustomed to be locked; but Ormond had found access, and, if all continued fast, it was incontestable that he was the author of this new impediment.

The other avenues were hastily examined. All were bolted and locked. The first impulse led her to call for help from without; but the mansion was distant from Laffert's habitation. This spot was wholly unfrequented. No passenger was likely to be stationed where her call could be heard. Besides, this forcible detention might operate for a short time, and be attended with no mischievous consequences. Whatever was to come, it was her duty to collect her courage and encounter it.

The steps of Ormond above now gave tokens of his approach. Vigilant observance of this man was all that her situation permitted. A vehement effort restored her to some degree of composure. Her stifled palpitations allowed her steadfastly to notice him as he now descended the stairs, bearing a lifeless body in his arms. "There!" said he, as he cast it at her feet; "whose countenance is that? Who would imagine that features like those belonged to an assassin and impostor?"

Closed eyelids and fallen muscles could not hide from her lineaments so often seen. She shrunk back and exclaimed, "Thomas Craig!"

A pause succeeded, in which she alternately gazed at the countenance of this unfortunate wretch and at Ormond. At length the latter exclaimed, –

"Well, my girl, has thou examined him? Dost thou recognise a friend or an enemy?"

"I know him well: but how came this? What purpose brought him hither? Who was the author of his fate?"

"Have I not already told thee that Ormond was his own avenger and thine? To thee and to me he has been a robber. To him thy father is indebted for the loss not only of property but life. Did crimes like these merit a less punishment? And what recompense is due to him whose vigilance pursued him hither and made him pay for his offences with his blood? What benefit have I received at thy hand to authorize me, for thy sake, to take away his life?"

"No benefit received from me," said Constantia, "would justify such an act. I should have abhorred myself for annexing to my benefits so bloody a condition. It calls for no gratitude or recompense. Its suitable attendant is remorse. That he is a thief, I know but too well; that my father died by his hand is incredible. No motives or means —"

"Why so?" interrupted Ormond. "Does not sleep seal up the senses? Cannot closets be unlocked at midnight? Cannot adjoining houses communicate by doors? Cannot these doors be hidden from suspicion by a sheet of canvas?"

These words were of startling and abundant import. They reminded her of circumstances in her father's chamber, which sufficiently explained the means by which his life was assailed. The closet, and its canvas-covered wall; the adjoining house untenanted and shut up – but this house, though unoccupied, belonged to Ormond. From the inferences which flowed hence, her attention was withdrawn by her companion, who continued: –

"Do these means imply the interposal of a miracle? His motives? What scruples can be expected from a man inured from infancy to cunning and pillage? Will he abstain from murder when urged by excruciating poverty, by menaces of persecution, by terror of expiring on the gallows?"

Tumultuous suspicions were now awakened in the mind of Constantia. Her faltering voice scarcely allowed her to ask, "How know *you* that Craig was thus guilty? – that these were his incitements and means?"

Ormond's solemnity now gave place to a tone of sarcasm and looks of exultation: – "Poor Constantia! Thou art still pestered with incredulity and doubts! My veracity is still in question! My knowledge, girl, is infallible. That these were his means of access I cannot be ignorant, for I pointed them out. He was urged by these motives, for they were stated and enforced by me. His was the deed, for I stood beside him when it was done."

These, indeed, were terms that stood in no need of further explanation. The veil that shrouded this formidable being was lifted high enough to make him be regarded with inexplicable horror. What his future acts should be, how his omens of ill were to be solved, were still involved in uncertainty.

In the midst of fears for her own safety, by which Constantia was now assailed, the image of her father was revived; keen regret and vehement upbraiding were conjured up.

"Craig, then, was the instrument, and yours the instigation, that destroyed my father! In what had he offended you? What cause had he given for resentment?"

"Cause!" replied he, with impetuous accents. "Resentment! None. My motive was benevolent; my deed conferred a benefit. I gave him sight and took away his life, from motives equally wise. Know you not that Ormond was fool enough to set value on the affections of a woman? These were sought with preposterous anxiety and endless labour. Among other facilitators of his purpose, he summoned gratitude to his aid. To snatch you from poverty, to restore his sight to your father, were expected to operate as incentives to love.

"But here I was the dupe of error. A thousand prejudices stood in my way. These, provided our intercourse were not obstructed, I hoped to subdue. The rage of innovation seized your father: this, blended with a mortal antipathy to me, made him labour to seduce you from the bosom of your peaceful country; to make you enter on a boisterous sea; to visit lands where all is havoc and hostility; to snatch you from the influence of my arguments.

"This new obstacle I was bound to remove. While revolving the means, chance and his evil destiny threw Craig in my way. I soon convinced him that his reputation and his life were in my hands. His retention of these depended upon my will, on the performance of conditions which I prescribed.

"My happiness and yours depended on your concurrence with my wishes. Your father's life was an obstacle to your concurrence. For killing him, therefore, I may claim your gratitude. His death was a due and disinterested offering on the altar of your felicity and mine.

"My deed was not injurious to him. At his age, death, whose coming at some period is inevitable, could not be distant. To make it unforeseen and brief, and void of pain, – to preclude the torments of a lingering malady, a slow and visible descent to the grave, – was the dictate of beneficence. But of what value was a continuance of his life? Either you would have gone with him to Europe or have stayed at home with me. In the first case, his life would have been rapidly consumed by perils and cares. In the second, separation from you, and union with me, – a being so detestable, – would equally have poisoned his existence.

"Craig's cowardice and crimes made him a pliant and commodious tool. I pointed out the way. The unsuspected door which led into the closet of your father's chamber was made, by my direction, during the life of Helena. By this avenue I was wont to post myself where all your conversations could be overheard. By this avenue an entrance and retreat were afforded to the agent of my newest purpose.

"Fool that I was! I solaced myself with the belief that all impediments were now smoothed, when a new enemy appeared. My folly lasted as long as my hope. I saw that to gain your affections, fortified by antiquated scruples and obsequious to the guidance of this new monitor, was impossible. It is not my way to toil after that which is beyond my reach. If the greater good be inaccessible, I learn to be contented with the less.

"I have served you with successless sedulity. I have set an engine in act to obliterate an obstacle to your felicity, and lay your father at rest. Under my guidance, this engine was productive only of good. Governed by itself or by another, it will only work you harm. I have, therefore, hastened to destroy it. Lo! it is now before you motionless and impotent.

"For this complexity of benefit I look for no reward. I am not tired of well-doing. Having ceased to labour for an unattainable good, I have come hither to possess myself of all that I now crave, and by the same deed to afford you an illustrious opportunity to signalize your wisdom and your fortitude."

During this speech, the mind of Constantia became more deeply pervaded with dread of some overhanging but incomprehensible evil. The strongest impulse was to gain a safe asylum, at a distance from this spot and from the presence of this extraordinary being. This impulse was followed by the recollection that her liberty was taken away, that egress from the hall was denied her, and that this restriction might be part of some conspiracy of Ormond against her life.

Security from danger like this would be, in the first place, sought, by one of Constantia's sex and opinions, in flight. This had been rendered, by some fatal chance or by the precautions of her foe, impracticable. Stratagem or force was all that remained to elude or disarm her adversary. For the contrivance and execution of fraud, all the habits of her life and all the maxims of her education had conspired to unfit her. Her force of muscles would avail her nothing against the superior energy of Ormond.

She remembered that to inflict death was no iniquitous exertion of self-defence, and that the penknife which she held in her hand was capable of this service. She had used it to remove any lurking obstruction in the wards of her key, supposing, for a time, this to be the cause of her failing to withdraw the bolt of the door. This resource was, indeed, scarcely less disastrous and deplorable than any fate from which it could rescue her. Some uncertainty still involved the intentions of Ormond. As soon as he paused, she spoke: –

"How am I to understand this prelude? Let me know the full extent of my danger, – why it is that I am hindered from leaving this house, and why this interview was sought."

"Ah, Constantia, this, indeed, is merely prelude to a scene that is to terminate my influence over thy fate. When this is past I have sworn to part with thee forever. Art thou still dubious of my purpose? Art thou not a woman? And have I not entreated for thy love and been rejected?

"Canst thou imagine that I aim at thy life? My avowals of love were sincere; my passion was vehement and undisguised. It gave dignity and value to a gift in thy power, as a woman, to bestow. This has been denied. That gift has lost none of its value in my eyes. What thou refusedst to bestow it is in my power to extort. I came for that end.

When this end is accomplished, I will restore thee to liberty."

These words were accompanied by looks that rendered all explanation of their meaning useless. The evil reserved for her, hitherto obscured by half-disclosed and contradictory attributes, was now sufficiently apparent. The truth in this respect unveiled itself with the rapidity and brightness of an electrical flash.

She was silent. She cast her eyes at the windows and doors. Escape through them was hopeless. She looked at those lineaments of Ormond which evinced his disdain of supplication and inexorable passions. She felt that entreaty and argument would be vain; that all appeals to his compassion and benevolence would counteract her purpose, since, in the unexampled conformation of this man's mind, these principles were made subservient to his most flagitious designs. Considerations of justice and pity were made, by a fatal perverseness of reasoning, champions and bulwarks of his most atrocious mistakes.

The last extremes of opposition, the most violent expedients for defence, would be justified by being indispensable. To find safety for her honour, even in the blood of an assailant, was the prescription of duty. The equity of this species of defence was not, in the present confusion of her mind, a subject of momentary doubt.

To forewarn him of her desperate purpose would be to furnish him with means of counteraction. Her weapon would easily be wrested from her feeble hand. Ineffectual opposition would only precipitate her evil destiny. A rage, contented with nothing less than her life, might be awakened in his bosom. But was not this to be desired? Death, untimely and violent, was better than the loss of honour.

This thought led to a new series of reflections. She involuntarily shrunk from the act of killing: but would her efforts to destroy her adversary be effectual? Would not his strength and dexterity easily repel or elude them? Her power in this respect was questionable, but her power was undeniably sufficient to a different end. The instrument which could not rescue her from this injury by the destruction of another might save her from it by her own destruction.

These thoughts rapidly occurred; but the resolution to which they led was scarcely formed, when Ormond advanced towards her. She recoiled a few steps, and, showing the knife which she held, said, –

"Ormond! Beware! Know that my unalterable resolution is to die uninjured. I have the means in my power. Stop where you are; one step more, and I plunge this knife into my heart. I know that to contend with your strength or your reason would be vain. To turn this weapon against you I should not fear, if I were sure of success; but to that I will not trust. To save a greater good by the sacrifice of life is in my power, and that sacrifice shall be made."

"Poor Constantia!" replied Ormond, in a tone of contempt; "so thou preferrest thy imaginary honour to life! To escape this injury without a name or substance, without connection with the past or future, without contamination of thy purity or thraldom of thy will, thou wilt kill thyself; put an end to thy activity in virtue's cause; rob thy friend of her solace, the world of thy beneficence, thyself of being and pleasure?

"I shall be grieved for the fatal issue of my experiment; I shall mourn over thy martyrdom of the most opprobrious and contemptible of all errors: but that thou shouldst undergo the trial is decreed. There is still an interval of hope that thy cowardice is counterfeited, or that it will give place to wisdom and courage.

"Whatever thou intendest by way of prevention or cure, it behooves thee to employ with steadfastness. Die with the guilt of suicide and the brand of cowardice upon thy memory, or live with thy claims to felicity and approbation undiminished. Choose which thou wilt. Thy decision is of moment to thyself, but of none to me. Living or dead, the prize that I have in view shall be mine."

CHAPTER XXIX.

It will be requisite to withdraw your attention from this scene for a moment, and fix it on myself. My impatience of my friend's delay, for some days preceding this disastrous interview, became continually more painful. As the time of our departure approached, my dread of some misfortune or impediment increased. Ormond's disappearance from the scene contributed but little to my consolation. To wrap his purposes in mystery, to place himself at seeming distance, was the usual artifice of such as he, – was necessary to the maturing of his project and the hopeless entanglement of his victim. I saw no means of placing the safety of my friend beyond his reach. Between different methods of procedure, there was, however, room for choice. Her present abode was more hazardous than an abode in the city. To be alone argued a state more defenceless and perilous than to be attended by me.

I wrote her an urgent admonition to return. My remonstrances were couched in such terms as, in my own opinion, laid her under the necessity of immediate compliance. The letter was despatched by the usual messenger, and for some hours I solaced myself with the prospect of a speedy meeting.

These thoughts gave place to doubt and apprehension. I began to distrust the efficacy of my arguments, and to invent a thousand reasons, inducing her, in defiance of my rhetoric, at least to protract her absence. These reasons I had not previously conceived, and had not, therefore, attempted, in my letter, to invalidate their force. This omission was possible to be supplied in a second epistle; but, meanwhile, time would be lost, and my new arguments might, like the old, fail to convince her. At least, the tongue was a much more versatile and powerful advocate than the pen; and, by hastening to her habitation, I might either compel her to return with me, or ward off danger by my presence, or share it with her. I finally resolved to join her by the speediest of conveyance.

This resolution was suggested by the meditations of a sleepless night. I rose with the dawn, and sought out the means of transporting myself, with most celerity, to the abode of my friend. A stage-boat, accustomed twice a day to cross New York Bay to Staten Island, was prevailed upon, by liberal offers, to set out upon the voyage at the dawn of day. The sky was gloomy, and the air boisterous and unsettled. The wind, suddenly becoming tempestuous and adverse, rendered the voyage at once tedious and full of peril. A voyage of nine miles was not effected in less than eight hours and without imminent and hair-breadth danger of being drowned.

Fifteen miles of the journey remained to be performed by land. A carriage, with the utmost difficulty, was procured, but lank horses and a crazy vehicle were but little in unison with my impatience. We reached not Amboy ferry till some hours after nightfall. I was rowed across the Sound, and proceeded to accomplish the remainder of my journey – about three miles – on foot.

I was actuated to this speed by indefinite but powerful motives. The belief that my speedy arrival was essential to the rescue of my friend from some inexplicable injury haunted me with ceaseless importunity. On no account would I have consented to postpone this precipitate expedition till the morrow.

I at length arrived at Dudley's farm-house. The inhabitants were struck with wonder at the sight of me. My clothes were stained by the water by which every passenger was copiously sprinkled during our boisterous navigation, and soiled by dust; my frame was almost overpowered by fatigue and abstinence.

To my anxious inquiries respecting my friend, they told me that her evenings were usually spent at the mansion, where it was probable she was now to be found. They were not apprized of any inconvenience or danger that betided her. It was her custom sometimes to prolong her absence till midnight.

I could not applaud the discretion nor censure the temerity of this proceeding. My mind was harassed by unintelligible omens and self-confuted fears. To obviate the danger and to banish my inquietudes was my first duty. To this end I hastened to the mansion. Having passed the intervening hillocks and copses, I gained a view of the front of the building. My heart suddenly sunk, on observing that no apartment – not even that in which I knew it was her custom to sit at these unseasonable hours – was illuminated. A gleam from the window of the study I should have regarded as an argument at once of her presence and her safety.

I approached the house with misgiving and faltering steps. The gate leading into a spacious court was open. A sound on one side attracted my attention. In the present state of my thoughts, any near or unexplained sound sufficed to startle me. Looking towards the quarter whence my panic was excited, I espied, through the dusk, a horse grazing, with his bridle thrown over his neck.

This appearance was a new source of perplexity and alarm. The inference was unavoidable that a visitant was here. Who that visitant was, and how he was now employed, was a subject of eager but fruitless curiosity. Within and around the mansion, all was buried in the deepest repose. I now approached the principal door, and, looking through the keyhole, perceived a lamp, standing on the lowest step of the staircase. It shed a pale light over the lofty ceiling and marble balustrades. No face or movement of a human being was perceptible.

These tokens assured me that some one was within: they also

accounted for the non-appearance of light at the window above. I withdrew my eye from this avenue, and was preparing to knock loudly for admission, when my attention was awakened by some one who advanced to the door from the inside and seemed busily engaged in unlocking. I started back and waited with impatience till the door should open and the person issue forth.

Presently I heard a voice within exclaim, in accents of mingled terror and grief, "Oh, what – what will become of me? Shall I never be released from this detested prison?"

The voice was that of Constantia. It penetrated to my heart like an icebolt. I once more darted a glance through the crevice. A figure, with difficulty recognised to be that of my friend, now appeared in sight. Her hands were clasped on her breast, her eyes wildly fixed upon the ceiling and streaming with tears, and her hair unbound and falling confusedly over her bosom and neck.

My sensations scarcely permitted me to call, "Constantia! For Heaven's sake, what has happened to you? Open the door, I beseech you."

"What voice is that? Sophia Courtland! O my friend! I am imprisoned! Some demon has barred the door, beyond my power to unfasten. Ah, why comest thou so late? Thy succour would have somewhat profited if sooner given; but now, the lost Constantia —" Here her voice sunk into convulsive sobs.

In the midst of my own despair, on perceiving the fulfilment of my apprehensions, and what I regarded as the fatal execution of some project of Ormond, I was not insensible to the suggestions of prudence. I entreated my friend to retain her courage, while I flew to Laffert's and returned with suitable assistance to burst open the door.

The people of the farm-house readily obeyed my summons. Accompanied by three men of powerful sinews, sons and servants of the farmer, I returned with the utmost expedition to the mansion. The lamp still remained in its former place, but our loudest calls were unanswered. The silence was uninterrupted and profound.

The door yielded to strenuous and repeated efforts, and I rushed into the hall. The first object that met my sight was my friend, stretched upon the floor, pale and motionless, supine, and with all the tokens of death.

From this object my attention was speedily attracted by two

figures, breathless and supine like that of Constantia. One of them was Ormond. A smile of disdain still sat upon his features. The wound by which he fell was secret, and was scarcely betrayed by the effusion of a drop of blood. The face of the third victim was familiar to my early days. It was that of the impostor whose artifice had torn from Mr. Dudley his peace and fortune.

An explication of this scene was hopeless. By what disastrous and inscrutable fate a place like this became the scene of such complicated havoc, to whom Craig was indebted for his death, what evil had been meditated or inflicted by Ormond, and by what means his project had arrived at this bloody consummation, were topics of wild and fearful conjecture.

But my friend – the first impulse of my fears was to regard her as dead. Hope and a closer observation outrooted, or, at least, suspended, this opinion. One of the men lifted her in his arms. No trace of blood or mark of fatal violence was discoverable, and the effusion of cold water restored her, though slowly, to life.

To withdraw her from this spectacle of death was my first care. She suffered herself to be led to the farm-house. She was carried to her chamber. For a time she appeared incapable of recollection. She grasped my hand, as I sat by her bedside, but scarcely gave any other tokens of life.

From this state of inactivity she gradually recovered. I was actuated by a thousand forebodings, but refrained from molesting her by inter-rogation or condolence. I watched by her side in silence, but was eager to collect from her own lips an account of this mysterious transaction.

At length she opened her eyes, and appeared to recollect her present situation, and the events which led to it. I inquired into her condition, and asked if there were any thing in my power to procure or perform for her.

"Oh, my friend," she answered, "what have I done, what have I suffered, within the last dreadful hour! The remembrance, though insupportable, will never leave me. You can do nothing for my relief. All I claim is your compassion and your sympathy."

"I hope," said I, "that nothing has happened to load you with guilt or with shame."

"Alas! I know not. My deed was scarcely the fruit of intention. It was suggested by a momentary frenzy. I saw no other means of escaping from vileness and pollution. I was menaced with an evil worse than death. I forebore till my strength was almost subdued: the lapse of another moment would have placed me beyond hope.

"My stroke was desperate and at random. It answered my purpose too well. He cast at me a look of terrible upbraiding, but spoke not. His heart was pierced, and he sunk, as if struck by lightning, at my feet. O much erring and unhappy Ormond! That thou shouldst thus untimely perish! That I should be thy executioner!"

These words sufficiently explained the scene that I had witnessed. The violence of Ormond had been repulsed by equal violence. His foul attempts had been prevented by his death. Not to deplore the necessity which had produced this act was impossible; but, since this necessity existed, it was surely not a deed to be thought upon with lasting horror, or to be allowed to generate remorse.

In consequence of this catastrophe, arduous duties had devolved upon me. The people that surrounded me were powerless with terror. Their ignorance and cowardice left them at a loss how to act in this emergency. They besought my direction, and willingly performed whatever I thought proper to enjoin upon them.

No deliberation was necessary to acquaint me with my duty. Laffert was despatched to the nearest magistrate with a letter, in which his immediate presence was entreated and these transactions were briefly explained. Early the next day the formalities of justice, in the inspection of the bodies and the examination of witnesses, were executed. It would be needless to dwell on the particulars of this catastrophe. A sufficient explanation has been given of the causes that led to it. They were such as exempted my friend from legal animadversion. Her act was prompted by motives which every scheme of jurisprudence known in the world not only exculpates, but applauds. To state these motives before a tribunal hastily formed and exercising its functions on the spot was a task not to be avoided, though infinitely painful. Remonstrances the most urgent and pathetic could scarcely conquer her reluctance.

This task, however, was easy, in comparison with that which remained. To restore health and equanimity to my friend; to repel the erroneous accusations of her conscience; to hinder her from musing, with eternal anguish, upon this catastrophe; to lay the spirit of secret upbraiding by which she was incessantly tormented, which bereft her of repose, empoisoned all her enjoyments, and menaced not only the subversion of her peace but the speedy destruction of her life, became my next employment.

My counsels and remonstrances were not wholly inefficacious. They afforded me the prospect of her ultimate restoration to tranquillity. Meanwhile, I called to my aid the influence of time and of a change of scene. I hastened to embark with her for Europe. Our voyage was tempestuous and dangerous, but storms and perils at length gave way to security and repose.

Before our voyage was commenced, I endeavoured to procure tidings of the true condition and designs of Ormond. My information extended no further than that he had put his American property into the hands of Mr. Melbourne, and was preparing to embark for France. Courtland, who had since been at Paris, and who, while there, became confidentially acquainted with Martinette de Beauvais, has communicated facts of an unexpected nature.

At the period of Ormond's return to Philadelphia, at which his last interview with Constantia in that city took place, he visited Martinette. He avowed himself to be her brother, and supported his pretensions by relating the incidents of his early life. A separation at the age of fifteen, and which had lasted for the same number of years, may be supposed to have considerably changed the countenance and figure she had formerly known. His relationship was chiefly proved by the enumeration of incidents of which her brother only could be apprized.

He possessed a minute acquaintance with her own adventures, but concealed from her the means by which he had procured the knowledge. He had rarely and imperfectly alluded to his own opinions and projects, and had maintained an invariable silence on the subject of his connection with Constantia and Helena. Being informed of her intention to return to France, he readily complied with her request to accompany her in this voyage. His intentions in this respect were frustrated by the dreadful catastrophe that has just been related. Respecting this event, Martinette had collected only vague and perplexing information. Courtland, though able to remove her doubts, thought proper to withhold from her the knowledge he possessed.

Since her arrival in England, the life of my friend has experienced little variation. Of her personal deportment and domestic habits you have been a witness. These, therefore, it would be needless for me to exhibit. It is sufficient to have related events which the recentness of your intercourse with her hindered you from knowing but by means of some formal narrative like the present. She and her friend only were able to impart to you the knowledge which you have so anxiously sought. In consideration of your merits and of your attachment to my friend, I have consented to devote my leisure to this task.

It is now finished; and I have only to add my wishes that the perusal of this tale may afford you as much instruction as the contemplation of the sufferings and vicissitudes of Constantia Dudley has afforded to me. Farewell.

THE END.

Notes on the Appendices

The goal of the appendices is to include documentary material contemporary with the publication of *Ormond* that will assist the reader in imagining the socio-cultural milieu in which the novel appeared.

Appendix A, Judith Sargent Murray's "On the Equality of the Sexes", was published as one of a series of Gleaner essays in 1790, nine years before the publication of *Ormond*. In this teasing and carefully argued essay addressed to the Gentlemen of the early republic, Judith Sargent Murray laments the ornamental status accorded to women in late eighteenth-century American society. Surely, she remarks, there is more to life than preparing a pudding or sewing a seam! Modelling the very intellectual abilities women are presumed not to have – classical and biblical knowledge, rhetoric, logic and wit – Murray argues that women are not limited by inferior capacities of imagination, reason, memory or judgment, but rather by not being given the same opportunities as men to acquire knowledge; if women were encouraged to use these faculties, they would demonstrate them more often. Like Constantia's father Mr. Dudley, Murray believes that women's education should include such subjects as geography and natural philosophy, customarily only taught to male students. Like Brown, Murray suggests that without equal education, independence will be impossible for American women.

Appendices B and C, excerpts from Professor John Robison's *Proofs of a Conspiracy against All Religions and Governments of Europe* and Reverend Jedidiah Morse's "Thanksgiving Sermon," document the growing paranoia in both Europe and America in the 1790s regarding rumours that the Illuminati – "a radical company of beings who discard the principles of religion and obligations of morality" according to Morse (295) – were threatening to subvert the powers of church and state. By the time Brown published *Ormond*, which associates Ormond with secret "political projects" (126), the term "Illuminati" had become a short form for all forms of radical thought that might threaten the conservative Federalist stronghold in the early Republic.

Judith Sargent Murray (1751-1820) was one of America's earliest professional writers. She contributed poems, essays and stories to local newspapers. She also published politically liberal essays, many with feminist sympathies, under the pseudonyms "The Gleaner" and "Constantia" in the *Massachusetts Magazine* from 1789 to 1796. Her feminism may have influenced Brown's early discussion of equal rights for women in *Alcuin*; her use of the pseudonym "Constantia" may also have given Brown the name of the heroine of *Ormond*.

Professor John Robison (1739-1805), General Secretary of the Royal Society of Edinburgh and scientific writer, was a lecturer in Chemistry at Glasgow University and, later, professor of Natural Philosophy at Edinburgh University. Robison had been a member of the Freemasons and visited several lodges in Europe. In 1797 he published *Proofs of a Conspiracy against All Religions and Governments of Europe*, an inflammatory work which aimed to prove that the Illuminati secret society had organized to overthrow the Christian church and governments throughout the world.

Reverend Jedidiah Morse (1761-1826) was a popular Congregational clergyman and staunch Federalist who feared the spread of the "contagion" of Republicanism in 1790s America. Like many New England ministers, including Brown's friend Timothy Dwight, Morse was inspired by Robison's inflammatory *Proofs of A Conspiracy against All Religions and Governments of Europe* to use the sermon form to generate popular hysteria over the rumoured spread of Illuminati principles in late-eighteenth-century America. Excerpted here, Morse's "Thanksgiving sermon" urged popular support for the Federalists' Alien and Sedition Laws, which attempted to stem the tide of pro-French sentiment in New England.

Appendix A

On the EQUALITY of the SEXES

[Judith Sargent Murray's essay was published in the *Massachusetts Magazine* (March 1790, 132-35; April 1790, 223-26)]

TO THE EDITORS OF THE MASSACHUSETTS MAGAZINE,

GENTLEMEN,

The following Essay is yielded to the patronage of Candour. – If it hath been anticipated, the testimony of many respectable persons, who saw it in manuscript as early as the year 1779, can obviate the imputation of plagiarism.

Is it upon mature consideration we adopt the idea, that nature is thus partial in her distributions? Is it indeed a fact, that she hath yielded to one half of the human species so unquestionable a mental superiority? I know that to both sexes elevated understandings, and the reverse, are common. But, suffer me to ask, in what the minds of females are so notoriously deficient, or unequal. May not the intellectual powers be ranged under these four heads – imagination, reason, memory and judgment. The province of imagination hath long since been surrendered up to us, and we have been crowned undoubted sovereigns of the regions of fancy. Invention is perhaps the most arduous effort of the mind; this branch of imagination hath been particularly ceded to us, and we have been time out of mind invested with that creative faculty. Observe the variety of fashions (here I bar the contemptuous smile) which distinguish and adorn the female world; how continually are they changing, insomuch that they almost render the wise man's assertion problematical, and we are ready to say, *there is something new under the sun*. Now what a playfulness, what an exuberance of fancy, what strength of inventive imagination, doth this continual variation discover? Again, it hath been observed, that if the turpitude of the conduct of our sex, hath been ever so enormous, so extremely ready are we, that the very first thought presents us with an apology, so plausible, as to produce our actions even in an amiable light. Another instance of our creative powers is our talent for slander; how ingenious are we at inventive scandal? what a formidable story can we in a moment fabricate merely from the force of a prolifick [*sic*] imagination? how many reputations, in the fertile brain of a female, have been utterly despoiled? how industrious are we at improving a hint? suspicion how easily do we convert into conviction, and conviction, embellished by the power of eloquence, stalks abroad at the surprise and confusion of unsuspecting innocence. Perhaps it will be asked if I furnish these facts as instances of excellency in our sex. Certainly not; but as proofs of a creative faculty, of a lively imagination. Assuredly great activity of mind is thereby discovered, and was this activity properly directed, what beneficial effects would follow. Is the needle and kitchen sufficient to employ the operations of a soul thus organized? I should conceive not. Nay, it is a truth that those very departments leave the intelligent principle vacant, and at liberty for speculation. Are we deficient in reason? we can only reason from what we know, and if an opportunity of acquiring knowledge hath been denied us, the inferiority of our sex cannot fairly be deduced from hence. Memory, I believe, will be allowed us in common, since every one's experience must testify, that a loquacious old woman is as frequently met with, as a communicative old man; their subjects are alike drawn from the fund of other times, and the transactions of their youth, or of maturer life, entertain, or perhaps fatigue you, in the evening of their lives. "But our judgment is not so strong – we do not distinguish so well. – Yet it may be questioned, from what doth this superiority, in this determining faculty of the soul, proceed. May we not trace its source in the difference of education, and continued advantages? Will it be said that the judgment of a male of two years old is more sage than that of a female's of the same age? I believe the reverse is generally observed to be true. But from that period what partiality! how is the one exalted, and the other depressed, by the contrary modes of education which are adopted! the one is taught to aspire, and the other is early confined and limitted [*sic*]. As their years increase, the sister must be wholly domesticated, while the brother is led by the hand through all the flowery paths of science. Grant that their minds are by nature equal, yet who shall wonder at the *apparent* superiority, if indeed custom becomes *second nature*; nay if it taketh place of nature, and that it doth the experience of each day will evince. At length arrived at womanhood, the uncultivated fair one feels a void, which the employments allotted her are by no means capable of filling. What can she do? to books she may not apply; or if she doth, *to those only of the novel kind*, lest she merit the appellation of a *learned lady*; and what ideas have been affixed to this term, the observation of many can testify. Fashion, scandal, and sometimes what is still more reprehensible, are then called in to her relief; and who can say to what lengths the liberties she takes may proceed. Meantime she herself is most unhappy; she feels the want of a cultivated mind. Is she single, she in vain seeks to fill up time from sexual employments or amusements. Is she united to a person whose soul nature made equal to her own, education hath set him so far above her, that in those entertainments which are productive of such rational felicity, she is not qualified to accompany him. She experiences a mortifying consciousness of inferiority, which embitters every enjoyment. Doth the person to whom her adverse fate hath consigned her, posses [*sic*] a mind incapable of improvement, she is equally wretched, in being so closely connected with an individual whom she cannot but despise. Now, was she permitted the same instructors as her brother, (with an eye however to their particular departments) for the employment of a rational mind an ample field would be opened. In astronomy she might catch a glimpse of the immensity of the Deity, and thence she would form amazing conceptions of the august and supreme Intelligence. In geography she would admire Jehovah in the midst of his benevolence; thus adapting this globe to the various wants and amusements of its inhabitants. In natural philosophy she would adore the infinite majesty of heaven, clothed in condescension; and as she traversed the reptile world, she would hail the goodness of a creating God. A mind, thus filled, would have little room for the trifles with which our sex are, with too much justice, accused of amusing themselves, and they would thus be rendered fit companions for those, who should one day wear them as their crown. Fashions, in their variety, would then give place to conjectures, which might perhaps conduce to the improvement of the literary world; and there would be no leisure for slander or detraction. Reputation would not then be blasted, but serious speculations would occupy the lively imaginations of the sex. Unnecessary visits would be precluded, and that custom would only be indulged by way of relaxation, or to answer the demands of consanguinity and friendship. Females would become discreet, their judgments would be invigorated, and their partners for life being circumspectly chosen, an unhappy Hymen would then be as rare, as is now the reverse.

Will it be urged that those acquirements would supersede our domestick [sic] duties. I answer that every requisite in female economy is easily attained; and, with truth I can add, that when once attained, they require no further *mental attention*. Nay, while we are pursuing the needle, or the superintendency of the family, I repeat, that our minds are at full liberty for reflection; that imagination may exert itself in full vigor; and that if a just foundation is early laid, our ideas will then be worthy of rational beings. If we were industrious we might easily find time to arrange them upon paper, or should avocations press too hard for such an indulgence, the hours allotted for conversation would at least become more refined and rational. Should it still be vociferated,"Your domestick employments are sufficient" – I would calmly ask, is it reasonable, that a candidate for immortality, for the joys of heaven, an intelligent being, who is to spend an eternity in contemplating the works of Deity, should at present be so degraded, as to be allowed no other ideas, than those which are suggested by the mechanism of a pudding, or the sewing the seams of a garment? Pity that all such censurers of female improvement do not go one step further, and deny their future existence; to be consistent they surely ought.

Yes, ye lordly, ye haughty sex, our souls are by nature *equal* to yours; the same breath of God animates, enlivens, and invigorates us; and that we are not fallen lower than yourselves, let those witness who have greatly towered above the various discouragements by which they have been so heavily oppressed; and though I am unacquainted with the list of celebrated characters on either side, yet from the observations I have made in the contracted circle in which I have moved, I dare confidently believe, that from the commencement of time to the present day, there hath been as many females, as males, who, by the *mere force of natural powers*, have merited the crown of applause; who, *thus unassisted*, have seized the wreath of fame. I know there are who assert, that as the animal powers of the one sex are superiour, of course their mental faculties also must be stronger; thus attributing strength of mind to the transient organization of this earth born tenement. But if this reasoning is just, man must be content to yield the palm to many of the brute creation, since by not a few of his brethren of the field, he is far surpassed in bodily strength. Moreover, was this argument admitted, it would prove too much, for occular demonstration evinceth, that there are many robust masculine ladies, and effeminate gentlemen. Yet I fancy that Mr. Pope, though clogged with an enervated body, and distinguished by a diminutive stature, could nevertheless lay claim to greatness of soul; and perhaps there are many other instances which might be adduced to combat so unphilosophical an opinion. Do we not often see, that when the clay built tabernacle is well nigh dissolved, when it is just ready to mingle with the parent soil, the immortal inhabitant aspires to, and even attaineth heights the most sublime, and which were before wholly unexplored. Besides, were we to grant that animal strength proved any thing, taking into consideration the accustomed impartiality of nature, we should be induced to imagine, that she had invested the female mind with superiour strength as an equivalent for the bodily powers of man. But waving this however palpable advantage, for *equality only*, we wish to contend.

I am aware that there are many passages in the sacred oracles which seem to give the advantage to the other sex; but I consider all these as wholly metaphorical. Thus David was a man after God's own heart, yet see him enervated by his licentious passions! behold him following Uriah to the death, and shew me wherein could consist the immaculate Being's complacency. Listen to the curses which Job bestoweth upon the day of his nativity, and tell me where is his perfection, where his patience – *literally* it existed not. David and Job were types of him who was to come; and the superiority of man, as exhibited in scripture, being also emblematical, all arguments deduced from thence, of course fall to the ground. The exquisite delicacy of the female mind proclaimeth the exactness of its texture, while its nice sense of honour announceth its innate, its native grandeur. And indeed, in one respect, the preeminence seems to be tacitly allowed us, for after an education which limits and confines, and employments and recreations which naturally tend to enervate the body, and debilitate the mind; after we have from early youth been adorned with ribbons, and other gewgaws, dressed out like the ancient victims previous to a sacrifice, being taught by the care of our parents in collecting the most showy materials that the ornamenting our exteriour ought to be the principal object of our attention; after, I say, fifteen years thus spent, we are introduced into the world, amid the united adulation of every beholder. Praise is sweet to the soul; we are immediately intoxicated by large draughts of flattery, which being plentifully administered, is to the pride of our hearts the most acceptable incense. It is expected that with the other sex we should commence immediate war, and that we should triumph over the machinations of the most artful. We must be constantly upon our guard; prudence and discretion must be our characteristicks [sic]; and we must rise superiour to, and obtain a complete victory over those who have been long adding to the native strength of their minds, by an unremitted study of men and books, and who have, moreover, conceived from the loose characters which they have been portrayed in the extensive variety of their reading, a most contemptible opinion of the sex. Thus unequal, we are, notwithstanding, forced to the combat, and the infamy which is consequent upon the smallest deviation in our conduct, proclaims the high idea which was formed of our native strength; and thus, indirectly at least, is the preference acknowledged to be our due. And if we are allowed an equality of acquirement, let serious studies equally employ our minds, and we will bid our souls arise to equal strength. We will meet upon even ground, the despot man; we will rush with alacrity to the combat, and, crowned by success, we shall then answer the exalted expectations which are formed. Though sensibility, soft compassion, and gentle commiseration, are inmates in the female bosom, yet against every deep laid art, altogether fearless of the event, we will set them in array; for assuredly the wreath of victory will encircle the spotless brow. If we meet an equal, a sensible friend, we will reward him with the hand of amity, and through life we will be assiduous to promote his happiness; but from every deep laid scheme for our ruin, retiring into ourselves, amid the flowery paths of science, we will indulge in all the refined and sentimental pleasures of contemplation. And should it still be urged, that the studies thus inlisted [sic] upon would interfere with our more peculiar department, I must further reply, that *early hours*, and close application, will do wonders; and to her who is from the first dawn of reason taught to fill up time rationally, both the requisites will be easy. I grant that niggard fortune is too generally unfriendly to the mind;

and that much of that valuable treasure, time, is necessarily expended upon the wants of the body; but it should be remembered, that in embarrassed circumstances our companions have as little leisure for literary improvement, as is afforded to us; for most certainly their provident care is at least as requisite as our exertions. Nay, we have even more leisure for sedentary pleasures, as our avocations are more retired, much less laborious, and, as hath been observed, by no means require that avidity of attention which is proper to the employments of the other sex. In high life, or, in other words, where the parties are in possession of affluence, the objection respecting time is wholly obviated, and of course falls to the ground; and it may also be repeated, that many of those hours which are at present swallowed up in fashion and scandal, might be redeemed, were we habituated to useful reflections. But in one respect, O ye arbiters of our fate! we confess that the superiority is indubitably yours; you are by nature formed for our protectors; we pretend not to vie with you in bodily strength; upon this point *we* will never contend for victory. Shield us then, we beseech you, from external evils, and in return we will transact *your* domestick affairs. Yes, *your*, for are you not equally interested in those matters with ourselves? Is not the elegancy of neatness as agreeable to your sight as to ours; is not the well favoured viand equally delightful to your taste; and doth not your sense of hearing suffer as much, from the discordant sounds prevalent in an ill regulated family, produced by the voices of children and many *et ceteras*?

Constantia

By way of supplement to the foregoing pages, I subjoin the following extract from a letter, wrote to a friend in the December of 1780.

AND now assist me, O thou genius of my sex, while I undertake the arduous task of endeavouring to combat that vulgar, that almost universal errour, which hath, it seems, enlisted even Mr. P —— under its banners. The superiority of your sex hath, I grant, been time out of mind esteemed a truth incontrovertible; in consequence of which persuasion, every plan of education hath been calculated to establish this favourite tenet. Not long since; weak and presuming as I was, I amused myself with selecting some arguments from nature, reason, and experience, against this so generally received idea. I confess that to sacred testimonies I had not recourse. I held them to be merely metaphorical, and thus regarding them, I could not persuade myself that there was any propriety in bringing them to decide in this *very important debate*. However, as you, sir, confine yourself entirely to the sacred oracles, I mean to bend the whole of my artillery against those supposed proofs, which you have from thence provided, and from which you have formed an intrenchment *apparently* so invulnerable. And first, to begin with our great progenitors; but here, suffer me to premise, that it is for mental strength I mean to contend, for with respect to animal powers, I yield them undisputed to that sex, which enjoys them in common with the lion, the tyger, and many other beasts of prey; therefore your observations respecting the *rib, under the arm, at a distance from the head, &c. &c.* in no sort militate against my view. Well, but the woman was first in the transgression. Strange how blind *self love* renders you men; were you not wholly absorbed in a partial admiration of your own abilities, you would long since have acknowledged the force of what I am now going to urge. It is true some ignoramuses have absurdly enough informed us, that the beauteous fair of paradise, was seduced from her obedience, by a malignant demon, *in the guise of a baleful serpent*; but we, who are better informed, know that the fallen spirit presented himself to her view, *a shining angel still*; for thus, saith the criticks in the Hebrew tongue, ought the word to be rendered. Let us examine her motive – Hark! the seraph declares that she shall attain a perfection of knowledge; for is there aught which is not comprehended under one or other of the terms *good* and *evil*. It doth not appear that she was governed by any one sensual appetite; but merely by a desire of adorning her mind; a laudable ambition fired her soul, and a thirst for knowledge impelled the predilection so fatal in its consequences. Adam could not plead the same deception; assuredly he was not deceived; nor ought we to admire his superiour strength, or wonder at his sagacity, when we so often confess that example is much more influential than precept. His gentle partner stood before him, a melancholy instance of the direful effects of disobedience; he saw her not possessed of that wisdom which she had fondly hoped to obtain, but he beheld the once blooming female, disrobed of that innocence, which had heretofore rendered her so lovely. To him then deception became impossible, as he had proof positive of the fallacy of the argument, which the deceiver had suggested. What then could be his inducement to burst the barriers, and to fly directly in the face of that command, which *immediately* from the mouth of deity *he* had received, since, I say, he could not plead that fascinating stimulous [*sic*], the accumulation of knowledge, as indisputable conviction was so visibly portrayed before him. What mighty cause impelled him to sacrifice myriads of beings yet unborn, and by one impious act, which *he saw* would be productive of such fatal effects, entail undistinguished ruin upon a race of beings, which he was yet to produce. Blush, ye vaunters of fortitude; ye boasters of resolution; ye haughty lords of the creation; blush when ye remember, that he was influenced by no other motive than a bare pusillanimous attachment to a woman! by sentiments so exquisitely soft, that all his sons have, from that period, when they have designed to degrade them, described as highly feminine. Thus it should seem, that all the arts of the grand deceiver (since means adequate to the purpose are, I conceive, invariably pursued) were requisite to mislead our general mother, while the father of mankind forfeited his own, and relinquished the happiness of posterity, merely in compliance with the blandishments of a female. The subsequent subjection the apostle Paul explains as a figure; after enlarging upon the subject, he adds, "*This is a great mystery; but I speak concerning Christ and the church.*" Now we know with what consummate wisdom the unerring father of eternity hath formed his plans; all the types which he hath displayed, he hath permitted *materially* to fail, in the very virtue for which *they* were famed. The reason for this is obvious, we might otherwise mistake his economy, and render that honour to the creature, which is due only to the creator. I know that Adam was a figure of him who was to come. The grace contained in his figure is the reason of my rejoicing, and while I am very far from prostrating before the shadow, I yield joyfully in all things the preeminence to the second federal head. Confiding faith is prefigured by Abraham, yet he exhibits a contrast to the affiance, when he says of his fair companion, she is my sister. Gentleness was the characteristick [*sic*] of Moses, yet he hesitated not to reply to Jehovah himself, with unsaintlike tongue he murmured at the waters of strife, and with rash hands he break the tables, which were inscribed by the finger of divinity. David, dignified with the title of the man after God's own heart, and yet how stained was his life. Solomon was celebrated for wisdom, but folly is wrote in legible characters upon his almost every action. Lastly, let us turn our eyes to man in the aggregate. He is manifested as the figure of strength, but that we may not regard him as any thing more than a figure, his soul is formed in no sort superiour, but every way equal to the mind of her, who is the emblem of weakness, and whom he hails the gentle companion of his better days.

Appendix B

Excerpted from *Proofs of a Conspiracy Against All the Religions and Governments of Europe, Carried on in the Secret Meetings of Free Masons, Illuminati, and Reading Societies.* Collected from good authorities, by John Robison, A.M. professor of natural philosophy, and secretary to the Royal Society of Edinburgh. *Nam tua res agitue paries cum proximus ardet.* The third edition. To which is added a Postscript.

Philadelphia: Printed for T. Dobson, No. 41, South Second Street, and W. Cobbet, No. 25, North Second Street. 1798. (pp. 80-184).

... This was in 1777. [Professor Adam] Weishaupt had long been scheming the establishment of an Association of Order, which, in time, should govern the world. In his first fervour and high expectations, he hinted to several Ex-Jesuits the probability of their recovering, under a new name, the influence which they formerly possessed, and of being again of great service to society, by directing the education of youth of distinction, now emancipated from all civil and religious prejudices. He prevailed on some to join him, but they all retracted but two. After this disappointment Weishaupt became the implacable enemy of the Jesuits, and his sanguine temper made him frequently lay himself open to their piercing eye, and drew on him their keenest resentment, and at last made him the victim of their enmity....

In the beginning of 1783, four professors of the Marianen Academy, founded by the widow of the late Elector, viz. Utschneider, Cossandey, Renner, and Grunberger, with two others, were summoned before the Court of Enquiry, and questioned, on their allegiance, respecting the Order of the Illuminati. They acknowledged that they belonged to it, and when more closely examined, they related several circumstances of its constitution and principles. Their declarations were immediately published, and were very unfavourable. The order was said to abjure Christianity, and to refute admission into the higher degrees to all who adhered to any of the three confessions. Sensual pleasures were restored to the rank they held in the Epicurean philosophy. Self-murder was justified on Stoical principles. In the Lodges death was declared an eternal sleep; patriotism and loyalty were called narrow-minded prejudices, and incompatible with universal benevolence; continual declamations were made on liberty and equality as the unalienable rights of man. The baneful influence of accumulated property was declared an insurmountable obstacle to the happiness of any nation whose chief laws were framed for its protection and increase. Nothing was so frequently discoursed of as the propriety of employing, for a good purpose, the means which the wicked employed for evil purposes; and it was taught, that the preponderancy of good in the ultimate result consecrated every mean employed; and that wisdom and virtue consisted in properly determining this balance. This appeared big with danger, because it seemed evident that nothing would be scrupled at, if it could be made appear that the Order would derive advantage from it, because the great object of the Order was held as superior to every consideration. They concluded by saying that the method of education made them all spies on each other and on all around them ...

... [According to the Founder of the Illuminati], "I have contrived an explanation which has every advantage; is inviting to Christians of every communion; gradually frees them from all religious prejudices; cultivates the social virtues; and animates them by a great, a feasible, and *speedy* prospect of universal happiness, in a state of liberty and moral equality, freed from the obstacles which subordination, rank, and riches, continually throw in our way. My explanation is accurate, and complete, my means are effectual, and irresistible. Our secret Association works in a way that nothing can withstand, *and man shall soon be free and happy.*"

"This is the great object held out by this Association, and the means of attaining it is Illumination, enlightening the understanding by the sun of reason, which will dispel the clouds of superstition and of prejudice. The proficients in this Order are therefore justly named the Illuminated. And of all Illumination which human reason can give, none is comparable to the discovery of what we are, our nature, our obligations, what happiness we are capable of, and what are the means of attaining it. In comparison with this, the most brilliant sciences are but amusements for the idle and the luxurious. To fit man by Illumination for active virtue, to engage him to it by the strongest motives, to render the attainment of it easy and certain, by finding employment for every talent in its proper sphere of action, so that all, without feeling any extraordinary effort, and in conjunction with and completion of ordinary business, shall urge forward, with united powers, the general task. This indeed will be an employment, suited to noble natures, grand in its views, and delightful in its exercise."

"And what is this general object? THE HAPPINESS OF THE HUMAN RACE. Is it not distressing to a generous mind, after contemplating what human nature is capable of, to see how little we enjoy? When we look at this goodly world, and see that every man *may* be happy, but that the happiness of one depends on the conduct of another; when we see the wicked so powerful and the good so weak; and that it is in vain to strive singly and alone, against the general current of vice and oppression: the wish naturally arises in the mind, that it were possible to form a durable combination of the most worthy persons, who should work together in removing the obstacles to human happiness, become terrible to the wicked, and give their aid to the good without distinction, and should, by the most powerful means, first fetter, and by fettering, lessen vice; means which at the same time should promote virtue, by rendering the inclination to rectitude hitherto so feeble, more powerful and engaging. Would not such an association be a blessing to the world?"

"But where are the proper persons, the good, the generous, and the accomplished, to be found; and how, and by what strong motives, are they to be induced to engage in a talk so vast, so incessant, so difficult, and so laborious? This Association must be gradual. There *are* some such persons to be found in every society. Such noble minds will be engaged by the heart-warming object. The first task of the Association must therefore be to form the young members. As these multiply and advance, they become the apostles of beneficence, and the work is now on foot, and advances with a speed encreasing [*sic*] every day. The slightest observation shows that nothing will so much contribute to increase the zeal of the members as secret union. We see with what keenness and zeal the frivolous business of Free Masonry is conducted, by persons knit together by secrecy of their union. It is needless to enquire into the causes of this zeal which secrecy produces. It is an universal fact, confirmed by the history of every age. Let this circumstance of our constitution therefore be directed to this noble purpose, and then all the objections urged against it by jealous tyranny and affrighted superstition will vanish. The Order will thus work silently, and securely; and though the generous benefactors of the human race are thus deprived of the applause of the world, they have the noble pleasure of seeing their work prosper in their hands."

Such is the aim, and such are the hopes of the Order of the Illuminated. Let us now see how these were to be accomplished. We cannot judge with perfect certainty of this, because the account given of the constitution of the Order by its founder includes only the lowest degree, and even this is liable to great suspicion....

... We are therefore suspicious of this Illumination, and apt to ascribe this violent antipathy to Princes and subordination to the very cause that makes true Illumination, and just Morality proceeding from it, so necessary to public happiness, namely, the vice and injustice of those who cannot innocently have the command of those offensive elegancies [sic] of human life. Luxurious taste, keen desires, and unbridled passions, would prompt to all this; and this Illumination is, as we see, equivalent to them in effect. The aim of the Order is not to enlighten the mind of man, but shew him his moral obligations, and by the practice of his duties to make society peaceable, possession secure, and coercion unnecessary, so that all may be at rest and happy, even though all *were* equal; but to get rid of the coercion which must be employed in the place of Morality, that the innocent rich may be robbed with impunity by the idle and profligate poor. But to do this, an unjust casuistry must be employed instead of a just Morality; and this must be defended or suggested, by misrepresenting the true state of man, and of his relation to the universe, and by removing the restrictions of religion, and giving a superlative value to all those constituents of human enjoyment, which true Illumination shews us to be but very small concerns of a rational and virtuous mind. The more closely we examine the principles and practice of the Illuminati, the more clearly do we perceive that this is the case. Their first and immediate aim is to get the possession of riches, power, and influence, without industry; and to accomplish this, they want to abolish Christianity; and then dissolute manners and universal profligacy will procure them the adherence of all the wicked, and enable them to overturn all the civil governments of Europe; after which they will think of farther conquests, and extend their operations to the other quarters of the globe, till they have reduced mankind to the state of one undistinguishable chaotic mass.

But this is too chimerical to be thought their real aim. Their

Founder, I dare say, never entertained such hopes, nor troubled himself with the fate of distant lands. But it comes in his way when he puts on the mask of humanity and benevolence: it must embrace all mankind, only because it must be stronger than patriotism and loyalty, which stand in his way ...

... Is it not astonishing, therefore, to hear people in this country express any regard for this institution? Is it not most mortifying to think that there are Lodges of Illuminated among us? I think that nothing bids fairer for weaning our inconsiderate countrymen from having any connection with them, than the faithful account here given. I hope that there are few, very few of our countrymen, and none whom we call friend, who can think that an Order which held such doctrines, and which practiced such things, can be any thing else than a ruinous Association, a gang of profligates. All their posessions [*sic*] of the love of mankind are vain; their Illumination must be a bewildering blaze, and totally ineffectual for its purpose, for it has had no such influence on the leaders of the band; yet it seems quite adequate to the effects it has produced; for such are the characters of those who forget God ...

... And all good men, all lovers of peace and of justice, will abhor and reject the thought of overturning the present constitution of things, faulty as it may be, merely in the endeavour to establish another, which the vices of mankind may subvert again in a twelvemonth. They must see, that in order to gain their point, the proposers have found it necessary to destroy the grounds of morality, by permitting the most wicked means for accomplishing any end that our fancy, warped by passion or interest, may represent to us as of great importance. They see, that instead of morality, vice must prevail, and that therefore there is no security for the continuance of this Utopian felicity; and, in the mean time, desolation and misery must lay the world waste during the struggle, and half of those for whom we are striving will be swept from the face of the earth. We have but to look to France, where in eight years there have been more executions and spoliations and distresses of every kind by the *pouvoir revolutionnaire*, than can be found in the long records of that despotic monarchy.

There is nothing in the whole constitution of the Illuminati that strikes me with more horror than the proposals ... to enlist the women in this shocking warfare with all that "is good, and pure, and lovely, and of good report." They could not have fallen on any expedient that will be more effectual and fatal. If any of my countrywomen shall honour these pages with a reading, I would call on them, in the most earnest manner, to consider this as an affair of the utmost importance to themselves. I would conjure them by the regard they have for their own dignity, and for their rank in society, to join against these enemies of human nature and profligate degraders of the sex; and I would assure them that the present state of things almost puts it in their power to be the saviours of the world. But if they are remiss, and yield to the seduction, they will fall from that high state to which they have arisen in Christian Europe, and again sink into that insignificancy or slavery in which the sex is found in all ages and countries out of the hearing of Christianity.

Appendix C

Excerpted from "A Sermon, preached at Charlestown, November 29, 1798. On the anniversary of thanksgiving in Massachusetts. With an Appendix, designed to illustrate some parts of the discourse; exhibiting proofs of the early existence, progress and deleterious effects of French intrigue and influence in the United States." By Jedediah [*sic*] Morse, D.D. pastor of the church in Charlestown.

Printed at Worcester, Massachusetts, by Daniel Greenleaf, July 10, 1799(88).

...The probable existence of *Illuminism* in this country was asserted in my Fall Discourse of May last. The following fact, related by a very respectable divine, while it confirms what is above asserted, shews that my apprehensions were not without foundation.

"In the northern parts of this state (Massachusetts) as I am well informed, there has lately appeared, and still exists under a licentious leader, a company of beings who discard the principles of religion, and the obligations of morality, trample on the bonds of matrimony, and separate right of property, and the laws of civil society, spend the sabbath in labour and diversion, as fancy dictates; and the nights in rioteous [*sic*] excess and promiscuous concubinage, as lust impels. Their number consists of about forty, some of whom are persons of respectable abilities, and once, of decent characters. That a society of this description, which would disgrace the natives of *Caffreria*, should be formed in this land of civilization and Gospel light, is an evidence that the devil is at this time gone forth, having great influence, as well as great wrath."

Here is certainly the *fruit* if not the *root*, the *practice* if not the *theory*, the *substance* if not the form of *Illuminism* ...

Works Cited And Recommended Reading

I. Works by C.B. Brown:

Brown, Charles Brockden. *Alcuin; A Dialogue*. New York: Printed by T. & J. Swords, 1798.

——. *Wieland; or, the Transformation. An American Tale*. New York: Printed by T. & J. Swords, for H. Caritat, 1798.

——. *Ormond; or, The Secret Witness*. New York: Printed by G. Forman, for H. Caritat, 1799.

——. *Arthur Mervyn; or, Memoirs of the Year 1793*. Philadelphia: Maxwell, 1799.

——. *Edgar Huntly; or, Memoirs of a Sleep-Walker*. Philadelphia: Maxwell, 1799.

——. *Clara Howard; In a Series of Letters*. Philadelphia: Dickins, 1801. (In England published as *Philip Stanley; or, The Enthusiasm of Love*. London: Lane, 1807.)

——. *Jane Talbot, A Novel*. Philadelphia: John Conrad; Baltimore: M. & J. Conrad; Washington City: Rapin, 1801.

——. *Carwin, The Biloquist, and Other American Tales and Pieces*. London: Henry Colbourn, 1822.

II. Bibliographic Checklists of Works by C.B. Brown:

Carpenter, Charles A. "Selective Bibliography of Writings about Charles Brockden Brown." *Critical Essays on Charles Brockden Brown*. Ed. Bernard Rosenthal. Boston: Hall, 1981. 224-39.

Parker, Patricia L. *Charles Brockden Brown: A Reference Guide*. Boston: Hall, 1980.

III. Works on C.B. Brown:

Axelrod, Alan. *Charles Brockden Brown, An American Tale*. Austin: U of Texas P, 1983.

Bennet, Maurice J. *An American Tradition — Three Studies: Charles Brockden Brown, Nathaniel Hawthorne, and Henry James*. New York: Garland, 1987.

Bradfield, Scott. *Dreaming Revolution: Transgression in the Development of American Romance*. Iowa City: U of Iowa P, 1993.

Brumm, Ursula. "Nature as Scene or Agent? Some Reflections on Its Role in the American Novel." *Vistas of a Continent: Concepts of Nature in America.* Ed. Andreas Riese. Heidelberg: Winter, 1979. 101-10.

Butler, David L. *Dissecting a Human Heart: A Study of Style in the Novels of Charles Brockden Brown.* Washington, DC: UP of America, 1978.

Christophersen, Bill. *The Apparition in the Glass: Charles Brockden Brown's American Gothic.* Athens: U of Georgia P, 1993.

Clark, David Lee. *Charles Brockden Brown: Pioneer Voice of America.* Durham: Duke UP, 1952.

Clemit, Pamela. *The Godwinian Novel: The Rational Fictions of Godwin, Brockden Brown, Mary Shelley.* Oxford: Clarendon; New York: Oxford UP, 1993.

Davidson, Cathy. *Revolution and the Word: The Rise of the Novel in America.* New York: Oxford UP, 1986.

Day, William Patrick. *In the Circles of Fear and Desire: A Study of Gothic Fantasy.* Chicago: U of Chicago P, 1985.

Dunlap, William. *The Life of Charles Brockden Brown together with selections from the rarest of his printed works, from his original letters, and from his manuscripts before unpublished.* Philadelphia: James P. Parke, 1815.

Elliott, Emory. *Revolutionary Writers: Literature and Authority in the New Republic, 1725-1810.* New York: Oxford UP, 1982.

Ferguson, Robert A. "Yellow Fever and Charles Brockden Brown: The Context of the Emerging Novelist." *Early American Literature* 14 (1980): 293-305.

——. *Law and Letters in American Culture* (Cambridge, MA.: Harvard University Press, 1984).

Fiedler, Leslie. *Love and Death in the American Novel.* New York: Criterion, 1960.

Fleischmann, Fritz. "Charles Brockden Brown: Feminism in Fiction." *American Novelists Revisited: Essays in Feminist Criticism.* Ed. Fritz Fleischmann. Boston: Hall, 1982. 6-41.

Goddu, Teresa. *Gothic America: Narrative, History and Nation.* New York: Columbia UP, 1997.

Grabo, Norman S. *The Coincidental Art of Charles Brockden Brown.* Chapel Hill: U of North Carolina P, 1981.

Hagenbuchle, Roland. "American Literature and the Nineteenth-Century Crisis in Epistemology: The Example of Charles Brockden Brown". *Early American Literature* 23 (1988): 121-51.

Hinds, Elizabeth Jane Wall. "Charles Brockden Brown and the Frontiers of Discourse." *Frontier Gothic: Terror and Wonder at the Frontier in American Literature*. Eds. David Mogen, Scott P. Sanders, and Joanne B. Karpinski. Rutherford, NJ: Fairleigh Dickinson UP, 1993. 109-125.

——. *Private Property: Charles Brockden Brown's Gendered Economics of Virtue*. Newark, DE: U of Delaware P, 1997.

Jordan, Cynthia. S. *Second Stories: The Politics of Language, Form, and Gender in Early American Fictions*. Chapel Hill: U of North Carolina P, 1989.

Kimball, Arthur G. *Rational Fictions: A Study of Charles Brockden Brown*. McMinnville, OR: Linfield Research Institute, 1968.

Krause, Sydney. "*Ormond*. How Rapidly and How Well 'composed, arranged, and delivered.'" *Early American Literature* 13 (1978-9): 238-49.

——. "*Ormond*: Seduction in a New Key." *American Literature* 44 (1973): 570-84.

Lee, A. Robert. "A Darkness Visible: The Case of Charles Brockden Brown." *American Horror Fiction: From Brockden Brown to Stephen King*. Ed. Brian Docherty. New York: St. Martin's, 1990. 13-32.

Levin, Harry. *The Power of Blackness*. New York: Knopf, 1958.

Levine, Robert. *Conspiracy and Romance: Studies in Brockden Brown, Hawthorne, and Melville*. Cambridge: Cambridge UP, 1989.

Looby, Christopher. *Voicing America: Language, Literary Form and the Origins of the United States*. Chicago: U of Chicago P, 1996.

Massé, Michelle A. *In The Name of Love: Women, Masochism and the Gothic*. Ithaca and London: Cornell UP, 1992.

Parrington, Vernon Louis. *The Romantic Revolution in America, 1800-1860*. New York: Harcourt, 1927.

Reising, Russell J. *Loose Ends: Closure and Crisis in the American Social Text*. Durham, NC: Duke UP, 1997.

Ringe, Donald A. *American Gothic: Imagination and Reason in Nineteenth-Century Fiction*. Lexington: UP of Kentucky, 1982.

——. *Charles Brockden Brown*. New York: Twayne P, 1966.

Rodgers, Paul C., Jr. "Brown's *Ormond*: The Fruits of Improvisation." *American Quarterly* 24 (March 1974): 4-22.

Rosenthal, Bernard, ed. *Critical Essays on Charles Brockden Brown*. Boston: Hall, 1981.

Samuels, Shirley. "The Family, the State, and the Novel in the Early Republic." *American Quarterly* (Fall 1986): 381-95.

——. "Infidelity and Contagion: The Rhetoric of Revolution." *Early American Literature* 22 (1987): 183-91.

——. *Romances of the Republic: Women, the Family and Violence in the Literature of the Early American Nation.* Oxford: Oxford UP, 1996.

Slotkin, Richard. *Regeneration Through Violence: The Mythology of the American Frontier, 1600-1860.* Middletown, CT: Wesleyan UP, 1973.

Smith, Allan Gardner. *The Analysis of Motives: Early American Psychology and Fiction.* Amsterdam: Rodopi, 1980.

Smyth, Heather. "Imperfect Dis(clothes)ures: Cross-Dressing and Containment in Charles Brockden Brown's *Ormond*." *Sex and Sexuality in Early America.* Ed. Merril D. Smith. New York: New York UP, 1998.

Stern, Julia A. *The Plight of Feeling: Sympathy and Dissent in the Early American Novel.* Chicago and London: University of Chicago P, 1997.

Tilton, Eleanor M. "In the Labyrinth of Charles Brockden Brown's Prose: The Bicentennial Edition." *Early American Literature* 19 (1984): 191-208.

Verhoeven, W. M. "Displacing the Discontinuous: or, The Labyrinths of Reason: Fictional Design and Eighteenth-Century Thought in Charles Brockden Brown's Ormond." *Rewriting the Dream: Reflections on the Changing American Literary Canon.* Ed. W.M. Verhoeven. Amsterdam: Rodopi, 1992. 202-09.

——. "Opening the Text: The Locked Trunk Motif in Late Eighteenth-Century British and American Gothic Fiction." *Exhibited by Candlelight: Sources and Developments in the Gothic Tradition.* Amsterdam: Rodopi, 1995. 205-19.

Vilas, Martin. S. *Charles Brockden Brown: A Study of Early American Fiction.* Burlington: Free Press Association, 1904.

Warfel, Harry R. *Charles Brockden Brown: American Gothic Novelist.* Gainesville: UP of Florida, 1949.

Warner, Michael. *The Letters of the Republic: Publication and the Public Sphere in Eighteenth-Century America.* Cambridge: Harvard UP, 1990.

Watt, Stephen. *The Romance of Real Life: Charles Brockden Brown and the Origins of American Culture.* Baltimore: John Hopkins UP, 1994.

IV. Secondary Sources on Backgrounds:

Allen, Richard and Absalom Jones. "A Narrative of the Yellow Fever in the Year of Our Lord 1793." *The Life Experience and Gospel Labors of the Rt. Rev. Richard Allen.* Rpt. New York: 1960.

Buel, Richard. *Securing the Revolution: Ideology in American Politics, 1789-1815.* Ithaca: Cornell UP, 1972.

Barruel, Abbé [Augustin]. *Memoirs, illustrating the history of Jacobinism: a translation from the French.* London: T. Burton, 1797.

Brown, Chandos Michael. "Mary Wollstonecraft, or, The Female Illuminati: The Campaign Against Women and 'Modern Philosophy' in the Early Republic." *Journal of the Early Republic* 15.3 (Fall 1995): 389-424.

Carey, Mathew. *A Short Account of the Malignant Fever, Lately Prevalent in Philadelphia with a statement of the proceedings that took place on the subject in different parts of the United States.* Philadelphia: 1793.

Davis, David Brion, ed. *The Fear of Conspiracy: Images of Un-American Subversion from the Revolution to the Present.* Ithaca & New York: Cornell UP, 1971.

Dayan, Joan. *Haiti, History and the Gods.* Berkeley: U of California P, 1995.

Dwight, Timothy. *Nature, and Danger, of Infidel Philosophy, exhibited in Two Discourses, Addressed to the Candidates for the Baccalaureate, in Yale College.* New Haven: 1798.

Fliegelman, Jay. *Declaring Independence: Jefferson, Natural Language and the Culture of Performance.* Stanford: Stanford UP, 1993.

——. *Prodigals and Pilgrims: The American Revolution against Patriarchal Authority, 1750-1800.* Cambridge: Cambridge UP, 1982.

Halttunen, Karen. *Confidence Men and Painted Women: A Study of Middle Class Culture in America: 1830-1870.* New Haven: Yale UP, 1982.

Johnson, Claudia L. *Equivocal Beings: Politics, Gender and Sentimentality in the 1790s: Wollstonecraft, Radcliffe, Burney, Austen.* Chicago: U of Chicago P, 1995.

Jordan, Winthrop D. *White Over Black: American Attitudes Toward the Negro 1580-1812.* Baltimore: Pelican, 1969.

Kann, Mark. *On the Man Question: Gender and Civic Virtue in America.* Philadelphia: Temple UP, 1991.

Kerber, Linda. *Women of the Republic: Intellect and Ideology in Revolutionary America.* New York: Norton, 1980.

Murray, Judith Sargent. *The Gleaner.* Introduction by Nina Baym. Schenectady, New York: Union College P, 1992.

Norton, Mary Beth. *Liberty's Daughters: The Revolutionary Experience of American Women, 1750-1800.* Boston: Little, 1980.

Smith, James Morton. *Freedom's Fetters: The Alien and Sedition Laws and American Civil Liberties.* Ithaca: Cornell UP, 1956.

Stauffer, Vernon. *New England and the Bavarian Illuminati.* New York: Russell, 1967.

Wood, Gordon. *The Radicalism of the American Revolution.* New York: Knopf, 1992.

——. *Creation of the American Republic, 1776-1787.* Chapel Hill: U of North Carolina P, 1969.

Wood, Sarah Sayward Barrell Keating. *Julia and the Illuminated Baron. A novel: founded on recent facts, which have transpired in the course of the late revolution of moral principles in France.* Portsmouth, NH: Oracle P, 1800.

Wollstonecraft, Mary. *A Vindication of the Rights of Woman.* Ed. Carol H. Poston. New York: Norton, 1975.

broadview literary texts

"This is a series in which the editing is something of an art form."
The Washington Post

"Broadview's format is inviting. Clearly printed on good paper, with distinctive photographs on the covers, the books provide the physical pleasure that is so often a component of enticing one to pick up a book in the first place.... And, by providing a broad context, the editors have done us a great service."
Eighteenth-Century Fiction

"These editions [*Frankenstein, Hard Times, Heart of Darkness*] are top-notch—far better than anything else in the market today."
Craig Keating, Langara College

The Broadview Literary Texts series represents an important effort to see the ever-changing canon of English literature from new angles. The series brings together texts that have long been regarded as classics with lesser-known texts that offer a fresh light—and that in many cases may also claim to be of real importance in our literary tradition.

Each volume in the series presents the text together with a variety of documents from the period, enabling readers to get a fuller, richer sense of the world out of which it emerged. Samples of the science available for Mary Shelley to draw on in writing *Frankenstein,* stark reports from the Congo in the late nineteenth century that help to illuminate Conrad's *Heart of Darkness;* late eighteenth-century statements on the proper roles for women and men that help contextualize the feminist themes of the late eighteenth-century novels *Millenium Hall* and *Something New*—these are the sorts of fascinating background materials that round out each Broadview Literary Texts edition.

Each volume also includes a full introduction, chronology, bibliography, and explanatory notes. Newly typeset and produced on high-quality paper in an attractive Trade paperback format, Broadview Literary Texts are a delight to handle as well as to read.

The distinctive cover images for the series are also designed (like the duotone process itself) to combine two slightly different perspectives. Early photographs inevitably evoke a sense of pastness, yet the images for most volumes in the series involve a conscious use of anachronism. The covers are thus designed to draw attention to social and temporal context, while suggesting that the works themselves may also relate to periods other than that from which they emerged—including our own era.